'I gather you want to talk.'

Nik spun back to her with the liquid grace of movement that had always caught her eye and frowned at her, black brows drawn down, wide, sensual mouth twisting in dismissal.

'No. I don't want to talk,' he told Betsy abruptly, before he tossed back the finger of Scotch whisky he had poured neat and set down the empty glass again.

'Then *why*—?' she began in confusion.

'*Se thelo*…I want you,' he heard himself admit, before he was even aware that the words were on his tongue.

So Nik—*so* explosively unpredictable, Betsy reasoned abstractedly, colour rushing into her cheeks as a hot wave of awareness engulfed her. Jewel-bright eyes assailed hers in an almost physical collision, and something low and intimate in her body clenched hard. Her legs turned so weak she wasn't convinced they were still there to hold her up, but she was held in stasis by the intensity of his narrowed green gaze.

'And you want m⸱⸱

THE LEGACIES OF POWERFUL MEN

Three tenets to live by:
money, power and the ruthless pursuit of passion!

Cristo Ravelli, Nik Christakis and Zarif al-Rastani know better than most the double-edged sword of their inheritance. Watching their father move from one wife to another, leaving their mothers devastated in his wake, has hardened each of these men against the lure of love.

But, despite their best efforts to live by the principles of money, power and passion, they find themselves entangled with three women who challenge the one thing they've protected all these years…

Their hearts!

Read Cristo's story in:
RAVELLI'S DEFIANT BRIDE
June 2014

Read Nik's story in:
CHRISTAKIS'S REBELLIOUS WIFE
July 2014

And read Zarif's story in:
ZARIF'S CONVENIENT QUEEN
August 2014!

CHRISTAKIS'S
REBELLIOUS WIFE

BY
LYNNE GRAHAM

MILLS &
BOON®

Published in Great Britain 2014
by Mills & Boon, an imprint of Harlequin (UK) Limited,
Eton House, 18-24 Paradise Road, Richmond, Surrey, TW9 1SR

© 2014 Lynne Graham

ISBN: 978 0 263 24666 7

Harlequin (UK) Limited's policy is to use papers that are natural,
renewable and recyclable products and made from wood grown in
sustainable forests. The logging and manufacturing processes conform
to the legal environmental regulations of the country of origin.

Printed and bound in Spain
by Blackprint CPI, Barcelona

Lynne Graham was born in Northern Ireland and has been a keen Mills & Boon® reader since her teens. She is very happily married, with an understanding husband who has learned to cook since she started to write! Her five children keep her on her toes. She has a very large dog, which knocks everything over, a very small terrier, which barks a lot, and two cats. When time allows, Lynne is a keen gardener.

Recent titles by the same author:

RAVELLI'S DEFIANT BRIDE
  (The Legacies of Powerful Men)
THE DIMITRAKOS PROPOSITION
CHALLENGING DANTE
  (A Bride for a Billionaire)
THE BILLIONAIRE'S TROPHY
  (A Bride for a Billionaire)

Did you know these are also available as eBooks?
Visit www.millsandboon.co.uk

To my daughter Rachel
with warm appreciation for all her support.

CHAPTER ONE

'A DIVORCE CAN be civilised,' Cristo Ravelli pronounced in a tone of studious tact.

Nik Christakis almost vented a derisive laugh at such a statement from the brother barely two months his senior. In reality only genuine respect for his sibling kept his cutting tongue silent. After all, what could Cristo possibly know about the blood and mayhem of a bitter divorce? Cristo was a newly and very happily married man without that experience...or that of many other unpleasant life events, in Nik's considered opinion. As a result, Cristo was as solid and straight as a ruler; he had no corners, no twists, no hidden places. He had no more concept of Nik's infinitely more complex and darker life experience than a dinosaur catapulted into a fairy story full of fluffy wings and magic.

'I know you're probably wondering where I get the nerve to offer advice,' Cristo remarked shrewdly. 'But you and Betsy did once have a good relationship and ratcheting down the current tension and cooling the aggro would be healthier for both of you—'

'Then you should be delighted to hear that Betsy and I are having a face-to-face meeting tomorrow in the presence of our lawyers in an effort to iron out a settlement,' Nik growled, his lean, darkly handsome features grim and hard.

'It's only money, Nik, and… *Dio mio…*' Cristo sighed, thinking wryly of the vast business empire that his workaholic tycoon brother had built from the ground up '…you have plenty of it—'

Nik ground his perfect white teeth together, his unusually light green eyes flashing bright with barely restrained fury. 'That's not the point!' he cut in harshly. 'Betsy's trying to take me to the cleaners and steal half of everything I have—'

'I can't explain why she's making such excessive demands. I would've sworn she didn't have a mercenary bone in her body,' Cristo fielded uncomfortably. 'Have you tried to talk to her, Nik?'

Nik frowned darkly. 'Why would I try to *talk* to her?' he asked in astonishment at a suggestion that clearly struck him as insane. 'She threw me out of our home, started a divorce and is currently trying to rip me off to the tune of billions!'

'She did have some excuse for throwing you out,' Cristo reminded his sibling in a rueful undertone.

In answer, Nik compressed his lips. He had his own very firm ideas about exactly why his marriage had imploded. He had married a woman who said she didn't want children and then she had *changed her mind.* It was true that he had chosen to withhold certain very private information from her in the aftermath of that revelation but he had understandably assumed that her change of heart was a whim or at best hormonal, an urge that might hopefully fade as quickly as it had first arrived.

'It was *my* house,' Nik responded flatly.

'So now you're planning to take Lavender Hall off her as well as the dog,' Cristo breathed heavily.

'Gizmo was *also* mine.' Nik glanced at the disputed dog, returned to his care two months earlier and still a study of deep doggy depression. Gizmo slumped by the window, an array of squeaky toys lying around him untouched, his short muzzle resting mournfully on shaggy paws. The animal had the best of everything that money could buy but, in spite of Nik's every effort to the contrary, the wretched mutt continued to pine for Betsy.

'Have you any idea how devastated she was when you took the dog off her?' Cristo enquired.

'The three pages of tear-stained care instructions that came with him did provide a hint,' Nik breathed sardonically. 'She was more worried about the dog than she ever was about me—'

'Less than a year ago, Betsy *adored* you!' Cristo shot back at his brother in condemnation of that unfeeling response.

And he had liked being adored, Nik acknowledged; he had liked it very much indeed. When adoration had turned to violent hatred and questions he couldn't answer he had had no appetite whatsoever for the new regime. Questions he *could* have answered had he been forced to do so, he qualified inwardly, but he could not have stood to see the look of pity or horror on her face should he have told her the truth. Some truths a man was entitled to keep private; some were simply too appalling to share.

'I mean…' Cristo hesitated. 'When you encouraged me to talk to Betsy, to become her friend after you split, I thought it was because you loved her and wanted her back and hoped to use me as an intermediary—'

Nik's devastatingly handsome face clenched hard. 'I didn't love her. I've never loved anyone,' he admitted coldly. 'I liked her, *trusted* her. She was a good homemaker—'

'A…*homemaker?*' Cristo was staggered by that description because it was such an old-fashioned term and there was nothing even remotely old-fashioned about Nik and his brand of contemporary cool.

'A good homemaker,' Nik repeated steadily, guessing that Cristo, who had always had a decent home, could not comprehend the draw of such a talent in a woman. 'But my trust in her was misplaced and obviously I don't want her back.'

'Are you absolutely certain of that?' Cristo pressed.

'*Ne*…yes,' Nik confirmed in Greek, his response instantaneous. He might not be divorced as yet but he had already moved on. After all, Betsy had always been an eccentric choice of bride for a Greek billionaire but she had appeared during a troubled period in his life and she belonged to that phase, most assuredly not to the new start and more promising future he now envisaged. In the space of the six months that had passed since their marriage broke down, Nik had changed and he was very proud of that change. He had shed his dysfunctional past, travelled from being a male with more excess baggage than a jumbo jet to a faster-moving, far more efficient version of himself. The very last thing he intended to do now was repeat past mistakes. And Betsy had been a *serious* mistake.

No matter how hard Betsy tried to hide it, she was so much on edge in the company of her polished legal team while they waited in the elegant conference room that a sudden noise would have seen her plastered to the ceiling.

Her nervous tension was understandable. After all, it had been six months since she had last seen Nik, six months during which her already broken heart had been repeatedly stamped on and then what little remained torn to pieces. He had refused to see her or make any explanation for his extraordinary behaviour. In the space of a moment she had travelled from being a happily married woman trying for her first baby to a betrayed, bitterly hurt and confused wife.

She had thrown Nik out but *he* had essentially abandoned *her*. After his heartless deception, the force of his counter-attack had almost destroyed her and he had walked away without a backward glance. He had reacted as if three years of marriage, and what she had honestly assumed was happiness, meant absolutely nothing to him. Too late had it occurred to her that she had married a man who had never said he loved her, who had said in fact that he didn't believe in love and who at all times and on all occasions had made his business affairs, rather than her, the top priority in his life.

So, after that shattering betrayal of trust and his very final rejection, it was hardly a surprise that she was finally hitting back. And she knew this course of action would take his feelings towards her from apparent indifference to actively *hating* her. And she didn't care; no, she definitely didn't care what Nikolos Christakis thought of her any more. Love had died when she was finally forced to acknowledge the degradingly low value he had set on her and their marriage, and she supposed that what she was now engaged in was a rather pathetic attempt at hitting back to punish him for the heartbreak he had callously inflicted.

Revenge. It was not a pretty or feminine word but it was also the very last thing a manipulative and cunning business shark like Nik Christakis would expect from his once submissive and soon-to-be ex-wife. He hadn't cared about her but he *did* care about his precious money. There was no greater goal in Nik's life than the ruthless pursuit of profit and the clever conservation of that vast store of personal wealth. Betsy knew that if she could significantly dent Nik in the wallet department, if in no other way, she would finally draw blood. After all, it had taken her outrageous claim of half of everything he possessed to persuade Nik into an actual face-to-face meeting with her again. Self-evidently money mattered to Nik more than she or their marriage had ever mattered.

Footsteps sounded in the corridor outside and

Betsy stiffened. The door handle made a slight noise but the door stayed shut and she froze, her heart leaping into her mouth.

'Let us do the talking,' her legal representative, Stewart Annersley, reminded her afresh.

He might as easily have said that Betsy was out of her league in such company but she already knew that, could barely credit that she had spent three entire years in Nik's world of rarefied wealth and yet contrived to remain easily shocked and gullible. What did that say about her? Was she stupid? A poor reader of people and their motivations? She had been distraught when Nik had taken Gizmo from her. The little dog had been her only comfort and even though Nik was by no means a doggy-orientated male, he had still insisted on taking the animal back. Why?

Betsy believed it was because Nik was the ultimate control freak. Evidently, what was his *stayed* his, unless it was a discarded wife. His most recent attack had been to go after the house that he had never liked but that she loved. Why? Certainly he owned it and he had paid for the restoration, yet he had only bought the property to please her. Or *had* he? Had he simply seen Lavender Hall as a promising investment? More and more Betsy doubted the assumptions she had once made about what motivated Nik.

Without warning, the door sprang open and framed Nik's very tall, well-built body. Her heart hammered madly for a split second and then felt as though it had stopped beating altogether because for a long timeless moment she couldn't move, couldn't breathe, couldn't speak, couldn't even blink. He radiated raw sexual charisma.

His extraordinarily light eyes glittered like gleaming emeralds in his lean, darkly beautiful face, startlingly noticeable eyes and shockingly astute. A thousand memories threatened to consume her—from the recollection of their disastrous first date to their idyllic honeymoon and the lonely challenge of her life once reality had set in—and she fought them off fiercely. He wasn't going to do this to her again, she swore with inner vehemence. He *wasn't* going to break her nerve again.

She lifted her chin, squared her stiff shoulders and stared back at him while carefully blanking him out because she could not face direct eye contact. Yet in the back of her mind she was still plunged into sudden agony by his presence, wondering how this had happened to them, how the man she had once adored could have become her worst enemy. Where had she gone wrong? What had she done to make him treat her with such hostility and unkindness?

And even while paranoia and self-pity threatened to overwhelm Betsy for a dangerous instant, it was Nik's voice she heard inside her head. *'Stop with the persecution complex and the blame game,'* he had once told her. *'Not everything's* your *fault. You're not being punished for some sin in this world or the next. The bad stuff is simply what life throws at you...'*

Nik scanned Betsy with compulsive intensity. Had she shrunk? She had never been very big in either height or size—indeed she barely weighed a hundred pounds soaking wet. Surrounded by her legal posse she was utterly overshadowed. She had definitely lost weight. He wondered if she was eating properly, an old protective instinct kicking in, instantly stamped down on hard and consigned to the back of his mind as inappropriate. It was none of his business any more, equally none of his business that her lawyer, Annersley, was leaning far too close to her, appreciative eyes pinned to Betsy's delicate profile as if she were a prize up for grabs. And of course, endowed with even a tithe of what Nik was worth, Betsy would be very much a trophy for some scheming male to snatch up in the future.

That idea didn't bother Nik, no, it didn't bother him at all, he told himself fiercely, sliding with a degree of unnecessary force into the chair spun out for him by his own team. Naturally there would be other men in Betsy's future; she was a beauty. His attention skimmed over her pale profile. She had always reminded him of a spun-glass figurine, fragile in every proportion, the sort of woman a man wanted to protect and cherish. And where had that chivalrous attitude, shown only to her, taken him? he asked himself cynically. On the road to the divorce court and a poorer future like a thousand other foolish men. *'I want a baby,'* she had said, all tearful blue eyes and trembling lips, breaking their premarital agreement, trying to selfishly, wilfully rewrite history... And she hadn't even noticed that the bottom had fallen out of his world the moment she spoke.

Obviously, Betsy would have that much-desired

baby with another man now. Without warning, Nik's stomach lurched. He gulped down the cup of hot black coffee offered to him and burnt his mouth. Betsy was trying to rob him blind just as his gigolo father, Gaetano, had once tried to rob Nik's mother, Helena. Helena Christakis, however, had been too clever to be conned by Gaetano Ravelli, and Nik's IQ left his mother's at the starting stakes.

More to the point, he didn't give a damn about Betsy now. Like an alcoholic he was taking the cure and the cure was *seeing* her again and feeling nothing. And there she was: tiny, exquisitely provocative in every detail from her cloak of silky pale blonde hair and porcelain skin to the luscious pout of her naturally pink lips. Hard jawline squaring, he searched out her flaws and underlined them in his head: the bump in her nose, the faint scattering of freckles, the ridiculous lack of height and the very modest curves. On a physical level she was very far from being perfect... What the hell had he ever seen in her?

Without warning Betsy glanced up, soft feathery lashes lifting to reveal eyes the colour of the deepest ocean, and instantaneous lust gripped Nik in an iron fist, punching through him so fast that his big, powerful body tensed, his muscles pulling defensively taut while the hungry swelling at his groin tightened the sleek fit of his tailored trousers. His response shocked him and it took a great deal to shock Nik. Indeed, the consternation that followed made sweat break out on his upper lip before he turned colder than snow, utilising every fibre of his single-minded character to crush his unwelcome response to her. Obviously, he reasoned grimly, his momentary arousal was nothing more complex than the knee-jerk reaction of an old habit around a sexually familiar woman.

Betsy stared fixedly at the table while the legal formalities got under way. Nik was at the far end, distant enough to be visually ignored, but every strand of her being was working against her will to turn her neck in that direction to snatch a glance at him. It had been so long, so agonisingly long since she had had the simple luxury of looking at him. Some instinct she could not suppress lifted her head up and for one explosive split second of time she collided with Nik's stunning green eyes, eyes that were positively startling in that lean, dark, devastatingly handsome face of his.

Suddenly she couldn't breathe or move again and the most primitive responses controlled her. Molten heat surged at the core of her and she literally *felt* her breasts stir inside her bra, her nipples prickling and straining into swollen buds. A welter of erotic images assailed her and burning colour drove off her pallor. Later it would hurt that Nik had the power to look away first but in the instant that disconnection occurred she was merely grateful to be set free of that terrible awareness and craving again. How could he still do that to her? How could she *still* feel the power of his scorching sexual attraction?

After all, Nik had put her through hell. He had stayed silent when he should have spoken up. He had even allowed her to go through the horrendous humiliation of discovering the truth that had made a mockery of their marriage from the lips of one of his brothers.

'You will regret this...' Nik had warned her forbiddingly the day she had thrown him out, but her sole regret then had been that she had not found out what he had been hiding from her sooner.

In retrospect she knew she had behaved like a madwoman that day. Temporary insanity had gripped her from the minute her whole world came crashing down around her. She had screamed, she had shouted, she had cursed and he had stood there like a granite rock battered by stormy seas—essentially untouched by her anger, her tears and her pleas for an explanation. In fact he had said nothing beyond the quiet, unemotional admission that what she had learned about him from his younger brother Zarif was indeed the truth: Nik had had a vasectomy at the age of twenty-two and there was absolutely no possibility of him ever having a child with her. But Nik had excluded Betsy from that secret and, unforgivably, he had allowed her to break her heart trying and failing to get pregnant for months on end. Why hadn't he just told her the truth? *'Why?'* she had demanded again and again, and he had stared back at her in resolute brooding silence, refusing to explain his behaviour.

Marisa Glover, the celebrated divorce lawyer by Nik's side, studied Betsy with cool blue eyes and quite casually asked her why she believed that a woman who had been a penniless, dyslexic waitress before her marriage and had not worked since should have a legal claim on half her husband's estate.

'Let's face it…you have no children to support,' the icy blonde beauty reminded the table at large.

All of a sudden, Betsy was bone-white and reeling from the stream of virtual body blows landing on her with the devastating efficiency of bombs, her skin squeezing tight over her bones in horror. Nik had *told* them; he had told them she was dyslexic and mortification drenched her like icy water thrown in her face. As for the reminder that she had no children, that was an even more cruel strike considering that Nik had comprehensively and deviously denied her what she had so desperately wanted.

Her lawyer stepped in to steer the topic in a more practical direction.

Nik scrutinised Betsy's pale, taut profile, the anxious flicker of her lashes, the tightness of her lips, and knew she was hurt, humiliated and still recoiling from Marisa's opening salvo. Marisa was the best divorce lawyer in London and an unashamed barracuda and Nik always employed the best. But now his perfect white teeth were gritted, brown fingers clenching into a fist against a long, powerful thigh. Had Betsy expected him to play nice? Had she thought anything could still be sacred, that anything could remain a secret in their divorce? Could she still be that innocent?

He was still waiting for her legal team to attack, for they certainly had the ammunition. It went without saying that he did not want the curious facts of his hush-hush vasectomy aired in an open court. That was private, considerably more so in his opinion than the dyslexia she was so ashamed of suffering from.

Even so the shaken look of pain and betrayal etched in her tightly controlled but oh, so expressive face got to him whether he liked it or not and distaste and impatience rose in Nik for degrading Betsy in front of witnesses.

Annersley was currently engaged in reminding Marisa that Nik had refused to allow Betsy to work during their marriage, implying that Nik was a dinosaur and a bully of no mean order but doing so in the politest of terms. Marisa was pointing out that Betsy lacked the education required to gain anything other than the most menial of jobs and that a man of Nik's social status could hardly be expected to tolerate a wife taking an unskilled, humble position.

Something suddenly snapped Nik's hold on his volatile temper. Without even thinking about what he was doing, he ground his hands down on the edge of the conference table and sprang upright with an abruptness that startled everybody present. Lean, strong face hawklike, he growled, '*Diavelos*...enough! This ends here. Marisa, you are well aware that Betsy single-handedly runs her own business at Lavender Hall—'

'Well, yes, *but*—'

'We are finished here for now,' he ground out with harsh finality. 'I will discuss this no further—'

'But nothing's been agreed,' Annersley complained.

Betsy stole a grudging glance at Nik, scarcely able to credit that he had brought the humiliating session to so swift a halt. Surely he could not have done that for *her* benefit? She refused to believe that; he had to have some clever ulterior motive. She felt wounded and degraded after having her dyslexia thrown in her face, not to mention the reminder that she had never completed her education to an acceptable level. It infuriated her that she could blame Nik for that last reality, for Nik had complained so bitterly when she was attending evening classes to study for her A levels that she had eventually given them up. Nik might have travelled the globe constantly during their marriage, but when he was at home he had made it very, very clear to her that he always expected her to be there. And she had finally given way to his selfish protests, naively believing that he was admitting to *needing* her and secretly gratified that the male who did not tell her he loved her could not bear to find her missing or unavailable.

'There will be another meeting,' Nik decreed, striding to the door without another glance in Betsy's direction.

Betsy got off the train and walked to her car.

She was angry with herself, as angry as she was ashamed that she had reacted to Nik on so basic a level, responding to his lethal sexual attraction like a silly young girl without self-knowledge or defences. She wanted to feel nothing, absolutely nothing around Nik. After all, nothing was what he deserved. Cristo's wife, Belle, had told Betsy that she should be dating again and that she would not get past her experience with Nik until she did. Unfortunately the last thing

Betsy needed after the heart-rending grief of her marriage breakdown was another man to worry about. Men were very high maintenance; Nik had taught her that.

Her troubled thoughts were already whisking her back in time. When she had first met Nik Christakis she had been working as a waitress at a little bistro across the road from his office.

She had enjoyed her job. *'If a job's worth doing, it's worth doing well,'* her late grandmother had told her when she was a child, and the truth of that homely maxim had never let Betsy down. She refused to let the fact that a job was humble or low paid colour her attitude, but she had always known that had her grandmother survived she would have been very disappointed by Betsy's lack of educational achievement. Her loving gran had taught her that with extra time and specialised tutoring she could overcome her dyslexia and that it was not an excuse for low expectations in life. That awareness in mind, she had chosen her job to fit the fact that she was studying several nights a week at evening class to get her A levels. Oh, she'd had *big* plans back then for a more promising future.

In those days it had never occurred to her that a man could come between her and her wits. She was twenty-one and boys had come and gone, but nobody special, nobody capable of engaging her heart or tempting her body. When she had first seen Nik, he had been sitting at one of her tables in the spring sunshine: a stunningly beautiful male sheathed in a black cashmere overcoat, light green eyes framed by impossibly long, lush black lashes, zapping her with instant tingling awareness as he ordered coffee. She hadn't noticed that Cristo was with him that first time, hadn't even registered the presence of plain-suited men by the wall, hovering with the protectiveness of bodyguards. As always Nik had commanded full centre stage. Her heart had beat so fast it had felt as if it were in her throat and she had feared its crazy acceleration would choke her.

When he had ordered a second coffee, she had left a complimentary biscuit on the table but he had handed it back to her. 'I don't touch sugar...*ever,*' he had told her softly, his foreign accent purring along the syllables with disturbing sexiness.

'Wish I could say the same,' Betsy had breezed back, popping the biscuit in her pocket for later. She had always been hungry, free meals or snacks not having been part of her employment terms. 'But I still have to bring you the biscuit with your coffee. It's management policy.'

'Wasteful,' he had pronounced with a sardonic curve to his handsome mouth. 'But you look like you could use the calories.'

'I'm just skinny. I've always been skinny,' Betsy had parried, dimly conscious of his companion's frowning, silent scrutiny.

'*Cute* skinny,' Nik had countered, whipping his keen gaze over her slender proportions, sending colour flying like a banner into her cheeks. 'Very, *very* cute.'

And she had rushed away to get that second coffee, wondering what on earth was wrong with her. He hadn't been the first customer to try to flirt with her and she had usually taken it in her stride as simple banter, infinitely preferring that approach to that of the occasional creeps who had let their hands stray if she'd got too close. It hadn't occurred to her that he might have actually meant anything by his remarks. After all, she had noticed his fancy coat and the sleek dark suit he had worn beneath it and already categorised him as some high-flying city-executive type and, as such, completely out of her league.

The next time she had served him he had offered her the biscuit first and she had flushed and said hurriedly, 'No, thanks. My boss told me we're not allowed to eat the biscuits because it looks bad.'

'Really?' Nik had quirked a black brow. 'Maybe I should have a word with him—'

'No, please don't say anything,' Betsy had urged in harried retreat with her tray.

'If it worries you that much I won't. My name's Nik, by the way,' he had responded casually.

A tin of incredibly expensive fancy biscuits had been delivered to her at work that afternoon, the gift card signed with a slashed 'Nik'. Betsy had been more embarrassed than pleased, particularly when her boss, Mark, had noted the delivery, asked her if the gift was from a customer and frowned in disapproval when she had confirmed it. When she had thanked Nik for the gift he had shrugged it off as if it was too unimportant to mention.

Nik had come in every Tuesday after that, settling down to chat in a foreign language to Cristo while constantly fielding calls on his mobile phone. Just seeing him had thrilled her and meeting his eyes had electrified her all over, sending heat laced with weird chills racing through her body in an uncontrollable surge. It had not escaped her notice that he watched her as well and that he left her ridiculously large tips that swelled the staff collection box as never before.

'Be careful around that guy,' Mark had warned her one morning. 'I've only just realised who he is. He's Nik Christakis and he owns the office block opposite—NCI, Nik Christakis Industries. And guess what? In his no-doubt vast portfolio of businesses he already has a large chain of coffee shops and I wouldn't like to get on the wrong side of him.'

'He *owns* the building over there?' Betsy had gasped.

'Haven't you ever noticed his bodyguards?' Mark had rolled his eyes at her lack of observation. 'He has to be an extraordinarily wealthy man to need security and you do have to wonder why he's slumming here with us.'

Betsy had felt foolish for not appreciating that Nik was as much a fish out of water in the bistro as snow in July. She had looked him up online and learned that he was Greek and that Cristo was his half-brother. She'd also discovered that Nik had grown up in a very different world from her own. Embarrassed by the adolescent daydreams she had been weaving round him until that point, she had become more circumspect in her behaviour when he was around.

'No smile for me?' Nik had queried on his next visit, catching her fingers in his to halt her and sharply disconcerting her with that move. 'Is something wrong?'

Azure eyes wide, she had reddened. 'No, nothing's wrong. We're just very busy and I'm a bit distracted.'

'Have dinner with me tomorrow night,' Nik had drawled without warning.

Jolted by the invitation, and scarcely believing that he was serious, Betsy had jerkily retrieved her fingers and clutched at her tray. 'Sorry, I can't. I've got a class—'

'The next night you're free,' Nik had interposed smoothly.

'We've got nothing in common,' she had protested.

'But I want you because you're different,' Nik had informed her huskily, making her drop her eyes in shock at that blunt admission and shiver as though her insides were being subjected to a force-ten gale.

'It wouldn't work,' she had argued in a low voice.

'If I say it will work, it will work. *When?*' Nik had pressed mercilessly.

'Er…Friday,' she had admitted in the suffocating silence, horrendously aware of his brother's incredulous scrutiny. 'I'm free Friday night.'

'I'll pick you up at half eight,' Nik had responded calmly and asked for her address.

As she had moved away to serve another customer she had heard Cristo arguing with his brother and she had just *known* it was about her and that Nik's sibling could not credit that his brother had invited a waitress out on a date.

Nik had steamrollered over her objections and she should have seen the writing on the wall then. Nik didn't quit until he got what he wanted. He was relentless, unstoppable and stubborn as a mule.

CHAPTER TWO

NIK WAS ENSCONCED in his limo with a very beautiful blonde. Jenna had seemed the perfect antidote to his difficult morning. She was light-hearted and fun and she wasn't looking for anything serious. She had invited him back to her apartment and neither of them had any illusion about what was to happen there. Now she snuggled up against him, her hand fastening possessively to a long, powerful thigh. He stiffened, resisting a strong urge to shake her off. He was getting a divorce, he reminded himself obstinately. He was a free man. It was past time he acted on that change of status.

Jenna shifted almost onto his lap to kiss him. In a defensive move, he threw his head back and her lips caught his jawline instead. The scent of her washed over him and she smelled wrong to him. Not bad, just somehow and inexplicably...*wrong*. He lifted a hand to her shoulder, long fingers accidentally brushing her hair. It felt coarse instead of silky and he didn't want to touch it. In a fury he willed himself to stop making crazy comparisons. Maybe that was why the normal, healthy male response to an approach from a willing, attractive woman wasn't happening for him.

Thee mou...his body was demonstrating all the reaction of a solid block of wood, he acknowledged in mounting frustration. Something was messing with his head and his libido and he didn't know what but neither was he prepared to discuss the problem with his therapist. He had been forced to explore quite enough unpleasant issues with the good doctor and, while he had every respect for the lady's common sense and discretion, there were still some things he refused to share. He might have unburdened himself of the dark weight of his dysfunctional past and felt stronger for it, but the freedom to return to his former taciturn habits was equally a relief. Sharing anything did not come naturally to a male with his reserved nature. And such acknowledgements were only one more unnecessary reminder that being involved in any way with Betsy was still ruining his life, cutting off his choices and reminding him of his boundaries while stifling the raw energy, the voracious sex drive and the sheer ruthlessness that had always healthily compelled Nik forward in life.

His mobile phone buzzed and he dug it out with an apology, but he already knew he wasn't going back to Jenna's apartment. Clearly she didn't attract him enough, he reflected grimly. When he added in the unthinkable, that for the first time in his life he might fail between the sheets, it was sufficient to crush his need to test himself and prove that he had left his marriage behind him.

No, to achieve that goal he required a rather more civilised approach, he conceded broodingly, momentarily forgetting his companion. Taking some of the aggro out of the situation between him and Betsy would be a good strategic move. That didn't mean he was going to give her a cartload of money or grant any of her ridiculous requests or, worse still, *talk* to her as Cristo had so ludicrously suggested. He didn't want to talk to Betsy. He wouldn't keep his temper if he talked to her and any gain from his breaking of the ice between them would be swiftly destroyed by a fresh flood of hostility and mutual resentment. No, talking of any kind was off the table. *Diavelos,* the lawyers could do the talking.

The day after the legal meeting, Betsy set out the items for sale on the new shelves in the shop and stepped back to assess the display.

She might have gone through hell since her marriage had broken down but, when it came to work, her overwhelming need to keep busy and mentally challenged had ironically ensured that the same months were astonishingly productive and creative in business terms. The little farm shop selling fresh veg, fruit and eggs, which Nik had grudgingly allowed her to open in one of the redundant farm buildings behind the hall, had tripled in size to house the baked goods and home-cooked ready meals she had sourced. Since then she had added the card and gift section, where she stocked everything from potpourri to local crafts. Across the yard, work was noisily progressing as a former ruined cottage was transformed into a small coffee shop.

Behind the counter, her manager, Alice, was chatting cheerfully to a regular customer stocking up for her weekly shop. Betsy had initially hired Alice to ensure that she was always available when Nik was at home, but even though she was now able to work much longer hours the arrangement still worked well. After all, the business had expanded and Alice was good at dealing with the financial side of things, while Betsy was happiest handling suppliers and sourcing new goods.

Furthermore, Alice had the wisdom to understand when not to ask awkward questions. Divorced from a cheating ex and raising three children, she knew all about sleepless nights and heartache. Alice had not said a word when she came into work some mornings and found all their produce rearranged, the fruit so shiny it looked polished and the tiled floor so clean you could see your face in it. Time after time Betsy had taken refuge in work when she couldn't sleep. But there was a far more practical reason behind her industry and the long hours she put in.

Betsy's ultimate goal was to make Lavender Hall self-sufficient because she was mortified by the prospect of hanging on Nik's sleeve for the rest of her days. If she built up the business enough it could support her and cover the wages bill for the staff required not only to run the business but also to maintain the house and garden. In truth, claiming a very large slice of Nik's fortune had not solely been an act of aggression or revenge but more of a counter-attack to his unreasonable demand that Lavender Hall be sold. The house offered Betsy an unparalleled resource as a business base from which she could earn her own living and she had lots of even more ambitious ideas on the back burner for the future.

The phone on the counter buzzed and Alice answered it. 'It's for you,' she told Betsy.

Edna, the hall housekeeper, was on the line. 'You have a visitor, Mrs Christakis. Is it still all right for me to take the afternoon off?' the older woman asked anxiously.

Edna and her husband, Stan, who kept the garden, had provided sterling ongoing support on the home front after Betsy had had to cut back on staff after Nik's departure. With Nik and his high expectations of instant service removed from the equation, there had been no need for a fancy private chef, a driver or a flock of maids.

'Of course it is,' Betsy assured her while abstractedly wondering why she had not named the visitor. Obviously someone familiar, possibly Cristo or even his wife, Belle, she thought hopefully, because she was in the mood for some uplifting company.

Betsy liked Belle, a leggy Irish redhead with boundless vitality and a great sense of fun. Belle had slowly become a trusted friend in spite of the fact that what Belle had to say about Nik was pretty much unrepeatable. Betsy, in turn, admired the way Belle and Cristo had taken on responsibility for the five kids Belle's mother had had during her long-running affair with Cristo and Nik's late father, Gaetano. Nik would never have sacrificed his personal freedom on such a score, she conceded painfully, wondering how she had contrived to be so blind to the reality that the man she wanted to father her child didn't even *like* children.

Smoothing her stretchy black skirt down over her hips and twitching down the pushed-up sleeves of her pink honeycomb-knit sweater, Betsy left the shop and cut through the walled garden to the door in the ten-foot wall that led straight into the hall's vast rear courtyard. When Nik had protested her desire for a commercial outlet at their home, she had reminded him of the size of that wall and had added that the opening up of the former farm lane would preserve their privacy from both customers and traffic. He had remained stalwartly unimpressed, giving way solely because he had known she needed something to occupy her while he travelled abroad so much.

And yet now here she was, running not the hobby shop *he* had envisaged but her own thriving business, she reflected ruefully, striving to raise her flagging spirits with that comforting reminder. Who would ever have thought she had that capability? Certainly not her parents, who had never expected much from her. It had been her grandmother, a retired teacher, who had ensured that Betsy got the help she needed with her dyslexia. In truth, Betsy's parents had never really had much time for Betsy and had been ashamed of her reading and writing difficulties. In fact she was convinced that she had been an accidental conception because even as a child she had been aware that her parents resented the incessant demands of parenthood, no matter how much her grandmother tried to help them out. Her parents had died in a train crash when Betsy was eleven. By then her grandmother had already passed away and Betsy had had to go into foster care, the first seed of her conviction that she would never ever want children already sown by her own distinctly chilly upbringing.

Cutting through the spacious empty kitchen, Betsy hurried through to the big hall and came to a startled halt when she saw the tall, broad-shouldered male with blacker than black hair, standing poised with his back turned to her by the still-open front door.

Nik had already surveyed his surroundings with keen interest, instantly noting the changes since his exit six months earlier. The furniture was a little dusty. There were no fresh flowers adorning the central table, not even a welcoming fire burning in the massive grate. But superimposed over that picture was a misty image of Betsy twirling round the same hall before restoration had made the building habitable.

'Isn't it just amazing?' she had exclaimed in excited appeal on their very first visit to Lavender Hall, her face lit up like a Christmas tree.

'It needs to be demolished,' Nik had countered, unimpressed.

'It's not past saving,' Betsy had argued. 'Can't you feel the atmosphere? The character of the place?

Can't you imagine what it would look like with a little work?'

A little work with a wrecking ball, Nik had thought grimly, uninspired by the chipped and broken bricks and the floor puddled by drips from gaping windows and a leaking roof. She had dragged him off on a tour, chattering with bubbling enthusiasm about how the Elizabethan property was a treasure chest of history and on the endangered historic buildings list. Right from the start he had thought it was a horrible house and about as far removed from his idea of a comfortable and suitable country home as it was possible to imagine. But he had recognised that Betsy had fallen madly in love with the dump and, even though it wasn't what he wanted, he had agreed to buy it for her, a generous act that had rebounded on him many times in the following months when the costs of restoration had risen to outrageous levels.

Ne...yes, he *had* been a decent, caring husband, Nik reflected with brooding hostility. He had tried to make his wife happy, had given her everything she had ever wanted with the single exception of that last impossible demand of hers, and he still could barely credit that their marriage had been destroyed by her desire for, of all things, a baby. Her careless dismissal of the idea of having a child had been so convincing before their marriage.

Lean, strong face tensed by the forbidding tenor of his thoughts, Nik swung round with a frown just as Betsy surged through the kitchen door. She looked harassed, her pale blonde hair tumbling round her delicate, flushed features, making her eyes look more mauve in hue than ever and emphasising the pink, pillowy, luscious shape of her unpainted lips.

Instantaneous desire lit Nik up inside in a firework burst of startling heat that took his breath away. Without the smallest warning everything he had failed to feel in the limo with Jenna the day before surged through him, tightening every muscle in his body and setting off a fast-beating pulse at his groin that made him want to smash something in sheer frustration.

'Betsy,' he breathed in growling acknowledgement.

One glimpse of her visitor and Betsy had frozen in place like someone who had run head first into a solid brick wall. Why on earth hadn't Edna warned her? His sexy-as-sin voice washed over her like rich vanilla ice cream coated in melted dark chocolate, vibrating down her taut spinal cord... Nik's voice, the first weapon in his considerable arsenal of attraction. Nik here at the hall where she had never expected to see him again! His sudden appearance was a huge shock and she blinked rapidly and snatched in a stark breath, striving to brace herself for what could only be bad news of some kind.

'What are you doing here?' she gasped strickenly before she could think better of openly revealing her dismay.

'I needed to see you.'

Unconvinced, Betsy simply stared back at him. His dark grey pinstripe designer suit was faultlessly fitted to every muscular angle of his lean, powerful body. Big and strong, he was a brutal force of nature beneath that sleek, sophisticated façade he wore to the world. In all the months they had lived apart he had made not one single attempt to see her, so why now? Her brain, however, was stuttering to a halt when confronted with Nik in the flesh. Those lean, darkly beautiful features of his drew her in like a fire on a freezing day. She didn't want to look but she couldn't help herself. He had the gorgeous face and classic body of a mythical god, eyes shimmering bright as emeralds, awakening a primal attraction that was rooted so deep inside her she didn't know where it began or how she would ever be free of its sway. Her skin prickled, tiny hairs rising at the nape of her neck as she subdued a responsive shiver. Her heart was racing.

And then mercifully a voice from outside broke into the smouldering silence. 'Come back here!' a man was shouting.

The pitter-patter of rushing paws and an unforgettably familiar bark made Betsy's eyes fly wide in recognition and she hurtled to the door to peer out. An ecstatic bundle of wriggling, whining terrier dog leapt up into her arms and covered every part of her he could reach with delighted doggy kisses.

'I'm very sorry, sir. He leapt through the window of the car,' Nik's driver confided in breathless pursuit.

Nik was tempted to remark that that had to be the most life Gizmo had shown in the two months since he had retrieved the dog from Betsy. With a nod of dismissal to his driver, he thrust the front door closed with an impatient hand and studied the tableau before him. Betsy was down on her knees on the tiled floor smiling and laughing and the terrier was bouncing and leaping around her, the pair of them enacting a mutually jubilant reconciliation scene that even Nik could not remain untouched by. He knew he had made the right decision.

'You brought him here to visit me?' Betsy questioned, glancing up enquiringly, utterly confused by the dog's sudden appearance.

'No, he's here to stay,' Nik informed her wryly. 'He's not happy away from you.'

'But he's *your* dog,' she framed uncertainly, gathering Gizmo into her arms and stroking him to calm him down.

'He was only mine until he met you,' Nik retorted, compressing his mouth into a sardonic line while he noted as she bent over the dog the slight definitive bounce of her small breasts below her sweater, which told him that she was wearing nothing underneath. He became so hard in that split second that he was in literal pain.

Giving Gizmo back to her was an extraordinarily generous gesture and an astonishing move from a male as cold-blooded and unforgiving as Nik, Betsy reflected in bewilderment while she struggled to understand his reasoning. Unfortunately, Nik might be gorgeous but he was also complicated, impossibly so. She had never had much idea what went on inside his handsome head and once again he had taken her very much by surprise.

Gizmo was a stray, who had been knocked over by Nik's limousine months before Betsy even met Nik. He had taken the dog to a veterinary surgery for treatment and when nobody came forward to claim him he had asked the vet to try and find him a home. When that had failed, Nik had baulked at the prospect of putting the little dog into a council home for strays where he would ultimately be put down if he still failed to attract a new owner. Against all the odds, Nik had taken in Gizmo himself, introducing the little animal to a roof garden and a life of luxury food, dog walkers and groomers.

While Betsy reflected on Gizmo's humble beginnings as a stray, Nik was wishing he had stayed safe at the office. Watching Betsy shower affection on his dog filled him with conflicting feelings. He wanted to look at her but he didn't want to be with her or note the way the sunlight flooding through the windows gleamed over her impossibly pale blonde hair, accentuating her porcelain-perfect skin and haunting blue eyes. He especially didn't want the intensely sexual arousal currently coursing through his big, powerful body like a runaway train.

'Thank you from the bottom of my heart,' Betsy told him with tears in her eyes. 'I've missed him so much.'

Restored to his proper home, Gizmo trotted off cheerfully to explore his old haunts.

Nik studied Betsy with smouldering green eyes and her heart gave a sudden jarring thud.

Betsy *knew* that look of hunger on Nik's hard,

handsome face and it burned through her like a lightning strike, riveting her to the spot. That light in his stunning gaze told her that he wanted her and she couldn't stop her body reacting to that lure. An unbearable ache stirred at the apex of her slender thighs and she pressed them tightly together as if she could lock it in and deny it. Her breasts swelled beneath her sweater, making her all too aware of their bareness as her nipples were grazed by the wool.

'Come into the sitting room,' she urged, scrambling upright to lead the way as if he were a genuine guest visiting an unfamiliar place. 'Why didn't Edna tell me it was you?'

'I asked her not to. I wanted to surprise you.'

'Well, you've certainly done that,' Betsy admitted truthfully, struggling to credit that he was actually with her in what had once been the home they shared, even if it did cross her mind that Nik had spent more time in hotel rooms round the globe than he had ever spent with her. But that look he had given her—her thoughts raced back to that, worrying at it like a dog at a bone. *Why* had he looked at her like that? Surely he could not still find her attractive? Nik had been a less than enthusiastic lover in the last months of their marriage, although, now knowing about the vasectomy as she did, she could finally comprehend his loss of interest. Back then she had only thought of sex in terms of getting pregnant and she had no doubt that he had found her attitude a turn-off. No, don't think about sex, *don't think about sex,* she urged herself feverishly.

Betsy hovered awkwardly. 'Would you like a coffee?' she asked, because she was eager for the chance to escape to the kitchen for a few minutes and pull herself back together again.

'No, thanks, but I'll take a drink,' Nik declared, long, powerful legs carrying him across the room to the drinks cabinet, where he proceeded to help himself.

Unnerved by the fact that he could still confidently make himself at home while remaining utterly impervious to the discomfiture some men might have felt in the same situation, Betsy breathed in slow and deep to ground herself. 'I gather you want to talk—'

Nik spun back to her with the liquid grace of movement that always caught her eye and frowned at her, black brows drawing down, wide, sensual mouth twisting in dismissal. 'No. I don't want to talk,' he told her abruptly before he tossed back the finger of Scotch whisky he had poured neat and set down the empty glass again.

'Then…er…*why?*' she began in confusion.

His spectacular green eyes zeroed in on her with penetrating force and a flock of butterflies was unleashed in her tummy while her heartbeat kicked up pace again. 'I'm only here to return Gizmo.'

'Oh…' Betsy framed for want of anything better to say. A few months ago she would have shot accusations at him, demanded answers and would have thoroughly upset herself and him by resurrecting the past, which consumed her. But that time was gone, she acknowledged painfully, well aware that any reference to more personal issues would only send him out of the door faster. Nik had always avoided the personal, the private, the deeper, messier stuff that other people got swamped by. From the minute things went wrong in their marriage she had been on her own.

Nik scrutinised her lovely face, willing himself to find fault, urging himself to discover some imperfection that would switch his body back to safe neutral mode again. And yet on another level he was relieved, even satisfied by his arousal, grateful for the discovery that there was nothing at all amiss with his sex drive. Nor could he think of anything that could quench the swelling fullness of desire holding him rigid, unquestionably not the tantalising awareness that Betsy, all five feet nothing of her and regardless of her lack of experience before their marriage, was absolutely incredible in bed.

'*Se thelo*...I want you,' he heard himself admit before he was even aware that the words were on his tongue.

So Nik, *so* explosively unpredictable, Betsy reasoned abstractedly, colour rushing into her cheeks as a hot wave of awareness engulfed her. Jewel-bright eyes assailed hers in an almost physical collision and something low and intimate in her body clenched hard. Her legs turned so weak she wasn't convinced they were still there to hold her up but she was held in stasis by the intensity of his narrowed green gaze.

'And you want me,' he told her thickly. It was classic, pure textbook Nik to tell her what she was feeling before she even knew it herself.

And Betsy knew she ought to argue and defend herself while telling him all the many reasons why that could not possibly be true, not least the fact that his deception and his willingness to turn his back on their marriage had made her *hate* him with the same passion that she had once loved him.

But, inexplicably, in that rushing silence filled only with the accelerated thump of her heart in her own ears, she said nothing, couldn't find the words, indeed was plunged into so much confusion her mind was a mess of barely formed thoughts and reactions.

CHAPTER THREE

NIK STALKED FORWARD with slow predatory grace, yet for all that there was barely a coherent thought in his handsome dark head. There was no reason, only re-action, no motive other than a desire that gripped him tighter than any vice, in fact a desire so powerful it made him throb and ache.

He reached for Betsy, tugging her arms round his neck, clamping her slim body close, sealing those soft curves to his with a raw exhalation of relief he could not suppress. Backing her to a wall, he raised her high to seize her mouth and claim it, opening his mouth over hers, using pressure to force an entrance and then delving deep with a hungry, devouring pas-sion that stole the breath from her lungs. He tasted of whisky and spice and Betsy drank him in like an ad-dictive drug, head spinning on an intoxicated high. He kissed her as if his life and hers depended on it and his raw urgency fired her up even more, her head falling back to allow him greater access.

Betsy whimpered beneath his lips, holding herself stiff while she fought a rearguard action in the back of her mind in which a voice was screaming that she didn't want to do what she was doing. Unfortunately, she very much *did* want to do it at that moment when only passion ruled and reason couldn't get a look-in. She was no victim either. Her tongue tangled with his and teased back, her small hands kneading his strong arms, rejoicing in the strength of him but frustrated by the barrier of his clothing.

Nik curved his hands to her bottom below her skirt, discovering to his satisfaction that her love of skimpy underthings still reigned supreme, and with one violent wrench the lacy knickers were torn away. Betsy gasped in shock.

'You want me,' Nik husked in hoarse excuse against her swollen mouth, his warm breath fanning her skin.

Oh, *how* she had wanted, night after night, day after day, craving what she had lost, missing the passion and the closeness and the intimacy that had once been so much a part of her life while wondering if she would ever trust anyone enough to let them touch her again. Every screaming skin cell was conscious of the proximity of Nik's hand to the hottest, neediest place in her body and she couldn't vocalise, couldn't think of anything but the deep-down, all-encompassing hunger for his touch.

Bracing her to the wall, he thrust her sweater out of his path with an impatient hand to enable him to close his mouth hungrily round a plump pink nipple while his palm cupped the firm pouting curve. Betsy moaned, eyes tight shut, sensation darting down to the hot, liquid heart of her. A wild pulse of need was mounting there while he teased that tender swollen tip with the edges of his teeth and his tongue. Clinging to his shoulders, she spread her thighs and clamped them to his waist. Finally she could feel him even through his clothing, learn the hard, urgent thrust of his erection as he ground his hips into the apex of her slender thighs, provoking an impatient cry from her lips. Arching her pelvis into him, she shuddered and moaned.

They were acting like horny teenagers, she registered suddenly, in a short-lived burst of mental clarity and embarrassment. This is not me, this is *not* me. And it was her last chance to shout stop and her lips actually parted and then he found her with his hand, a long, knowing finger sliding into the hot, wet sheath of her body. In reaction, an explosion of fiery heat shot through her and she jerked against him, overwhelmingly eager for his touch, for anything that would assuage the intolerable scream of need building up so fast inside her that she could not contain it.

Nik struggled to support her at the same time as he unfastened his trousers. Betsy emitted a breathy moan when she felt him push against her. She was on a high of uncontrollable excitement, her hands biting into his shoulders, urging him on. He aligned their bodies, spreading her open before bringing her down on him. He sank into her slowly, stretching the sensitive tissue with his length and girth to the burning edge of pain. But it was so much a pleasurable pain that she almost wept at the thrill of his invasion be-

cause for the first time in many months she felt like
a living, breathing woman again.

'Nik…?' she whispered shakily.

'No talk, *hara mou,*' he gritted, tilting her back
at an angle, using the wall to partially support her as
he slammed back into her again with sensual, dominant force. '*Thee mou,* what you do to me! Don't tell
me to stop!'

At that moment Betsy wasn't capable of such a
feat. She was already at fever pitch. An agony of desire and helpless need controlled her. Gripping her
slender thighs, ebony-lashed green eyes blazing with
emerald fire, Nik surged and retreated, keeping up
the erotic pace with perfect timing. Her excitement
rose with every driving thrust, pushing her higher
and higher until finally she reached the crest and it
shattered her, making her writhe and sob and cry out.

'That was spectacular…' Nik breathed raggedly as
he lowered Betsy's legs slowly back to the floor. She
was weak, dizzy, unsteady on her feet, and even he
was trembling. What had he done? *Diavelos,* what had
he done? Yet in spite of that rational voice inside his
head, Nik shed his jacket, yanked free his tie, contriv-
ing both instinctive actions without once letting go
of Betsy. He tugged her by the wrist across the floor
to the rug by the dying fire and drew her down on it
to face him on her knees. He laced both hands into
her tumbled hair, palms framing her cheekbones, and
kissed her again, sliding his tongue between her lips,
skating it over the sensitive roof of her mouth until she

quivered and her hands curved over his arms again to support herself.

She couldn't think, could barely breathe and could hardly believe that that single kiss had sent the heat surging again like a gushing river of liquid fire in her belly. Satiation was washed away by a renewed tingling and prickling of potent awareness that covered her entire skin surface with heat. He pulled her down, rearranging her legs to cradle him, pinning her beneath the weight and bulk of his lean, muscular body.

'I'm not done yet, *hara mou,*' he confessed thickly, luxuriant black lashes low over scorching emerald eyes, lean, strong face taut, cheekbones flushed.

Her hand rose of its own volition and she ran her fingertips along the mobile line of his often hard-set mouth. It had a softer, more flexible cast now. She thought of him bringing Gizmo home and she gazed up at him, curiously at peace with what had happened, her heart full to overflowing. After all, she never had been able to second-guess Nik's next move and she guessed she never would have that power because he was very much a law unto himself.

He shifted against her, lithe and dynamic as a jungle cat, and she felt him hard and ready again against her stomach. 'Don't ask me to stop,' he groaned.

'Take off your shirt,' she whispered, amazingly relaxed in his arms, marvelling at how right it felt to be there again although even in that instant, in a part of her brain, she wouldn't acknowledge she knew she would never be able to justify what she had done.

He levered back from her and hauled roughly at

the garment. A couple of buttons went flying and a long, brown, mouth-watering wedge of a six-pack male torso appeared between the parted edges. Her mouth ran dry, tiny little slivers of excitement sparking again. She arched up against him, revelling in the skin-to-skin contact she had never thought she would feel again with him. With a hungry sound in the back of his throat he kissed her again, sliding between her slender thighs, hitching her skirt with impatient hands.

'This time...*slow,*' he framed in raw promise.

'Am I the hare or the tortoise?' she teased.

'Something about you turns me into the hare every time.'

Betsy laughed. 'Is this us again?' she mumbled wonderingly.

'This is now, *only* now,' Nik contradicted with innate precision, covering her mouth again with his to silence her and stop the questions and then lingering to savour her.

He sank into her again as slowly as he had promised. The taste of him was still on her lips and she was achingly sensitive to his every movement. A long, breathy sigh was extracted from her.

'Too much?' he prompted, staring down at her.

'Not enough,' she said daringly. 'I'm not made of glass... I won't break!'

Her heart and her body jumped in concert when he twisted his lithe hips and added a more dominant flavour to his possession, sensation winging through her in slow, delicious waves. She closed her eyes to contain her feelings, the excitement catching at her again and flaring bright as a falling star, making every nerve ending strain in longing for the ultimate peak. He quickened his pace and delicious friction intensified the electrifying pleasure. She moaned and her voice rose against her volition into a cry of shocked release, her whole body shaking with the soul-deep force of it as he emitted a raw groan of pleasure.

Nik eased back from her, righting his clothing, reaching down to scoop her up into his arms.

'What are you doing?' she framed limply, eyes flying open.

'Taking you to bed, where we should have gone in the first place,' Nik informed her, striding across the hall towards the heavily carved staircase.

'What we did was more exciting,' Betsy mumbled, thinking of how very long it had been since they had done anything this instantaneous or uninhibited. For the first time she recognised how much her campaign to fall pregnant had cost them in terms of intimacy. Nothing had been the same once that process had started.

Nik carried her into the room they had once shared and froze by the side of the bed, scanning the unfamiliar surroundings. The décor had changed and even the furniture was new. His mouth quirked. The reality jolted him, pushing him in the direction of thoughts he was determined not to think just then. He settled her down on the wide, low bed and undressed her with cool efficiency, tugging off the sweater, unzipping her skirt and slipping off her shoes before pulling the duvet over her.

'I need a shower,' he admitted. 'Is there still one in the bathroom? Or have you got rid of that as well?'

Betsy almost laughed. 'Of course the shower's still in there.'

She lay watching him strip, a sight she had never thought to see again, and the experience felt utterly unreal. He strode naked into the bathroom, yet she had recognised his unease with his surroundings. He didn't like change; he never had. The new colour scheme and furniture had made him tense and uncomfortable. Well, what had he expected? That she would continue to live with the bed they had once shared, allowing her home to inflict constant wounding with memories of what they had once shared together and lost? No, at least Belle had helped Betsy to make that much of a fresh start.

Nik emerged from the bathroom still towelling dry his black hair. She was startled to notice that he was still fully aroused. Nik had assumed that Betsy would fall asleep, but she was awake, wide, evocative azure eyes pinned to him. She was snuggled down under the duvet, hair as pale as a young child's trailing across the pillow in tousled disarray. Would he simply have got dressed and left had she been conveniently asleep? He honestly didn't know the answer to that question. What he did know as he looked at her was that he wasn't yet ready to leave, and without hesitation he tossed back the duvet and climbed in beside her.

'It's the middle of the day,' she reminded him, colour heating her face.

'Are you only remembering that now?' Nik traded sardonically, and she might have snapped back had he not closed his arms round her and tugged her reassuringly close. 'What does it matter what time it is?'

'It doesn't,' she conceded and then said in a different tone altogether, *'Nik?'*

'Shush,' he breathed, fearful of what she might say, curving her up against his still taut and aroused length with an exhilarating sense of extraordinarily intense satisfaction.

'You're *still*—' she began.

'I am,' Nik agreed, draping her tiny body over top of him with care. 'Do you think you could do anything about that?'

'You're not joking, are you?' Betsy knew he wasn't joking because she could feel him hard as an iron bar beneath her.

'Evidently you make me insatiable, *hara mou.*'

Her palms curved to his broad shoulders. Nik had enormous reserves of charm when he chose to utilise them but it was a very long time since he had bothered to show her that side of him. As a result, the slashing charismatic smile that lit up his lean dark features literally mesmerised her, leaving her defenceless. He lifted his head and tasted her parted lips with an intensity that set up a chain reaction of response that slivered through her bloodstream and sprang a sneak attack on her. He tasted so good and his lean hands were stroking up and down her slender spine, finding spots that felt erogenous even though she knew they were not. Even sealed to the heat and hard muscularity of him, she shivered, her heart hammering again, astounded by events and yet covertly flattered by his unquenchable hunger for her.

'One more time and then you can sleep,' Nik husked, rolling her back against the pillows and leaning over her, his devastatingly dark and masculine attraction enhanced by the shadow of stubble beginning to roughen his lower cheekbones and jawline.

'Time off for good behaviour?' she teased.

Claiming her mouth hungrily again in answer, he caught a swollen nipple between finger and thumb and rubbed the tender tip. A flame darted anew through her slender length and centred at her core, renewing the throb of awareness she had believed quenched. 'You could always make me want you,' she breathed in a helpless admission.

'Once you only wanted me when it was the right day on your temperature chart,' Nik reminded her with more than a hint of ice in his dark deep voice.

Something shrivelled and died inside Betsy and she would have done anything not to have roused that memory, which tore an ugly hole in the cocoon of togetherness she had spun for them in her mind. She pressed up against him, flattening her breasts to his broad, hair-roughened chest, and nipped at his full lower lip in reproof. 'I don't have a chart any more—'

'*Siopi*...quiet,' he urged and kissed her until she couldn't remember what they had been talking about and, furthermore, no longer cared.

He tasted wonderful. He even smelled wonderful, the evocative scent that was uniquely him flaring her nostrils, firing her senses with a tormenting familiarity that made her feel ridiculously safe. Expert fingers traced her breasts and skimmed up the inside of her thigh, teasing, taunting until the torment made her squirm and twist and whimper in frustration, wanting, by then *needing* so much more. Only when the hunger he had skilfully awakened rose to an unbearable intensity did he shift over her, sliding into the honeyed welcome of her body with an ease and dexterity that made her cry out and arch her spine. And from that point on, once an answering passion had fully seized her, the tenor of his approach changed and his shallow thrusts became deep and strong and she could feel what control she retained slipping away as the excitement built and built until finally she came, screaming his name, and almost instantly fell into the deep sleep of complete exhaustion.

Darkness had fallen beyond the windows when a slight sound awakened Betsy. She lifted her head from the pillow and everything came flooding back with much the same effect as having a bucket of cold water thrown over her and she sat up with an abrupt start of energy. Nik was engaged in tying his tie in front of the cheval mirror in the corner and hot, mortified colour enveloped her from top to toe. She hugged the sheet, afraid to think, shrinking from the prospect of passing judgement on herself.

'You're leaving?' she whispered as she switched on the bedside lamp.

Nik swung round, eyes light and glittering in the shadows, reticence etched in every angle of his lean, strong face. 'I should've gone hours ago—'

'Were you planning to walk out without speaking to me first?' Betsy pressed tightly because her throat was closing over. She edged the sheet as high as she could, so tense that her muscles ached from the strain.

'That might have been easier for both of us,' Nik quipped, striding to the foot of the bed to gaze down at her from his considerable height.

'How so?'

'I've heard that *this*...' he shifted a fluid brown hand in a gesture that encompassed both her and the bed '...is quite common for couples going through a divorce.'

Betsy felt as if he had punched her in the stomach and she lost colour, her skin pulling taut across her fragile bone structure. 'Really?' she queried with no expression at all.

'Yes, really,' Nik fielded drily. 'It happens but it doesn't mean anything, doesn't change anything.'

For the very first time in her life, Betsy wanted another human being lying stone dead at her feet. But even then she wouldn't forgive Nik, she reckoned wildly, plunged as she was into an abyss of mortification and pain and, worst of all, the dreadful conviction that it was *her* mistake that had unleashed such a humiliation on her.

'Obviously, we're still getting a divorce,' Nik assured her, underlining the point quite unnecessarily as though he feared that she might be too stupid to get that message.

'Yes,' she agreed, knowing that even the sight of him falling down dead at her feet wouldn't satisfy her sufficiently. Hatred now leapt through her as fierily as the passion that had betrayed her. In spite of everything he had done to her, she had missed him, missed sex, and she was paying the price for her wretchedly poor judgement now.

'We both need to move on,' Nik breathed curtly.

'Until now I never appreciated what a taste you have for platitudes,' Betsy responded grittily. 'You have patronised me, insulted me and used me. Now I know what it feels like to be a booty call.'

Nik ground his teeth together. He had said what he had to say. He was exceptionally intelligent and he knew the score, even if calling it was insensitive. They had both made a mistake and it was his place to spell that out. He wasn't built to closely connect with another human being. After the abusive childhood he had endured, how could he possibly be? There was a lack in him, not in her, and he could never give her what she wanted and deserved.

'I'll let you keep the house as well,' he told her flatly.

'It's good to know I profited from prostituting myself,' Betsy hurled back at him shakily, tears burning the backs of her eyes like acid. 'For goodness' sake, *go!*'

And without fanfare that was exactly what Nik did. The door snapped shut in his wake but not before

Gizmo had inserted himself through the gap and hurtled towards his only recently rediscovered mistress.

'Oh, Gizmo...' she gasped, her voice catching on a sob as she hugged the shaggy little dog to her chest.

Nik had just walked out on her again. His driver would have sat outside waiting for him all these hours. That wouldn't bother Nik and he wouldn't apologise for his thoughtlessness either. The only child of a fabulously wealthy Greek heiress, Nik was accustomed to staff who never questioned or complained and he paid highly for a very high standard of service. A wife with a similar attitude would have suited him so much better than Betsy ever had. She had wanted too much from him and had fought her own corner too hard while demanding an independence of thought and action that had frequently infuriated him. But then bearing in mind his behaviour on their first catastrophic date, she really couldn't say that she hadn't been warned that nothing would be plain sailing with Nik Christakis at the helm...

And because the far distant past was less threatening than the turmoil of the present, she let her mind drift back to that evening and a wry smile formed on her lips. Nik had taken her to a glitzy party, where her little black dress unembellished by jewellery or a designer bag or shoes had failed to cut the mustard. Ten minutes after their arrival, Nik had excused himself and abandoned her, leaving her alone in a sea of strangers to be hit on by strange men and visually crucified by much-better-dressed women. After an hour and a half during which she had failed to find him she had angrily embarked on the long journey home by bus and train. He had turned up on her doorstep after midnight to furiously demand to know why she had walked out on him. And they had had their first row, a flaming no-holds-barred argument where he insisted he had only left her alone for about fifteen minutes.

'You were away well over an hour… You treated me like dirt. I should've known what kind of treatment I was in for when you picked me up and then spent the entire drive to the party talking to someone on your phone!'

He had forgotten the time; she knew that. It was also possible that he had even forgotten he had brought Betsy to the party in the first place because an old friend had offered him a deal and business always took precedence with Nik. He had sent her flowers every day for a week afterwards and had then visited the bistro for coffee every day the following week.

'You're acting like a stalker,' she had warned him.

'Give me one more chance. I'll treat you like a queen,' Nik had promised.

'You know, Mr Christakis doesn't usually go to so much trouble with women,' one of his bodyguards had told her chattily. 'You must be special.'

And when she had returned with Nik's coffee and those brilliant green eyes clung to her, she had realised that he did make her feel special. Everyone made mistakes, she had thought forgivingly; she would give him the chance to prove that he could act differently. And for a very long time afterwards she had not regretted that decision because Nik, she now recognised, had been on his very best behaviour. She even remembered the day he had asked her how she felt about having children. She couldn't remember how the dialogue had progressed in that direction but with hindsight suspected that he had guided it there.

'I don't want children!' she had proclaimed, wincing at the very idea. 'I spent my teenage years in foster homes and I spent a lot of time helping to look after the younger ones and the babies. Kids are so much work and such a tie. I don't think I'll ever want any.'

But Betsy had discovered the hard way that Mother Nature had amazing ways of working her wiles to persuade a woman that what she wanted most in the world was a little baby. When she'd first married Nik she had been Cinderella and he had been Prince Charming. He had given her so much in terms of material things that she had somehow never dared to complain that he was rarely at home and was invariably preoccupied with business even when he was. He had missed her birthday and their first anniversary and slowly but surely she had become incredibly lonely and had begun to crave what she had never dreamt she would crave—a baby to love and keep her company.

In the grip of that desire she had made stupid optimistic assumptions, believing that Nik would spend more time at home if they had a child, that a child to share would bring them closer, hopefully breaking through his reserve as she had already discovered she could not.

She had made so many mistakes with Nik, Betsy acknowledged wretchedly, dabbing her damp cheeks dry on the sheet, soothing Gizmo when he whined and pushed his muzzle under her hand. But Nik had made just as many mistakes with her. Getting back into bed with him again, however, had to qualify as her crowning act of stupidity. Her face burned hot while her body ached in silent evidence of her weakness. Afterwards, Nik had been so cold, so sure that their renewed intimacy meant nothing. Why? Because it had meant nothing to him and he had been appalled by the idea that she might think otherwise.

Once again, Nik had taught her a hard lesson. A woman worthy of being treated like a queen had to maintain standards to exercise that power over a man. When she abandoned those standards, she was infinitely more likely to be treated like a booty call.

CHAPTER FOUR

'BETSY?' CRISTO'S WIFE, Belle, questioned eagerly. 'Why haven't you been answering your phone? Where have you been? What have you been up to?'

It was a bad moment for her friend to have phoned because Betsy couldn't concentrate. Betsy sank weakly down on an armchair and contemplated the results of her insane shopping trip to the nearest pharmacy: no less than *five* separate pregnancy-testing kits. And each and every one of the kits had given her the same answer. Ironically she was deeply familiar with such testing procedures. When she and Nik had still been together, whenever her menstrual cycle had shown the slightest deviation, she had rushed out to buy a test, inwardly praying for a positive result and each and every time she had been disappointed it had broken her heart afresh.

This time around, however, everything was very different. Betsy had been feeling out of sorts for weeks before she finally went to visit her GP and she had gone there without the smallest suspicion of the truth now facing her. Indeed she didn't know how she would ever walk through the door of the doctor's surgery again without feeling embarrassed. A simple test had disclosed the fact that she had inexplicably conceived and her response to the news had been more than a little hysterical while she told first the doctor and then the nurse that there had been a mistake, that they must have mixed up her results with someone else's and that in any case, a pregnancy was a complete impossibility.

'*Betsy?*' Belle exclaimed. 'Are you still there?'

'Yes, sorry, I'm just a little preoccupied right now.'

'It's the divorce, isn't it?' her friend said grimly. 'You've been upset. That's why you haven't been in touch. What has that wretched man done to you now?'

Betsy compressed her lips, because astonishingly it seemed that Nik *had* contrived the impossible. In spite of the fact that he'd had a vasectomy and he was sterile, or whatever people chose to label it, and she had endured many months of striving to get pregnant by him and failing, a miracle or a catastrophe— depending on one's viewpoint—had occurred and she was now carrying Nik's baby. How on earth *could* that be possible? Betsy breathed in deep and slow because even sitting down she felt giddy and more than a little nauseous.

'It's not something I can share,' Betsy said, inwardly wincing at that severe understatement.

'Something happened when Nik brought Gizmo back to you…didn't it?' Belle prompted worriedly. 'You haven't been yourself since then—'

'Yes, something happened,' Betsy confirmed

reluctantly. 'But not something I can talk about right now—'

The pregnancy that she had once craved had actually materialised but she no longer had the support system of either a marriage or a father for her unborn child. That awareness put a very different complexion on the situation.

'I just knew it was too good to be true when he gave you the dog back!' Belle exclaimed heatedly. 'And then the house, for goodness' sake! Nik Christakis suddenly starts playing Santa Claus! There's something wrong with that image—'

'I promise I'll phone you in a few days when I've sorted stuff out,' Betsy cut in ruefully. 'I'm sorry but I just can't talk about this yet.'

Betsy switched off her phone and stared into space, rather than at the testing kits and packaging. There was no avoiding her next step: she needed Nik to explain how she could have fallen pregnant by a man who'd had a vasectomy. She could not possibly keep her condition a secret from him. Nik had to be told that he was going to be a father, whether he liked the idea or not. No, without a doubt, Nik had to be informed that he had got her pregnant and he had to be forced to accept that fact even if it meant the humiliation of having to undergo DNA testing as evidence after their child was born. Betsy was already excruciatingly aware that Nik would not want their child and would probably much prefer to believe that she had fallen pregnant by some other man, thereby absolving him from all responsibility and the threat of a continuing connection to the wife he could hardly wait to divorce.

Over the past two months Betsy's spirits had steadily sunk into the doldrums. Coming to terms with the explosive passion that had plunged her into renewed sexual intimacy with her estranged husband had proved a mammoth challenge. The emotional wound Nik had inflicted was almost as great as the agony of feeling that she had seriously let herself down. Yet she wasn't a victim, wasn't a weakling, wasn't one of those women who forgave a man no matter how badly he treated her. She had *not* forgiven Nik and she was mortified that she had gone to bed with him again.

What had made her feel even worse was the painfully obvious fact that Nik could not wait to draw a double black line below their marriage and mark it finished. He had returned Gizmo, and just two weeks earlier had offered her a very generous final financial settlement through his lawyers. All the writing was on the wall. He wanted out of their marriage fast. She knew how Nik operated. He was stubborn and impatient and as cutting as a polished steel blade. He didn't waste time with anything he didn't want, and anything he did want he wanted it yesterday and he most definitely *wanted* the divorce.

So, how was she to approach a male so eager to cut their final ties and forget about her and tell him news that he couldn't possibly want to hear? Her small shoulders straightened with sudden spirit and purpose. Well, tough for Nik! He had got her pregnant, hadn't he? He was the one who had neither warned her of that risk nor guarded her against it and the consequences were as much his fault as her own. He might not want children but the warmth stealing through Betsy at the knowledge that she carried her first child was already infiltrating the shock value of the same discovery. She wanted *her* baby and she knew he would not. The facts were there. A male who had had a vasectomy at such a young age could *never* have wanted a child. But mercifully what Nik wanted no longer needed to influence her, Betsy acknowledged with relief, and allowing herself to be intimidated by a development for which they were both equally responsible would be silly and spineless, and Betsy was neither of these things.

'It's not convenient. Inform her that I will be in touch.' With difficulty Nik swallowed his ire at the polite lie he was being forced to utter before setting his phone down and returning to his business meeting.

Evidently Betsy had shown up uninvited and was waiting outside his office to see him. What on earth had come over her? She was well aware that he hated being interrupted for any reason during working hours. His perfect white teeth gritted, anger at her lack of consideration stirring. If she had something she needed to say to him she had a lawyer to act as her spokesperson, as did he. He did not want personal contact with her; he wanted a smooth, clean and civilised divorce.

Even so, a defiant image glimmered in the back of

his mind, a frankly licentious image of Betsy's slender, perfect body splayed across that bed at Lavender Hall, and outraged by that unwelcome intrusion, he kicked the image out again, wide, sensual mouth settling into a tense line of compression. Sleeping with Betsy again had been like turning over a stone, because all sorts of things he would rather not deal with had come tumbling out in the aftermath. Given time, however, the memories would fade and disappear, he assured himself resolutely.

He had paid absolutely no heed to his therapist's suggestion that he was deeply conflicted on the subject of his marriage. In that line the lady talked a lot of nonsense! Nik believed in keeping things simple and he fully understood why he had done what he had done. He had gone off the rails and fallen back into a better-forgotten past for a few hours…that was *all*. Soon his marriage would be as decently buried as the terrifying nightmares and flashbacks that had plagued him for years already were.

Betsy listened with a polite smile to the message Nik's stalwart PA, Steve, passed on with fervent apologies that she was persuaded had not fallen from Nik's lips. But Steve, unlike his boss, was a nice guy. Once upon a time Betsy's very rare visits to Nik's office building had been greeted with disconcerting attention and servility because she had been deemed a person of importance in Nik's world. Now, however, it was clear that she had lost that polished passport to special treatment and was viewed as being about as relevant to Nik as yesterday's newspaper.

'Thanks, Steve,' she said, sweeping up her sensible leather rucksack bag, ruefully conscious that her casual jeans and plain black pea coat had attracted raised brows of surprise since her arrival.

But then probably for the very first time ever, Betsy was happy to simply be herself in Nik's sophisticated radius, not the more glossy, artificial self she had long believed he found infinitely more attractive. So, she hadn't dressed up for his benefit and wasn't wearing high heels, designer clothing or even very much make-up. Nik was the husband who had deceived her, hurt her and humiliated her and she was determined to seek neither his approval nor his admiration.

As the PA walked away Betsy moved purposely in the opposite direction to head straight for Nik's office. Nik had wasted enough of her morning and she wasn't prepared to kick her heels any longer on his behalf! Why should she? She was no longer eager to please and conform to nonsensical rules that had once made her feel more like an irrelevant nuisance than a legally wedded wife with rights and needs of her own.

Betsy thrust Nik's office door wide, scanning the half-dozen men seated round the small conference table with flaring midnight-blue eyes of enquiry before settling her attention on Nik's lean, hard-boned face. 'I need to see you…*now*,' she declared without hesitation.

A feverish glimmer of dark colour rose to accentuate the exotic line of Nik's hard cheekbones, his green eyes flaring like emeralds in bright sunlight to betray more than a glint of outrage. He stood upright, lithe and fit as the predator he was, and shifted a hand in dismissal as Steve raced through the door a mere breathless step in Betsy's wake.

'Gentlemen, we'll have to take a break. I'll see you in an hour,' Nik informed his companions flatly.

The other men filed out and the door snapped shut behind Betsy. Her attention had not once wavered from Nik. Even his business suit couldn't hide the lean, powerful perfection of his athletic body. She remembered the appalling nightmares he used to have and how even though it was the middle of the night he would go down to the basement gym to work out afterwards, before finally falling back exhausted into bed still wet from the shower.

Immobile as a statue now, she could hear her own breath scissoring audibly through her tight throat while her heart thumped so hard with stress she would have liked to press a hand to her chest to slow it down. But that, much like apologising, would have been a dead giveaway of her inner turmoil and Betsy had no intention of making such a crucial error in Nik's forceful and assured presence.

'What the hell are you playing at?' Nik demanded in a harsh undertone, appraising her unfamiliar appearance with a frown of incomprehension.

For some inexplicable reason she was dressed like a student and she looked impossibly young, blue eyes huge in her delicate heart-shaped face. She was five years younger than him, *only* five and yet sometimes the distance between them had seemed an unbridgeable gulf because she had a quality of innocence and a level of trust in other people that he had lost at a very early age. But then if he was honest that difference in their outlook had been a strong part of her appeal, he acknowledged reluctantly. He had known she would always need his strength to protect her while also knowing that love made her loyal and naively trusting and that she would always be there waiting for him in the background.

And even with her dressed as carelessly as she was now, Betsy's beauty still rocked him where he stood. That awareness shook him because it seemed as though all his mental prompts that she was imperfect had only highlighted the fact that she somehow made imperfection the absolute definition of pure exquisiteness on his terms. Instinctive desire kindled in him, his temperature rising, his libido purring into gear. His keen gaze lingered on the lush curve of her mouth and the tender white of her fragile throat where it emerged from a roll-neck sweater while he remembered the taste of her mouth and the feel of it on him.

'It's payback time…the magic moment when all your sins come home to roost,' Betsy told him in direct challenge, absolutely determined not to be apologetic or, indeed, understanding of the mistake he had made. 'And you have to explain something to me. You had a vasectomy, so how the heck did you get me pregnant?'

Disconcerted by that highly provocative opening assault, Nik froze to the carpet in front of her, sleek ebony brows rising, nostrils flaring. Betsy worked really hard at not noticing his glossy gorgeousness. But memory was flashing debilitating images through her brain: her fingers sliding through the shiny black silk of his hair, her thumb smoothing the sexy line of that full, wonderfully sensual lower lip. With great difficulty she suppressed her wandering thoughts.

'*Pregnant?*' Nik repeated that word in outright disbelief. 'What are you talking about?'

Betsy recognised that she still had the advantage because she had taken him totally by surprise. 'I'm pregnant and I haven't been with anyone but you,' she informed him bluntly. 'So explain to me how that is possible.'

For the first time in his life, Nik was speechless. *Pregnant?* All his natural colour drained from beneath his bronzed skin as he took a sudden step back from her, stunned eyes locked to her in unconcealed shock while a shard of bone-deep fear sliced unequivocally through his big frame. 'You're…pregnant?' he breathed in a roughened undertone, his scepticism concerning her claim blatant.

'*Explain* that to me,' Betsy urged impatiently.

Nik raked long brown fingers through his blue-black hair, a dazed aspect to his usually shrewd gaze as he stared steadily back at her. 'You've found out that you're pregnant? *Seriously?*'

'Do I look like I'm joking?' Betsy shot back at him defensively.

A deep frown line pleated Nik's brows and there was a pause before he spoke again because his brain refused to accept what she had just told him. 'I had the vasectomy reversed,' he admitted without any expression at all.

Betsy took a sudden step forward, moving closer to him without even being aware of the movement. 'Reversed...*when?*' she queried, suddenly desperate to hear that answer.

'After you threw me out—'

'But...*why?*' she prompted, wondering if he had hoped to get her back with that news and if so why he hadn't approached her at the time.

'I realised it was time that I trusted myself to be in charge of my own fertility. I didn't even know the vasectomy *could* be reversed when we broke up. I always assumed it was final,' he admitted curtly, speaking with a candour she was unaccustomed to him using. 'When I found out that a reversal may well be successful if done within ten years of the original op, I decided to go for it. I was supposed to return for tests after the procedure to see if it had worked but I'm afraid I was so busy I never got around to it...'

Betsy's lashes wavered slowly up and down as she tried to process that unexpectedly detailed reply. But no matter how often she thought that response over she couldn't make sense of it. What did he mean about trusting himself to be in charge of his own fertility? What on earth was he talking about? And why the heck would he have had the procedure reversed *after* they had separated and not even bother to tell her about it? Well, that was one question answered loud and clear, she acknowledged painfully. Evidently his decision to have his vasectomy reversed had had nothing whatsoever to do with either her or her longing for a baby or the saving of their marriage. It was yet another slap in the face for Betsy, another wounding reminder that she never had understood and never would understand what made Nik Christakis tick.

'You are honestly pregnant?' Nik pressed her, studying her with frowning intensity and a lingering sense of disbelief because that possibility still didn't feel real to him. He might now have the proof that the reversal had worked but he was equally appalled by the risk he had unwittingly run and the unthinkable consequences of his evidently restored fertility. This result was his fault, solely *his* fault for neglecting to recall the fact that for the first time ever with Betsy he would need to take precautions.

Diavelos, suppose he *had* slept with another woman? Suppose he had been having this exact same conversation with a woman who was almost a stranger? But then would he have been so careless with anyone other than Betsy? He didn't think so. Once again familiarity had worked against him with Betsy, but then it had been so many years since he had had to guard against the risk of an unwanted pregnancy that he had behaved as imprudently as a teenager eager to have sex for the first time at any cost.

'One hundred per cent pregnant,' Betsy extended curtly, whipping her attention off his lean, darkly beautiful face when she felt it wanting to loiter, stifling her reaction to him with every fibre of her self-discipline because it was screamingly inappropriate. For the sake of the future and her unborn child she had to stick to cold, hard facts. 'So you accept that you're to blame for this pregnancy and that this will be *your* child?'

Lush spiky black lashes narrowed over suddenly astute green eyes, bright chips of colour in his lean, strong face. 'Have you any doubt on that score?' he questioned drily.

Betsy lifted her chin, azure eyes full of scornful dismissal. 'None at all.'

'Are you pleased?' Nik asked her without warning because he literally couldn't think of anything else to say and was wary of saying the wrong thing. A baby. Betsy was having a baby, *his* baby. Her announcement had plunged him deep into shock. He couldn't compute a concept so foreign to him for he had never once actively considered becoming a father. Reversing the vasectomy had been much more of an intellectual and philosophical exercise than an actual wish to see a child of his own blood born. Indeed that was a development that even at his most optimistic he had never once dared to envisage. After all, children were so vulnerable and no matter how hard one might endeavour to protect a child bad things still happened to them. At the thought, Nik paled.

Betsy breathed in so deep and long that she felt giddy. 'Am I *pleased?*' she repeated in charged disbelief, her small body turning rigid with the force of her feelings. 'Are you kidding? I wanted a baby when we were married. I wanted a family. *This*...' she spread her arms wide in emphasis, as if encompassing the distance now between them '...is not what I wanted!'

'So you don't want the baby,' Nik assumed, wondering how he felt about that but still too shaken by her news to know. A baby. Betsy was going to have a baby, the first Christakis infant to be born since his own birth.

'It's my baby...*of course* I want it!' Betsy slung back at him with an aggression she had never shown him before, no, not even on the day their marriage had tumbled down like a pack of cards and she had virtually thrown him out of their home. 'You need to know now upfront that there's no way I'm having a termination—'

'I am not that stupid,' Nik fielded flatly. 'Nor would I ask you to do such a thing.'

'*No?*' Betsy's voice was steadily rising in volume even though she was struggling to stay calm, well aware that a loss of temper was a handicap she didn't need. 'Wouldn't you? Wouldn't a termination suit you much better than the birth of a child you don't want?'

'Don't put words in my mouth. I didn't say I didn't want the child,' Nik countered darkly. 'Obviously, you do—'

Betsy was in no mood to allow him to make assumptions and she was frustrated by his failure to give her a single hint of his true feelings. 'Why? What's obvious about it? Because you're wrong— everything's changed. I never wanted to be a single parent raising a child alone!'

Nik clenched his teeth together on an ill-considered retort. She was pregnant. Betsy was pregnant, he reflected abstractedly, marvelling at the development that had come too late to save them. Whether she would admit it or otherwise, he had finally contrived to give her the one thing she truly wanted and he was violently disconcerted by the flare of satisfaction that infiltrated him at that acknowledgement. He didn't want to think about the baby; he wanted to think about what the baby would mean to *her,* and he was convinced that that child would mean the world to Betsy.

He remembered the secret stash of baby clothes he had stumbled on in the back of the closet and the sickening sensation of futility and powerlessness that had engulfed him that evening. He couldn't tell her the truth about his past; he could *never* tell her the truth, for how would she regard him afterwards? He had only had his pride left to sustain him. He had known from the outset that silence was his only possible defence, but her announcement had engulfed him like a hurricane, throwing into chaos everything he had believed he felt and thought.

'*You* made it that way for me!' Betsy continued in angry condemnation. 'You didn't give me a choice. You didn't warn me I *could* get pregnant—'

Nik released his breath in an impatient sound and replied with innate practicality, 'I don't think contraception was uppermost in either of our minds that day. I didn't think about anything that prosaic—'

'Oh, I can believe *that* all right!' Betsy flamed back at him, eyes hurling furious derision, ripe mouth curved with unfamiliar scorn. 'All you were thinking about was sex!'

'Be practical...what else would I be thinking

about?' Nik traded evenly, not one whit perturbed by that indictment. 'You didn't hold back either.'

Betsy wanted to slap him for that insolent reminder. Had she behaved like a sensible, self-respecting woman, nothing would've happened. She would have looked at him in shock and said no straight away when he came on to her. But she had never found it possible to look at Nik and say no and that went right to the heart of their relationship. The balance of power in the sex department had always been his until she had thrown a spanner into the works by craving a child and a whole new schedule during which Nik's desire for her had noticeably declined. Colour infusing her cheeks, she studied his desk. 'I totally hate and despise you—'

'We must be practical,' Nik murmured softly, much as if she hadn't spoken. 'Drama and accusations of blame will get us nowhere—'

'That's very easy to say from where you're standing,' Betsy riposted bitterly. 'Your whole life isn't going to be disrupted by single parenthood!'

'Both our lives will be disrupted,' Nik countered drily. 'But as lack of resources is not a problem I believe we will survive the challenge. I will naturally ensure that you have all the support you require from this point on—'

People he would pay to take the physical work and round-the-clock responsibility out of parenting, Betsy interpreted in even greater disgust. He wasn't volunteering himself; he wasn't willing to make a single sacrifice. And why would he be when he didn't want to be a father in the first place? she asked herself painfully.

'Stuff your blasted resources!' Betsy slung at him, vitriolic in the grip of her resentment, her heart-shaped face flushed with fury, eyes hurling don't-give-a-damn defiance. 'All I ever wanted was a *father* for my baby, not access to your wallet!'

Nik settled lacerating sea-green eyes on her, derision shimmering in every angle of his lean dark features. 'Am I supposed to be impressed by that statement? Until very recently you were claiming half of everything I own,' he reminded her with razor-edged cool.

Betsy squared her slim shoulders and hitched her bag, determined not to show weakness. 'And instead I've done even better,' she quipped. 'A baby has to be a virtual lifelong meal ticket!'

Nik surveyed her with chilling detachment. 'Go home, Betsy, before I lose my temper,' he urged.

And Betsy couldn't get out of his office fast enough and didn't breathe again until she was safe in the lift, whirring back down to the ground floor. Playing up to his view of her as a gold-digger might momentarily have seemed a way to save face, but in the long term it was a very bad idea, she reflected shamefacedly, particularly if it soured relations between them even more. What happened to her brain around Nik? She had just called her baby a lifelong meal ticket and she cringed at the awareness, knowing that even screaming abuse at Nik would have been preferable to the not so subtle weapon she had employed to fight her own corner.

And why had she behaved that way? She hated the way he had made her feel, hated that a moment that should have been exceptional and a cause for celebration had been destroyed by his shocked recoil in the face of her news. But then why was she still looking for the kind of response from Nik that he could never give her? He didn't want a child and she was having a child. Being disappointed wasn't an option, she told herself angrily. It was time to grow up and accept her world as it was, not as she would like it to be. In any case, hadn't Nik reacted better than she had hoped? There had been no demand for DNA testing, no suggestion that he suspected she might have fallen pregnant by another man.

Emerging into the fresh air, Betsy glanced across the street to where the bistro in which she had once worked had long since been replaced by an upmarket estate agency. Her troubled face tensed and then softened when she allowed herself to remember that, with savage irony, Nik Christakis had truly treated her like a queen *before* their marriage.

Sadly, Betsy had fallen in love with Nik so fast and so terrifyingly deeply that she had lost herself in him. When he had been with her he had become all that mattered and when he had been abroad he had been all she could think about and she had been wretchedly unhappy without him. Until she had met Nik she had not even known that she *could* feel such powerful emotion. She had begun skipping her night classes when Nik had wanted to see her and soon she had fallen behind with her assignments and stopped attending altogether. She was still ashamed of that short-sighted loss of drive back then and the inherent weakness of dropping her life plan in favour of a man and a relationship that might not have lasted. She had never dreamt that she was that kind of woman, but loving Nik had humbled her.

When Nik had asked her to marry him, she had been stunned, for she'd had no idea that he was that serious about her. At that point she hadn't even slept with him and his restraint in that department had already surprised her.

'You're a virgin, aren't you?' he had prompted after dinner in a trendy restaurant one evening. 'I don't mind waiting until you feel ready to share my bed. In fact the very act of waiting is refreshing and remarkably exciting.'

They had married in a welter of orange blossoms and flash photography, surrounded by hundreds of guests she hadn't known and only a handful that she had. Within weeks of the wedding, however, Nik had begun to change and recently she had wondered if he had changed towards her for the most demeaning reason of all. With the exciting chase ending on their wedding night when he finally got her into bed, had her driven alpha-male husband then begun to steadily lose interest because he was bored with her? After all, an inexpert non-virgin had little in the way of novelty to offer a sexual sophisticate.

But Betsy had predictably hung on in there, struggling to make a success of a marriage with a constantly absent partner. She had foolishly believed that a baby would bring them closer together and break through Nik's increasing detachment and reserve. And then one evening when Nik was abroad on business she had attended a dinner party at Cristo's, where Zarif, Nik's royal kid brother, had made an effort to chat to her and get to know her. When he had asked her how she managed when Nik was out of the country so often, she had briefly mentioned that now that the work on Lavender Hall was complete she was hoping to start a family soon, and Zarif had given her a startled look and asked how she planned to achieve that when Nik had had a vasectomy. That bombshell had come at her out of nowhere and within days had blown their marriage sky-high.

Now the world seemed to have turned full circle, Betsy acknowledged forlornly. She was getting the baby she had once craved but she no longer had a husband or a man willing to play the role of father. Their marriage was over even though the divorce had yet to be finalised.

CHAPTER FIVE

NIK WAS HAVING a very bad day. It had crashed and burned the minute Betsy had given him her news and he had found it impossible to concentrate after her departure. Having cancelled his meetings and told his PA to hold his calls, Nik walked out onto the roof garden of his apartment. He was home in the middle of the day and not working and it felt seriously strange. It was quiet and there was not even a breath of a breeze and only the dulled roar of the traffic far below. He would never have admitted it but he missed Gizmo, who had at least been company of a sort.

In the past, Nik had been a serious loner until he'd met Cristo and somehow contrived to bond with his brother in spite of the fact that they were very different men. Now he stared out unseeingly at the skyline and the rooftops. He led an immensely privileged existence and nobody needed to remind him of that fact. In almost every corner of his life his great wealth had smoothed his progress and thrust him onward and upward. But in one department his billions had always failed him and that was in the sphere of personal happiness.

It was possible though, he conceded broodingly, that he just didn't have what it took to experience joy. A lifetime of repressing his emotions and keeping secrets had damaged him, not to mention his ability to trust and sustain relationships. He had fought that truth for a long time and only recently come to accept that it was an inescapable fact.

Just as his dark and dreadful background was inescapable, he acknowledged grimly, Betsy's announcement along with her condemnation had unleashed some seriously unwelcome memories. Just at that moment he was recalling his first day at school, or, more accurately, the nightmare journey there in a chauffeur-driven car with a mother who had an uncontrollable temper.

'Having you has totally wrecked my life!' Helena had screamed at him resentfully, her clenched fist flying out to catch him a stinging blow across the cheek because she was enraged that his grandfather had insisted she get out of bed to accompany her four-year-old son. 'You ruined my body, you ruined my social life, you're preventing me from travelling or doing *anything* I enjoy… What else are you going to ruin, you little freak?'

Helena Christakis had never wanted to *be* a mother but when her deeply conservative father threatened to disinherit her after she conceived a child with her latest lover, Gaetano Ravelli, Helena had been forced for the first time in her self-indulgent life to deal with penalties. Faking a marriage to Gaetano to satisfy her father had been the first consequence and one that had ultimately paid off in terms of conserving her fortune. Unfortunately the ongoing responsibility of a child and the curtailment of Helena's freedom to do exactly as she liked had been a much more onerous punishment.

Not for one moment did Nik credit that Betsy could ever be as cruel, selfish or violent as his own mother had been throughout his childhood. He couldn't believe she would ever hate her child as his mother had often hated him while blaming him for every disappointment in her life. Even so, Nik could certainly accept that Betsy had conceived their child in far less rosy circumstances than those that she had originally foreseen. *Their* child? Even inside his head that label felt unnatural, unreal because he could not even begin to imagine the reality of such a development, for he had never had the smallest thing to do with pregnant women or children.

But what was done was done and Nik had always been a pragmatist. He had no doubt that if he failed to step up to the plate some other man would replace him as both husband to Betsy and father figure in their child's life. And that development would be totally unacceptable to Nik. There could be no halfway measures, he conceded broodingly. Either he became fully involved in his child's life or he would find himself excluded because a young and rich divorcee with Betsy's looks would not remain single for long. Yet how *could* he embrace everything that he had *always* avoided and feared? Fatherhood, with all the concerns and dangers that came with the responsibility. He breathed in slow and deep, eyes bleak, wide, sensual mouth clenching hard with constraint. He would do it the same way he had survived his brutal childhood: by never looking back to relive a better-forgotten past and taking only one step forward at a time.

'So, *spill,*' Belle urged. A tall, vibrant redhead, she threw herself back into the comfortable embrace of a purple velvet sofa and regarded Betsy with unconcealed expectancy in her lively eyes.

'I'm pregnant,' Betsy blurted out, having come to visit to make exactly that announcement.

Perceptibly disconcerted, her sister-in-law sat forward in a sudden movement. 'How the heck did you sneak having a man in your life past my radar?' she demanded in disbelief.

'Because he was already there…well, sort of,' Betsy muttered ruefully. 'It's Nik's baby—'

'Nik? How *could* it be Nik's?'

'You must not mention this to Cristo yet. It's private…between Nik and me,' Betsy extended awkwardly, wishing that Cristo's wife would stop studying her as though she were waiting for the clowns to come trooping in and provide a comic act. In as few words as she could manage she revealed that Nik had had the vasectomy reversed.

Belle blinked slowly. 'OK,' she conceded. 'And then he gave you the dog back and clearly you slept with him out of gratitude—'

'It wasn't like that,' Betsy countered quietly.

'I know you. You're very soft-hearted. He took advantage—'

'Maybe I took advantage of him…'

Belle was shaking her head in wonderment. 'Wow…just wow. Nik's going to be a dad. Considering that he can't even bear to be in the same room with my siblings that scenario takes quite a stretch of the imagination—'

Betsy was fond of Cristo's wife but had never appreciated her outspokenly critical attitude towards Nik. 'You're not being fair, Belle. Nik never knew his own father and has never had anything to do with children. Gaetano Ravelli walked out of his life when he was a baby and Nik never saw him again, so it's a lot harder for him to feel that there's a family connection with the younger brothers and sisters that you and Cristo have adopted.'

Franco, the youngest of those children, an adorable toddler with curly black hair and big brown eyes, clambered onto his half-sister Belle's lap and hugged her with easy affection. It was clear that he regarded Belle very much as his mother, yet Franco and his four siblings were actually the progeny of Belle's late mother's long-running affair with Nik and Cristo's now-deceased father.

For the first time though, Betsy was also registering an odd fact that made her brow furrow in surprise. Almost *everything* she knew about Nik's family background had come from either Cristo or Belle because Nik never ever talked about his childhood. His relationship with his mother was quietly dysfunctional and something he politely refused to discuss.

Betsy had only met Helena Christakis once when the older woman had evidently surprised Nik by choosing to attend their wedding. Helena had arrived with her latest boyfriend in tow and had avoided all but the most fleeting contact with her son and his bride. Even so, Helena's presence must've proved more of a punishment than a pleasure for her son because she had worn a dress more suited to a teenager, had got distinctly drunk and at one stage had chosen to recline on her toy boy's lap and behave like a sex kitten. Nik had seemed impervious to his mother's behaviour and had made no comment. At the time Betsy had naively assumed that he was hiding his embarrassment but she had since learned to appreciate that virtually nothing embarrassed Nik.

'It was a challenge for Cristo as well,' the other woman reasoned. 'He wasn't into kids either but I don't think he was ever as set against the idea of them as Nik has always seemed to be. When do you plan to tell him about the baby?'

'I've already told him… This morning, in fact. That's why I came up to London.' Betsy compressed her lips because she had no intention of sharing any further information, but then she could scarcely have hoped to conceal a pregnancy from close friends and family. And more than anything else that was what Cristo and Belle had become to Betsy—family, the family she'd never really had. They had both made time in their busy lives for her during the gloomy, heartbreaking months of her marriage breakdown, always ready to listen and support and offer soothing words.

'And?'

'Well, at least Nik didn't suggest that the baby might be some other man's—'

'Why would he when you've been living like you've taken a vow of celibacy?' Belle demanded with a wry roll of her eyes. 'A child is going to make everything so much more difficult and complicated for you.'

'I don't see why,' Betsy replied in a fiercely upbeat tone as she tilted her chin. 'I have a business, a home and a devoted dog. The baby will slot right in there perfectly and life will go on.'

Soon after that, Betsy got up to leave because the emotional turbulence of her day had exhausted her and she was looking forward to getting home and relaxing in front of the fire with Gizmo as a foot warmer. Belle pulled open the drawing room door for her. 'Oh, before I forget, you're booked to come to my birthday party a week on Friday. I've even arranged a lift for you—'

'A…lift?' Betsy repeated in surprise.

'Chris Morrison. He lives by you and he said he'd be happy to bring you with him, so you won't even have to stay the night here because he'll take you home again as well,' Belle revealed with satisfaction. 'I passed on your number so that he can contact you to arrange a time.'

'Who is he?' Betsy prompted with a frown, recognising how Belle had cleverly boxed her in and made it impossible for her to refuse to attend. Her momentary spark of resentment at being managed, however, evaporated when she pictured herself sitting home alone every night moping. Nik wasn't moping; no, her soon-to-be ex was regularly linked to society beauties, whom he escorted to clubs, art galleries and opera performances. Indeed, Nik, who had rarely taken Betsy out anywhere after marrying her, had turned into a maddeningly visible male, whose social success was mapped by a trail of revealing photos in gossip columns and both glossy and worthy magazines.

Across the hall in the very act of emerging from Cristo's study where a couple of brandies had chased the increasing chill from his stomach, Nik had frozen into immobility at the unexpected sound of Betsy's voice. A glance at his brother revealed that even tolerant, laid-back Cristo had tensed at the obvious fact that the feisty Belle was already making dates for Nik's still legally wed wife. And with a womaniser like Chris Morrison, of all people! Only Betsy would have to ask *who* the man was! Only one of the richest bankers in the City! *Diavelos!* Nik's eyes flashed pure emerald brilliance as he fought down a tide of pure toxic rage because no matter how he felt he couldn't strangle his brother's provocative wife.

'Ah, boys together too...' Belle trilled teasingly, not one whit perturbed by the awkward meeting. 'Isn't this cosy?'

'Betsy...' Cristo gave Betsy an uneasy smile that

warned her that Nik had confided in him. She wondered if Nik's brother even appreciated how extreme an honour that was, because Nik was one of the most secretive men she had ever met. She finally dared to shift her attention to Nik. His sheer physical impact as he stood there poised with his arrogant black head held high and his broad shoulders thrown back hit her like a thunderclap. The amount of stress she had been fighting at his office had shielded her from the full effects of his compelling sexual magnetism. Now suddenly she was bare to the elements, reliving X-rated moments of their passionate encounter weeks earlier. She remembered the hard, jolting thrust of his demanding body into hers, the wild, screaming sensitivity of every nerve ending and the mad excitement that had engulfed her. A flush of heat travelled from her pelvis up through her already tender breasts and burned her face.

But behind that unwelcome response smouldered an anger and a resentment that Betsy had always repressed because as a child she had been taught to regard such emotions as destructive, rude and undesirable.

'Betsy won't need a lift from Morrison,' Nik announced, tight-mouthed. 'As I'm coming to the party as well, I'll organise her transport.'

Betsy could not credit her hearing because Nik had spoken as though she were a crate requiring shipping. Or a personal possession that he still had the right to move about at will. *This,* from a male who had deceived her, deserted her and who was racing to divorce her! Without warning a volcanic fury beyond anything Betsy had ever felt before funnelled up through her diminutive figure like hot, scorching lava and she stalked forward, blue eyes ablaze.

'Where do you get the nerve?' Betsy spat out, her small face a mask of raging indignation as she confronted Nik and jabbed a small forefinger hard into his shirtfront. 'Where the hell do you get the nerve to think you have the right to organise anything for me?'

As taken aback as if a chair had suddenly lifted up and attacked him, Nik gazed down in disbelief at Betsy, the most conciliatory person he had ever known and without an ounce of aggression, facing up to him like a miniature warrior on the battlefield.

'I—'

'Shut up...I don't want to hear your voice!' Betsy seethed up at him, head tipping back because she refused to focus on his chest, but it was a challenge to seek eye-to-eye contact when he was so much taller than she was. 'You've got nothing to say that I could possibly want to hear! You don't own me and you don't have any say in what I do or where I go or who I do it with! Only last week you were wrapped round an Amazonian blonde at some New York party. I didn't interfere. I didn't offer you an opinion. Why not? Because it was *none of my business!* And my life now is none of your business either!' she completed with a final stab of her forefinger on his broad chest. 'Do you get that, Nik? Or do I need to write it down for you, put it in business language so that you might actually grasp it?'

'That is enough,' Nik warned her, hard cheekbones rigid beneath his flushed golden skin. 'What has got into you?' he demanded, incredulous at her daring in attacking him.

'You've got into me, Nik…literally and figuratively. You were a rotten, selfish husband and you went out of my life on an even worse note—'

Cristo swung wide the door of his study in an almost comically inviting gesture. 'You and Nik can talk in there—'

'But I wouldn't miss a minute of the mouse finally roaring,' Belle confided without shame. 'You go, girl!'

Even white teeth gritting together, Nik breathed curtly, 'You're pregnant—obviously you don't want to be forced into the company of another man—'

'Why should being pregnant stop me? And who said I was being *forced?*' Betsy queried, still as furious as she had started out because Nik's many, many sins and omissions were piled up like coffin dust in the back of her mind. She wrenched her arm free the instant he closed long brown fingers round it in an effort to hustle her into the study. 'Lay one hand on me, Nik, and I'll charge you with assault—'

'You will not stage a public argument with me in my brother's house!' Nik thundered down at her, green eyes so startlingly light with rage they shimmered like polished gems in his lean dark features.

'That's fine. I wasn't planning to stay and waste my breath on a lost cause.' Azure eyes like jewels assailed his irate stare with a boldness that stunned him. 'Just don't you ever *dare* to tell me what to do again!

Subject someone else to the control-freak stuff...
You're not my husband any more. I spent three years
trying to be the very best wife I could be, submitting
to your every demand and expectation and fitting myself into your world, and thank heaven I don't have
to do it any more!' she slung at him with a sudden
sense of freedom as she walked with determination
towards the front door.

'We're still married,' Nik reminded her stubbornly,
his attention locked to her like a powerful force beam
that could not be evaded.

And Betsy spun round, rigid with so much annoyance at that provocative claim that she was instantly
ready to storm into round two of the battle. '*Really?*
Where have you been for the past eight months?
Oh, yes, divorcing me, repossessing the dog you always ignored, trying to take the roof from over my
head while running round with other women. If I
did choose to sleep around, consort with lots of men
and generally act like a very embarrassing ex-wife,
well, I might as well, because playing nice with you
all those years certainly didn't do me any favours!
You lied to me—'

'I didn't... I have never *ever* lied to you,' Nik
breathed grittily, big, strong hands clenched into fists
by his sides, pale as death below his year-round tan.
A claustrophobic silence fell while she waited to see
if he would say anything else but, predictably, Nik
sealed his firm masculine lips together.

'You lied by omission,' Betsy conceded and a belated flush of mortification that they were fighting in

Cristo and Belle's home engulfed her and she cringed inwardly at the lengths her loss of temper had taken her to. 'And trust you to make that distinction. You're too clever for your own good, Nik, and I was never h-half clever enough… You broke my heart, Nik, and I'll never forgive you for it.' Something very like the start of a sob clogged in her throat and her eyes burned and in more haste than ever she wrenched the front door open, starting down the steps, only halting when a heavy hand settled on her shoulder.

'Let me take you home—'

'That would be ridiculous,' she said tightly, staring fixedly out at the quiet residential street, refusing to turn her head. 'In any case my car's parked at the train station at home.'

Nik said something in Greek and a man side-stepped Betsy to yank open the passenger door of the limo parked by the kerb. One of Nik's security team, Betsy registered, her head swimming a little with the mental and physical exhaustion threatening to overwhelm her. Yet even in that condition, she couldn't help wondering and beating herself up about whether or not Nik's security men had also been witnesses to her diatribe. She had harangued Nik like a shrew, had gone up like a firework, experiencing a rage entirely new to her, and it had totally overcome her every inhibition. Sadly, in the aftermath of it, she only felt drained, ashamed and achingly weary.

Nik watched her narrow shoulders droop, her head bow, concern clawing at him even while he remained astonished by her behaviour. She had given him a glimpse into her outlook and he was reeling from it.

You broke my heart, Nik, and I'll never forgive you for it.

He turned her round, slowly, carefully. She looked up at him, eyes bright with unshed tears in the street light. His mouth came crashing down on hers without warning and suddenly he was lifting her up to him to part her soft lips and drink deep of the sweet, tender interior of her mouth. She felt as if her head were swimming as her body ran from cold to very hot and she wanted to climb him like a tree and cling. Molten desire laced with helpless self-betrayal powered her treacherous response, a wild but necessary release from the unbearable tension. He tasted so good. He tasted hotter than the flaming heart of a fire. Nothing had ever been as primitive as that devouring kiss and yet nothing could have drawn her down so efficiently from her distressed emotional high and grounded her again. He steadied her with both hands as he set her down on her own feet again because she was tottering, dizzy, in another place altogether from the mood she had been in before he reached for her.

'My car will drop you at the station... I'll stay on here,' Nik murmured in a hoarse undertone, but it was the only outward sign he gave that what had just transpired had had any kind of effect on him.

It was a huge challenge but Betsy contrived to relocate her brain and, shaken though she was, she made it down the steps, across the pavement and into the upholstered comfort of the limousine, breathing again only when the car drew away from the kerb. That kiss… No, she wasn't even going to think about that. It was just part of the craziness that happened when people lost their temper and fought and she wasn't used to fighting with Nik. Even the day she had told him to get out of Lavender Hall there had been no *real* fight. While she had ranted about the vasectomy he had kept secret he had stood in brooding silence without explaining, excusing or even attempting to justify his behaviour.

As the limo departed, it finally occurred to Nik that he had set himself much more of a challenge than he could ever have imagined. Telling Betsy that he was coming home to look after her and their unborn child would go down like a brick thrown through a glass window because *she didn't want him back.*

Returning indoors, Nik turned in a blind, unco-ordinated half circle in the hall of his brother's el-egant town house and he wasn't aware of anything, of where he was or even of who might be watching for such a moment of weakness. Why had he just as-sumed that she would want him back? Women had always wanted Nik and it was simply a reality he took for granted. But then he had made that mistake with Betsy before when she'd ditched him on their first date, he recalled abstractedly, an iron bar pounding painfully behind his temples. Of course, Betsy had never been like other women, which was why he had married her in the first place.

When he had brought her flowers she had admit-ted she would simply prefer an apology for his long absences and more frequent phone calls and texts while he was away.

When he had brought her gifts she had scolded him for wasting his money as if he were an extravagant child. *'You can't impress me with that stuff,'* she had once told him gently. *'That's not why I'm with you. I'm here because I love you and you can't put a price on that.'*

Perspiration dampening his brow, Nik asked himself for the first time why Betsy had tried to claim half his wealth, because that claim from her had never made sense with what he knew of her character. He wondered what love really felt like, never having experienced it except when it came to her loving him. That love had given him the strangest sense of security... Ridiculous! As if he were *insecure*. He almost laughed out loud at that idea but somehow couldn't crank up even a shadowy atom of his sense of humour.

He wondered if it would be possible to kidnap Betsy and take her abroad where she would have to listen to him. Would she really call the police? Ultimately, she *had* to listen to him. Catching himself up on that peculiar kidnapping fantasy, he raised his brows and wondered if he had taken a sudden nose-dive into insanity.

Like Betsy, acting so oddly, attacking him like that. What was the matter with her? Was it possible that it had only happened because she was pregnant? How had he forgotten that for even as long as five minutes? Pregnant ladies had to be very hormonal, he thought vaguely. Betsy had definitely not been herself; in fact she had behaved like someone possessed, displaying a change of character he was happy to lay at argumentative Belle's door. After all, he knew that Belle didn't like him and was likely to use his worst mistakes and flaws against him. Although, Nik reasoned with a frown, it was more probable that the only demon possessing Betsy was the result of unstable pregnancy hormones. He was more than a little relieved to have worked out that obvious explanation. That raving virago of a woman had borne no resemblance whatsoever to the soft and gentle Betsy he had once lived with. And would be living with again soon, Nik reminded himself with satisfaction.

Betsy would be surprised but pleased, ultimately *very* pleased, he told himself with charged conviction. Since the day Betsy had told him to get out of Lavender Hall, Nik had been pursued and propositioned by other women on a daily basis. He had met with seductive looks and bold advances everywhere he went and after three years of marriage such bold invites had proved disconcerting and a passion killer, but, even so, if other women who didn't even know him could want him so much that they dropped all finesse and dignity, Betsy must want him back more, mustn't she?

She had let him take her up against the wall that day. Just thinking about it, Nik got hard as steel. She couldn't honestly hate him if she had had sex with him again, could she? Why the hell was he thinking about all this stupid relationship stuff? For a split second of seething frustration Nik wanted to bang his head on the wall to clear it of the chaotic madness of his thoughts and then he finally registered his brother's presence several feet away.

'Are you OK?' Cristo was watching him worriedly.

Nik flexed his stiff shoulders and straightened to his full height. 'Why wouldn't I be?'

Cristo was not subtle but he knew that telling Nik he was acting weird would be more of a hindrance than a help. In any case Cristo was operating in full sympathy mode. Nik had married a mouse who had started roaring like a lion and naturally he couldn't cope with that unnerving switch of personality on top of the prospect of a baby as well.

Nik was very much a man's man, short on the imagination and empathy stakes, Cristo thought understandingly. Cristo had long since noticed that in complete contrast to his brother's brilliant intellect and polished business negotiation skills, Nik was downright backward and all at sea when anything emotional got involved in a situation. But Nik was trying to understand; Cristo could see quite clearly that Nik was *trying* and struggling, and he just hoped that, sooner rather than later, Betsy would see it too.

CHAPTER SIX

IT WAS EARLY evening and Betsy was staring down
the front steps at the huge removal van and the crew
standing beside it and said for the second time, 'Obviously you've got the address wrong. I'm not moving any place and nobody is moving in…'

Simultaneously with that statement came the loud
thwack-thwack of rotor blades sounding overhead and
drowning out her words. Everyone, including Betsy,
looked up into the sky but only Betsy was in a position to identify the logo on the helicopter coming in to
land on the helipad Nik had had built. Betsy blinked,
blindsided by yet another baffling event. Was Nik
flying in to visit her? To discuss the baby and future
arrangements between them? But why wouldn't he
have done that through the medium of their respec-
tive legal advisors? Surely that would have been less
challenging than yet another traumatic meeting?

Five days had passed since Betsy had confronted
Nik in Cristo and Belle's home and she was still cring-
ing, inwardly raging and squirming at the memory
of how she had finally given her almost ex-husband

a few much-needed home truths. It was unfortunate that she had done that in front of an audience; indeed she felt she owed Nik an apology on that score for having lost control to that extent. On the other hand, Nik was not given to introspection and had probably shaken off her criticisms within minutes of her departure. He wasn't a sensitive male and he didn't love her, so why should he care about what she had said about the past when their marriage was over, barring the final legal ratification? And why the heck had he kissed her afterwards? What kind of sense had that move made?

Sky-blue eyes opening very wide, Betsy watched Nik striding through the shrubbery that concealed the helipad and her blood ran cold as she worried again about what might have prompted him to make yet another personal visit. He delegated responsibility whenever he could to free himself up for the much more stimulating arena of the business world.

She concentrated on guiltily trying not to notice how amazing Nik looked in his charcoal-grey designer suit, how exotically, wonderfully handsome with that luxuriant black hair and those stunning light eyes of his that were so striking against his bronzed skin. Her colour fluctuated, her chilled blood started heating up dangerously in her veins and she wanted to slap herself for reacting to his compelling sexual charisma even after all he had done to her. It was just stupid chemistry, she told herself in exasperation. That was why, in a nutshell, she had kissed him back that night; it was a sad fact of life but she found him utterly irresistible.

She was surprised when Nik paused at the rear of the removals van to address the hovering work crew and wondered what he was saying to them. At least as a male with very little patience for inefficiency and other people's mistakes, he would soon send them about their business.

'Betsy…' Nik purred, mounting the steps in a couple of graceful strides of his long, powerful legs, his jewelled gaze locking to hers like a guided missile trained on a target, she thought dimly, little hot and cold tremors winging through her in an unnerving wave of response.

'What are you doing here?' Betsy asked, striving this time around to be cool and sensible in her reaction to his arrival. 'Couldn't you at least have called to say that you were coming?'

A hairy mop of dog provided an interruption by hurling himself cheerfully against Nik's legs in welcome.

'Gizmo…' Betsy scolded.

'He must like having us both in the same place again,' Nik pronounced, actually laughing and reaching down to pet a flyaway doggy ear.

'Well, he'll be disappointed then when you leave again,' Betsy remarked tightly. 'Honestly, Nik, you should've phoned to at least mention that you would be visiting—'

Nik frowned. 'Could we have a word in private?' he was careful to enquire.

Glancing behind him, her brow furrowing in be-musement when she registered that the removal men were actually opening up the back of their lumbering behemoth of a truck, Betsy murmured, 'Of course. Has something happened?'

'Nothing you need to worry about,' Nik asserted, a lean brown hand settling into the indent of her slender spine as he urged her in the direction of the drawing room and, having got her there, he prudently closed the door.

'So, something *has* happened,' Betsy assumed, searching his lean, darkly beautiful features, recog-nising his tension and constraint in growing dismay.

Nik breathed in slow and deep. Moving back in had seemed so simple a solution when he had thought of it but, faced with Betsy's sheer bewilderment at his appearance, it suddenly seemed rather more compli-cated than that. Cristo had urged him to go and talk to her first but Nik had wanted to avoid drama and the unthinkable possibility of rejection. Presenting Betsy with a fait accompli and checking out his legal position in advance had impressed him as a more workable and efficient approach. After all, he didn't warn a company that he was about to take over what he was planning to do in advance, did he?

'Why aren't you saying anything? You're scaring me… What's wrong?' Betsy gasped, her nervous ten-sion reaching an unbelievable high. 'Are Cristo and Belle all right?'

'Of course they are.' Nik scanned his wife in a swift all-over appraisal that missed not a single detail of her jeans-clad, relaxed appearance. She still didn't look pregnant and he wondered when her tiny, slender proportions would show change. He glanced away, colour lining his cheekbones, marvelling at the amount of instant hunger coursing through him. Evidently she owned the key to his libido, or perhaps it was just that he was an exceptionally faithful married man with some mental kink that had prevented him from seeking release with another woman even during a legal separation. With some relief he reached for that practical explanation.

'Nik...what is it?' Betsy pressed worriedly, stiff as a walking stick as she stood in front of him.

'I'm moving back in.' Nik let the announcement hang there and watched Betsy's mouth fall open to display two rows of small pearly-white teeth. 'I've decided to come home—'

Betsy almost fell over in shock. In fact her head swam and her ears buzzed as those words rhymed back and forth inside her head and she refused to credit them. 'I beg your pardon?' she said limply.

'I want to come home,' Nik spelt out in case she had yet to get the message. 'Make a go of our marriage again...'

He's certifiably insane, Betsy decided dizzily. The last time he had seen her she had been screaming at him and now, all of a sudden and without the smallest warning, he was telling her he wanted to come back and live with her again. And, worst of all, he spoke as if such a far-reaching decision were entirely one-sided and his alone to make.

'You mean…that removal van out there—?'

'*Ne*…yes. It's mine,' Nik admitted, relieved that she had finally understood without him having to spell anything out in greater or potentially embarrassing detail. 'Don't worry, you won't be put out in any way. I called Edna and warned her—'

'You phoned our housekeeper to tell her you were moving back in and *you didn't tell me?*' Betsy demanded in a charged voice, thinking that the arrival of his possessions was a great deal less perplexing than his own arrival, only he didn't seem to grasp that obvious little fact.

'Only an hour ago,' Nik confided as though that might mitigate the offence.

Betsy breathed in so deep that her head swam again and she studied him in disbelief. 'Nik…you can't just decide you want to try again at our marriage without discussing it first with me,' she pointed out a little shakily, hysteria gathering somewhere deep inside her chest because she just could not believe what she was hearing.

'I'm discussing it with you now,' Nik countered levelly, strolling over to the blazing fire. 'I want you to be pleased.'

It wasn't the first time in their relationship Nik had told her how she ought to feel before she could decide on her own account, so she wasn't surprised by that seemingly careless aside. 'Nik…you left eight months ago. This is my house and home now—'

Nik swung back round, lean, strong face taut. 'No,

it's not. The settlement papers have yet to be signed. The hall still belongs to me—'

'Oh, that's all right, then,' Betsy told him with spirited sarcasm. 'I'll just pack up me and Gizmo and sleep on Belle's couch! I'm sure she'll squeeze us in somewhere—'

'What on earth are you talking about?' Nik demanded darkly. 'Why would you leave now that I've moved back in again?'

'We are getting a divorce, Nik,' Betsy reminded him doggedly, wondering on what planet his reasoning had been formed. 'You *can't* just move back in and spring a reconciliation on me without my agreement—'

'I don't want a divorce. We have a son or a daughter on the way and we should be together to raise him or her,' Nik informed her without fanfare.

'Ideally speaking…' Betsy commented weakly. 'I had no idea you felt that way about the baby when you never wanted one.'

'But the baby's now a fact of life,' Nik replied. 'We're going to be parents and I won't allow my child to grow up without me.'

Betsy was afraid her legs would give out as support and she sidled over to a sofa and literally dropped down on it in a desperate attempt to clear her light-headedness. 'Nik? All this is coming at me out of nowhere and I'm very confused—'

'Why?' Nik queried with apparent sincerity, crossing the rug to crouch down at her feet so that he could still see her face. 'I'm home again—'

'But that's not a unilateral decision you can make!' Betsy exclaimed in a raw outburst. '*Obviously* it concerns me as well. I know it's best for a child to have two parents if possible but there's the question of *our* relationship—'

His wide, sensual mouth quirked. 'There wouldn't be a child to worry about in the first instance if it wasn't for our relationship.'

'Depends on how you look at the situation.' Betsy lifted her head, cobalt eyes sparking with annoyance. 'I saw it as just sex and straight afterwards you did as well when you said that you believed it was quite common for divorcing couples to fall into bed together again.'

'It was the wrong thing to say.' Nik raked restive brown fingers through his silky black hair as he made that confession. 'But I was…er…very confused that day. I didn't know what I felt or what to say to you—'

Betsy found herself strangely touched by that uncharacteristically frank admission but it did not silence her. 'No, you just *ran*—'

Nik's green eyes flared with macho male defensiveness. 'I did *not* run—'

'Take it from me…you *ran* as if I was a one-night stand you regretted. Only a week ago you were divorcing me. How can you go from that level to suddenly saying you want to be married to me again?' she prompted shakily.

Nik paced restively in front of the fire because he hadn't expected so many questions or the barrier of resistance she was engaged in raising between them. But she wasn't screaming at him, which he deemed a plus and an improvement. 'You have to start somewhere—'

'But all that's changed is that I'm pregnant,' Betsy reminded him, trying not to listen to the opening and closing of doors in the hall and the sound of voices and noise that accompanied Nik's possessions returning to what had once been the home they shared. She was traumatised and trying not to show it. Not for the first time, Nik's conduct had stunned her into silence. He had stopped the divorce, returned to her... But why? She didn't understand. 'I can't believe that you care that much about a baby you never wanted—'

Nik tensed. *'Believe,'* he urged. 'I also care about you and I want to be here for both you and the baby now and in the future.'

'It's an amazing turnaround,' Betsy told him numbly. 'I don't know how I feel about it.'

Nik hunkered down athletically again at her feet and reached for both her hands in an unusual demonstration for a male who was normally very reserved. 'Be pleased. I want to come home, *glikia mou.* I suppose I'm asking you for a second chance...'

It was so humble, so unlike the proud, fiercely independent male she knew that tears stung the backs of Betsy's clear eyes. She stared at him, her gaze locked to the sleek, dark, fallen-angel beauty of his lean, taut face and she could literally sense how keyed up he was waiting for her to agree. It meant a great deal to him; she could *feel* that. And she thought that only a male of Nik Christakis's complexity could think it was normal to move back in with the wife he was divorcing without even talking the idea over with her in advance. There had always been something about his sheer lack of emotional intelligence that pierced her heart deep as an arrow. He was so clever but so out of touch with ordinary things that she took for granted and she had always recognised that eccentric quality in him, right from the night of his equally startling wedding proposal, which had also come out of nowhere at her.

'I'm not sure I could trust you again,' she told him honestly. 'So much has happened…and the other women—'

'I haven't slept with anyone but you.'

Betsy was astonished until she recalled him falling on her like a hungry wolf and it was that recollection that convinced her that he was telling the truth. 'Even so, you've been photographed out and about with a lot of other women—'

'But I've only been with you,' Nik declared afresh. 'I only *want* to be with you.'

Betsy lifted uncertain fingers and traced his darkly shadowed jawline, fingertips brushing the stubble already formed there. She wondered what she was doing. But she was realising that her supposed hatred of Nik had only provided a useful bolster to her pride and her survival, and that when she went looking for its strength to stiffen her spine with resistance, it was mysteriously absent. She didn't hate him; she wanted him back. Did that make her the biggest female fool in the Western world? Was she crazy to even consider reconciling with a guy who arrived with a removals van as if eight months of separation and all the bitter turns and twists of the divorce proceedings had never happened?

'But you *never* wanted a baby,' she heard herself remind him hoarsely.

'A child is a big responsibility,' Nik said seriously, evidently indifferent to the reality that he already had responsibility for a vast business empire and thousands and thousands of employees round the world. 'And children are very vulnerable. That was why I never wanted the responsibility of protecting one.'

Betsy didn't follow his reasoning. He seemed to be thinking of some kind of doomsday scenario in which a child could get hurt, but she could see that he was deadly serious and for that reason she nodded as if she totally understood what he was saying. 'And that's why you had the vasectomy?' she prompted.

Nik nodded in silence, having given the explanation that he had already worked out beforehand. He wished he could have come up with those words eight months earlier when it might have saved them both a lot of grief. But at the time, in shock at her discovery that he had had a vasectomy, he had thought he could only tell her the truth and that was an option he could not even contemplate, would *never* contemplate.

Betsy searched his lean dark face, noticed the shadows below his eyes, the indented lines of extreme tension bracketing his mouth, and tried to think straight. But with no warning whatsoever, emotional overload and exhaustion were together hitting her like a freight train hurtling downhill. 'I can't give you an answer right now,' she told him shakily. 'I need to think about it and I think I need to lie down for a while...'

Rigid with dissatisfaction at that response, Nik backed away as Betsy levered herself upright and then, without a jot of warning, her eyes rolled up in her head and she just dropped where she stood without a sound. Betsy had fainted. There was something seriously wrong with her. Nik, usually ice cool in a crisis, experienced an intense wave of panic as he scooped her up and strode out to the hall again, where their housekeeper, Edna, was supervising the removal team.

'Oh, dear, has Mrs Christakis fainted again?' Edna prompted in a mild tone of acceptance as she moved towards him.

'*Again?* You mean this has happened before?' Nik pressed in consternation.

'Some women are prone to it in early pregnancy,' the older woman told him calmly. 'We all watch out for her as best we can.'

Nik pictured Betsy fainting as she crossed a road and falling beneath the wheels of a car. He saw her tumbling downstairs and breaking her neck. Even when he envisaged her falling and simply bruising herself he felt sick, and determined that it wasn't going to happen any more. Having a baby could kill her, he reflected in horror. He couldn't have her fainting all over the place; it was too dangerous, too risky.

He needed proper medical advice and somewhere to keep her safe.

Betsy drifted back to consciousness to find that she was lying across Nik's lap in the back of a limousine. 'Where on earth are we going?' she whispered, her fingers fluttering up to brush her clammy brow. 'I did it again, didn't I? Sometimes if I stand up too fast I pass out. Sorry if I gave you a fright. I'm just so tired—'

'I'm taking you to see a doctor—'

'That's not necessary—'

'When you're ill *I* decide what's necessary.'

'But I'm not ill. I'm only pregnant,' Betsy countered gently, recognising his concern and his stress level. Nik did not like the unexpected. In the same way she knew that every piece of furniture he had taken with him would be returned to pretty much the same position it had occupied eight months earlier. He had a thing about familiar order and structure, which had once thoroughly irritated her because she liked to move stuff around and try it in different places. But then everyone had their little quirks and preferences, she conceded ruefully.

'I think you need to rest,' Nik spelt out.

Her nose was almost buried in his shirtfront and the musky, sexy scent of his skin was so familiar it made her eyes prickle with tears. Her fingers clenched round the front edge of his jacket and she lowered her lids. She loved him but that didn't mean she could live with him again or raise their child with him. It would mean a return to being a business widow because he would always be travelling, unavailable when she needed and wanted him. It would be lonely and thankless because he wouldn't appreciate how much she missed him. Their child would hardly see him, would even struggle to recognise him when he was away for weeks on end. Was a part-time father better than none at all?

Odd electronic beeps and loud voices roused her again.

'Betsy, tell them that you know where you're going,' Nik instructed, turning up her face to horrendously bright lights so that she shut her eyes fast again.

''Course I do,' she mumbled, willing to say anything if it meant being left in peace again.

'My wife can't help being unwell,' he breathed, anger in his voice now fracturing his Greek accent as he tightened his arms round her.

Her head was pounding and the familiar weariness settled back over her like a blanketing fog because it had been so many long weeks since she had enjoyed a decent night's sleep. She blocked the anxious thoughts battering to be heard inside her heavy head; she would think through all the complexities of her marriage and Nik with a clearer head some other day…

Betsy shifted on the comfortable mattress and a low sigh escaped her as she opened her eyes on the shadowy room. There was a low drone in the background. 'What's that noise?' she mumbled sleepily.

'Go back to sleep… It's late,' Nik advised from the foot of the bed. 'I shouldn't have come in but I wanted to check on you… Instead I'm afraid I woke you up.'

Remembering what had happened earlier, Betsy tensed, her gaze darting round what little she could see of the dim and seemingly quite small room. She could only assume she was in one of Nik's guest rooms in London. Where else would he take her to see a doctor? And why hadn't she argued, for good-ness' sake? Because arguing with Nik had always been pointless. When Nik was convinced that he was doing something in her best interests he was impos-sible to shift.

'Why were you checking up on me?' she framed.

Unshaven and decidedly tousled with his black hair ruffled and his tie and jacket missing, Nik loomed large as a twenty-storey building, poised beside the bed. 'You collapsed,' he reminded her almost accus-ingly. 'That's not normal—'

'I had a silly little faint…more embarrassing than serious,' Betsy fielded sleepily, realising that for some reason she felt strangely soothed by his presence.

'You seem to be incredibly tired—'

'I haven't been sleeping well recently,' Betsy ad-mitted before she could think better of that revealing confession. 'And fatigue is normal in the early stages of pregnancy.'

'The doctor will tell us tomorrow what's normal and what is cause for concern.'

'It's not like you to fuss over something trivial—'

'The state of your health is not a triviality.'

He sounded so serious that a drowsy smile of amusement lit her tired face before she shut her eyes again.

Betsy wakened to light flooding through a porthole window and blinked in confusion. She clambered slowly out of bed and, even before she reached the window to get a good view of the clouds beyond it, she knew she was on board a plane. The lights that had blinded her the night before, the questions Nik had been angrily parrying, must have taken place at airport security the night before. How stupid am I? she asked herself in consternation. Why am I on a plane? Why did he put me on a plane without mentioning it? But then why did Nik *do* anything?

The clothes she had been wearing were in the wardrobe but she was relieved to find that a selection of other items had evidently been packed for her and she yanked out fresh underwear before rushing impatiently into the en suite to freshen up. The discovery of her toiletries and her make-up bag did nothing to mollify her. She felt like Alice in Wonderland, only, instead of her falling, Nik had *thrown* her down the rabbit hole. The bright blue sky beyond the porthole persuaded her to choose a light floral skirt and tee from the sparse selection of clothing and, dressed, she walked out into the main cabin with the light of battle in her eyes.

Nik was working at a laptop for all the world as though he were in an office. He glanced up through lush black lashes, green eyes gleaming. 'I heard you get up. Breakfast should be here soon—'

'Where on earth are we?'

'In thirty minutes we'll be landing in Athens—'

'Athens?' Betsy yelled.

'I told you that I was taking you to a doctor. Mikis Xenophon is the world's leading authority on pregnant women,' Nik informed her with distinct satisfaction. 'And you have an appointment with him this morning—'

'I don't care who the heck he is!' Betsy shot back at him, out of all patience. 'I was willing to see a doctor but I wasn't willing to fly to Greece to do it!'

'Xenophon is the best. I want you to see the best,' Nik countered stubbornly. 'His research is first class and his patients speak very highly of him—'

'But bringing me to Greece without *asking* me,' Betsy began half an octave higher.

'You fell very deeply asleep. You must've badly needed the rest. I was determined not to disturb you,' Nik assured her tautly.

At that point a knock sounded on the door and the breakfast he had ordered arrived. Expelling her pent-up breath in a rush, Betsy sat down because, having missed dinner the night before, she was truly hungry. But as she nibbled she quietly seethed in frustration. He had done it again, taken over, steamrollering over her options and wishes as if only he knew best. The one and only occasion when he had ever let her choose anything had been the time when he had finally agreed that she could try for a baby if she wanted to. Of course that had been a safe choice from his point of view when he had known that his vasectomy had meant that there was then no prospect of her falling pregnant.

'Why on earth did you ever agree to me trying to get pregnant last year?' Betsy found herself asking him abruptly. 'I mean, when you knew it *couldn't* happen, why did you give way?'

Unprepared for the question, Nik stared fixedly back at her. 'I thought it would satisfy you. I…incorrectly, perhaps even foolishly, assumed you'd go off the idea again… After all, you didn't want children when we got married and somehow I never expected that to change—'

'Unfortunately, people do change. I thought I didn't want children because my parents never really wanted me—that was a major turn-off. I also spent a lot of time helping to look after the younger kids when I was a teenager in the foster system and I saw kids back then as nothing more than a time-consuming responsibility who stole away your freedom,' Betsy explained ruefully. 'I genuinely didn't *ever* expect to start wanting a baby, but I was too young when I made that decision and shared it with you.'

Nik nodded grimly. 'I will give you that. So, what changed?'

Her small face stiffened. 'You were away on business so much. I was bored, lonely, and then one day I woke up and somehow I believed a baby would be the best thing that ever happened to me and that everything would be improved with a child in the picture.'

'But you became obsessed by your desire for a child.' Nik sighed. 'I'm afraid I didn't understand how

important having a baby had come to mean to you…
that it was as much an emotional as a physical desire.'

Betsy tore her croissant into at least ten pieces
and then began buttering each one while deciding
that nothing less than honesty would suffice. 'Yes, I
was obsessed,' she agreed, thinking back to the vita-
mins she had taken, the temperature charts to check
when she was ovulating, the acupuncture and yoga
sessions, the state of mind and pure desperation that
had persuaded her that she would do literally *anything* to become pregnant.

Nik hadn't expected her to admit that. 'I felt shut
out and extremely uncomfortable because I knew that
no matter what you did it would be in vain.'

'Obviously,' Betsy conceded, glad to hear that guilt
had afflicted him even if he didn't have the right word
to quantify the feeling.

'I assumed you would just give up and forget about
it eventually,' he admitted with what would have been
poignant ignorance had it only related to a less sensitive subject.

'No, what you can't have, you just want *more,*'
Betsy whispered ruefully.

And now she had finally got it and she was almost
in Greece and Nik was back in her life. Was that what
she wanted? Betsy was ashamed to realise that she
truly didn't know any more. Her troubled gaze rested
on him, skimming over his bold bronzed profile before skipping down the long, straight slope of his
perfect nose to linger on the full curve of his sensual
mouth, and as if aware of her scrutiny he turned his

handsome dark head. Eyes that were glittering slivers of bright green ringed by luxuriant black lashes transfixed her with stunning effect. Her mouth ran dry and her tummy flipped a helpless somersault.

But that was her body reacting, not her mind, Betsy reasoned shamefacedly. Sadly, her brain was going round and round in ever-shrinking circles without reaching any definitive conclusion and it had been doing that for weeks. What did she want? Could she forgive him? *Was* he sincere? How could he simply walk away and then walk back? Could he *really* care about their baby's future? And what about her? Her needs? Her wants? Her happiness?

CHAPTER SEVEN

MR XENOPHON PLEATED his fingers and surveyed his anxious patient and her even more anxious husband. He had run a battery of standard tests and reached certain obvious conclusions.

'You are *very* stressed, Mrs Christakis,' he told Betsy gently. 'And although you don't yet seem to be aware of the fact, you are carrying twins. A twin pregnancy will be a heavier burden—'

'She's *stressed?*' Nik demanded as if the concept was entirely foreign to him.

'You are both very stressed,' the doctor pronounced mildly. 'Why is not my concern but you both need to find some way of reducing that stress for the sake of your wife's health.'

Betsy finally unpeeled her tongue from the roof of her mouth. 'I'm expecting…*twins?*' she finally pressed for clarification.

'My grandfather was a twin,' Nik commented, very much in the tone of someone owning up to a regrettable secret.

Not one but *two* babies, Betsy reflected in a daze.

Nik was probably filled with horror at the prospect of what might well strike him as a positive *horde* of babies.

'Mrs Christakis is in poor condition right now for a twin pregnancy, which will demand more of her and her body,' Mr Xenophon informed them calmly before focusing his attention on Betsy to continue. 'You are underweight even for your petite frame. You are anaemic. Clearly, you're not eating enough for a pregnant lady who needs all her strength. Your blood pressure is not good either. It's not bad but it is not what it should be. Thankfully, all those problems are easily curable with a sensible approach. The stress is most probably causing the rise in your blood pressure but you need to find your own solution to dealing with that. It should involve lots of rest and reasonable exercise. There is a higher risk of premature birth with twins. You must both make the mother-to-be's health your top priority.'

While listening, Nik had slowly lost all his natural colour. It was beginning to sink in to him that just being pregnant could be dangerous, seriously dangerous, for a woman's health. The mere idea of anything happening to Betsy sent a queasy roll through his stomach and he swallowed hard. 'Whatever it takes to improve Betsy's state of health, it will be done.'

'Twins,' Betsy mused in a complete stupor as they emerged onto the sunlit pavement to climb back into the waiting limousine. 'I saw the nurse pointing during the scan but, of course, I couldn't understand what she was saying. Didn't you?'

'I wasn't looking at the screen or listening. I was looking at you because you looked so worried—'

'I never dreamt... *Twins!* I mean, I've barely changed shape—'

The concept of *two* babies battling to occupy Betsy's tiny, fragile body at one and the same time only filled Nik with guilt and fear. Had he been more careful, had he thought to use precautions, had he suppressed his desire for her, none of this would have happened, he acknowledged angrily. But then, had she not fallen pregnant, would he have her back in his life? He thought not. And oddly enough, that acknowledgement banished all the razor-edged regrets attacking him.

Cristo's wife, Belle, phoned when they were walking back through the airport.

'Where the heck have you been?'

'Greece. Nik flew me to Athens to see an obstetrician.'

'As you do,' Belle mocked after a disconcerted pause. 'When will you be home?'

Betsy asked Nik. He veiled his gaze. 'I don't plan for us to return immediately,' he admitted. 'After what the doctor said I thought a week of rest and relaxation here would be a wiser idea... What do you think?'

The addition of the 'what do you think?' question was a groundbreaking improvement from Nik's domineering corner.

'I'll phone you later,' Betsy told her sister-in-law,

and in the VIP travel lounge she sat down beside her husband. 'Where are you planning on taking me?'

'The island of Vesos, where I spent my first years in my grandfather's home.'

Betsy hadn't known even that small fact about his childhood and even had she been furious with him, which for once she was not, she would not have missed the chance to see the island. In any case she knew Nik well enough to recognise that he was seriously worried about her physical condition and the doctor's sober pronouncements had filled her with dismay and guilt as well. Obviously she had not been looking after herself and her pregnancy as well as she had dimly imagined.

She felt humbled by that knowledge. After all, she had longed to have a child for so long and here she was gifted with the prospect of two babies and her body wasn't doing the job it should be doing because she had stressed and fretted, skipped meals and lain awake too many nights. Now she felt duly punished and arguing with Nik was the last thing on her mind. Indeed she was willing to do virtually anything to get her blood pressure back to normal and her condition improved to the level where she could carry a twin pregnancy safely to term.

'How on earth will Alice cope without me?' Betsy groaned. 'There's deliveries arriving every day—'

'I've already instructed her to hire temporary help to provide cover during your absence.'

'You think of everything—'

'No, I don't. If I did, we wouldn't be in this situation now. Xenophon was right. We're both stressed out of our minds. The divorce, the unexpected pregnancy, the constant conflict,' Nik bit out in a tone of harsh regret. 'How could we be anything else but stressed?'

'I'm going to be a lot more sensible,' Betsy swore.

'And instead of playing points, I will do what I can to support you, *glikia mou*.'

Nik lifted Betsy out of the helicopter as though she were fashioned of spun glass and Betsy suppressed a groan of frustration. Nik in rare conscience-stricken mode was entertaining for a while but she was convinced that the lion's share of the problems she was suffering were down to her own obstinate refusal to make adjustments to her schedule. She hadn't felt well but she had kept on pushing herself, determined to maintain the same workload and hours, refusing to consider that her condition might force changes on her usual routine. After all, she knew that most women worked through their pregnancies and had assumed she would be no different, but perhaps she ought to have sought medical advice when the fainting had started and she had realised that she was feeling consistently under par.

Nik set her down below the pine trees, where she breathed in the salt-laden air with a helpless sigh of pleasure and stood gazing down the grassed slope to the pale glistening stretch of beach washed by the surf. 'It's beautiful. Where do we stay?'

'I built a house here.'

'Did you? I assumed you had inherited your grandfather's home,' she said in surprise.

When she glanced at him enquiringly, his lean dark features were clenched hard, his eyes shuttered. 'I signed it over to my mother, although island life is too quiet for her tastes and I have been told that she only makes occasional use of the property. We flew over it coming in. It's that sprawling marble monstrosity on the cliffs. Did you notice it?'

'Yes…the villa with the massive pool area?'

Tight-mouthed, he nodded confirmation with a jerk of his stubborn chin and splayed a hand to the base of her slender spine to lead her through the trees. 'Lunch should be waiting for us. I want you to eat and go straight to bed—'

'I'm not an invalid. You know, you never even mentioned that you owned a house here in Greece,' Betsy reminded him as the trees slowly thinned out and an ultra-modern and graceful white villa surrounded by gloriously colourful gardens appeared in front of them. 'Especially one so beautiful. Why didn't you suggest we come here for our honeymoon?'

Nik gritted his even white teeth together, reluctant to admit that his memories of his time on the island had haunted him for years. 'I originally built the house solely as an investment I intended to sell but I never got around to it. To be frank, I left the island to go to boarding school and, after my grandfather died, I had no good reason to return here—'

'So not much in the way of sentimental attachment to this place, then?' Betsy guessed, recognising the taut flex of long fingers against her spine, aware that he was very uneasy beneath the barrage of her questions and wondering why.

But then that was Nik, a fascinatingly complex male, layered with mystery with nothing as you expected and no information granted for free. It had always been that way and she had learned to live with that wall of reserve. When they were first married she had walked in awe of him and his achievements, unable to understand why such a magnificently handsome, clever and wealthy male should choose to marry a lowly waitress when he might have married some rich socialite or successful businesswoman instead. She had never stopped being grateful that he had picked her, which was why she had never felt she had the right to complain when he left her alone so much.

Every paradise has thorns, she had thought, striving to be practical, knowing that many women would have been content simply to have a beautiful home and a string of credit cards at their disposal. Loving him to distraction, however, had made Betsy much greedier for his time and attention. Unfortunately she didn't think any human being would ever engage his interest to the extent that his business empire did, and wishing for more from him was like wishing for the moon.

Even so, it was unfortunate that Nik's former inability to grant her much of his personal time should have reminded Betsy of her years in foster care, when she had never been anyone's priority and her needs had been more often a second thought rather than a first. Nik had left her isolated at Lavender Hall, much as she had been isolated in a series of foster homes without close connections to the other inhabitants or loving carers. In those days, she had wondered if she was inherently unlovable.

They walked into a cool white hall, decorated with lush plants, to be greeted by a pleasant middle-aged housekeeper called Stephania. At the foot of the winding elegant staircase, Nik bent and lifted Betsy into his arms, ignoring her protests.

'No stairs for you,' he pronounced drily. 'If a dizzy spell hit you at the wrong moment you could have a nasty accident.'

'You always think in worst-case scenarios,' Betsy censured, amazed by the level of his pessimism while looking up at him to marvel at the length and lushness of his eyelashes, amused that she had to wear falsies to get even a hint of such luxuriance. It was wasted on him too, she thought abstractedly, for he was the least vain man she knew.

'No, I'm taking sensible precautions for your benefit,' Nik countered, reaching the wide decorative landing without an iota of breathlessness. But then in the wake of the doctor's comments, Betsy didn't think that carrying her could offer a well-built male much of a challenge.

The bedroom was a huge, dreamy space furnished with pale oak furniture, natural stone walls and draperies fluttering lightly at the open windows. Nik rested her down on a wide, sumptuously dressed bed.

Betsy rested her head approvingly back on a crisp white linen pillow. 'This place reminds me of a five-star boutique hotel.'

Nik slipped off her shoes and a knock sounded on the door to herald the entrance of a maid with a tray. Betsy sat up against the banked pillows while Nik collected the tray. He handed her a fork and sat down on the side of the bed. 'Eat before you sleep,' he urged.

It was a chicken casserole and very good but his reference to sleep had roused her interest. 'I was just wondering,' Betsy began abruptly, putting curiosity ahead of tact when it came to what had once been a touchy subject. 'Do you still suffer from the nightmares you used to get?'

Before her very eyes, Nik stiffened defensively, his bright eyes immediately veiling. 'No. It seems that was just a phase. I was working too hard last year, not allowing myself enough downtime to chill,' he parried with resolute cool.

'You never would tell me what the nightmares were about,' Betsy could not resist reminding him.

Nik shrugged a broad shoulder with careful unconcern. 'Telling you about them would have given them undue importance and lodged them in my mind even deeper,' he proffered in explanation. 'I have always preferred not to dwell on negative events.'

He had removed his jacket and tie. Lean muscles flexed beneath his silk shirt as he reached for the tray when she finished eating and set it aside. He closed his hand over hers. 'Now, you go to sleep.'

While she studied him with wondering blue eyes,

his thumb caressed the soft inner skin of her wrist in a soothing motion and he lifted her hand, spread her fingers and pressed a kiss to her palm.

Her heart thumped in the smouldering silence, gooseflesh erupting on her exposed skin, tiny hairs rising at the nape of her neck while low in her pelvis she felt the sweet, all-pervasive tug of the hunger that only he could stir. Her breath shortened in her throat as she stared back at him. It was no use, his gut-wrenching sensuality plundered her defences like an invading army. That fast she wanted his mouth, wanted his hands on her body...and a great deal more. Colour blooming in her cheeks, she felt her nipples strain and push against the bodice of her dress while her thighs pressed together to ease the ache he had induced at the heart of her.

'*Later,*' Nik breathed with hoarse emphasis, sexual anticipation written boldly in every line of his hard, angular features and the blaze of his eyes. 'If you sleep now, I'll make a late-night banquet of you.'

Betsy was taken aback by that proposition. 'But we...*can't*—'

Nik rested a silencing fingertip against her parted lips. 'Right at this moment the only thing that matters is that you get stronger and healthier. You don't have to make *any* big permanent decisions while we're here,' he assured her with determined emphasis.

Her eyes opened very wide. 'Sex *isn't* a big decision?'

In answer, Nik flashed her a wickedly amused grin. It filled his lean, darkly beautiful features with such charisma that the roof could've fallen in without her noticing. 'Not when we're married and you're already pregnant. What is the worst that could happen now?' he drawled silkily. 'That you might enjoy yourself?'

The warmth in her cheeks increased and she tore her gaze from his in self-protection, ashamed of her susceptibility. She had always enjoyed herself with him in bed. From the very first time to the very last time, sex with Nik had been a guaranteed passport to a wickedly seductive world of euphoric physical sensation. Long brown fingers gently circled her ankle and smoothed along the bare skin of her calf. A little tremor ran through her slight body and her lashes shot up again to focus on his lean, hard-boned face. In self-defence she closed her eyes but the predatory blaze of explosive hunger that had greeted her in his intense gaze was seared on the inside of her eyelids. *Nik wanted her every bit as much as she wanted him*. The awareness soothed her stinging pride but did nothing to assuage the flickers of eager warmth tingling through her lower body.

'Allow me…' Nik bent over her to run down the side zip on her dress and then without hesitation he gathered up the hem and lifted the garment off over her head.

'What are you doing?' Betsy whipped defensive hands over her bared breasts as they spilled free of the supportive bodice.

'Tucking you in.' Nik slid a hand below her hips to ease her free of the bedding, flipped it back and settled her down on the cool sheet. 'Drop the modesty. Let me enjoy the view.'

Her heart beating very fast, Betsy lowered her hands, feeling a little foolish for that belated cover-up. After all, they were married. And he had already told her that they could have sex without him assuming that it meant they were reconciled. Could she take that cool, sensible stance too? Her every emotion battled against such a concept. But at the same time there was no way she was ready yet to give him a final answer on whether or not she believed they could rebuild their marriage.

'There's more of you now to appreciate and you were already beautiful, *yineka mou,*' Nik husked, appraising the fuller contours of her small breasts before lowering his dark head to lick the lush, prominent peak of a swollen pink nipple while his fingers delicately shaped the new ripeness of her flesh. 'This, however, is for your pleasure, not mine. I want you to relax.'

Her breath hitched in her dry throat and she slumped back against the pillows, weak with longing and more than willing to let him play with her treacherous body but very far from being in a relaxed state. He dallied with the straining buds, utilising every ounce of skill in his armoury to tease her sensitised flesh. Heat thrummed to another level between her slender, trembling thighs, while her hips shifted back and forth in a movement she couldn't control. He tugged off her panties and leant back to slowly run his hands up the full length of her extended legs and ease them apart. Eyes hot on hers, he vented an appreciative masculine growl when his fingertips came into contact with the honeyed moisture coating her hidden core.

He drew her back into the hard heat of his taut, muscular body, covering her mouth with his. His tongue delved and explored and desire burned higher in Betsy than a firework shooting into the sky. Her hands clutched at his shoulders before lacing into his luxuriant black hair to hold him fast. He was a very sexy kisser. While he engaged her lips his hands roved until, freeing her mouth, he pulled her back against him and gently, softly, touched her between her trembling thighs.

Between one heartbeat and the next, her whole body became a mass of screaming nerve endings and she quivered and shook in response against him, her breath releasing in muffled sobs and gasps. Against her hip she could feel him hard and ready even through the barrier of his trousers. 'Make love to me,' she urged helplessly.

'Later,' Nik husked, burying his mouth against her exposed throat and licking and nipping at the sensitive cords of muscle pulling taut there to send another wave of painfully erotic stimulation through her already tormented body. 'Come for me…'

His stubbled jawline rasped against her cheek as he touched her with aching expertise and suddenly there was nothing she could do about it, her body was racing for the finish line all on its own. A liquid flame ran through her as unstoppable as a tide and the tightness in her pelvis suddenly clenched and convulsed in an explosion of almost intolerable pleasure as spasm after spasm of ecstatic release gripped her.

Nik settled her limp length back against the pillows. 'Now you sleep,' he rasped.

Betsy's face felt hot enough to fry eggs on and she didn't open her eyes as he tugged the cool linen sheet over her hot, damp body. She was limp with shame at having succumbed to temptation and taken the pleasure he offered. Once again she had stomped all over her own most deeply held principles. But then hadn't she always done that to keep Nik in her life? She had married a man who did not love her and from that moment on *everything* had become a compromise. In the same way, if they reconciled to raise their unborn children, she would never have the security of knowing herself loved and would have to live with the truth that only her fertility had brought him back to her.

And that was a toxic truth, she acknowledged painfully, one that would twist and grow inside her like Jack's beanstalk and eventually smother her self-esteem. But if the only alternative was to stay separated and continue the divorce, would that be any easier? After all, with her being pregnant they could not have a clean break now. Could she live with Nik always on the periphery of her life as the father of her children? Look on with detachment when he eventually chose another woman to share his life?

Pain slammed through her in answer to that question. Her lashes lifted as she stole an anguished glance at his bold bronzed profile, insecurity clawing at her.

For a split second she wanted his arms round her so badly it hurt. *Later,* she recalled, a little bubble of heat warming her chilled limbs at the promise of that word. And in the back of her mind, she cringed at what loving Nik had done to her pride. Would she only feel secure now when he demonstrated desire for her body?

CHAPTER EIGHT

OVER BREAKFAST ON the sunlit terrace the following morning, Betsy studied Nik's lean bronzed face with its sleek yet hard-edged charisma, feminine appreciation sending prickles of awareness slivering through her pelvis. At the same time she was wondering why he hadn't joined her in bed the previous night. She assumed it was because her long and very sound sleep had convinced him that her need for rest was more important.

'So, what would you like to do today?' Nik enquired lazily.

'Obviously I want to see where you grew up...in fact every place on this island that's associated with your childhood!' Betsy confessed with helpless enthusiasm.

Seriously taken aback by that chirpy admission, Nik briefly froze. A split second later he concealed his reaction by forcing a transient smile to his lips while he scanned Betsy's happy and relaxed expression. No, she had not the slightest suspicion that she had dropped a brick. And Vesos was, after all, where he had grown up. Her expectation that, having brought her here, he would want to share childhood experiences was simply normal. Acknowledging that truth, Nik cursed his decision to come to the island in the first place. Why hadn't he just hired a villa some-where? Vesos and this house had seemed the most sensible choice when they were already in Greece. But it had also been the very *last* place he had wanted to revisit, he reflected grudgingly.

Rising with something less than his usual grace from his seat, Nik stood gazing out through the trees towards the sea, mastering the powerful emotions threatening to roar through him like a hurricane, his broad back and wide shoulders rigid with tension. My mistake, he conceded heavily, and what could he do but play along to satisfy her natural curiosity? And why not when he was an adult now and no longer a weak and frightened child? Betsy wanted pretty, cosy pictures and he would give her pretty, cosy pictures, not the awful, pity-inducing truth.

'You started school here?' Betsy prompted over an hour later as she studied the small brick-built build-ing beside the harbour and the young children play-ing outside with fascination.

Nik nodded and barely repressed a shudder. He thought of the bruising a teacher had once questioned and the lies he had been forced to tell to hide the re-ality of what went on within his own home. School had been difficult, not, of course, in academic terms but in the pain of the gradual dawning realisation that other children did not appear to suffer the treatment that he did. It had been a challenge for him to make friends, set apart as he was by his family's wealth, even more of a challenge to play when he didn't know *how* to play.

'I really wish we could go and see your grandfather's house—' Betsy admitted.

No, no, no, *no,* Nik reflected sickly, nausea stirring at such a disturbing prospect.

'But I know it's your mother's house now,' Betsy allowed ruefully. 'Couldn't we drive past it?'

Nik was willing to settle for that less menacing suggestion. He drove along the coast road towards the cliffs.

'Did you play on this beach?'

'I was never allowed to leave the grounds of my grandfather's home unless I had an adult with me,' Nik fielded wryly, struggling to think of some single sunny recollection of his earliest years that would satisfy her desire to know more, but coming up with nothing.

Betsy peered at the house through the tall wrought-iron electric gates while Nik stared out through the windscreen without turning his dark head, lean brown hands flexing round the steering wheel of the sports car. 'It's an enormous place,' she commented, glancing at him, wondering why he was so quiet and *so...* She struggled and failed to come up with an adequate label for his attitude. 'Which bit of it did you live in?'

'The wing furthest away from the gate,' Nik related flatly. 'It was entirely self-contained—my mother insisted on having her privacy.'

'Were you happy here?' Betsy prompted gently.

'Of course I was,' Nik lied.

'So, when are we leaving?' Betsy asked casually over dinner almost a week later.

Nik frowned and studied her with questioning green eyes clear as emeralds ringed by spiky black lashes. 'Why would we be leaving?'

It was Betsy's turn to be disconcerted. 'Because we have to be back for Belle's birthday party on Friday night,' she pointed out.

'I don't see why,' Nik countered, cradling his wine lazily in one lean, elegant hand. 'We'll send her a special present instead—'

Betsy stiffened. 'No. I want to attend her party. I always assumed we'd be returning in time for it.'

Nik shrugged a broad shoulder while studying her with quiet satisfaction. Even in the short time they had spent on the island Betsy had blossomed. Her skin had acquired a light golden tint and her eyes were no longer shadowed. Her face was fuller, softer, the previous tension etched there banished by a regime of good food, afternoon naps and regular swimming sessions. When the local doctor had checked her blood pressure the day before, the reading had been normal and Nik believed that his decision to stay on Vesos had been fully vindicated. Here on the island, Betsy had nothing to do but get out of bed in the morning. Rest and relaxation had proved to be all she truly needed to regain her strength.

'It never occurred to me that you would want to attend Belle's party,' he admitted levelly. 'You're doing so well here. I think we should stay on for at least another week.'

Betsy had stiffened defensively. 'No, I can't do that—'

'Of course you can,' Nik told her in a 'subject closed' tone of voice lightly tinged with impatience and dismissal. 'Belle will understand that your health must come first—'

'For goodness' sake, there's nothing wrong with me any more!' Betsy argued, planting her hands firmly to the table and pushing herself upright as she thrust her chair back. 'I'm feeling a lot better and you know it!'

Nik uncoiled his long, lean length from the seat opposite with a positively slothful grace that mocked her angry, impatient movements. 'I don't understand why you're getting so annoyed—'

'Of course you don't. You're too accustomed to me doing everything you ask!' Betsy condemned, angry with him, angry with herself, for hadn't she taken the path of least resistance too often in recent days? For almost a week she had been painfully sensible and she had followed all Mr Xenophon's advice while at the same time taking on board Nik's suggestions. 'But I'm not going to go on acting like a doormat!'

His lean dark features hardened. 'I have not treated you like a doormat—'

'That's what I used to behave like and how you're used to dealing with me,' Betsy reasoned bitterly. 'But I'm not the same woman I was before you started the divorce, so laying down the law, giving me your opinion and making it clear what *you* want isn't going to make me change my mind about what *I* want to do!'

Nik ignored that direct challenge and said instead, 'Why is this party so important to you?'

'Because it's important to Belle and she and Cristo are family, not to mention my best friends…or haven't you realised that?' Betsy prompted, happily leaping off on another tangent because even before he had spoken she had not been in the best of moods. 'Who do you think supported me when the divorce started? Your brother! Cristo was really, *really* good to me—'

Nik chose not to mention that he had encouraged that connection but he was taken aback by her vehemence. 'Don't think I'm not grateful for that—'

'Like you cared at the time!' Betsy slung back at him in furious rebuttal. 'Cristo *listened* to me, talked to me, helped me through the worst period of my life. And Belle was generous enough to offer me her friendship from the very beginning—'

'Well, she never offered it to me,' Nik responded drily.

'Belle resents the fact that you've never shown the smallest interest in her mother and your father's children!'

'I never knew Gaetano. Why would his other children interest me? It's different with Cristo—he's an adult and we have a genuine bond—'

'Well, just you remember that those same children are going to be our babies' uncles and aunts!' Betsy reminded him tartly. 'Let's hope they feel friendlier towards our children in the future than you are to them.'

Lean dark features clenching hard, Nik gazed steadily back at her and slowly compressed his sculpted lips. 'I hadn't thought of that aspect. It does put a different complexion on the situation.'

Disconcerted by that concession though she was, Betsy made no comment. Instead she said, 'Why are you always so negative about Gaetano Ravelli?'

'Why wouldn't I be? As a father, he was an embarrassment. He lived off women like a gigolo—'

'But he was married to your mother, Cristo's mother and Zarif's,' she contradicted in surprise at his opinion.

'Surely you must have appreciated that Gaetano only ever married rich women for what he could get out of them? He got no money from my mother solely because their beach wedding in South America wasn't legal,' Nik advanced with derision. 'Helena deliberately neglected to file the right documents because she already suspected Gaetano of infidelity with Cristo's mother. Once she had the proof of it, she got rid of him and he couldn't claim a penny from her. How can you expect me to have any respect for a man that calculating and greedy?'

'Well, hopefully Gaetano's children by Belle's mother will grow up into decent people. You shouldn't hold their parentage against them. After all, you don't hold it against Cristo or Zarif,' she reminded him.

His mobile phone rang and she walked away, leaving him to answer it, and went out to the terrace.

There she perched on a low wall to listen to the distant sound of the surf washing the shore beyond the trees while striving to breathe in deep and let her bad mood simply evaporate.

His unbuttoned shirt blowing back in the breeze, Nik strolled along the terrace talking on the phone in measured Greek. His strong shoulder muscles bunched and kicked back as he gave a languorous stretch, arching his long spine so that his washboard abs pulled tight into mouth-watering definition. Betsy couldn't take her eyes off his spectacular body or the downy little furrow of hair that swam into view above his shorts as he breathed in, chest swelling, stomach tightening, causing the waistband to drop even lower on his lean brown hips. Heat flooded her face and her body and, half angry, half amused at her own behaviour, she tore her gaze from him and stared out into the darkness instead.

Considering that 'later' had never come around a week ago, looking was the only sensual pleasure she had, Betsy reflected, tensing at the thought and the feelings of hurt and rejection it evoked. For some reason, Nik had backed away from the idea of intimacy. Not only did he cart her up and downstairs with the detachment of a block of wood but he had also chosen to sleep in the bedroom next door. His retreat on that front had taken Betsy by surprise because Nik had always been very highly sexed. Even worse from her point of view, her body was awash with hormones and raring to go with an enthusiasm she had never experienced before.

She remembered that sexy little interlude on the evening of their arrival and breathed in deep and slow to cool her rising temperature. What had changed for Nik since that night? Did the very fact that she was pregnant make her less attractive on his terms? She supposed that was perfectly possible, particularly to a male who had never wanted children. Now that children were on the way, Nik might be ready to take responsibility as a parent but who was to say how he *really* felt about the development? A man wasn't committed simply because he said and did the right things. It was even possible that her less than enthusiastic reaction to the offer of reconciliation had annoyed and offended him. Nik was a proud man. He had tried to build a bridge between them and she was still standing frozen in the middle of that bridge, moving neither forward nor back, paralysed by indecision and terrified of doing the wrong thing.

Yet he had given her every opportunity to discuss her insecurities. Only, when had deep, meaningful conversations *ever* worked with Nik? When he didn't talk back it was a waste of her breath and when he brooded in silence she felt even worse. And when, as now, he might feel that for the sake of her health and peace of mind he had to tell her whatever she wanted to hear, how likely was it that he would feel that he could be honest? Throughout the week, Nik had displayed endless concern about her well-being. Fortunately her appetite had returned and she was sleeping soundly again, pleasantly tired after daily swimming sessions and walks on the beach. But the emergency, such as it had been, was over now and he needed to accept that and stop treating her like an invalid.

Tossing his phone down on the table, Nik came to a sudden halt in front of her. His wide, sensual mouth compressed. 'Look, if Belle's party is *that* important to you, we'll leave tomorrow,' he delivered grimly. 'But I don't agree with it—'

Surprise and pleasure darted through Betsy that he had given way. He might not understand the depth of her friendship with Cristo and Belle but he was trying to respect it. Without thinking about it, she stretched up on tiptoe to link her arms round his neck. 'You'll enjoy seeing Cristo, and Belle told me that Zarif is trying to clear his schedule to attend as well...'

The warmth of her smile lit up her heart-shaped face. It was relatively easy to make Betsy happy; Nik had realised that a long time ago but he had fallen out of the habit. But then in the early days he had had to negotiate a welter of misapprehensions before he had found the right path. It was not the cost of the gift that mattered but the thought and the effort behind it. It could be as simple as making a phone call, regardless of how busy he was, or of sharing the minutiae of his busy day to make her feel a part of it. Back then an unexpectedly sunny morning, the random kindness of a stranger or a casual compliment could leave Betsy wreathed in smiles.

'Oh, joy, my brother the king with the big mouth,' Nik derided as he looked down at her and slowly closed his arms round her slight body.

Betsy groaned out loud, having forgotten that complication. 'I think Zarif did you a favour, so cut him some slack. I had to find out about the vasectomy at some stage,' she pointed out ruefully. 'You had backed yourself into a corner by not telling me about it and I don't think you knew how to get out of it.'

Nik was genuinely stunned by that shrewd assessment of his behaviour. Ebony lashes shielded his reflective gaze but his thoughts were short-circuited by the soft, full mouth pressing to the corner of his with unstudied warmth. Betsy smelled of peaches and vanilla, and every barrier he had raised against temptation was washed away as if a tidal wave had engulfed him. His hands slid down to her delicately curved hips and he hoisted her up against him and brought his mouth crashing down on hers with hungry enthusiasm.

'Why did I have to wait so long for that?' Betsy moaned helplessly, struggling to relocate her breath while every skin cell in her body erupted into sudden life.

Nik stiffened defensively at the question and then set her circumspectly down again. 'Because if I can't finish, I don't want to start,' he told her frankly.

Brow furrowing, Betsy stared up at him. 'Why can't you finish?'

Nik groaned. 'You're supposed to be resting, taking it easy—'

Betsy flushed. 'But Mr Xenophon told me that making love would be OK.'

Nik froze in surprise. 'And when did he tell you that?'

'While I was getting dressed and you were in his office, because that's when I asked him what I should be avoiding—'

'*Diavelos!* Why didn't you tell me?' Nik suddenly demanded, studying her in disbelief.

'Well, the first night here, you seemed perfectly comfortable—'

'And then I came downstairs while you slept...' Nik exclaimed, stretching out his arms in emphasis. 'And I thought, what the hell am I doing here? Why am I assuming that a pregnant woman is in any fit state for a sexual marathon? That has to be the very *last* thing she needs in her current state of health!'

Betsy blinked, putting the facts together, amazed that she had been as foolish in her own way as he had been. He had assumed he should keep his distance and she had assumed that he simply didn't want her enough. 'We don't talk enough,' she murmured ruefully.

'And we're not going to talk very much tonight or indeed for the remainder of our stay,' Nik forecast, a breathtaking smile of intent slashing his beautiful stubborn mouth as he scooped her up into his arms and headed straight for the stairs. 'I have other plans.'

'Extensive, I hope,' Betsy encouraged, turquoise eyes locked to his lean, darkly handsome face, true energy leaping through her for the first time in days because the desire he couldn't hide in his possessive gaze restored her battered self-esteem.

'*Very* extensive,' Nik promised, laying her down on her bed, pulling off her shoes, flipping her over to unzip her dress and flipping her back to trail her out of its concealing folds to leave her exposed in a lacy bra and panties set. 'You look amazing—'

Betsy shifted uneasily. 'No, I don't… I'm losing my waist—'

'You *do* look amazing. I don't say anything I don't mean.' Nik shrugged off his shirt, loosed the button at the waist of his shorts. 'I've hardly slept this week. It's been so hot and the nights are very long when you have a hard-on that won't quit…'

Betsy watched his spectacular lean bronzed length emerge as the garments slid away. Her heartbeat was racing. He was fully erect and ready for action and her self-consciousness ebbed as though he had thrown a switch inside her. She sat up, unclasped her bra and skimmed off her panties with an eagerness she had never really dared to show him before. A predatory grin of appreciation slashing his mouth as she unveiled her succulent breasts, Nik came down on his knees on the bed.

'Multiply amazing by ten,' he advised, brushing his mouth across a straining pink nipple.

'You're just sex-starved—'

'Totally,' Nik agreed without shame. 'I haven't had sex since I got you pregnant…'

'Or after leaving me,' she reminded him, stroking an appreciative hand down the velvety length of his boldly aroused shaft in a way that made him jerk and suppress a moan.

Nik lounged back against the tumbled white pillows, the very image of sleek, dark, sexy masculinity.

Blue eyes bright with hunger, Betsy bent over him. Silky blonde hair fanned his abdomen and brushed his lean, hair-roughened thighs, and his breath caught on a groan of pleasure. He wanted her so much. He had never ever wanted anything so much.

'Enough,' he urged hoarsely, tugging a strand of pale hair to restrain her. 'Words can't describe the pleasure of what you're doing to me but I want to come inside you.'

Heat was already throbbing between her thighs and she could feel the moisture gathering there. He tugged her up into his arms and fastened his mouth to a lush rosy nipple, lashing the prominent bud with his tongue, and her spine arched and her pelvis brushed against his arousal. She came down with her knees either side of him and instinctively glided the neediest part of her back and forth over him.

'Hot,' Nik pronounced appreciatively, green eyes glittering like jewels in his lean, strong face. 'Am I allowed to assume that you've found the nights long and unsatisfying too?'

'You are,' Betsy confided, quivering over him, alight with so many different sensations she was intoxicated by that physical contact.

He took her mouth, his tongue plunging deep, his hand knotted in her hair to hold her fast. His dominance excited her beyond bearing. His other hand was engaged in darting explorations of whichever part of her was within reach and she immediately shifted up higher on him, squashing her tingling breasts against the hard, solid wall of his chest, settling her hot, damp core down to ride astride a lean, powerful thigh, and attempted to rock away the tormenting ache of emptiness afflicting her.

'Be patient…we've got all night,' Nik growled urgently.

'To heck with patience!' Betsy almost sobbed against his wildly demanding mouth, her fingers biting into the satin-smooth width of his shoulders.

A disconcerted sound of amusement was wrenched from Nik. He reached for her and lifted her, rearranging her over him to realign their bodies. He angled up his lean hips, initially sliding against her before finding entry with a sudden precision that wrested a sob of wonder and pleasure from her parted lips.

'Never say I can't take a hint,' Nik teased breathlessly, settling her over him and driving deep and then finally, with a revealing sound of frustration, he eased her over and pinned her flat to the mattress under him. 'Better?'

He thrust into her hard and she felt every inch of him and the delicious friction of the movement sent tiny convulsive tremors rippling through her womb.

'Perfect,' she told him, barely able to find her voice.

And it was, absolutely perfect in every way. With every driving stroke of his possession he unleashed a storm of pleasure on her eager body. She lifted her hips and bucked beneath him, matching his insistent rhythm while the consuming, tormenting delight grew and soared to a blinding high of raw excitement. Her heart thumping like crazy in her ears, she flew higher than ever before, carried by the wild throbbing pleasure to a stormy climax that lit her up inside and out with joy and sweet release.

'So, Cinderella shall go to the ball,' Nik mused huskily into her damp, tumbled hair. 'In fact if this is your response to the chance of attending a family party, I will find a party for you every night.'

A choked giggle escaped Betsy. He rolled onto a cooler patch of the bed, taking her with him, draping her over his sprawled powerful length with careful hands, fingers smoothing down her slender spine. It was a long time since anything had felt so right to her as the peace she experienced in the protective circle of his arms. She was tempted to tell him that she loved him but she swallowed the words that she had once offered so freely and with such trust, impervious to the reality that he did not return those words. She was not so naïve now. She rubbed her chin against a broad bronzed shoulder and drank in the hot, musky scent of him like an addict, happy, content but frightened that she was being foolish and short-sighted about the future.

Could she dare to trust Nik Christakis again? Could he be persuaded to make more of an effort this time around? Perhaps she should negotiate with him before she agreed to a proper reconciliation. Sometimes she thought Nik understood business deals much better than he did human relationships. If she laid out her needs as terms and conditions, would he listen then? What could she offer him in return? That second chance he had mentioned and as much sex as he could handle? Hot-faced, she grinned against his shoulder, struggling to pin her dizzy feet to planet earth again and be sensible. She had to learn to be as logical as Nik was and address future problems in a positive rather than critical way.

CHAPTER NINE

Nik studied Betsy as if she had gone insane without him having noticed, with wonder and disbelief and, yes, unfortunately, just a little amusement. 'Let me get this straight…you want to negotiate the terms of our marriage *before* you'll consider making a reconciliation permanent?'

In the background the hum of the jet engines provided a surprisingly soothing backdrop to Betsy's ears. Nik was a trapped audience when he was airborne. He couldn't walk away, make an excuse about pressing business or lose his temper because he would dislike the risk of the cabin crew overhearing him arguing with his wife.

'Yes. I think it's the practical approach. We failed the first time around, so we should try to foresee the potential problems there might be and endeavour to avoid them this time,' Betsy responded doggedly, lifting her chin as Nik sprang restively out of his seat and frowned down at her.

'But we didn't *have* any problems the first time— you decided you wanted a baby, I knew I couldn't give you one and it all went downhill from there,' Nik recited drily.

'It only went downhill because *you* decided that you couldn't tell me the truth about your vasectomy,' Betsy contradicted.

His green eyes glittered with challenge and his strong jawline clenched hard with tension. 'How many men want to tell a woman that they can't give her the one thing she most wants in the world?' he demanded in a harsh undertone. 'How do you think I felt when I stumbled on the baby clothes you had hidden in a bag at the back of the closet?'

Betsy was taken aback by that bold and unusually emotional question. It made her appreciate for the first time that Nik's macho spirit had been crucified by her desire for what he had known he could not give her; she had made him feel inadequate. When he mentioned the secret cache of baby items she had bought as a gesture of continuing hope and then shamefacedly hidden, she didn't know where to put herself. She was deeply embarrassed by that revelation, did not even want to think about how that discovery must have made him feel, and her face burned with discomfiture.

'I didn't know you'd found those clothes… Why didn't you tell me?' she pressed weakly.

'I knew I was in way over my head, so it was easier and safer to avoid the subject,' Nik admitted grimly. 'There was no way out for me that I could see. As far as I knew then the vasectomy was irreversible and no matter what I did you were going to break your heart for what I could *never* hope to give you…'

'I'm so sorry,' Betsy whispered feelingly, finally recognising what that troubled phase of their lives had cost him as well. Her desire for a child had become an obsession that had ruled her existence *and* his and he had been trapped by a truth that he could not bear to share with her.

But now everything had changed, she reminded herself impatiently. Against all the odds, she had conceived that much-wanted baby and what she was fighting for now was the need for them to create a viable blueprint for their marriage to thrive in the future.

'These terms you mentioned…' Nik prompted softly but she wasn't fooled by his tone. He stood straight and tall, lean, darkly beautiful face taut as if he was daring her to suggest conditions that he would find unacceptable.

'You were always travelling and I was home alone. That would have to change,' Betsy told him ruefully.

Nik viewed her in astonishment. 'But I wasn't away on pleasure trips. I was travelling for business reasons—'

'I know, but you were never at home and I got very lonely,' Betsy forced herself to admit with bald honesty. 'I was lucky to see you one week a month. It wasn't enough.'

Nik was sharply disconcerted. 'As a husband my most basic function is surely to be a good provider for you?'

'That would sound very impressive and I could

forgive your absences if your business was in trouble or you weren't already richer than Croesus. But you don't have either excuse. Ideally, I want a husband who thinks that his most basic function should be to make me happy,' Betsy confided valiantly. 'And it would make me much happier if you were at home more, particularly once the children are born. You need to be on the spot to be a good father.'

Nik was broodingly silent. It had never occurred to him that she could be lonely when he wasn't around. After all, in the first years of their marriage she had never once complained about the amount of time they spent apart. It was true that she had once said that loneliness had initially led to her desire for a child, but he had assumed that that was a momentary source of unhappy frustration, more of an excuse on her part than an actual fault that could be laid at his door.

'A long time ago, my grandfather taught me that the only person you can really trust in business is yourself and you're asking me to delegate important functions to subordinates,' he informed her heavily. 'I don't know if I can do that…'

He was so serious, so very serious. She had asked him to travel less, stay home more, but the way he was reacting she might as well have asked him to give her a daily pint of his blood or sacrifice a limb. Her hands knotted by her sides to prevent her from reaching out to him because until that moment she had never appreciated just how deep his distrust of others went or that that distrust had been fostered in him at an early age by a close relative.

'But you could *try*,' she pointed out gently. 'Try and see how it goes because if you don't try another way of living I can't see how I'll ever be happy with you.'

Nik was taken aback by that underwritten threat. He knew men who would be grateful to learn that their wives wanted to see more of them. He knew even more how grateful he had always been to come home to Betsy, even during the baby-obsessed phase of their marriage. Then, quick as a flash, another acknowledgement gripped him. In a few months' time they would have two young children in their lives and that fast and that easily Nik understood where his first priority should lie. He could not protect children whom he rarely saw. He could not be a good father or a good husband without making compromises. But, as always, when sudden change threatened, Nik froze, filled with sudden dread and disquiet at the prospect of his careful routine being disrupted.

'What's wrong?' Betsy queried.

'Nothing,' Nik declared instantly, veiling his gaze and breathing in slow and deep in a control exercise he had been taught to utilise at the tender age of ten. No child of his would ever be similarly afflicted. The knowledge that he would do everything possible to protect his children soothed him.

Betsy moved forward, painfully aware that Nik was locked in an intense introspection that took hold of him occasionally and shut her out. She ran her palms up over his shirtfront, exulting in the heat and hard strength of him, wishing he would share what was troubling him. 'You and I…it can work,' she told him steadily. 'We can *make* it work.'

His lean, powerful length tensing for a different reason as his body's natural instincts took over from his brain, Nik stared down into anxious azure eyes and a hundred memories threatened to entrap him: Betsy struggling to hide her difficulty in reading the menu at their first dinner date; Betsy laughing in the rain when her umbrella broke and she got soaked; Betsy teaching Gizmo to return a ball rather than chewing it to pieces; Betsy telling him he had got her pregnant. She was both fearless and frank with that take-it-or-leave-it honesty that he had always cherished. It was a shame he couldn't match that honesty, couldn't tell her what had happened to him, but he believed that the truth would only weaken him in her eyes and ultimately frighten her and she depended on him to protect her. He was caught between a rock and a hard place.

'Betsy…' he husked not quite evenly, fingers lacing into her silky blonde hair to brush it back from her cheekbone.

'We can make each other happy. We can make it work,' she repeated with dogged conviction.

'Shut up,' he told her in Greek and he kissed her with urgent claiming force.

It was a kiss filled with lust and frustration and it was hotter than the fires of hell, burning through Betsy like a flaming arrow that ignited a wanton ache between her slender thighs. She fell into that kiss like a falling star and burned up. When he gathered her up in his arms and carried her through to the sleeping compartment, she looked up at him with her heart in her eyes, warmth and fear and longing all tangled up together, but she still didn't give him the words of love she had once given so trustingly. Once she said those words, she couldn't take them back again, couldn't impose any distance between them and couldn't make the same demands. Once she said them he would know her for a fake; he would know she wouldn't turn her back or walk away. Not because she didn't want to but because she simply *couldn't*...

CHAPTER TEN

BETSY GRIMACED AT her reflection in the mirror. She was getting ready for Belle's party but her thoughts were far removed from frivolity.

If Nik had loved her, she was convinced she could have buried every atom of her insecurity for ever. As it was, unhappily, she was convinced that her husband had only returned to her because she was pregnant and that knowledge was a humiliation that would only fester with every passing year. Her troubled blue eyes dampened. Blinking ferociously fast, she quickly grabbed up a tissue to soak up the tears before she could smudge her mascara.

But it was a fact that Nik didn't love her and never had loved her. He lusted after her like crazy, a chemical connection that had evidently kept him true even while they were separated. Be grateful for what you have rather than yearning for what you can't have, Betsy urged herself in frustration. After all, some people would kill for the power to ignite such high-voltage passion in a partner. It should be enough. It *had* to be enough.

It was barely twenty-four hours since they had returned to Lavender Hall and a good deal of that time they had spent in bed. Her face burned at the recollection. She couldn't stop wanting Nik, couldn't put the brakes on the wild, greedy hunger he invoked every time she looked at him. But if she continued to be so easily available, how long would it be before Nik recognised that he had her exactly where he wanted her? In the palm of his hand to treat as he saw fit. A position of such weakness and vulnerability could never be a good starting point, particularly for a shiny new reconciliation.

Pale blonde hair, freshly washed and dried, swung in a silken bell round her shoulders as she walked back into the bedroom. Almost simultaneously, Nik strode out of the dressing room, fully dressed and immaculate. In a designer jacket teamed with close-fitting black trousers that enhanced his height, narrow hips and long, muscular legs, he looked absolutely gorgeous, all dark and sleek and the very ultimate in raw sexual power.

Heat pooled low in Betsy's pelvis and she fought that sizzle of awareness with every fibre she possessed. After all, there was no point trying to play it cool with Nik to keep him on his metaphoric toes while at the same time falling into the nearest bed with him at every possible opportunity. Wasn't that what she had been doing? Whenever she looked at Nik, she could barely keep her hands off him.

Nik studied her with unconcealed appreciation. 'Blue is definitely your colour, *kardoula mou*.'

Betsy's midnight-blue evening dress was fitted at breast and hip and the sleeves and skirt were made of lace. Her pale skin gleamed with the shimmer of a pearl through the mesh and her bright eyes reflected that rich blue like a mirror.

'I appreciate you coming to this with me. I know you don't like parties unless you're tucked away somewhere quiet talking solely about business,' Betsy remarked ruefully. 'But you'll have your brothers there for company—'

'And all the little half-brothers and sisters,' Nik reminded her wryly. 'I'll make an effort to get to know them but, as I lack small talk and Belle's probably already given them a poor impression of me, I can't make any promises.'

'A little bit of an effort is all that is required from you,' Betsy assured him, trying not to smile at his willingness to extend an olive branch to Gaetano Ravelli's youngest children. He had listened to her and he was prepared to change the status quo and to her way of thinking that was more than enough to earn him four gold stars.

'Obviously I'm willing to make any effort required,' Nik countered.

Betsy looked up at him with her very blue eyes. 'Why?'

Nik linked his arms round her still-slim waist, slowly easing her slender body into connection with his while he stared down at her with green eyes that had flared to jewelled brilliance with desire. 'I want you to be happy with me, Betsy.'

'I *am* happy,' she assured him, colour rising in her cheeks, hugely erotically aware of his big, powerful body and the erection he was making no attempt to hide. She stared up at him, treacherously enthralled by his sleek, dark, masculine beauty. The knowledge that in every way that mattered he was still hers in spite of the separation they had endured thrilled her and played merry havoc with her defences. Her body hummed at her feminine core, desire stirring in her, even while common sense fought to suppress it and remind her that she was all dressed up and keen to arrive on time for the party.

Nik lowered his handsome dark head and in an abrupt motion Betsy twisted her head aside, fighting her natural inclinations before he could succeed and wreck her lipstick. 'I'm all done up now,' she reasoned in breathless excuse and then glanced up at him, disconcerted when she recognised a fleeting flash of wounded uncertainty in his gaze. Her heart leapt in dismay at the memory that look provoked. He had looked at her precisely like that the day he had walked out, as if he didn't understand quite what he had done by making a secret of his vasectomy, couldn't credit her reaction to the revelation and was incredibly hurt by it. She hadn't understood it then but it still wasn't an expression she could be comfortable seeing him wear again.

In an equally sudden movement she pulled free of his arms and spun to present him with her back. 'Unzip me,' she instructed.

'But I *thought*—' he began in apparent mystification at her change of heart.

'Since when was I so fussy?' Betsy teased shakily, eyes over-bright with sudden tears, her pregnancy hormones all on override because she wanted him, she *always* wanted him and she marvelled that he should not immediately grasp that little fact.

The dress shimmered down to the floor and she stood revealed in lacy underwear. He feasted his eyes on her tiny, increasingly curvy body while she scooped up the gown and laid it carefully over a chair. 'Sometimes I want you so much it almost hurts,' he told her in a hoarse undertone.

Colour mounted in her cheeks as he shed his jacket and shirt with none of the care she had employed. She strolled back to him and unfastened his trousers, slender hands delving beneath to find the long, hard evidence of his arousal and stroke his velvet-smooth, rigid shaft with wondering fingers until he swore in guttural Greek under his breath and wrenched off the remainder of his clothing with less patience than he had shown a moment earlier. She knelt at his feet pleasuring him with her lush mouth and knowing fingers, excitement lancing almost painful waves of arousal through her heated body with every groan she wrenched from him.

'I want to make love to you,' Nik growled, bending down to scoop her up and plant her down squarely on the end of the bed. He skimmed off her knickers and ran the tip of his tongue across the pointed evidence of her achingly sensitive swollen nipples before testing the honeyed welcome between her thighs with the single dip of a long, appreciative finger.

Even before he came down over her, Betsy was gasping and arching, unbearably eager for the finale she longed for. Nik tipped her legs over his shoulders and sank into her slick channel hard and fast, stretching her with delicious force.

'You're incredible in bed, *kardoula mou*,' he told her rawly, angling back his hips before thrusting back deep inside again in a movement that wrenched a helpless cry from her convulsed throat.

Her heart raced and she struggled to breathe as the excitement built, backed by the ever-tightening constraint of tension gripping her pelvis. His fast, fluid rhythm became rougher, rawer as he pounded into her and finally she lost control, overwhelmed by the passion and the wild explosion of pleasure that assailed her when she could hold it back no longer. Even afterwards little tremors of delight continued to rock through her in rippling waves while she buried her face in Nik's damp shoulder and drank in the hot, musky scent of the lean, powerful body pinning hers to the mattress.

'I think we'd better make a move if we want to make the party before midnight.' Mocking light green eyes rested on her dazed expression and he laughed as awareness reclaimed her, dismay flashed across her face and she shoved against his shoulders, scrambling to get up and reclaim her party finery.

'I was really chuffed to see Nik taking some time to chat to Bruno about his art course,' Belle confided as she urged Betsy into the conservatory at the rear of the vast and luxurious London town house she and Cristo lived in. It was two in the morning and most of the party guests had already taken their leave.

'Nik probably finds Bruno less intimidating than his sisters,' Betsy joked.

'I invited far too many people tonight. I haven't been able to get five minutes alone with you all evening,' Belle complained, waving her glass of champagne in an emphatic gesture of annoyance, which sent a quantity of the golden liquid spilling over the lip of the goblet and down the stem.

Betsy laughed because the birthday girl was definitely a little tipsy. 'It's your party. Naturally everyone here wanted to speak to you personally—'

'But you and Nik…it's *definitely* all back on again?' the lively redhead asked with a fascination she couldn't conceal. 'When Cristo first told me that Nik had moved back into the hall, I refused to believe it.'

Betsy resisted an urge to admit that she too had initially been incredulous about that development. But some things were better kept private. 'The divorce is off,' she confirmed. 'We're going to try again.'

Smooth brow furrowing, Belle studied her with keen curiosity. 'In spite of everything that's happened between you? Regardless of everything he's done?'

Betsy chose to respond to those thorny questions with honesty. 'Apart from the fact that Nik's not the only one of us to have made mistakes, I never stopped loving him. I thought I had but then once I was with him again, I realised I'd only been kidding myself.'

In receipt of that confession, Belle unexpectedly looked surprisingly thoughtful and then she sighed in grudging surrender to the argument. 'I think we've all been there at some stage,' she confided with unexpected feeling. 'When I thought Cristo was in love with you, I honestly thought I hated him because I was devastated and so unbelievably jealous.'

Betsy froze to the spot in disbelief and wondered if she had misheard the other woman. 'You thought that Cristo could be in love with *me?* For goodness' sake, *when?*'

'After we got married I discovered that he carried a photo of you in his wallet,' Belle admitted ruefully. 'Before that find I had assumed that you were only friends—'

'But we *were* only friends,' Betsy retorted with uncomfortable stress, wondering just how much alcohol Belle had imbibed that evening. 'There was never anything else, not even a minor flirtation between us—I swear it—'

Belle wrinkled her nose in embarrassed dismissal. '*Of course* I know that now but I didn't know that back then and Cristo had quite a job convincing me because, let's face it, you are beautiful and very feminine, Betsy, so obviously I could see your appeal. At the time I was so afraid that you were much more Cristo's type than I could ever be—'

At that instant Belle's rambling speech was interrupted by a sudden noise behind Betsy and a harsh bitten-off masculine exclamation. She spun in consternation, just in time to see Nik's tall, broad-shouldered figure swinging round in the doorway to fire back out into the corridor.

'Nik?' she called after him anxiously while she wondered how long he had been standing there waiting for her to notice his presence. 'Were you looking for me? Wait for me...'

'Oh, *hell!*' Belle gasped in undiluted horror. 'Nik must've heard what I told you about Cristo...'

The two women raced out of the conservatory to return to the party and reached the hall just as Nik grabbed his brother Cristo by the shoulder and punched him in the face. A split second later Nik had Cristo physically pinned to a wall, black fury and outrage etched in every flushed line of his lean, rigid features. 'My wife...you were in love with *my* wife?' Nik was growling with enraged incredulity.

Betsy realised that Nik had indeed overheard Belle's deeply damaging admission that she had once believed that Cristo was in love with Betsy and she gritted her teeth in frustration at the realisation, because it was not at all the sort of revelation that Nik was likely to take lying down or with a large forgiving pinch of salt. Nik was a proud and possessive man and even his close friendship with his brother would not excuse what Nik would regard as an unforgivable betrayal of trust. Even so, it was all a stupid storm in a teacup, Betsy thought in exasperation, reluctant to credit that Belle's suspicions could ever have had any foundation in fact.

'Calm down, Nik. Think this through,' Cristo was urging with admirable cool for a male who had blood running from the corner of his mouth. 'You've got this all wrong—'

'You had a photo of Betsy in your wallet?' Nik was roaring, apparently deaf to any plea for calm.

'It's not like it sounds,' Cristo protested.

'My *own* brother? I trusted you, *totally* trusted you around my wife and you deceived me!' Nik growled as if Cristo hadn't even spoken and with that embittered accusation he threw back his arm and hit Cristo again.

Cristo finally tore himself free of Nik's punishing hold and shot a string of words at his brother in fast, fluent Italian.

'For goodness' sake, someone stop them!' Betsy exclaimed in consternation as the two brothers began to exchange punches in earnest with both of them so well matched in powerful build and strength that there was no hope of a quick conclusion to the fight.

Belle darted across the hall to the main reception room, which still contained a handful of lingering guests, and called her brother-in-law Zarif out to join them.

Zarif appeared in the doorway. Tall and startlingly handsome with olive skin and very dark eyes, the young King of Vashir took in the situation at a glance and waded between his brothers, ducking a blow that would have sent him flying had he not been so agile. Mercifully that near miss of their sovereign was all it took to provoke Zarif's four accompanying guards into plunging straight into the fight to forcibly separate the battling siblings. An exchange of furious Italian and Greek followed but Zarif flung open the door of Cristo's study and said drily, 'We will discuss this in a more private setting.'

Betsy dealt the younger man an appreciative appraisal, grateful for his intervention. While Zarif was technically merely a kid brother, he had been raised as an Arab prince in a royal palace and, having trained as a soldier and seen actual combat, he had a habit of command and a mature and level-headed presence far beyond his years.

'Oh, my heaven, what have I done to this family?' Belle was whispering, distraught, dashing her auburn hair off her brow in a feverish gesture. 'I've caused so much trouble between the brothers. Cristo will never forgive me for opening my big mouth.'

'No matter how he felt, Nik shouldn't have just exploded like that and assumed the worst,' Betsy breathed ruefully. 'He should have talked it over with Cristo first.'

'Nik would *still* have hit him,' Belle opined without hesitation. 'Nik's very much the dark, jealous, passionate type.'

Somehow Betsy had never viewed her husband in that light before and her lashes fluttered in confusion.

'And Cristo explained to me once that Nik's not good with emotional things, which I suppose explains why you almost got all the way to the divorce court before it finally dawned on Nik that you're *still* the most important person in his world.'

'I wouldn't put it quite like that,' Betsy muttered uncomfortably, wishing that she could crash into

Cristo's study to find out exactly what was happening between the three brothers. It was the very first time that she had seen Nik lose his temper and his self-control to that extent and she was still in shock, her legs feeling a little wobbly at having been witness to the kind of violence she abhorred, even more particularly when it broke out between members of the same family. That welter of exchanged blows had torn apart the brothers' close relationship and she was distressed by that reality.

'Nik's absolutely crazy about you!' Belle protested. 'And Cristo says he always has been…from the first moment he saw you.'

A lump formed in Betsy's throat. Was it possible that Nik truly cared about her? That he could have been as misled as she had been about her own feelings? After all, hadn't she believed that she hated Nik for a while? Hadn't that been her way of coping without him? Her way of getting by and surviving life without him?

'Cristo is just going to kill me for this mess,' Belle muttered guiltily, tears sparkling in her lovely eyes. 'I don't always think before I speak. Deep down inside me, I never forgot that time when I believed Cristo might care more for you than for me—'

'I don't believe that could ever have been the case,' Betsy countered staunchly.

'Maybe I wanted to test you, see how you reacted,' Belle acknowledged shamefacedly.

'I've just never seen Cristo as fanciable.' Intercepting Belle's rather chagrined glance, Betsy smiled wryly. 'There's never been anyone but Nik for me.'

Her steps uncertain, Betsy approached the study door and knocked on it before opening it. From the threshold she peered in at the brothers, all three of whom were posed with varying degrees of strain and annoyance etched in their remarkably similar lean features. 'I think we should go home now,' she told Nik flatly.

'Good idea.' Nik crossed the room with a flash of his long, powerful legs.

'And when you get there, you should explain some things to Betsy,' Cristo urged ruefully.

'That kind of interference is not within our remit,' Zarif chimed in, his tone one of reproach at that offering of advice.

As he listened to his brothers a line of colour flared along Nik's high cheekbones and then receded, leaving him curiously pale and extremely tense. Lush black lashes dipped down over his bright eyes as he dropped a protective arm round Betsy's slim shoulders. 'Home,' he agreed with unconcealed relief.

'Did you apologise to Cristo?' Betsy prompted as the limousine drew away from the town house.

Nik flashed her a stunned glance. 'No, I did not. Why would I apologise?'

Betsy breathed in slow and deep. 'You attacked him—'

'He got what he deserved,' Nik countered with caustic bite. 'It may be a little late in the day that he's getting it but he did deserve it. You're my wife and I trusted him with you—'

'And he never once betrayed that trust,' Betsy declared, choosing to be tactful rather than point out that during that period of their lives Nik had turned his back on their marriage and left her alone to sink or swim. 'If it's true that he did develop some sort of silly crush on me, I had no suspicion of it because he never said or did anything around me that even suggested that.'

'Never?' Nik pressed, shooting her a troubled and still-unconvinced appraisal. 'And how did you feel about Cristo at the time? I had gone, the divorce had started and you were alone but for my brother's *supportive* visits.' He spoke the word 'supportive' with deeply derisive emphasis.

'I was grateful for his support and the fact that he was willing to listen to me rambling on,' Betsy admitted honestly. 'I had nobody else to talk to. He was your brother. Talking about you to Cristo didn't feel disloyal and I *knew* that anything I said wouldn't go any further.'

'I encouraged him to connect with you,' Nik confided grittily, his jawline clenching hard at the recollection. 'I had total trust in him. I should have known better—'

'You *encouraged* him to be my friend?' Betsy repeated in surprise. 'But why?'

Nik shifted uneasily in his corner of the back seat. 'I wanted to know that you were all right, that you had everything you needed—'

'But I wasn't all right,' Betsy responded in a small, tight voice of commendable restraint. 'How could I have been? You had refused to even discuss your vasectomy and why you'd had it done and then you simply walked out on our marriage.'

Nik frowned, clearly thinking that evaluation unjust. 'Because you told me to leave. You said you could never forgive me, never look at me again and that I had killed your love. You said our marriage was over,' he replied.

Betsy studied his lean, darkly handsome face, taken aback to have her words of many months earlier thrown back at her when she'd least expected to hear them. 'But that's just the sort of thing people say when they're angry and hurt and crazily confused—'

'Only you can't afford to say stuff like that to me because I took it all literally and I believed that you meant every word that you said,' Nik admitted in a raw undertone.

Her brow indented. 'We should have talked again more calmly back then.'

'There were issues I wasn't prepared to discuss with you,' Nik vented grittily. 'I'm useless at discussing emotional stuff. If I don't even know quite how *I* feel, how am I supposed to know what anyone else is feeling?'

Frustration and bitterness roughened his dark deep drawl and she turned her head away, dropping her eyes, wondering what he was talking about but reluctant to put pressure on him after the upsetting evening they had had. 'Have you made up with Cristo?' she asked baldly.

'Were… *Are* you attracted to him?' Nik asked abruptly, his eyes light and bright in the dimness of the car interior. 'Most women would prefer him to me. I'm darker, rougher round the edges, a lot less smooth.'

Betsy swallowed hard, astonished that Nik could still seem so insecure and marvelling that he was still shaken up by Belle's revelation to continue feeling suspicious. 'All I can tell you is that I met the two of you together the same day at the bistro and I never really noticed him. I mean, I realised that there was a guy with you and I eventually worked out that you were brothers, but Cristo might as well not have been there for all the interest he inspired in me,' she confided quietly. 'It was you I noticed, you I couldn't take my eyes off—'

'And…later?' Nik pressed, closing a lean brown hand round hers where she had braced it on the leather seat. 'How did you feel later after our marriage broke down?'

'That he was my only friend, for listening and not judging. For being there when I needed a shoulder. He was very good to me—'

'He said I was a rotten husband, that I didn't treat you properly and that he felt sorry for you,' Nik breathed harshly. 'Is it true? Did I treat you badly?'

'You just travelled a lot and you were very… detached. You never explained anything. But aside of the vasectomy you kept quiet about, I wouldn't have termed you a rotten husband,' Betsy said truthfully. 'I was happy with you most of the time—'

'But it should have been *all* of the time,' Nik fielded grimly. 'I let you down. But with the exception of your desire for a child, I really thought I was doing OK in the husband category. Unfortunately I'm not perfect, in fact I'm seriously flawed and I've done as much as I can to remedy that. But then you're not quite perfect either. When I realised that you suffered from dyslexia I felt so comfortable with you. At first it was a wildfire physical attraction I felt for you, but once I got to know you and realised that you had restrictions as well, you seemed so perfect for me...'

The limousine drew up outside the hall and for a split second Betsy simply sat there, fixedly staring at Nik. *You had restrictions as well* was still ringing in her ears with the last two words ringing the loudest. 'When you said you were seriously flawed, what did you mean...?'

The passenger door whipped open and crisp, cool night air flooded in. Nik retained her hand and tugged her out of the car to guide her up the steps. 'I owe you the truth,' he intoned with a bitterness he couldn't hide. 'But it's a truth I would never have chosen to share with you.'

A chill of foreboding was sliding down Betsy's taut spinal cord and rousing goosebumps on her exposed skin. She searched his bold bronzed profile, only to be taken aback by the harsh lines of tension underscoring his spectacularly strong bone structure.

'I don't know what you're talking about,' she whispered apologetically.

Nik thrust open the drawing room door and went to pour them both a drink. In silence he extended a pure orange to her and she grasped the moisture-beaded glass of juice tightly, unable to take her attention off him.

'Didn't it ever occur to you that I was a little off the wall sometimes?' he framed with sardonic bite.

Without responding, Betsy watched him toss back a brandy and registered the strain he was striving to control.

'Well?' he prompted grimly.

'You're a little different…occasionally,' she acknowledged reluctantly, thinking of the wedding proposal that had come out of nowhere and the reconciliation he had chosen not to discuss before moving back in. 'But nothing I can't handle or live with—'

'Let's see if you can work it out for yourself,' Nik framed with dark, driven derision, a muscle jerking taut at the corner of his unsmiling mouth. 'I'm no good at empathy. I find it hard to know what someone is thinking. I instinctively distrust most people. On the plus side, I don't play games in relationships. Even so, my flaws have caused me endless problems in the field of personal relationships.'

Betsy was in a daze. Her head started to thump with the onset of a tension headache because what he was trying to tell her was so much more important than anything she could have foreseen.

'As a child, I was brutalised by a severe level of

abuse,' Nik admitted gruffly, watching her with his beautiful green eyes as if he was suddenly expecting her to start screaming or shouting at him. 'My mother was the perpetrator—'

'Your...*mother?*' Betsy exclaimed in horror.

'My mother...yes—women can be violent too,' Nik extended grittily. 'I've always suspected she had some kind of personality disorder. Whatever, she was very violent. She never wanted a child in the first instance and, worst of all, I reminded her of Gaetano, whom she hated. She believed my father had made a fool of her by getting Cristo's mother pregnant as well and she focused her hatred and resentment on me because I resembled him.'

Betsy was dizzy with shock. 'I had no idea, Nik. Why didn't you ever tell me about this? Those nightmares you used to suffer—?'

'Childhood memories... I also began suffering from flashbacks of the abuse,' Nik confessed in a raw, reluctant undertone. 'It takes me longer to understand emotional stuff...like tonight with Cristo. I went into meltdown because I was very angry and upset. I felt betrayed. I was afraid that you might have developed feelings you shouldn't have where he was concerned, feelings you couldn't acknowledge because you knew you shouldn't have them. I wondered how the hell I would ever get to the real truth and believe it in such a situation...because difficult as it would be for anyone in that position, it's even worse for me.'

'Oh, Nik...' Betsy breathed painfully, her heart going out to him because so much that she had never understood about him was finally falling into place for her.

This was why he struggled when she hurled angry accusations at him, fell silent and brooded when she began to talk about feelings, and ultimately it was why he had misunderstood how she felt about him and walked out on their marriage. He had genuinely thought she didn't love him any more, that she had told him the literal truth. He couldn't comfortably assess such a confrontation and sometimes, regrettably, people threw wild, wounding insults and made threatening announcements purely to shock when they were hurt and angry. After all, that was exactly what she had done with him.

'And this is what I would have done anything to avoid,' Nik admitted angrily, throwing his proud dark head high. 'I never wanted you to know and to think less of me—'

'I don't think less—' she argued in dismay.

'I didn't want you to see me as being damaged and I don't want your sympathy or your pity now,' Nik told her curtly, pale beneath his bronzed skin as he stared back at her in challenge. 'You thought I was perfect and I *wanted* so badly to be perfect for you. I wanted you to look up to me, to respect me—'

'I still do, for goodness' sake!' Betsy swore in passionate rebuttal of his obvious concern. 'You're ten times cleverer than I am and a brilliant, highly successful businessman. Of course I respect you and I could never think less of you. In fact I probably think more of you because you've chosen to struggle very bravely in silence… Why is that? I appreciate the macho aspect of hiding what you deem to be a weakness, but why couldn't you tell me years ago? I mean, for goodness' sake, we were *married!*'

'I was taught always to hide it from people, the bruises, the scars. I became an expert at redirecting people away from my pain and suffering. My own mother saw me as a freak because I would never react to the abuse she put me through. I learnt quickly that if I did react, or cry, or beg her to stop, it would only be worse for me. So I stopped crying, stopped feeling and closed off from her and everyone else completely,' Nik volunteered in the most shockingly calm voice as though his mother's attitude to him had been perfectly understandable. 'She had me in behavioural conditioning sessions by the time I was four years old.'

Betsy studied him in horror but clamped her lips shut on an exclamation that would have revealed her true feelings. He didn't want to hear that her heart was breaking on his behalf. Evidently his childhood had been an endurance test of unkindness and pain. His mother hadn't nurtured or loved him; she had called him a freak. From an early age he had been forced into self-reliance, a fact that could only have increased his innate distrust of others and his isolation.

Emboldened by her lack of embarrassing reaction to his admission, Nik continued doggedly, determined to tell her everything now that he had started. 'Helena despised me. It was bad enough that she had a baby she didn't want but she was ashamed of me too.'

Tears stung Betsy's eyes but she kept her eyes wide, determined not to let him see them. She couldn't bear to think of what his childhood must have been like. By all accounts, his mother had been a less than loving parent and he must have felt that was his fault because he wasn't good enough for her, wasn't perfect. How confused and lost he must often have felt when he didn't understand, she reflected in positive anguish at the thought of the unhappiness he must have suffered.

'My mother was physically abusive,' Nik admitted curtly. 'But the nightmares only began shortly after I met you. I had suppressed all the memories of her cruelty—it was my way of coping. I hadn't forgotten what she did to me. I just didn't want to dwell on the memories. But when I met you I opened myself up to feeling things for the first time and then without any warning I started suffering flashbacks and nightmares about the violence.'

Betsy sucked in oxygen like a drowning swimmer and then she simply couldn't contain her feelings any longer. She crossed the distance between them and wrapped her arms round his lean, powerful body as though she would never let him go. 'You should never have allowed your mother to come to our wedding,' she condemned for want of anything better to say, fearful of revealing her sympathy and damaging his pride, for she was painfully aware that such honesty, such soul-baring, had to be very tough for so reserved and secretive a male. 'Why didn't your grandfather protect you?'

'We lived in an entirely separate wing of his home. He never saw or heard anything suspicious and he assumed I picked up the bruises being bullied at school because I wasn't very good at playing with the other children,' he explained wryly.

Betsy rested her brow against his shirtfront, the solid, reassuring thump of his heartbeat thrumming against her and his warmth sinking into her chilled bones like an addictive drug. 'Why didn't you tell him what your mother was doing to you?'

'I thought I deserved it for not being the son she wanted.'

Her hands linking round his waist, Betsy swallowed so hard that she hurt her throat. He was a man of steel forged in fire and she had never truly appreciated that. He was tough because he had had to be tough to survive, hard because he knew that weakness meant vulnerability and distrustful because too many people had let him down.

'The abuse I suffered is the reason why I chose to have a vasectomy,' Nik spelled out in a harsh undertone. 'I didn't want to have a child in case I too felt the same way my mother felt about me. I couldn't bear to put a child through the same pain as I had suffered. However, I know that I am not like my mother and I decided that the vasectomy was an overreaction on my part.'

His explanation was so simple and yet it rocked her where she stood for it had really never occurred to her that Nik might have had a very good reason to make that choice while he was still so young. She had thought only of more selfish and less presentable motivations relating to reluctance to have his freedom curtailed by the responsibility of becoming a parent. She pressed her rounded tummy to his big, powerful frame and leant against him. 'You are a kind and caring man. I know that you will protect and cherish these babies with your life. You are nothing like your mother—don't ever think you are,' she breathed shakily.

Nik closed his hand to her chin and tipped up her face to look down at her. 'I was scared that when I told you the truth you would hate me for having got you pregnant—'

'I could never hate you,' Betsy whispered, wide azure eyes locked to his lean, darkly beautiful features. 'I love you too much for that and I'll love our children the same way...'

His level black brows pleated, his stunning eyes glittering with surprise and curiosity below a fringe of luxuriant black lashes. 'You're saying you still love me? How is that possible?'

'I never stopped. When I said you'd killed my love the day I threw you out, I was being a drama queen,' Betsy confided guiltily. 'I was angry but I didn't mean it—'

'Don't say stuff like that to me,' Nik advised, long brown fingers cradling her delicate jawbone. 'I thought I'd lost you for ever. I went to see a therapist about the flashbacks and nightmares when they got worse,' he admitted gruffly. 'Being honest about my childhood lightened the load and helped me come to terms with it as an adult. I put it behind me. I just don't look back…except where you're concerned.'

'And why am I different?' Betsy prompted intently.

'Because you've always inspired feelings inside me that nobody else does,' Nik confessed. 'But I didn't realise what they were until it was almost too late. I know you weren't happy when we were first married, but *I* was. Just having you in my life and my home was enough for me. Without you, everything went to hell and I was hopelessly unhappy.'

Betsy rested up against him with a sigh of pleasure. 'It was the same for me. I think we belong together.'

'And I think missing you and wanting you and needing you all the time means that I love you,' Nik confessed in a tone of self-derision. 'I'm sorry it took me so long to work out that you make me happy but at least I got there in the end—'

Betsy gazed up at him with wonder in her eyes. 'You *love* me?'

'Without you there's nothing to look forward to,' Nik admitted baldly. 'Even the sound of your voice on the phone lifts me…'

Happiness foamed up inside Betsy, banishing the pain, the worry, the insecurity, and opening up a view of the future that was gloriously inviting. 'I was really scared that you only came back to me to give our marriage another chance because I was pregnant.'

'That was only my excuse. The truth is that I wanted to come back and once I got the idea in my head I couldn't wait to do it,' he confided, looking at her with tender appreciation. 'I can't face my life without you in it.'

Betsy pushed her face into his throat, breathing in the familiar scent of him with huge satisfaction, knowing he was finally home with her in every way. 'Will Cristo ever forgive you for what happened tonight?'

'We've made our peace. He knows he was in the wrong.'

Betsy studied him in dismay. 'That's *not* what—'

'He shouldn't have had any feelings for you at all and he knows it,' Nik parried stubbornly.

'I'm tired,' she whispered, briefly resting her heavy head down on his shoulder. 'Let's go to bed before it gets any later.'

In the hall, Nik lifted her up to carry her upstairs.

'You don't need to do that any more,' she reminded him gently.

'Carrying you gives me a kick, *latria mou*.' Nik laid her down on their bed and a charismatic smile flashed across his wide, sensual mouth. 'And when one of you becomes three and the babies are born, life will be even better because I'll have two extra people to take care of.'

'And we'll all be very demanding,' Betsy forecast in warning as he unzipped her gown and helped her to take it off.

'I love you enough to put up with anything you care to throw at me, *pethi mou*,' Nik asserted, sliding into bed beside her to reach for her slight body and ease her close. 'I think I must have fallen for you the very first time I saw you because I couldn't get you out of my mind.'

Her pale fingers skated lovingly through his silky black hair as she relaxed into the circle of his arms. 'It was mutual,' Betsy confirmed drowsily, winding her arms round his neck. 'I need to get up and take my make-up off. Don't let me fall asleep...'

But Nik was much too content holding his sleeping wife to wake her up. Wide awake, he luxuriated in his wonderfully new sense of peace and contentment. Betsy stirred and snuggled into him with a faint sigh of satisfaction as even in sleep he was the source of her security. In the darkness, Nik smiled. *This,* he was convinced, was the essence of being happy...

Baby giggles filled the air as Nik chased his twin daughters across the beach. 'Come back here!' he yelled, finally acknowledging defeat.

From the picnic rug, Betsy waved baby cups of juice and Dido and Ione hurried back to claim them, little toddler legs moving fast and confidently. In the sunlight the diamond-studded eternity ring that Nik had presented her with when they became parents glittered on her wedding finger. Their daughters were almost two years old now and full of spirit. They were identical twins, rejoicing in black curls, olive skin and their mother's blue eyes.

Rolling his eyes at the ease with which Betsy had contrived to recall the two little girls, Nik folded his long, lithe sun-bronzed body fluidly down on the rug beside his wife. 'Why don't they do what I tell them to?' he demanded.

'You spoil them and you never tell them off,' Betsy pointed out as the toddlers arrived to claim their cups and drink thirstily from the plastic spouts.

Nik studied his daughters with a frown. If only he didn't adore them, if only they didn't remind him of Betsy at every turn, it would have been easier to play the disciplinarian. But the girls had inherited Betsy's eyes and cuteness as well as her sense of mischief. Being a father was both more enjoyable and more demanding than he had expected but he wouldn't have exchanged a day of their often chaotic, busy life for a day without their children.

Whenever they had a few days free they flew out to Vesos to stay at the villa and spend time together as a family. The girls loved the beach while Betsy simply enjoyed relaxing and having Nik all to herself. Nik rarely left Lavender Hall now for more than three days at a time. He had rigorously cut back on his business trips abroad. That lifestyle change had begun when Betsy was still pregnant because he hadn't wanted to leave her, and had continued after the twins' birth when he had soon realised that he wanted to be as fully involved in their daughters' lives as Betsy was.

While the girls munched sandwiches, Betsy watched Nik's lean, darkly handsome face soften as he appraised his daughters. She had never dreamt that she could be as happy as Nik had made her. With no secrets left between them and a great deal of love and mutual understanding, their lives had changed for the better, becoming richer and more absorbing. They still saw a lot of Belle and Cristo and the half-siblings the other couple had adopted. Thankfully, Nik and Cristo's confrontation had not left lingering bad feelings on either side and the brothers were as close as ever. Sometimes they all got together to fly out to Zarif's fantastically opulent palace and enjoy the desert sunshine. But more than anything else, Nik enjoyed being a father and enjoyed being at home.

Of course, not everything between them had been perfect, Betsy acknowledged wryly. Once Nik had appreciated the size of the business operation she was running at the back of their home he had been taken aback and had insisted that the farm shop and its attendant outlets be moved to another site. There had been several heated arguments on that score before that move finally took place to a neighbouring farm that Nik had purchased for the purpose. Now it took Betsy time to drive to work but she had had to concede that with access to the new site lying off a busy main road, business had increased exponentially. Thanks to his business acumen, Nik could really not be bettered as an invariably silent partner.

When they had all finished eating lunch, their daughters' nanny came down to the beach to collect the toddlers and led them back up to the villa for their afternoon nap.

'Adult time,' Nik sighed with rich satisfaction, rolling over with alacrity to stare down at Betsy, who was sunbathing in a red bikini composed of three small triangles. 'How long will it take you to remove that?'

'I'm not taking it off. We could be seen from a passing fishing boat,' Betsy pointed out, her cheeks warming at the thought and the risk.

Nik laughed out loud and tugged wickedly at the tie on the bikini bra to loosen it while stealing her breath with a hungry demanding kiss that made her toes curl shamelessly. 'You may be beautiful and amazing but you can be a complete prude, Mrs Christakis—'

'I admit it, but I do love you very much,' Betsy said in her own favour while craving that wide, sexy mouth of his on hers again, fire dancing across her skin as his hand spread across her midriff, his long, elegant fingers tantalisingly close to her breasts.

'I love you too,' Nik husked, emerald-green eyes gleaming with appreciation as he gazed admiringly down at her. 'For ever isn't long enough to be with you.'

He kissed her again and delight and joy flared through her every skin cell. When he untied the bikini briefs she pretended not to notice, but it was a long, long time before they returned to the villa.

* * * * *

'Hold on!' She shook her head decisively. 'That's not going to happen, Dante.'

He pulled her to her feet and stood staring down at her. 'We made a child together—'

Rose held her ground. 'I didn't tell you about Bea to force you to marry me, Dante. I don't want—or need—a husband.'

'But this is not all about you, Rose,' he flung at her. 'My daughter needs a father. You have not considered this?'

'Are you serious? Of course I have!' She sighed wearily. 'But I like being in charge of my own life— and of hers. If I married you, Dante, I suppose you would expect me to uproot us to live with you in Italy?'

'*Naturalmente*. I have a home ready for you,' he said swiftly.

Rose shook her head firmly. 'It's not the basis for a marriage, Dante.'

'You would find it so hard to be my wife?' he demanded, eyes glittering.

In some ways not hard at all, but that wasn't the point. 'I think it's a mistake to rush into anything, Dante,' she said at last.

Dante stood with long legs apart and arms folded as he stared down at her. 'I will do whatever it takes to make it happen.'

ONE NIGHT WITH CONSEQUENCES

A high price to pay for giving in to temptation!

When succumbing to a night of unbridled desire it's impossible to think past the morning after!

But with the sheets barely settled that little blue line appears on the pregnancy test and it doesn't take long to realise that one night of white-hot passion has turned into a lifetime of consequences!

Only one question remains:

How do you tell a man you've just met that you're about to share more than just his bed?

If you enjoy **DANTE'S UNEXPECTED LEGACY** why not try these?

A SECRET UNTIL NOW by Kim Lawrence

A DEAL WITH BENEFITS by Susanna Carr

PROOF OF THEIR SIN by Dani Collins

DANTE'S
UNEXPECTED
LEGACY

BY
CATHERINE GEORGE

Published in Great Britain 2014
by Mills & Boon, an imprint of Harlequin (UK) Limited,
Eton House, 18-24 Paradise Road, Richmond, Surrey, TW9 1SR

© 2014 Catherine George

ISBN: 978 0 263 24666 7

Harlequin (UK) Limited's policy is to use papers that are natural,
renewable and recyclable products and made from wood grown in
sustainable forests. The logging and manufacturing processes conform
to the legal environmental regulations of the country of origin.

Printed and bound in Spain
by Blackprint CPI, Barcelona

Catherine George was born in Wales, and early on developed a passion for reading which eventually fuelled her compulsion to write. Marriage to an engineer led to nine years in Brazil, but on his later travels the education of her son and daughter kept her in the UK. Instead of constant reading to pass her lonely evenings, she began to write the first of her romantic novels. When not writing and reading she loves to cook, listen to opera, and browse in antiques shops.

Recent titles by the same author:

THE ENIGMATIC GREEK
A WICKED PERSUASION
UNDER THE BRAZILIAN SUN
THE POWER OF THE LEGENDARY GREEK
  (Greek Tycoons)

This one's for Justin

CHAPTER ONE

ROSE SAT RIGIDLY, every nerve on edge as the plane took off. No turning back now. For years she'd been turning down invitations to Florence, flatly refusing to be parted from her little daughter, or to take her child with her. But this time refusal had been impossible.

'Please, *please* come,' Charlotte had begged. 'Just you and me in a luxury hotel for a couple of days. God knows you can do with a break, and I'll pay for everything and send you a plane ticket, so absolutely no expenses on your part. You know Bea will be fine with your mother, so don't say no this time. I really need you, Rose. So come. Please!' she'd added, and because Charlotte was her oldest and closest friend and she loved her like a sister, Rose had finally given in.

'Oh, all right. If it means that much to you I will. But why a hotel and not your place?'

'I want you all to myself.'

'Fabio can't be cool about this. It's your wedding anniversary, isn't it?'

'He'll be away for it on some business trip,' said Charlotte miserably. 'Besides, he doesn't know about the hotel yet. But I've already booked, so there's nothing he can do about it—not that he would, of course.'

Rose wasn't so sure. A possessive husband like Fabio

Vilari would surely be anything but cool if his wife took
a hotel break in Florence without him, even if it was with
her lifelong friend and the bridesmaid at their wedding.
But from the moment Rose had said a reluctant yes to the
trip Charlotte rang every day to make sure that she hadn't
changed her mind, and in her final call sprang a surprise
with instructions to take a taxi from Santa Maria Novella
railway station to the hotel. 'I'll meet you there later in
time for dinner, Rose. I can't wait!'

Money, if the hotel brochure was anything to go by, was
obviously not part of Charlotte's problem, but if something
was going wrong with her marriage Rose couldn't see
what earthly help a single parent like herself could give
her friend, other than to provide a sympathetic ear. Still,
the note of tearful desperation in her friend's voice had
been so worrying that Rose had enlisted her mother's willing help, covered her child's face with kisses and made for
Heathrow with her shoulder ready for Charlotte to cry on.

On terra firma in Pisa Airport, Rose concentrated on
collecting her luggage and finding the train for Florence,
but once she'd boarded it the Tuscan scenery passed her
by almost unnoticed in her worry about possible problems
left behind and the all-too-probable ones awaiting her at
journey's end. Her daughter was used to spending time
with her beloved gramma while Rose went out to work,
but Mummy had always been home before bedtime. Rose
blinked hard. The thought of her darling Bea crying for
her in the night was unbearable. Yet Charlotte had been
there for Rose through thick and thin in the past, and now
her friend was the one needing help and support for once
Rose had no option but to get to her as quickly as possible to provide it.

Rose came to with a start as the train pulled into Santa
Maria Novella and was soon wheeling her suitcase through

the heat and bustle of the crowds streaming from the lofty station into the late afternoon Florentine sunshine, so very different from the cool mists left behind. The taxi driver who eventually picked her up took a look at her hotel brochure and whisked her on a fast, chaotic drive past tall old buildings in narrow streets filled with honking cars and scooters en route to the banks of the River Arno. Rose stared, impressed, when they reached the hotel. Charlotte was certainly pushing the boat out for her. A flight of stone steps with a red carpet runner led up to an arched doorway crowned by a fabulous Venetian glass fanlight. Rose paid the driver, wishing she'd worn something more elegant than denim jeans and jacket for her red carpet entrance as she trailed her suitcase past marble statues and urns of flowers in the vaulted foyer. She approached the man behind the reception desk at the foot of a sweeping staircase and gave him her name.

'Buonasera,' he said courteously, but to her relief continued in English. 'Welcome to Florence, Miss Palmer. If you will just sign the register? I am to inform you that Signora Vilari has ordered dinner for two in the hotel restaurant this evening.'

Rose smiled gratefully. 'Thank you.'

'Prego. If you require anything at all, please ring. Enjoy your stay.'

A porter took charge of the luggage to escort Rose to a lift rather like an ornate brass birdcage. It took them up two floors at such a leisurely rate she could have walked up faster, but she was utterly delighted when she reached her room. She tipped the porter and went straight out onto a balcony looking down on the River Arno, her feelings a heady mix of trepidation and excitement as she recognised the sun-gilded bridge farther upstream as the famous Ponte Vecchio. She was actually, unbelievably, here in Florence at last. She sent a text to Charlotte to confirm her arrival, and then rang her mother.

'No problems, darling; Bea's as happy as a lark,' Grace Palmer assured her. 'She's playing with Tom in the garden before her bath. Do you want to speak to her?'

'I just long to, Mum, but I won't in case it upsets her. If she's happy let's keep her that way.'

'She'll be fine. You know we'll take good care of her, so for heaven's sake, relax and enjoy yourself.'

Rose promised to try, said there was no news from Charlotte yet, but would report tomorrow. She chose a tonic from the minibar and sat back on one of the reclining chairs on the balcony to breathe in the scents and sounds of Florence as she watched the traffic stream past across the river. For the first time in for ever at this time of day she had absolutely nothing to do—but missed her child too much to enjoy it. *Stop it*, she told herself irritably. Now she was here it was only sensible to make the most of her short break in this beautiful city. But what on earth was going on with Charlotte and Fabio? Could Fabio be cheating on her? Rose glowered. In the unlikely event that she ever acquired a husband herself her gut reaction would be grievous bodily harm if the man started playing away. She checked her silent phone again, took a last look at the sparkling waters of the Arno and went inside to soak in the bath for as long as she liked for once.

With still no word from Charlotte, the uneasiness grew as Rose got ready for the evening. To keep occupied, she took longer over her appearance than she ever had time for normally and even coaxed her newly washed hair into an intricate up-do. She nodded at her reflection in approval. Not bad. Her long-serving little black dress looked pretty good now she'd lost a pound or two. Charlotte's clothes were always wonderful, courtesy of a wealthy, besotted

husband—Rose bit her lip, wondering if there lay the problem. Maybe Fabio Vilari was no longer so besotted. Or,
worst scenario of all, was now besotted with someone else.

She leapt away from the mirror as the phone rang. At
last!

'Hello,' she said eagerly, but her face fell at the news
that a letter had arrived for her.

A *letter*?

'Thank you. I'll come down for it right away.' And wait
for Charlotte downstairs with a drink.

Too impatient to wait for the lift, Rose hurried down
the imposing staircase as fast as she could in her kept-
for-best heels and crossed the foyer to the reception desk.
The bulky envelope, addressed in Charlotte's unmistakable scrawl, was handed to her, along with the information that the gentleman who'd delivered it wished to
speak with her.

'*Buonasera*, Rose,' said a voice behind her. 'Welcome
to Firenze.'

Her heart, which had taken a nosedive at the sight of
Charlotte's handwriting, flew up to hammer Rose in the
ribs. To hide her horrified reaction, she turned very slowly
to confront a tall, slim man with dark curling hair and a
face that could be straight out of a Raphael portrait. A face
she had never forgotten, though heaven knew she had tried.
Here in the handsome, irresistible flesh was her reason for
refusing all invitations to Tuscany—to avoid meeting up
with her daughter's father again.

'Good heavens—Dante Fortinari,' she said lightly when
she could trust her voice. 'What a surprise!'

'A pleasant one, I hope?' He took her hand, a light in
his blue eyes that made her want to turn tail and run. 'I
am so very happy to see you again, Rose. Will you have a
drink while you read your letter?'

Her first reaction was to refuse point-blank and tell him to get lost, but after a pause she nodded warily. 'Thank you.'

'Come.' He led her to a table in the hushed sophistication of the lounge bar. 'You would like wine?'

She felt in crying need of something even stronger than wine after the shock of seeing him again, but to keep her wits about her opted for water. 'Sparkling water, please. Will you excuse me while I read this?'

Dante Fortinari gave the order to a waiter then sat watching intently while she read her letter. Rose Palmer had changed in the years since their last meeting at Charlotte Vilari's wedding over four years ago. Then she had been an innocent just past her twenty-first birthday, but now she was very much a woman. Hair still the colour of *caramello* was swept up in a precarious knot that made his fingers yearn to bring it tumbling down. Combined with the severe dress, it gave her a look of sophistication very different from his memory of her. His mouth twisted. She had been so irresistible in her happiness for her friend that day, but the carefree young bridesmaid had now matured into a poised, self-contained adult who was very obviously not pleased to see him. This was no surprise. He had half expected her to snatch her letter and walk away, refusing to talk to him at all.

Rose, in the meantime, was reading Charlotte's note in dismay.

You'll want to hit me, love, when you read this—I don't blame you one bit. Fabio woke me up yesterday morning with flowers, a gorgeous gold bracelet, plus tickets for a surprise trip to New York for today of all days.

God, Rose, the relief was enormous. I came across the tickets and hotel reservation by ac-

*cident a while ago and immediately pole-vaulted
to the wrong conclusion—that Fabio was taking
someone else and pretending it was a business
trip. And on our wedding anniversary! That was
why I needed you so badly.*

*Sorry to be such a drama queen—I've been a
total idiot. I was about to ring you to grovel and
cancel your trip when Fabio insisted a little holiday would be very good for you after all your efforts to get away. I agreed wholeheartedly, so take
it easy, Rose, and enjoy a taste of la dolce vita
before you fly back. Lord knows you deserve it.*

*Enclosed is some spending money for meals
and shopping—and Fabio says don't dare refuse
it or he'll be very hurt. Buy presents, if nothing
else. I'll fly over to catch up very soon.*
Love always, Charlotte.

'Bad news?' asked Dante.

Rose gave him a dazed look. 'I flew here to meet Charlotte for a little holiday, but Fabio's taken her on a surprise
trip to New York today instead.' She smiled valiantly to
mask her crushing disappointment. 'Never mind. I've always wanted to visit Florence.'

'But in company with your friend, not alone.' Sympathy gleamed in the vivid blue eyes that had haunted her
dreams and given her many a disturbed night in the past.
Not that she was ever short of those in the present.

Rose shrugged philosophically. 'I'd prefer that, of
course, but I certainly won't lack something to do in a
city like Florence. I'll explore as many museums and galleries as possible, enjoy glorious meals and gaze into shop
windows as much as I like.' And even swallow her pride
and spend some of the money sent with the letter.

'But all that is for tomorrow. Tonight, it is time to dine. Charlotte has made a dinner reservation for two here tonight.' Dante reached across to touch her hand. '*Allora*, since she cannot join you, it would give me much pleasure to take her place.'

Rose snatched her hand away. 'Will you bring your wife along, too?'

'*Cosa?*' He sat back, his eyes suddenly arctic. 'You forget. I no longer have a wife.'

Rose winced. Had his wife *died*? 'I…I apologise. I didn't know.'

He raised a cynical eyebrow. 'Charlotte did not tell you that Elsa left me?'

'No.'

'You surprise me! In Fortino it was such a hot topic of conversation I was grateful when my travels took me to the vineyards of California for a while.' He drained his glass. 'But now you know I am *solo* again, and have been for years, may I have the honour of your company at dinner tonight, Miss Palmer?'

She studied him in silence. Her first instinct was to refuse. But she was secretly daunted by the thought of dining alone in such opulent and formal surroundings. Even so, after refusing for years to come to Italy in case she ran into Dante Fortinari again, it would be wiser to have some food sent to her room rather than accept the company of the man who'd caused total upheaval in her life after their first and only meeting. Her brain, which was still furious with him, ordered her to refuse point-blank, but her heart, the unruly organ which had got her into trouble in the first place, was urging her to forget wisdom for once. And, idiot that she was, that was what she was going to do. She would never come here again, so what harm in making use of him?

'You are taking much time to decide, Rose,' Dante pointed out. 'Do you wish for my company or not?'

'Yes. Thank you.' She eyed him curiously. 'How did you get involved in acting as delivery boy for Charlotte?'

He shrugged. 'Fabio offered to deliver a package to a friend of mine in New York and Charlotte requested a favour in return. I was most happy to do this because it meant meeting you again, Rose.' He signalled to a waiter for some menus.

'But do you have a place here in Florence these days? I vaguely remember that you lived in the family home at the Fortinari vineyards.'

'I did at one time, but now I own a house a few kilometres from our vineyards at Fortino. Now my father is retired I help run the business with my brother, Leo. He is maestro of production; I am good at the selling,' Dante said without conceit.

No need to tell her that. 'You came a long way just to deliver a letter.'

'A trip to Firenze is always a pleasure,' he assured her, and held her eyes very deliberately. 'Also, I wanted very much to see you again.'

'I'm surprised you even remembered me after all this time,' she said tartly.

'I have never forgotten you, Rose,' he assured her, and for the first time gave her the bone-melting smile that had caused all the trouble in the first place. '*Allora*, what do you like to eat?'

'Practically anything I don't have to cook myself!'

He eyed her over the top of his menu. 'You live alone?'

'No. I share a house not far from my mother.'

'I remember her well—a very lovely lady who looks much too young to be your mother.'

'That she does.' Rose returned to her menu. 'What do you recommend?'

'If you like fish the salmon will be good here. Or there is the *bistecca alla Fiorentina*, the famous steak of the region. You have travelled a long way today, Rose; you must be hungry.'

'I am, but not enough to attempt a steak. I'll have the salmon.' Her stomach was in such knots that she was sure she'd only be able to manage a bite or two at the most.

Rose listened as he gave the order to the waiter, wishing she could understand the rapid, melodious interchange. She had once fancied learning Italian to add to her schoolgirl French, but studies of a different kind had taken up all her time.

Later, experiencing the effortless service Charlotte had described, Rose was glad of Dante's company among the elegantly dressed diners. She would have felt uncomfortable dining alone. Instead, now she was over the first shock of meeting up with him again, she enjoyed the ravioli in sage-fragrant butter sauce Dante insisted she try for a first course, and ate her share of the exquisite little vegetables served with their main course. But she kept firmly to water instead of the wine he offered.

'You drank champagne the first time we met,' Dante reminded her. 'You were such a delight in that charming dress.'

'It was a long time ago,' she said coolly.

'You do not remember the occasion with pleasure?'

Her eyes clashed with his. 'Of course I do. It was Charlotte's wedding day. She was on cloud nine and I had just left university with a respectable degree. Euphoria all round.'

He held the look in silence for a moment then got up to

escort her to the bar. 'Will you take a little cognac with your coffee?'

'Since I abstained over dinner, I will, please.' Rose needed some kind of stimulant for once. A sip of the fiery spirit helped her to relax a little as she looked across at her companion. Now she could study him objectively without wanting to hit him, he looked a lot older and harder-edged than the effervescent charmer who'd made Charlotte's wedding so memorable for the bridesmaid. There had been other young Italian men among Fabio's relatives and friends at the wedding, but Dante had monopolised Rose so completely she'd had no eyes for anyone else.

'You are very quiet,' he observed.

'It's been a very eventful day.'

'So tell me all about your life, Rose.'

'I run a bookkeeping business from home.'

His eyebrows rose. 'You did not take up your career in accountancy?'

'No, though the qualifications come in very handy in my line of business.' She changed the subject. 'Dante, I know it's a bit late to say this, but I was very sorry about your grandmother.'

'*Grazie*. I miss her very much.'

'Do you miss your wife, too?'

'No. Not at all.' His eyes hardened. 'The marriage was a bad mistake. When Elsa soon left me for another man my brother said I should thank God for such good fortune. Leo was right.'

Rose looked him in the eye. 'Odd you forgot to mention Elsa when we first met.'

His mouth twisted. 'I did not forget. I refused to let thoughts of her spoil my time with you. I was very angry because she refused to cancel a fashion shoot to accompany me to Fabio's wedding.'

'So you made do with me.'

'No! This is not true, Rose. I took great delight in your company.' His eyes held hers. 'Am I too late to apologise for leaving you so suddenly?'

'I completely understood when I heard that your grandmother had died.' She held the brilliant blue gaze steadily. 'Not so much when I was told about Elsa.'

His jaw clenched as he beckoned to a waiter. 'I need more cognac. Will you join me?'

'No, thanks.' She got up. 'I'm a bit tired, Dante, so—'

'No!' He sprang up. 'It is early yet. Stay a little longer with me, Rose, *per favore*.'

Since only sheer pride had forced her to make the first move, she nodded graciously and sat down again, eyeing Dante's glass. 'Should you be drinking that before a long drive?'

'I am not driving. I have reserved a room here at the hotel tonight so that I can be your guide to the city tomorrow.'

Rose stiffened. 'Charlotte asked you to do this?'

'No, she did not. It was my idea.' He lifted a shoulder, his eyes cold again. '*Non importa*, if you do not desire my company I will leave in the morning.'

That would be the best move all round, as Rose knew only too well. But she was a stranger in a city foreign to her and didn't speak a word of Italian, so it was only practical to take advantage of someone native to the place. After all the trouble he'd caused her, he might as well make himself useful.

'I'd appreciate your services as guide, Dante. Thank you.'

'It is my great pleasure, Rose!' He reached across the table to touch her hand, eyes warm again. 'I will try to make your stay memorable.'

He wouldn't have to try hard. In spite of her initial rage at the sight of him, it had taken only a minute in Dante's company again to remember how easy it had been to fall in love with him all those years ago. He'd been a charming, attentive companion who'd shown unmistakable signs of returning her feelings on Charlotte's wedding day, which had made it all the more devastating when she'd learned about his missing fiancée after he'd gone. In sick, outraged reaction to the blow, she had immediately blanked him out of her mind and pretended she'd never met him. And because she'd flatly refused to listen whenever his name came up, Charlotte had eventually given up mentioning him. Yet Charlotte had sent Dante to the hotel with her letter. Rose made a note to have words with Signora Vilari on the subject next time they spoke.

She took her hand away. 'Won't it be boring for you, Dante, showing me round a city you know so well?'

He shook his head. 'Firenze will seem new to me, seen through your eyes. But why have you not been here before, Rose? I had hoped so much to see you again when you visited Charlotte, but you never came.'

'Too much work to get away. And I see her regularly when she comes to visit her father.'

'She told me Signor Morley shares his life with your mother. You are happy with this?'

Rose nodded. 'It's a happy arrangement all round.'

'It was plain that you were all close at the wedding. I am fortunate to possess both my parents, but no longer, alas, my grandmother. I adored her and miss her still.' Dante's eyes lit with sudden heat. 'Only the message telling me she was dying could have torn me away from you so suddenly that night, you understand? But, *grazie a Dio*, because I left immediately I arrived at the Villa Castiglione in good time to say goodbye to Nonna and hold her hand in mine before she…she left us.'

'I'm glad of that,' said Rose quietly. Though at the time she hadn't believed a word of it, convinced the call had been from some girlfriend—a theory which had seemed proved beyond all doubt next morning when she found out about Elsa.

'Nonna left her house to me.' Dante's eyes darkened. 'At first I did not want the Villa Castiglione, afraid I would miss her there too much. But because it was Nonna's greatest wish my parents persuaded me to live there.'

'Alone? You've found no replacement for Elsa yet?'

'No.' He arched a wry black eyebrow. 'You think such a thing is easy for me?'

'I don't think about you at all.' She shrugged. 'After all, I only met you once.'

His eyes narrowed to an unsettling gleam. 'And you did not look back with pleasure on that meeting!'

'Oh, yes, most of it. I had a great time with you all day. But once I knew you were spoken for I never gave you another thought.' She smiled sweetly and got to her feet. 'Now I really must go to bed.'

He walked with her to the ornate lift. 'I shall take much pleasure in our tour of Firenze, Rose.'

'You must tell me what to see.'

'When do you fly home?'

'Thursday morning.'

'So soon!' He frowned. 'But that gives you only one day for the sightseeing. We must meet early for breakfast.'

'I thought I'd have it sent up—'

'No, no.' Dante shook his head imperiously. 'I will take you to breakfast in the Piazza della Signora to begin on the sightseeing as we eat. We shall meet down here at nine, *d'accordo*?'

Rose nodded. 'I'll enjoy the luxury of a lie-in for once.'

'You rise early for your work?'

'Much too early.' She smiled politely as the lift glided to a halt and pressed the button for her floor. 'Which one for you?'

'The same.' He showed her his room number. 'So if you are nervous in the night you can call me and I will come.'

Rose shot him an arctic look. 'Not going to happen, Dante.'

'Che peccato!' When they reached her room, Dante opened the door and stood aside with a bow. 'Now lock your door to show me you are safe.'

Rose nodded formally. 'Thank you for your company this evening, Dante.'

His lips twitched. 'Because it was better than none?'

Rose let her silence speak for her as she closed and locked the door.

Dante made for his room and went out onto his balcony, deep in thought as he stared down at the Arno. Rose Palmer was very different now from the girl he'd fallen more and more in love with as the hours passed during that memorable day. Even in the rush to reach his grandmother's side, and the searing grief that followed, it had been impossible to stop thinking of the girl he'd been forced to abandon so suddenly that night. He had made a vow to apologise to Rose in person when she first visited the Vilaris. But she never came and the apologies were never made.

It was no surprise that she had been hostile at first tonight. Whereas he had felt a great leap of his heart at the first sight of her, and an urgent need to offer comfort when she found Charlotte wasn't joining her. He had seized the chance to propose his own company instead. He smiled sardonically, well aware that Rose had accepted the offer only because it was marginally preferable to spending her brief time in Florence alone. Tomorrow, therefore, he must do everything in his power to make her stay pleasurable before she went back to her bookkeeping. He shook his head in wonder. Could she not do something more interesting with her life?

Convinced, for a variety of reasons, that she'd lie awake all night, Rose fell asleep the instant she closed her eyes. When she opened them again the room was bright with early sunshine, and with a gasp she shot upright to grab her phone, and smiled in relief when she saw a message from her mother. Grace Palmer had come late to the skills of texting, and the message was brief:

Everything fine. Have lovely day.

Reassured, Rose sent off a grateful response and then stretched out in the comfortable bed, feeling rested after the surprise of the best night's sleep she'd had for ages. Eventually, she wrapped herself in the hotel robe and went out on the balcony, face uplifted to the sunshine. Since she *was* here at last, doing the last thing she'd expected to do, pride urged her to make herself as presentable as possible now Dante Fortinari was to be her guide.

In the years since she'd last seen him she'd persuaded herself he couldn't possibly be as gorgeous as she remembered. And she was right. Now Dante was in his early thirties maturity had added an extra dimension to his dark good looks—something her wilful hormones responded to even while the rest of her disapproved. So since a capricious fate—or Charlotte—had brought them together again, she would make use of his escort for a day and then tomorrow, back home in the real world, erase him from her life. Once again.

Dante had worn a suit cut by some Italian master of the

craft the evening before, so if he'd decided to stay on the spur of the moment it seemed likely he'd have to wear the same thing again today. With that in mind, Rose went for pink cotton jeans instead of the denims worn for travelling. With a plain white cotton tee, small gold hoops in her ears and her hair caught back with a big tortoiseshell barrette, she slid her feet into the flats brought for sightseeing with Charlotte and felt ready to take on the day.

Dante was waiting in the foyer when she went downstairs shortly before nine, his look of gleaming appreciation worth all her effort. '*Buongiorno*, Rose. You look delightful!'

So did Dante. She raised an eyebrow at his pale linen trousers and crisp blue shirt. 'Thank you. You've been shopping?'

He shook his head. 'It is my custom to keep a packed bag in the car.'

Her lips twitched. 'Ready for unexpected sleepovers?'

He grinned, looking suddenly more like the youthful Dante she remembered. 'You are thinking the wrong thing, *cara*. I do this to impress the clients. Here in Italy, image is everything.' He looked at her feet with approval. '*Bene*, you are prepared for walking.'

'Always.' As they left the hotel she looked at the sparkling river in delight. 'Though my daily walks at home are in rather different surroundings from these.'

'But the town you live in is a pleasant place, yes?'

She nodded. 'Still, it's good to take a short break from it. My only time away from home before was in university.'

'I remember your pleasure at doing well in your final exams, and the celebrations which followed them.' He frowned as they began to walk. 'But you did not continue with the accountancy.'

'No, I didn't.' She waved a hand at the beautiful buildings they were passing. 'So talk, Signor Guide. Give me names to go with all this architecture.'

Dante obliged in detail as they walked with the river on one side and tall, beautiful old buildings on the other. But eventually he steered Rose away from the Arno to make for the Piazza della Signora with its dominant fifteenth century Palazzo Veccio that still, Dante informed her, served as Town Hall to Florence. He steered her past the queues for the famous Uffizi Gallery and the statues in the Loggia dei Lanzi on their way to the Caffe Rivoire. 'You may look at all the sculpture you wish later,' he said firmly and seated her at an outdoor table with a view of the entire Piazza. 'But now we eat.'

Rose nodded. 'Whatever you say. Breakfast is a rushed affair at home, so I shall enjoy this.' In the buzz of this sunlit square packed with people—and pigeons—she could hardly fail. She sat drinking it all in to report on later.

'I will buy you a guidebook so that you may show your mother what you have seen,' said Dante as the waiter brought their meal. 'You will take orange juice?'

'Thank you.' As she sipped, her eyes roved over the statuary she could see everywhere, and felt a sudden stab of envy for the man sitting so relaxed beside her.

'That is a very cold look you give me,' commented Dante, offering a plate of warm rolls.

'I was thinking how privileged you are to live in a place like this. You probably take all this wonderful sculpture for granted.'

'Not so. I do not live in the city,' he reminded her. 'Therefore, I marvel at it every time I return. And, Signorina Tourist, these statues were erected for more than decoration. The big white Neptune in the fountain with his water nymphs commemorates ancient Tuscan naval victories.'

'How about the sexy Perseus brandishing Medusa's severed head over there? Just look at those muscles!'

Dante laughed, his eyes dancing at the look on her face. 'He is a Medici warning to enemies, while the replica of Michelangelo's *David* represents Republican triumph over tyranny.' He shook his head. 'Enough of the lessons. What would you like to do next?'

'Could we just sit here for a while, Dante?' Rose refused to feel guilty because she was enjoying herself so much. She could go back to resentment and hostility later.

'Whatever you wish.' He beckoned to a waiter for more coffee.

Rose tensed as her phone beeped; she read the text, replied to it quickly and put the phone away. 'Sorry about that—one of my clients.' She smiled radiantly at the waiter who topped up her cup. *'Grazie.'*

'Prego!' The man returned her smile with such fervour Dante frowned.

'It is good I am here with you,' he said darkly when they were alone.

'Why?'

'To keep my beautiful companion safe from admirers.'

Rose shook her head impatiently. 'Hardly beautiful—I'm just reasonably attractive when I make the effort.' But sometimes the effort was hard.

'You are far more than just attractive, Rose,' he said with emphasis, and signalled to the offending waiter. 'I will pay, and then we shall see more of Firenze.'

'Dante,' she said awkwardly, 'could I pay, please?'

He stared at her in blank astonishment. *'Cosa?'*

She felt her colour rise. 'You've given up your time to show me round. I can't expect you to feed me as well.'

'It is my privilege,' he said, looking down his nose. 'Also a great pleasure.'

'But I feel I'm imposing.'

Dante shook his head. 'You are not.' He took her hand and stayed close enough to make himself heard as they threaded their way through the crowds in the Piazza. 'I was forced to rush away from you last time, Rose, with only a brief apology. This time perhaps you will think better of me after we say goodbye tomorrow.'

Less likely to murder him, certainly. 'When you've been so kind, how could I not?' she said lightly. She stood looking up in wonder as they reached Perseus and his grisly trophy. 'Wow! I've seen Renaissance art in books but the bronze reality is something else entirely.'

'Cellini was a master,' he agreed, and moved on to the next, graphic sculpture. 'So was Giambologna, yes? You like his *Rape of the Sabine Women*? It is carved from a single block of marble, but it is flawed, as you see.'

Rose wrinkled her nose. 'I'm not so keen on that one.'

'Then let us go to the Bargello, which was once a prison, but now houses sculpture. Donatello's bronze *David* from a century earlier is there. You will like that, I think. Then you cannot leave Firenze without a visit to the Accademia to gaze in wonder at the greatest statue of all—the marble *David* by Michelangelo.'

Rose found that Dante was right when they arrived at the rather forbidding Bargello. On the upper loggia, it needed only one look at Donatello's jaunty David, nude except for stylish hat and boots, for Rose to fall madly in love. She turned to Dante, her eyes bright with recognition. 'I've seen him before on a television programme.' She grinned. 'The handsome lady in charge of his restoration couldn't help smoothing his bottom!'

He laughed, his eyes alight as he squeezed her hand. 'You have not changed so much after all, *bella*. But now you must have a *tramezzini* and a drink. We may have to wait for some time in the Accademia.'

She shook her head. 'I don't need anything yet after all that breakfast, Dante. Let's go now.'

As Dante had forecast, at the Academy of Fine Arts they had quite a wait among throngs of tourists with cameras and students with backpacks, but when they finally gained entrance to the star attraction Rose stood motionless in pure wonder at the sight of the monumental white figure gazing sternly far above their heads, the sling he would use to kill Goliath at the ready over one shoulder.

'You are impressed?' murmured Dante in her ear.

'How could I not be?' With reluctance, she dragged her eyes from the statue. 'Thank you so much for bringing me here.'

'It is my pleasure as much as yours, Rose. But now, if you have looked at David long enough, we shall go in search of food. Shall we go back to Caffe Rivoire, or would you like to try a different place?'

'The Rivoire again, but just coffee and a snack, please.'

'You shall have whatever your heart desires.'

CHAPTER TWO

To Dante's amusement Rose took surreptitious glances at her phone from time to time when they were seated among the greenery at a table close to the building, a little away from the press of crowds and pigeons in the Piazza.

'You are expecting a call from your lover?' he demanded at last.

'Sorry. Just checking for any client problems,' she lied. No way was she telling him she was checking on her child—who just happened to be his daughter. She thrust the phone in her bag, feeling suddenly cold. Would Dante try to lay claim to Bea if he found out about her? No way was she sharing her child with him. Bea was hers and hers alone.

'You look tense. Forget the work for today,' commanded Dante. 'Let us enjoy this unexpected gift of time together. First you must rest for a while in your room and then later we shall go wherever you wish.'

Rose forced a smile and insisted that she couldn't waste precious time in resting, but after some of the café's famous hot chocolate conceded that Dante's idea was a good one after all.

'*Bene,*' he said as they walked back to the hotel. 'Those beautiful eyes look heavy. We shall meet in the foyer at three, yes?'

She frowned. 'Look, Dante, I'm taking up a lot of your time. If you have other things to do—'

'What could be more important than spending time with you, Rose?'

'If you're sure—' A yawn overtook her mid-sentence, and Dante laughed.

'You see? A rest is good, yes?'

Rose nodded, embarrassed to feel glad of the rococo gilded cage instead of trudging up the stairs. 'If I stayed in Florence for any length of time I'd get very lazy.'

Dante smiled indulgently. 'It is good to be lazy sometimes, Rose. I shall see you at three—unless you would like to sleep longer than that?'

She shook her head. 'I'll be ready on the dot.'

Rose rang her mother for a brief update and learned that Tom had collected Bea from nursery school, and afterwards the three of them had gone for a walk in the park to feed the ducks and buy ice cream.

'Did she cry for me in the night, Mum?'

'No, darling. She told me I wasn't quite as good at reading stories as Mummy, but otherwise settled down fairly well, and went off happy to school this morning. So do stop worrying. Enjoy yourself.'

Reassured, Rose had a brief rest on the bed, showered herself awake afterwards and changed the white tee for a navy polo shirt. When she saw Dante waiting for her in the foyer downstairs her unruly heart gave a thump as his eyes lit up at the sight of her. He was too good-looking by half, she thought resentfully as he took her hand.

'You slept, Rose?'

'I had a shower instead.'

'So did I.'

Since he was wearing a fresh shirt, his black curls

were damp and he smelt delicious, Rose had already gathered that.

'Where now?' she asked as they left the hotel.

'To look at shops, *naturalmente*!'

Their first stop was on the Ponte Vecchio to look at the jewellery on display, but with her eyes popping at the prices Rose soon abandoned the jewellers for a shop selling silk ties.

'You want a gift for the boyfriend?' asked Dante.

Tempted to lie and say yes, she shook her head. 'For Tom, Charlotte's father.' She pointed to one in cream-dotted bronze silk. 'What do you think?'

'A good choice. What will you buy your mother?'

'I think I'll go for one of these silk scarves. Which do you fancy?'

Dante pointed to one in colours similar to the tie. 'That one, yes?'

Rose was very pleased with her purchases, sure she would have paid a lot more without Dante's help. Later, window-gazing at designer clothes in the Via da Tornabuoni, they spent fantastic pretend fortunes on a wardrobe for her before Dante took her to the Piazza della Repubblica to browse through La Rinascente, a department store where Rose could have spent hours.

'Next time stay longer and linger here as long as you wish. Also explore the Palazzo Pitti and the Tivoli Gardens,' Dante told her. 'But now, if you are not too tired, let us walk to Santa Croce to visit the Bar Vivoli Gelateria. The best ice cream in the world is made there.'

'An offer I can't resist!' She laughed up at him and saw his eyes light up. 'What?'

'At last you laugh! For a moment I saw the younger Rose again.'

The smile faded. 'A fleeting illusion, Dante.'

Their progress was slow on the way to the Vivoli due to the lure of the small shops in the Santa Croce area. In one of them Rose spotted attractive plaques in papier mâché painted with vegetables and bought a pair for her mother and Tom. 'They both love gardening, and these will be light enough to stow in my suitcase.'

He smiled. 'You have done much shopping for others, but nothing for yourself.'

'I don't need anything,' she assured him. She felt guilty enough about spending Fabio's money as it was. 'I'll settle for this ice cream you promised.'

At the Bar Vivoli Rose rolled her eyes in ecstasy when she tasted her strawberry ice cream. 'It's gorgeous—aren't you having any, Dante?'

He shook his head, smiling indulgently. 'I will protect the shopping from your gelato while you enjoy. Is there more you wish to buy? Or we could explore the great church of Santa Croce here.'

'I'd like to very much, but I'd better leave that for another time.' Not that there would be another time. She looked up at the magnificent facade with regret. 'Shall we go back now?'

'Whatever you wish, Rose. Where would you like to dine tonight?'

So he meant them to dine together again. Irritated by her pleasure at the prospect, she told him that at that moment, her palate still rocking with strawberry gelato, it was difficult to think of food. 'Maybe we could eat in the hotel again?' At least that way the cost of dinner would appear on her hotel bill and she would feel less obligated.

Dante frowned. 'If you really wish to. But there are many restaurants in Firenze. One of my favourites is right here in Santa Croce. We could take a taxi if you are tired. You can decide later when you have rested.'

She nodded. 'Fine.'

'I will see you at nine then, Rose.'

'I'll be ready. Are you taking a rest, too?'

He nodded. 'Also I must make a few phone calls, touch base, as you say. *Ciao.*'

Rose waited to make sure Dante stayed put in his room and then, praying she wouldn't get lost, hurried out of the hotel to make her way back to the Piazza della Repubblica to buy some of the delightful things she'd seen earlier in the department store. It might be Fabio's money, but he would approve of presents for Bea. When she got back she stowed her packages away in her suitcase and, feeling hot and grubby after her rushed, guilty shopping spree, checked her messages, grateful to find a brief but totally reassuring one from her mother. The other, at last, was from Charlotte, so obviously happy Rose felt a searing pang of envy for an instant before stepping into the shower, but afterwards fell into instant sleep so heavy it took the phone to wake her.

'Willow House Bookkeeping,' she muttered sleepily, and bit her lip at the sound of Dante's chuckle.

'You are in Firenze now, *cara*. You obviously slept well!'

She stifled a yawn. 'Very well.' She sat bolt upright after a look at her watch. 'And much too long!'

'*Bene.* You obviously needed this. Sleep longer if you wish.'

'No, indeed. Just give me half an hour and I'll be ready.'

'I shall knock on your door.'

Rose shot off the bed to wash and get to work on her face. Wishing she had something different to wear, she brushed her hair loose to ring the changes a little with the faithful black dress, and flung the scarf bought for her mother over one shoulder.

'You glow, *cara*,' Dante told her when she opened the door to him later.

'Surprising what a little nap can do for a girl.' She smiled guiltily. 'I thought Mum wouldn't mind if I wore her present just once first, but I must be careful not to get anything on it—no more gelato, for a start.'

'Should such a tragedy happen, I will buy you another. So, Rose, do you still wish to dine here, or would you like something more *animado*, where locals eat?'

'*Animado* with locals, definitely. And I'm perfectly happy to walk.' Maybe she could persuade him to let her go halves with the bill.

'Then I shall take you to a trattoria near the bar where you had your gelato. It is basic and traditional, and so popular it is always crowded.'

'Sounds good. Lead on.'

After her hot, furtive dash earlier on it was dangerously pleasant to stroll with Dante through the balmy warmth of the Florence evening. For one night like this she would pretend he was just a friend she was enjoying an evening with, rather than the man who'd once broken her heart and turned her life upside down. The trattoria was packed, as he had forecast, but a place was found for them in a long red-walled dining room filled with laughing, talking, gesticulating diners sitting elbow to elbow, in total contrast to the formality of the night before, and Rose loved it.

After discussion with the waiter who brought their menus Dante ordered wine and mineral water and sat back, amused to see Rose so obviously enjoying the proximity with her fellow diners.

'This is more like it,' she said with satisfaction, sneaking a look at the dishes set down at the next table. 'Will you help me choose, Dante?'

He leaned close to translate the names of the dishes,

and after much discussion about the various delights on offer Rose settled on a mixed grill of fish with spinach. 'I don't cook fish much at home, so this is a treat for me. What are you having?'

'I like your choice. I will have the same.' Dante nodded in approval as he studied the bottle of wine a waiter offered for his inspection. '*Grazie*. Try the wine, *cara*, and give me your opinion.'

'Mmm,' she said with relish. 'Gorgeous. What is it?'

'A Fortinari Classico,' he said with pride. 'I am impressed that they keep this range here.'

'Which means it's very pricey.' Rose drank a little more. 'I can see why.' She raised embarrassed eyes to his. 'I'm putting you to so much expense, Dante. Please let—'

'No!' he said flatly. 'To see you enjoy your dinner is reward enough.'

'I'm enjoying everything.' She looked round the packed, noisy dining room with pleasure. 'I love it here.' Her eyes sparkled as plates were set in front of them. '*Grazie,*' she said to the waiter.

Dante laughed indulgently as she sniffed in rapture. 'Enjoy, *carina*.'

'I will! It's a long time since that gelato.'

'So tell me about this house you live in,' Dante said later, after Rose had refused a *dolce* in favour of coffee.

'It's my own family home. Mum signed it over to me when she moved in with Tom. He wants them to get married,' she added, 'but Mum is happy the way things are, afraid that formalising the arrangement might change it. She believes in the saying "If it ain't broke don't fix it".'

Dante's eyes darkened. 'She is wise.'

Rose looked at him questioningly. 'Were you heartbroken when your wife left you?'

He gave a mirthless laugh. '*Dio*, no! My brother, as always, was right. I had a fortunate escape—forgive me, Rose. You cannot want to hear this.'

How wrong could a man be? 'Is Elsa still with the new man she left you for?'

'Yes, though *new* is not the right word.' Dante's expressive mouth turned down. 'Enrico Calvi is old enough to be her father, but so wealthy Elsa is now enjoying a life of idle luxury.'

'She wanted to do that?'

'Oh, yes.' He smiled sardonically. 'Younger faces—and bodies—were winning the top jobs. She was glad to abandon her career while still known as a supermodel. *Allora*, I no longer see her face on magazine covers everywhere to remind me of my folly.'

'Is she very beautiful still?'

He nodded carelessly. 'I have not seen her since she left, but Elsa was obsessed with her looks and I doubt she has changed much. Calvi has children from a former marriage and does not demand the babies that would ruin his trophy wife's perfect body. I, fool that I was, wanted children very much.'

Rose drank some water, suddenly sorry she'd eaten so much as her stomach lurched at Dante's heartfelt admission.

His mouth tightened. 'She waited until our wedding night to tell me she had no intention of having babies. Ever. But no more talk of Elsa.' Dante looked at Rose in silence for a while, his blue eyes intent. 'Now I must take you back. I wish you could stay longer, Rose.'

'Not possible, I'm afraid.'

'*Que peccato*! In the morning I will drive you to the airport in Pisa—unless you would prefer the train journey?' He beckoned to a waiter to bring the bill.

'No, indeed. But won't that take up too much of your time?'

'It is not far out of my way home,' he assured her, 'and will give me the pleasure of more time with you before you leave. But this will not be goodbye, Rose. I shall see you when I come to England again next.'

Her heart lurched. If Dante still wanted babies no way was she letting him anywhere near Bea. He took her arm to steer her past an approaching entwined couple as they walked back, the contact raising her pulse rate even higher.

Rose paused when they reached the foot of the hotel steps, her eyes raised to the handsome, intent face. 'This has been a lovely evening, Dante. Not the kind of thing that features much in my life as a rule.'

'Yet Charlotte told me you have someone in your life.'

'He's a friend from my college days.'

'But surely you will marry one day, Rose?'

She shrugged. 'I doubt it.'

Dante held the door open for her. 'When you see Charlotte so happy with Fabio, do you not wish for a relationship like theirs?' His eyes darkened as they made for the lift. 'I have always envied them their marriage.'

'They're very lucky.'

Dante halted when they reached her room. '*Ascolta*, it is early yet, Rose. I would so much like to sit with you on your balcony and talk for a while longer like old friends. I can order tea. You would like that?'

She looked at him in silence for a moment. 'All right, Dante.' She gave him a wry smile. 'But only because you said the magic word.'

His smile mirrored hers. 'Friends?'

'No—tea!'

Dante laughed and rang room service. After a waiter arrived with a tray Dante tipped him and closed the door behind him then pulled up two of the chairs to the metal table on the balcony overlooking the moonlit Arno. Rose poured tea and the coffee Dante had ordered for himself, and sat back in her chair, eyeing him warily.

'So what shall we talk about?'

'You, Rose. Tell me why you started your own business.'

'I applied for accountancy jobs but didn't get the ones I wanted, so I decided to use my training for something else and eventually hit on bookkeeping.'

'Ah,' said Dante, nodding. 'You went to college again for this?'

'No. I did an eighteen-month home study course accredited by the Institute of Certified Bookkeepers, and managed to complete it in just over three months.' Rose drained her cup and refilled it. 'My mother was a huge help. So was Tom. He found a web designer for me and made sure I informed HM Revenue and Customs, and took out indemnity insurance to cover me while working in clients' offices. I also got a practising licence...' She paused, biting her lip. 'This is probably boring you rigid, Dante.'

He shook his head decisively. 'I am enthralled. You were so young to achieve all this, Rose. I am impressed.'

'I had a lot of things going for me,' she reminded him. 'With such wonderful support from my mother and Tom, a home of my own with a room I can use for an office— and with my brain still in gear from my finals—I managed to get the new qualification quickly. I now divide my time between working at home and in travelling to small businesses grateful enough for my help and my reasonable charges to pass on my name to new clients.'

'You make a good living from this?'

'It was a slow start, but I've now done well enough to pay back the money my mother lent me for the original expenses for certification and optional exams and the web design and so on.' Rose took a look at the clear-cut profile outlined by the light from her room. 'So now you know all about me, Dante.'

He shook his head. 'I think not. One day I hope to learn much, much more—but not tonight. I will leave you now to your sleep.' He raised her hand to his lips. '*Buonanotte*. I shall see you in the morning. Since we must leave early, you would like breakfast brought to your room?'

Rose nodded. 'Will you order it for me, please?'

'*Subito*. And in the morning I shall ring you when it is time to leave.' He went to the door and turned to smile at her. 'Now lock it, *per favore*.'

Rose spent a restless night after the conversation with Dante. His talk of babies terrified her. If he found out that Bea was his child what would he do? What would she do, if it came to that? She eventually lapsed into a restless doze but woke early, and after a horrified look in the mirror stood under a hot shower until she felt, and looked, more human. By the time her breakfast arrived her hair was dry and she was dressed for travelling, her bags packed.

Soon afterwards, Dante rang. '*Buongiorno*, Rose.'

'Good morning. I'm ready. I just have to sort the bill.'

'I will be with you in one second.'

When Rose opened her door Dante smiled at her denim jeans and casual jacket. 'You look so young, like a student again.' He took her suitcase. 'I will put this in the car, which is waiting outside. Forgive me if I stay there with it until you are ready to leave.'

'Of course. I'll join you as quickly as I can.' Armed with her credit card, Rose approached the suave receptionist to ask for her bill.

'All was settled in advance; there is nothing to pay.' He

handed her a receipted bill. 'Signor Fortinari waits out-side in the car,' he added. 'I trust you enjoyed your stay?'

She smiled. 'I did. Very much. Goodbye and thank you.'

'*Arrivederci* and safe journey, Miss Palmer.'

Rose felt uneasy as she left the hotel, wondering if she should have asked for an itemised version of the bill for Fabio, but forgot her worries when she saw the car wait-ing at the foot of the steps. It was sleek and scarlet and as handsome as the man who jumped out of the driver's seat as she approached.

'Wow, Dante, great car!'

He laughed as he handed her inside. 'This is my one indulgence—she's a sports car but also practical. She has four doors, also four-wheel drive, which is of much use to me in some parts of the country. You like her?'

'What's not to like? She's obviously the love of your life.'

'*Davvero*—see how she responds to me?'

Rose laughed and sank back in the seat, feeling the power vibrate through her body when Dante switched on the ignition. 'What more can a man ask?'

He shot her a sidelong glance as he drove away from the hotel. 'Those things a machine cannot do for a man.'

Annoyed to feel her face flush, Rose made no response as she settled down to enjoy the drive, content just to look at the passing landscape as they left the city. She relaxed as she breathed in the aroma of expensive new car, and whatever Dante had used in the shower. 'This is a big im-provement on the train journey,' she commented when they were speeding along the *autostrada*. 'I tried to look at the scenery I was passing through on the way here in the train, but I couldn't concentrate.'

'Why not?'

'I was tired after all the effort it took to juggle appoint-

ments and so on before getting away.' Plus her worries that
Bea might be unhappy without her, and the strain of wondering what was wrong with Charlotte.

'If your mother is looking after your business while
you are away she will be pleased to see you back, Rose.'

'Unless she's cross with me for buying presents.'

Dante laughed. 'If so, you may blame me for encour-
aging your extravagance. But you are very close to your
mother, yes?'

Rose nodded, smiling. 'But we have clashes of tem-
perament sometimes.'

'My mother had many with my sister Mirella in the past,
but now she is Nonna to several grandchildren the clashes
happen only when she spoils them too much.'

'How many nieces and nephews do you have?'

'Five. Mirella and Franco have two sons and a daughter, and Leo and Harriet one of each.'

'Harriet?'

Dante nodded. 'My brother's wife is English. You would
like her.'

Rose was intrigued. 'How did they meet?'

'It is such a strange story I shall leave it until next time
I see you. I must concentrate now as the traffic is heavy.'

Dante insisted on waiting at Galileo Galilei Airport
with Rose until she was ready to board the plane, and took
note of her telephone numbers and her address while passengers surged around them as constant announcements
filled the air. 'I will be in London next month to meet an
old friend of mine, Luke Armytage,' he told her. 'He is a
master of wine and owner of a chain of wine stores which
retail our best vintages. I shall come to see you then, Rose,
but I will consult you first to make sure you are free.'

'Goodbye then, Dante.' Rose smiled at him brightly as
her flight was called. 'And thank you yet again.'

'*Prego.*' Without warning, he seized her in his arms and kissed her full on the mouth. He raised his head to stare down into her startled eyes and then kissed her again at such length they were both breathless when he released her. '*Arrivederci*, Rose.'

Afraid to trust her voice, she managed a shaky smile and hurried away after the other passengers.

Dante stood watching as his heartbeat slowed, his smile wry when it became obvious that Rose had no intention of looking back.

The flight home was tiring. Rose spent most of it convincing herself that there was no danger of falling in love with Dante Fortinari again, even after the electrifying effect of his goodbye kiss, which, from the look on his face, had affected Dante in pretty much the same way. She was human and female enough to find this deeply gratifying, but she would make sure it never happened again. No way could she let him back into her life. She would have to tell him about Bea, and then she would be forced to tell her mother the truth at last, that Dante Fortinari was her child's father. And then Tom would know, and so would Charlotte, and Fabio, and everyone else involved once she started the ball rolling. By the time Rose boarded the Pennington coach at Birmingham Airport, she had decided against any such dramatic upheaval in her tidy little life. If Dante did ring to ask to see her again she would take the coward's way out and refuse to see him.

CHAPTER THREE

WHEN THE CAB stopped outside Willow House the front door flew open while Rose was paying the driver, and a little girl dressed in jeans and T-shirt hurtled down the garden path with the tall figure of Tom Morley in hot pursuit. Rose abandoned her suitcase and swept her child up in her arms, kissing her all over her rosy, indignant face.

'Where you *been*, Mummy?' demanded Bea, struggling to get down. 'You didn't sleep in your bed for lots of nights!'

'Only *two* nights, darling. Have you been a good girl?'

Beatrice Grace Palmer nodded happily. 'Lots of times.' She tugged on her mother's hand. 'Come *on*. Me and Gramma did baking.'

'The cakes smell delicious, too,' said Tom, taking charge of the suitcase. He kissed Rose's cheek. 'You look tired, pet.'

'Only from travelling.' Rose smiled as Grace Palmer appeared in the doorway, looking too youthful in jeans and jersey to be anyone's grandmother. 'Talking of tired, how's Gramma?'

Grace hugged her daughter. 'I'm just fine.' She grinned triumphantly at Tom. 'We coped very well, if I do say so myself.'

Rose allowed herself to be towed straight to the kitchen,

where little iced cakes sat on a wire tray. 'Look, Mummy,' said Bea, bouncing in her little pink sneakers. 'Fairy cakes!'

'They look gorgeous. Let's have them for pudding after our lunch, which is something delicious from the yummy smell coming from the oven.'

'Nothing fancy, darling,' said Grace. 'I offered several menu suggestions to celebrate your return from foreign parts, but cottage pie won the majority vote. So come on, Bea. Let's put the cakes away in the tin so we can lay the table, and we all need to wash before we eat.'

'Bea and I will lay the table,' said Tom, 'and let Mummy wash first.'

'Hurry *up*, Mummy,' ordered Bea. 'I'm hungry.'

'I need another kiss,' said Rose huskily, and picked her daughter up to hug her.

Bea obliged her with a smacking kiss. 'I cried for you last night, so Gramma cuddled me.'

Rose blinked hard. 'Then you were a lucky girl. Gramma's the best at cuddling.'

Tom nodded in vigorous agreement over the curly fair head, winning a flushed, sparkling look from Grace as he took Bea from her mother. 'Come on, Honey Bea. Let's wash those paws.'

Rose hurried upstairs to her room and took a depressed look in the mirror as she hung up her clothes. Far from benefiting from her little holiday, she looked as weary and wan as she felt.

Lunch was a lively affair with much input from Bea about her activities in her mother's absence. 'I went to school *all* day yesterday, then to the park with Gramma and Tom.'

'I bet they enjoyed that!' said Rose, grinning.

'We did,' agreed Grace, and relieved her granddaughter of her plate. 'What a star—you ate the vegetables, too. You liked that, darling?'

'Yummy!' said Bea, and gave Rose a smile exactly like her father's. 'Cake now?'

Rose waited expectantly, eyebrows raised.

'Please!' Bea beamed in triumph.

'Good girl.'

After cakes had been devoured, Rose said casually, 'I'd better find some things I bought in Florence.'

'Where's that?' demanded Bea.

'It's a town near where Auntie Charlotte lives in Italy. I had to fly there on a plane. You can help me carry the parcels.'

Later that evening, after a rapturous Bea had tried on her new jeans and T-shirts, and the exquisite little dress that Rose hadn't been able to resist, the child was finally tucked up in bed with her new cuddly Pinocchio before Rose could finally relax over supper with her mother and Tom and give details of her trip. She told Charlotte's tale with care, not sure how much she was supposed to divulge to Tom.

'Good God!' He eyed Rose in disbelief as she finished. 'Charlotte finally got you there, only to take off somewhere else?'

Grace put a hand on his arm. 'No harm done, love. Rose had her first real break since Bea was born, and hopefully she was able to enjoy it, knowing that her baby girl was safe with us.'

He frowned. 'But the fact remains that Charlotte stranded Rose alone in a strange country while she went swanning off to New York with Fabio. How did you manage, pet?'

Rose braced herself. 'Charlotte asked Dante Fortinari

to deliver a letter to the hotel to brief me. You remember him from the wedding, Tom?'

'Of course I do. Charming fellow—got married shortly after Charlotte.'

'But his wife left him pretty quickly, stupid woman,' said Grace, eyeing her daughter. 'You got on with him very well at the wedding, I seem to remember.'

Rose nodded. 'He was great fun.'

Tom shook his head in disapproval. 'I shall have words with my daughter next time she rings. Now, tell me why she was so determined to get you to Florence. Lord knows she's asked you often enough before, so what made this occasion so different?'

'Tom,' said Grace gently, 'perhaps Rose thinks Charlotte should tell you that.'

Rose sighed. 'I do, but on the other hand, Tom, if it's going to worry you it's pointless to keep you in the dark.' She recounted Charlotte's suspicions about Fabio, followed by her remorse afterwards when she discovered the truth. 'Fabio insisted I should stay at the hotel anyway, all expenses paid.'

Grace shook her head in wonder. 'How on earth could Charlotte suspect Fabio of straying? The man adores her!'

'And spoils her far more than I ever did,' said Tom and raised an eyebrow at Rose. 'So where does Fortinari come into this?'

'He volunteered to show me round Florence.' Rose smiled brightly. 'Which was kind. I would have been a bit lost on my own.'

'I should damn well think you would.' Tom got up to hold out his hand to Grace. 'Come on, love, we must let this girl get to bed. She looks done in.'

'I could stay, if you like, Rose, and get up with Bea if she's wakeful tonight?' her mother offered.

'Absolutely not,' said Rose, laughing. 'You've done more than enough, both of you. Though I'm afraid I'll need you tomorrow afternoon for a couple of hours, Mum, if you can? A client got in touch while I was away so I'm driving to see her.'

'Of course.' Grace kissed her daughter good-night, and thanked her again for the presents. 'You shouldn't have been so extravagant.'

Rose smiled. 'Dante got a far better price for them than I would have done, and in any case it was Fabio's money.'

'Then we'll both enjoy our booty free of guilt,' said Tom, eyes twinkling.

Later Rose checked on her sleeping child, longing to kiss the rosy cheek but too tired to risk waking her up. Yawning, she went next door to her own room, glad to crawl into bed. It had been an odd sort of holiday. The stay in Florence had been too short, the air travel too tiring and her taste of the *dolce vita* with Dante too unsettling. It would take effort to knuckle down to routine again. Not that she had a choice. And though most people, like Dante, thought her job boring, her travels to meet with clients made it far less so than being confined to an office all day. As she reached to turn out the light her phone rang.

'Rose?' said a husky, unmistakable voice.

She sat bolt upright. 'Dante!'

'Did all go well on your journey?'

'It did, and now I'm back where I belong.'

'I do not agree with that,' he said, surprising her. 'In Firenze you belonged there. I shall be in London soon and will drive to see you.'

Rose was about to veto the idea when Dante went on without pausing.

'Now I know you are safe I will let you sleep. *Buona-notte*, Rose.'

'Good night. Thanks for ringing,' she said politely.

His chuckle sent tremors down her spine. 'You knew that I would. *Ciao.*'

Rose switched off the light and slid down in the bed, but thanks to Dante's call she was no longer tired. The mere sound of his voice had conjured up not only his goodbye kiss but all her doubts and fears about keeping his daughter secret from him. But he had no legal right to claim Bea as his daughter, she reassured herself with a resurgence of the old resentment. His sole contribution to her existence was a fleeting episode of sexual pleasure before he'd returned to the fiancée he'd neglected to mention.

When Bea had been dropped off at nursery school the next morning Rose got down to work right away to make up for lost time. Usually she did some household chores before settling at her desk, but Grace had left the house in remarkably immaculate condition for someone in charge of a lively child. Rose sighed. In the beginning, after Bea was born, she had tried hard to transform herself from slapdash student into perfect mother, housekeeper and eventual wage earner. She'd learned the hard way to get her priorities right. As long as Bea was happy, clean and well fed Rose took her mother's advice and kept her brief spells of spare time for taking the baby for walks, or resting while Bea napped. The chores could wait until Rose had time and energy to spare for them. Or, said Grace, she could accept money to pay for a little help in the house.

Rose switched on her computer, smiling at the memory of her indignation at the suggestion. She'd been so determined to be the most efficient single parent it was possible to be. And if she was sometimes desperate for a good

night's sleep, or to be out clubbing or shopping with girl-
friends again, or even just taking a walk without pushing
a buggy, she never admitted it to a soul. She sighed irritably and settled down to work in the brief window of time
before she collected her daughter.

Bea's face lit up when she saw her mother waiting for
her. 'Mummy! You came today.'

'Of course I did.' Rose took her leave of the young
teacher and held Bea's hand. 'I told you I would.'

'You didn't come yesterday.'

'I was away, so I asked Gramma and Tom to fetch you.'

Bea nodded as she was buckled into her car seat. 'They
fetched me lots of times.'

'Only two times, darling.'

Bea looked unconvinced by the maths. 'Are you going
to work today?'

'Yes, but only for a little while this afternoon. Gramma
will stay with you and I'll be home in time for tea. And
tomorrow it's Saturday and we can go to the park.'

Rose was soon so firmly entrenched in her usual routine
again it was hard to believe the trip to Florence had ever
happened until Charlotte rang to grovel with apologies
and demand every detail of Rose's taste of *la dolce vita*.

Rose brushed that aside. 'Did you ask Dante Fortinari
to show me round, Charlotte?'

'Certainly not. I just asked him to deliver your letter
by hand because there was cash in it.' Charlotte paused.
'Though Dante seemed pretty keen on meeting up with
you again.'

'He was very kind,' said Rose colourlessly. 'And,' she
added with more bite, 'I would have been a bit lost in Florence if he hadn't turned up.'

'I know, I know,' said Charlotte remorsefully. 'But if Dante looked after you it all worked out in the end.'

'As did your problem,' Rose pointed out. 'You were mad to think Fabio would cheat on you!'

'Hormonal, not mad.' Charlotte drew in an audible breath. 'I behaved like a total idiot because—wait for the roll of drums—I'm pregnant at last.'

Rose gave a screech of delight. 'Oh, Charlotte, how *wonderful*. I'm so happy for you. Have you told your father?'

'No. I'll ring him right away now I've told you. I waited until I was absolutely sure before spreading the glad news. I didn't even tell Fabio until we were in New York.'

'But surely he was wondering?'

'Of course he was, but I've been late before so he was afraid to say a word, especially because I'd been a bit standoffish with him due to my crazy suspicions. But now I'm so happy I don't even mind the morning sickness part—at least not too much.' Charlotte came to a halt. 'So, Rose, are you still mad at me?'

'For giving me a luxury, all-expenses-paid holiday in one of the most beautiful cities in the world? No, Signora Vilari, I'm not. Now, hurry up and ring Tom so I can share the glad news with Mum.'

Once the excitement about Charlotte's news had died down Rose was soon back in her usual dual role of mother and businesswoman, until Dante rang one morning to say he would be with her the next day to take her out to dinner. She stiffened her resolve and told him that she was working and wouldn't be available.

'Is this true, Rose, or do you mean you have no wish to see me?'

She sighed. 'All right, I'm not working, but I think it's best we don't see each other again.'

There was silence on the line for a moment. 'I frightened you with my kiss?'

'Of course not. The thing is, Dante, I'm grateful for the time you took to show me round Florence, but it was just a one-off kind of thing.'

'You are refusing to see me any more?' he demanded, his voice hard.

'Yes. I am. You live in Italy and I live here, so it would be pointless, anyway.'

'*Allora*, you have not forgiven me.'

'For what, exactly?' she snapped.

'For making love to you and then leaving you so suddenly that night.'

'Oh, that. No forgiveness necessary. These things happen.'

'If not that, then I demand to know what is wrong, Rose.'

'Do you, indeed! Goodbye, Dante.' Rose switched off her phone and slumped down on the sofa, determined not to cry. She'd done enough crying over Dante Fortinari in the past. But no matter how hard she tried to control them, the tears came pouring down her face just the same and she had to do some hasty face scrubbing in case Bea saw Mummy crying.

Grace popped in later for coffee and frowned when she saw Rose's swollen eyes. 'Darling, what's wrong?'

'Dante rang. He wanted to take me out to dinner tomorrow.'

'But that's good, surely, not something to cry about?'

Rose sniffed inelegantly. 'I turned him down.'

Grace stared at her blankly. 'Why?' Her eyes narrowed suddenly. 'This is about Bea, isn't it?'

'What…what do you mean?'

'You don't want him to know about her. Bea's not a dark secret, darling—it's time you got that idea out of your system.'

Rose's heart settled back into place again. 'You're right. Lord knows, my situation is hardly unusual. I saw the percentages of single parent families in the headlines on my computer only this morning.'

'And, as one of them, you do brilliantly, darling.'

'Ah, but I wouldn't be without help from you and Tom. And,' Rose added with sudden passion, 'don't ever think I forget that, not for a minute.'

'I don't. So why not ring Dante back and say you've changed your mind? We'll have Bea for a sleepover and keep her out of the way if that would make things easier for you?'

Rose shook her head obstinately. 'I'm not going to see him again.'

'Why not? How often will you have a date with someone like Dante Fortinari?' Grace gave a wicked grin as she straightened. 'Your old pal Stuart Porter is very nice, but gorgeous and Italian he isn't.'

Rose laughed ruefully. Her mother had hit the nail on the head. Quite apart from Dante as escort, expensive dinners were not part of her social life. A night out with Stuart meant a trip to the cinema and sometimes coffee or a drink afterwards, all of which she enjoyed occasionally. But dinner with Dante would have been in a different league.

'Look, darling, why don't we have Bea for a sleepover tomorrow anyway, and you have a whole evening to yourself and a good night's sleep afterwards? You look as though you could do with it.'

'I know that.' Rose eyed her mother doubtfully. 'I love my daughter, but a night to myself does sound tempting.'

'Right. We'll come for her about four. She can eat with us as a special treat and we'll take her to school next morning, too, so you can make the most of *your* special treat.'

Bea was wildly excited the next day when she learned about the sleepover with Gramma and Tom. She loved the bedroom they had created for her there, so useful if Rose was ever travelling away overnight for work.

'Are you going out with Stuart?' asked Bea suspiciously as they packed her shiny pink holdall.

'No, not tonight. Why? Don't you like him?' On the odd occasions that she'd run into Stuart while out with Bea his embarrassment had been so plain her bright little daughter had picked up on it.

Bea shook her curly head in disdain. 'He calls me little girl.'

'Ah. His mistake, because you're a *big* girl! Shall I put Pinocchio in here with Bear or will you carry him?'

'Carry him.' Bea hugged the toy to her chest possessively, and then beamed as the doorbell rang. 'Gramma! Can I open the door?'

'Go down slowly,' called Rose. She collected a couple of books and followed with the bag, suddenly aware that it was very quiet below instead of Bea's usual joyful reunion with Grace. She flew down to the hall to find her daughter scowling at the man smiling down at her.

'*Buonasera*, Rose,' said Dante. 'Will you introduce me to this beautiful young lady?'

Struck dumb for a moment, Rose's first reaction was fury because all her cloak and dagger efforts had been useless. Dante was face to face with her child and, as a second strike against him, Mummy looked a mess while he, as always, looked wonderful. 'Why are you here?' she demanded.

His smile faded. 'I hope to change your mind about dining with me. But I make a mistake, yes?'

Dante's English was usually so good it was obvious she'd thrown him off balance.

'Not at all,' said Rose coolly. 'Do come in.'

Bea clutched Pinocchio to her chest, glaring balefully at the visitor.

'My name is Dante Fortinari,' he told her. 'What is yours, *bella*?'

'Beatrice Grace Palmer,' she announced militantly.

'My daughter,' said Rose, in case he was in any doubt.

'You are very fortunate,' said Dante, looking up from the fair curls to meet Rose's eyes. 'Perhaps we could dine early and take Beatrice with us?'

'No!' wailed Bea, incensed. 'I want to go to Gramma's.'

To Rose's relief, the doorbell rang again. 'Go and open the door again then, darling. This time it *is* Gramma; Tom, too, I expect.'

'Mrs Palmer, Mr Morley, I am delighted to see you again,' said Dante, shaking hands with the surprised pair in turn as they exchanged greetings. He smiled wryly. 'I came with hope to change Rose's mind about dining with me.'

'I'm sure she'd be delighted to do that,' said Grace, narrowing her eyes at her daughter as Bea swarmed up into Tom's arms and sat there, secure and hostile, scowling at Dante.

'Are you packed and ready, Honey Bea?' asked Tom. 'If so, we'll take you home to supper.'

'Yes, come along, darling,' said Grace, manfully ignoring the undercurrents simmering in the hall of Willow House. 'It was lovely to meet you again, Dante.'

'My pleasure, *signora*.' He smiled at the little girl in Tom's arms. 'It was a pleasure to meet you, too, *bella*.'

Another scowl was the only response.

'Bea,' said Rose in a tone the child knew well.

'Sorry,' she said and then, to everyone's surprise, gave Dante her most irresistible smile. 'Not Bella. I'm Bea.'

He returned the smile in delight. 'I apologise!'

'Bye-bye,' she said firmly, hugging Pinocchio closer.

'Be a good girl for Gramma and Tom,' Rose reminded her.

'She always is,' said Tom, bending the truth a little.

Rose waved as the trio went down the garden path then closed the door and turned to face her visitor.

'Why did you not tell me you had a daughter?' Dante demanded before she could say a word.

Rose's chin lifted. 'If you're inferring that I'm in any way ashamed of her, I assure you I'm not!'

He held up a hand. '*Pace, pace.* How could you be ashamed of such a beautiful child? Yet if I had not ignored your refusal to see me I would not have met her. You did not want me to?'

'No, I didn't.'

His eyes narrowed. 'Because her father objects?'

'No, nothing like that.' Rose sighed. 'Oh, well, now you're here, come into the kitchen. I'll make coffee.'

Dante shrugged off his suede jacket as he followed her. *'Permesso?'*

'Of course. Do sit down.'

He took a chair at the table, his eyes on the artwork adorning the walls. 'These are by Beatrice?'

Rose nodded. 'Yes. As you can see, she's heavily into red and orange. And, as she informed you, we call her Bea.' She made coffee, then laid a tray and brought it all over to the table. 'Would you like something to eat?'

'Nothing, *grazie.*' Dante's eyes met hers. 'You are angry with me for intruding, Rose?'

'Only because I would have preferred to tell you about Bea before you met her.'

'But since you refused to see me again, when would you have done that?' he demanded, looking down his nose with hauteur. 'You are obviously uneasy because I have come here against your wish. Is there a jealous lover or, worse, a husband, who would object to my presence here?'

'Neither.' She sat down wearily. 'I suppose you may as well know the truth. Bea is the result of a one-night stand with someone who has no idea he's a father. I'm not ashamed of my child, only of the circumstances that brought her into the world.'

Dante sat down abruptly, colour draining from his olive skin. He leaned forward and grasped her hand. 'You were—forced, *cara*?'

'No, nothing like that! I just drank one glass of wine too many one night to celebrate my results.'

'And you did not tell this man what happened?'

'No.' Rose felt her face heat. 'At the time I was working as a waitress while I applied for jobs, and put my lack of energy—and other things—down to being on my feet so much. It was a couple of months before it even dawned on me that I could be pregnant.'

Dante's grasp tightened. 'What happened then?'

Rose drew in a deep, unsteady breath. 'I told my mother and gave her the glad news that I had no intention of contacting the father. Tom, of course, was ready to hunt him down and force him to take responsibility. Fabio and Charlotte too.'

'*Naturalmente,*' said Dante harshly. 'Did they find him?'

'No. I refused to give his name.'

'*Dio!*' He raked a hand through his hair. 'Your mother found this hard, yes?'

Rose nodded. 'So did Charlotte. But she was hugely

supportive, flew over to see me a lot during the pregnancy and even insisted on being present at the actual birth.'

'She is a good friend,' said Dante, nodding. 'She was very unhappy about deserting you in Firenze, Rose.'

'Is that why you volunteered to look after me?'

'No. I was most delighted to do so.' He eyed her narrowly. 'I so much enjoyed our brief time together there, but you think it is a mistake to meet again, yes?'

'I'm sorry I was so rude, but finding you talking to my daughter was a shock.' She sighed. 'When I first found out I was pregnant I was in such a state I begged Charlotte and Fabio to keep it secret from the wedding guests I'd met because there's no father in the picture.'

'Yet there is one somewhere who has no idea he has a daughter.' Dante shook his head. 'Having met your child, I feel sympathy for him.'

'Too late to tell him now; he'd never believe me,' said Rose flatly.

Dante looked at her in silence for a moment, his eyes intent on hers. 'You are going out tonight?'

'No.'

'Yet your child has gone to stay overnight with your mother and Signor Morley, yes?'

'Yes.' Rose coloured. 'Mum thought I could do with some time to myself.'

'So what will you do? Read, watch television?'

'Probably.'

'While I go back to my hotel for a lonely dinner.' He reached across the table and took her hand. 'Change your mind. Dine with me, Rose.'

Now he was here, with the touch of his hand sending heat rushing through her, Rose found it hard to imagine why she'd ever said no to him in the first place. 'All right.'

She ignored the warning bells going off in her head. 'But you'll have to wait while I made myself more presentable.'

His smile took her breath away. '*Bene*! I will go back to the hotel to make myself more presentable also and return for you later.'

'Thank you,' said Rose, wondering if she'd made a huge mistake. At least her mother and Tom would be pleased. They worried about her lack of social life.

'And this time I will be more welcome, yes?'

Her eyes softened. 'Sorry I was so hostile, Dante.'

'*Non importa,*' he assured her, and smiled as he collected his jacket. 'Your daughter was even more hostile, no?'

'It was a new experience for her.'

'The friends who take you out do not call for you here?'

'No. I meet them in town.'

Dante nodded. 'And drive yourself home afterwards so you can leave when you wish?'

'Exactly.'

'I shall return at seven-thirty—and not a minute sooner. *D'accordo*?'

Rose nodded. 'I'll be ready.' She opened her front door and smiled when she saw the sleek hire car. 'Nice wheels again, Dante.'

'Not as nice as my own, though,' he said with regret and returned the smile, his eyes warm again. 'I look forward to our evening, Rose. *Ciao.*'

'*Ciao,*' she echoed as he drove off, and shook her head. Her efforts to keep her life private had been a total waste of time.

Rose hurried upstairs to shower and give herself a makeover. She couldn't compete with Dante's faithless Elsa, but she could look pretty good when she made the effort. When she was ready she eyed her reflection critically and took heart in the fact that even in the clinging caramel jersey of her Christmas present dress her baby bulge was hardly noticeable now, due to constant boring exercises.

She went downstairs, wondering why she was doing this. After the delight Dante had taken in Bea earlier, she should have sent him packing right then to avoid any future danger. But she'd silenced her head and given in to the heart which urged her to make the most of an opportunity that would probably never happen again.

When she opened the door to Dante later the heated look he gave her was worth all her hard work. 'Rose, you are ravishing!'

'Thank you, kind sir. You look pretty good yourself. Nice threads.'

'*Cosa?*'

'Great suit.'

'*Grazie*. I like your dress also.'

'Thank you.'

Rose had expected Dante to treat her to dinner at the Chesterton, the best hotel in town, but she stiffened as she realised he was driving out into the country to a venue they eventually approached down a long tree-lined drive. The Hermitage was so well-known for luxurious comfort combined with the warmth of a family-owned hotel that Charlotte had chosen it for her wedding.

Before Rose could ask why Dante had brought her there, a large, vaguely familiar man came out to greet them, hand outstretched to clap Dante on the shoulder.

'Introduce me, then.'

'This lovely lady is Miss Rose Palmer, Tony.' Dante turned to Rose. 'Rose, allow me to present my cousin, Anthony Mostyn, owner of the Hermitage—also of the Chesterton in town.'

Rose smiled as Tony Mostyn shook her hand. 'How do you do?'

'A pleasure to meet you, Miss Palmer. A shame my wife's taken the children to her mother's for a couple of days. We could have made a foursome for dinner.'

'Give Allegra a kiss from me and tell her we look forward to seeing her next time. What is good on the menu tonight, Tony?' asked Dante.

'Everything,' said Tony promptly, 'including your usual choice. So enjoy the meal. I'll catch up with you later.'

'What is wrong, Rose?' asked Dante when they were seated in the bar.

'This is where we met at Charlotte's wedding,' she said tonelessly, and looked him in the eye. 'I remember seeing Tony Mostyn at the time, and thinking he looked young to run the Hermitage. You didn't tell me you were related.'

'It is not the dark secret. My aunt, Anna Fortinari, married Huw Mostyn, Tony's father, but tragically they were killed in an air crash a few years ago. Tony is now managing director of the company that runs both hotels. His sister used to work in the business with him, but she married a Frenchman and lives in Paris now.' Dante surveyed the crowd in the bar. 'Tony does well.' His eyes were sombre as he turned back to her. 'I thought you would like to come here again, Rose, to the place where we first met. But this is another mistake, yes?'

'Yes,' she said bluntly, her eyes narrowing as a waiter arrived with a bottle of champagne.

'Mr Mostyn's compliments, sir,' he said, and filled their glasses.

Dante told him to convey their thanks and turned to Rose with a frown. 'Why did you look at me so?'

'I thought you were reminding me that I drank too much champagne last time I was here.'

His mouth tightened. '*Dio*, you find it very easy to think badly of me. For which you have good reason.' He lifted a shoulder, his eyes taking on the cold, hard look she'd seen before. The silence lengthened between them. 'This evening is a bad idea, yes?' he said at last.

'No.' Rose felt sudden remorse. 'It's lovely here, Dante, and a great treat for me.' Oh, God, that sounded so pathetic. 'But if you prefer to drive me home right now I wouldn't blame you. I've been utterly petty and graceless—'

'Because I brought you here, where we first met?' Dante moved closer. 'I hoped it would bring back pleasant memories. But perhaps all you remember is the way I left you so suddenly—'

'And then went on to marry the fiancée you forgot to mention to me.' To her angry dismay, her eyes filled with tears.

'For which I felt great guilt afterwards.' Dante gave her a pristine white handkerchief and then filled their glasses. 'Do not cry, *bella*. We must drink some of this champagne or Tony will ask questions.'

Rose dabbed at her eyes, thankful they were seated in a corner where no one would notice. She managed a smile and picked up her glass. 'Has my mascara run?'

Dante checked them out. 'No, Rose. Those beautiful dark eyes are still perfect.'

She raised her glass. 'What shall we drink to?'

'To more evenings together like this, but without the tears!' Dante drained his glass and signalled to a waiter that they were ready to order.

'You know, Dante,' said Rose, thinking about it, 'I've eaten more meals with you recently than with anyone other than Bea.'

'That pleases me very much.' He smiled at her over one of the huge menus. 'What would you like tonight? I always choose roast beef with the Yorkshire pudding when I am here.' He laughed as she looked at him in astonishment. *'Davvero!'*

Now she'd recovered from their disturbing little exchange Rose found her appetite had recovered with it. 'Actually, that sounds really good. Make it two.'

Dante gave the order to the waiter then sat back. 'Perhaps next time we can take your little Bea out for a meal. Would she like that?'

'She would.' Though Rose had no intention of letting it happen.

He smiled and refilled her glass. 'I also. I often take my nephews and nieces out, though not all of them at once! You must bring little Bea to meet them next time you come.'

Rose sighed. 'That won't be any time soon.'

'Because of your work?'

'Partly, yes.'

He eyed her questioningly. 'If the expense is also a problem I would be happy—'

'Certainly not!' she said, so sharply people nearby looked round. 'Sorry,' muttered Rose, crimsoning. 'But I can't take money from you, Dante. I feel beholden enough already because you paid for so much in Florence.'

'Is it so hard to accept things from me?' he demanded in a fierce undertone. 'I ask for nothing in return, if that is your fear.'

'I know that.' She bit her lip. 'The thing is, Dante, ever since Bea was born I've tried very hard to live on what I earn from my business. I refuse hand outs, even from my mother. Though she paid for what I'm wearing today by calling it a Christmas present.'

'She is a clever lady.' Dante relaxed slightly. 'Also I doubt that Charlotte keeps to such rules.'

'No. She comes laden with presents every visit, including the suede jacket you gave to someone to put away.'

'You cannot hurt your dearest friend by refusing her as you refuse me.' Dante got up, holding out a hand to Rose as a waiter informed him their table was ready.

She was thoughtful as she accompanied him to a small, intimate dining room very different from the large one used for Charlotte's wedding breakfast. Had her refusal actually hurt Dante?

The room was full, the atmosphere lively with the buzz of conversation, and though not as loud as at the trattoria in Santa Croce a great improvement on the hushed elegance of her first dinner in Florence.

Dante nodded when Rose mentioned it. 'I was surprised that Charlotte chose that particular hotel for your stay. You liked it there?'

'I was a bit intimidated when I first walked through the doors. But at the time I was so worried about Charlotte—' She halted, biting her lip.

'Fabio told me why,' Dante assured her quickly. 'Charlotte suspected him of taking some other woman to New York on their wedding anniversary. *Incredibile*!' He shook his head. 'There are many men who do such things, of course, but Fabio Vilari, never. And now Charlotte is about to give him a child he is the happiest man alive. What will you drink, Rose?'

'No more wine for me, thanks. I'll have some lovely Welsh water.'

'Because I will drive you home I will drink the same.'

'If you send me back in a taxi you won't have to.'

Dante glared at her. 'You think I would do that so I could drink another glass of wine?'

'Just a thought,' she murmured as they were served with miniature Welsh rarebits.

From then on Rose made sure she was as good company as possible as they ate their appetisers and then watched, impressed, as a huge roast of beef was carved on a trolley at the table and perfect high-rise Yorkshire puddings served to them with locally grown vegetables.

'Do you cook roast beef like this, Rose?' asked Dante as they began eating.

'I've never tried,' she confessed. 'Mum does it on Sundays sometimes, but usually goes for roast chicken, Bea's favourite. At home I cook pasta a lot—and, of course, the inevitable fish fingers, which my daughter would eat every day if allowed.'

'You make the pasta?'

'Alas, no. I buy the fresh kind from a supermarket. But I do make my own sauces.' Rose smiled at him as she went on with her meal. 'I see why you always order this here, Dante. It's superb.'

'Yet I think you enjoyed our meals in Firenze also, yes?'

'I certainly did.' Her eyes met his. 'You made my little holiday there very special, Dante.'

He smiled warmly. '*Grazie*. It was special for me, too. You must come again soon. And this time, perhaps, you will bring your daughter?'

Rose suppressed a shiver at the thought as Dante leaned nearer, the warmth of his breath on her cheek. 'I hope very much that you will come. You have forgiven me at last, Rose?'

'For coming to see me today?'

His eyes held hers. 'No. For leaving you here so suddenly all those years ago, when I wanted so much to stay.'

'Oh, that,' she said airily. 'Of course I have. Forgiven and forgotten years ago.'

Dante's smile was wry. 'You put me in my place, I think.'

Her eyes fell. 'Let's not talk about it any more, Dante. It was a long time ago and we're two different people now.'

'*Certo,*' he agreed. 'You are the successful one with your own business and your beautiful daughter—'

'While you help run the exalted Fortinari vineyards.'

'But I made a bad marriage,' he said bitterly.

She shrugged. 'My record's hardly faultless in one instance.'

'You speak of Bea's father?' He frowned. 'Are you sure you will not search out this man and tell him about her?'

'Absolutely sure. Can we talk about something else, please?'

'I shall do whatever you wish, *carina.*'

Tony Mostyn joined them shortly afterwards for coffee. He showed them the latest photographs of his children and received the news that Rose was a single parent with much interest when Dante told him she ran her own business.

'When you take a day off you must bring your little girl over to meet Allegra and my two,' he told her. 'My wife would like that very much.'

Rose thanked him and looked at her watch. 'And now I'm afraid I must be getting home. It was a wonderful meal, Tony. My sincere compliments to the chef.'

'I'll pass them on.' Tony grinned at his cousin. 'Though next time try something different. Dante here always goes for the same thing.'

'Why not? I eat it nowhere else. Also it is your national dish and your man does it to perfection,' said Dante, unmoved. 'I shall see you in the morning, Tony, but now I must drive Rose home.'

To Rose's surprise, Tony Mostyn asked for her telephone number as they left, so he could get in touch when his wife came home.

'I like your cousin,' she said on the way to the car park.

'He is a great guy,' Dante agreed. 'You will like Allegra also.' He gave her a searching look as he helped her into the car. 'Will you visit her, Rose?'

'If she asks me to, yes, I will.' Rose found she liked the idea a lot. She'd lost touch with most of the friends she'd made in college, mainly because they were now pursuing high-profile careers, or if they had children they also had a husband. And Charlotte, her closest friend of all, lived in Italy.

'You enjoyed the evening, Rose?' asked Dante as he drove off.

'Very much. Thank you for taking me there.'

'Even though it was where we first met?'

'Even so.'

When they arrived at Willow House, Dante switched off the ignition and gave Rose a wry sidelong glance. 'This is where we say goodbye, unless you will invite me in to talk for a while before we part.'

Rose nodded. It was relatively early, and who knew when she would have another evening like this? 'I could make more coffee—'

'I have no wish for more coffee,' he said and smiled. 'But I would very much like more of your company.'

CHAPTER FOUR

ROSE UNLOCKED HER front door and led Dante into the small sitting room, which was unusually tidy, partly due to Bea's absence, and partly because Rose had whirled round it like a dervish in case Dante came in when they arrived home. She took off her jacket and laid it on the back of a chair.

'Are you sure you won't have coffee?' she said, suddenly awkward now they were alone together in the silent house.

He shook his head and took her hand to draw her down on the comfortable velvet sofa that dated from Rose's childhood. 'This is a very warm, welcoming room,' said Dante, surveying it appreciatively.

'All my mother's work,' she assured him. 'I'm lucky. Not many single parents own a fully furnished home, complete with willing babysitters close at hand.'

'Davvero!' Dante smoothed a hand over the upholstery. 'There is a sofa a little like this in my house also, Rose. My grandmother was fond of velvet.'

'Have you kept all her furniture?'

'Yes.' He sighed. 'At first I thought this was a mistake. I kept waiting for Nonna to walk through the door to join me. But now, every time I go home I feel her warmth and love welcoming me.'

'Your wife didn't feel the same about it, obviously,'

Rose said, and wished she hadn't as his face hardened into a mask.

'I do not like to discuss her,' he said, looking down his nose.

She nodded coldly. 'How true. You certainly made no mention of her the first time we met.'

'I have apologised for this already, more than once,' he said wearily and got up. 'I think it is best I leave.'

Rose jumped to her feet, chin lifted. 'So leave.'

For a moment she was sure that Dante, his eyes blazing blue flames, was about to storm out of the house there and then, but with a choked sound he pulled her into his arms and kissed her fiercely. *'Arrivederci, tesoro.'*

By supreme effort of will Rose detached herself, her eyes glittering hotly. 'That's what you said last time.'

He frowned. 'At the airport in Pisa?'

'No. When you left my bed after the wedding.' She smiled sweetly. 'Goodbye, Dante. Thank you for dinner.'

'Tell me, Rose,' he demanded angrily, 'why did you accept my invitation tonight? At one moment I think we are friends, but then in the blink of the eye I am enemy again.' His eyes narrowed. 'It amazes me that you agreed to my company in Firenze.'

It had amazed Rose at the time. 'I was alone in a foreign country, remember?' She eyed him narrowly. 'If it comes to that, why did you offer? Did Charlotte ask you to take pity on me?'

Dante looked down his nose again. 'I felt pity without being asked.'

Rose glared at him, incensed. 'So Saint Dante escorted Charlotte's little friend out of the goodness of his heart!'

He raised a shoulder. 'You could say that, yes. Though I am no saint.'

'No. Neither am I. As you have discovered for yourself

since meeting up with me again, my disposition has deteriorated.' She felt sudden shame. 'So have my manners.'

Dante's smile stopped short of his eyes. 'You have reason. You work hard with no husband to provide for your daughter, and you do well. She is a credit to you.'

'But Bea has a temper, too, which is definitely down to me, because her father—' She stopped dead at the sharp look Dante gave her.

'Her father is of better disposition?'

She nodded, flushing.

'You know this from just one night?' he demanded. 'Rose, I think you know much more than that, so why do you not contact him? He deserves to know the truth.'

She took a leaf from Dante's book and stared down her nose at him. 'It's absolutely none of your business, Dante Fortinari.'

He stiffened, and inclined his head with hauteur. 'You are right. It is not. Goodbye, Rose.'

He strode from the room and straight out of the house. Rose gave a choked sob as she heard the outer door close, and then began to cry in earnest as Dante drove away. She curled up in a heap on the sofa, and for the first time in years gave way to engulfing, bitter tears that only died down at last when she remembered the dress. Head thumping, stomach suddenly unhappy after the rich dinner, she trudged upstairs, hung up her dress and pulled on her bathrobe. She took off her make-up and pressed a wet cloth to her swollen eyes then stiffened, heart hammering, at the sound of the doorbell. Rose raced down the stairs, almost falling in her haste to wrench open the door, and found Dante holding out something that caught the light.

'Your earring, Rose. It came off in the car, I think.'

'Oh. Thank you.' She swallowed convulsively, trying to blink away the black spots dancing in front of her eyes.

'Dante I'm...I'm so sorry, but—' She uttered a sick little moan and would have crumpled in a heap if he hadn't sprung to catch her.

Rose came round on the sofa with Dante leaning over her, an expression of desperate anxiety on his face as he bombarded her with a flood of questions she couldn't understand.

'English,' she croaked, and his eyes lit with a smile so brilliant she closed her own in defence.

'Forgive me, *bella*, in my panic my English deserted me. What is wrong?'

'I passed out.'

'*Certo*! But why?'

'I panicked when you rang the bell.'

'Ah, Rose. I am so sorry. Though it is not so very late.'

'I know. But my immediate thought was Bea. Mothers tend to be wired that way.'

Dante slid an arm beneath her and slowly and very carefully raised her to a sitting position. 'Your head still spins?'

Rose thought about it. 'A bit. Could you hang on to me a little longer?'

He muttered something under his breath.

'What did you say?'

'I will hold you all night if you permit.' He smiled. 'But I will not expect that.'

Her lips twitched. 'I won't, either. I meant until the room stands still.'

Dante sat beside her, holding her close. '*Allora*, you are comfortable like this?'

'Yes.' Much too comfortable.

He looked down into her swollen eyes. 'You have been weeping, *cara*. Because we parted in anger?'

She nodded again and, to her dismay, her eyes filled again. 'And now my head is aching, and I look *awful*.'

'You do not,' he assured her, and gathered her closer. 'You need some of your tea, perhaps?'

Rose managed a smile. 'Do you know how to make tea, Dante?'

He shrugged. 'I put the tea-bag in the cup and pour the hot water, yes?'

'Absolutely. But I won't have any just now.' The scent and warmth and muscular security of his embrace were far more effective than tea. And, unlike tea, were not normal features of her life. 'Sorry I was such a shrew earlier. I enjoyed our evening, Dante. At least until the moment you stormed off and left me sobbing my heart out.'

Dante turned her face up to his. 'You cried because I left?'

'Yes.' She drew in a deep, shuddering breath. 'I was utterly horrible, and you didn't give me the chance to say I was sorry.'

His eyes held hers with a look which turned her heart over. 'We have both made enough apologies now, *bella*, yes?'

She nodded, her bottom lip quivering as she tried to smile. 'Are we friends again?'

Before the words were out of her mouth, Dante's lips were on hers, and she gave herself up to his kiss with a relishing little sound that tightened his arms round her as he kissed her swollen eyelids and her red nose and then returned to her quivering parted mouth with a sigh of such pleasure she melted against him, shivering in response to his urgent, caressing hands. Emotions heightened by the quarrel, their kisses grew wild with such hunger that history repeated itself with inexorable rapture. Hands and lips came together as clothes flew in all directions, restraint gone up in smoke as they came together in a pulsating, overpowering rush of desire that hurled them both to orgasm, and left them panting and breathless, staring at each other in shock.

'*Dio,*' Dante said hoarsely at last. 'From the moment I saw you again in Firenze I have wanted this, but I swear I did not intend it tonight, *tesoro.*'

Rose pushed him away and suddenly hotly aware of her nakedness, snatched up her robe. 'My fault as much as yours, Dante.' She swallowed hard. 'I don't know what to say, so please go now.' Before she did something really insane and begged him to take her to bed and make love to her all night.

Dante pulled on his clothes at top speed and then turned to her, his blue eyes lambent with a light which sent a streak of heat right down to her toes. '*Arrivederci, amore.* But this is not goodbye. I shall return soon. Very soon.' He took her in his arms. 'I have no wish to leave you now, Rose, but it is late and you need your bed.'

She looked at him searchingly. 'Why did you come back, Dante?'

'Because nothing has changed since that first time we met,' he said huskily, smoothing a hand down her cheek as he released her. 'You are as irresistible to me now as you were then. *Buonanotte, carissima.*'

Rose watched him stride down the path to the car at the gate, wishing her heart would resume its normal beat. Dante turned to wave, and she lifted a shaking hand in return, then closed the door and went upstairs to stand under a hot shower to recover. Fool! How could she have allowed that to happen again? Allowed? She gave a mirthless laugh. She could no more have prevented it than stopped breathing.

Grace had insisted on giving Bea her breakfast and then driving her to school so Rose could enjoy the added luxury of a lie-in the next morning, but Rose was showered and dressed and ready to start work by the time her mother called in before going home.

'I've made some coffee,' she said, smiling.

'Good. I need it.' Grace sat down at the kitchen table and watched her daughter filling cups.

'Was Bea all right last night, Mum?'

'Fine. How about you? Did Dante change your mind about going out?'

'Yes. We went to the Hermitage.' Rose set the cups on the table, eyeing her mother narrowly. 'What's wrong? Are you sure Bea didn't play up last night?'

'She was as good as gold.' Grace took a deep breath. 'Look, Rose, there's no easy way to say this, but it's time you told me the truth. Is Dante her father?'

'*What?*' Rose went cold. 'Why on earth should you think that?'

'Because,' continued Grace relentlessly, 'yesterday when Bea smiled at him and Dante smiled back, the resemblance stared me in the face, not least the blue eyes. Your father's eyes were dark like yours and mine. And I'd better warn you that Tom, not normally observant in such matters, commented on it first.'

'Which doesn't make it true.'

'Doesn't it? I couldn't sleep last night as I thought back to the wedding, how Tom and I preferred to drive home once Charlotte and Fabio left on their honeymoon, but booked a room for you so you could enjoy the party with the other guests. Then Dante Fortinari had to leave in a hurry because his grandmother was ill.'

'So you think he somehow sandwiched in a quickie with me before he took off?' snapped Rose.

Her mother winced. 'I wouldn't have put it quite like that, but it would certainly explain a lot.' Her eyes remained locked with her daughter's. 'I'm right, aren't I?'

The backbone Rose had always managed to keep so rigid suddenly crumbled. Unable to look away, she slumped down on a kitchen chair. 'Yes, you are. But this doesn't change anything. I have absolutely no intention of telling Dante.'

'Why not?' Grace reached to take her hand. 'Can you tell me what happened after we left that night, darling?'

Rose nodded reluctantly.

She had been dancing to something slow with Dante late in the evening when it struck her that Charlotte's home would now be in Italy with Fabio, and her lifelong friendship with Rose would naturally take a back seat. When Dante had asked why she was sad she'd confided in him and blinked away her tears, suddenly desperate to get to bed. Dante had insisted on escorting her to her room, where he'd held her in his arms to comfort her, at which point she'd found she was no longer tired and within seconds they'd been kissing and caressing wildly, shedding their clothes to fall on the bed and join together in a maelstrom of heart-stopping bliss. They had still been locked in each other's arms, breathless as they came back to earth, when Dante's phone rang. Cursing, he had reached over Rose to pick it up, then with a wild exclamation he'd withdrawn to leap to his feet to dress, all the while continuing an impassioned conversation with the caller in Italian. Rose had pulled the sheet up to her chin as Dante, face ashen and haggard, begged forgiveness for his sudden departure, his English erratic in his distress as he explained he had to return home immediately because his grandmother was very ill. 'I will contact you soon. *Arrivederci, tesoro,*' had been the parting words she'd never forgotten.

She smiled bitterly. 'After he'd gone I lay in a rose-tinted afterglow, dreaming of a future relationship with Dante, only to discover the next morning that he had a fiancée he'd forgotten to mention.'

Grace winced. 'And you'd had unprotected sex!'

Rose gave a mirthless laugh. 'Not a bit of it. He used a condom, but it was faulty. In his rush to get away he didn't realise that, so I knew it was unlikely he'd believe he was the father of my child.' She eyed her mother ruefully. 'Not that it was possible to tell him, anyway. By the time I realised I was pregnant I was two months along, as you well know, and Dante Fortinari was well and truly married by then. So there was no way I could name him as Bea's father. Dante is one of Fabio's closest friends, and Fabio is married to *my* dearest friend, so I just couldn't spoil things for Charlotte and perhaps even risk affecting the relationship between you and Tom.'

'So you invented a one-night stand after a college party.' Grace got up and pulled her daughter into her arms. 'My darling girl, what are you going to do now?'

'Nothing.' Rose swallowed hard. 'I was such a fool to go to Florence. I'd been refusing to all this time just in case I met Dante again. And then Charlotte actually sent him to see me at the hotel, and I took one look at him and knew exactly why I'd fallen in love at first sight all those years ago. Because, Mum, if I hadn't fallen so hard for him it wouldn't have happened.' Her face flamed. 'And in case you're wondering, Dante was no way to blame. It was completely consensual.' Not only then but last night, too. Would she ever learn?

Grace stood back and looked at her daughter searchingly. 'Are you still in love with him?'

Rose nodded miserably. 'But I don't *want* to be. Part of me still blames him for what happened, and now and then my resentment gets the upper hand.'

'Did you part on good terms last night?'

'Eventually, yes. But there were a few awkward moments during the evening *and* when he brought me home. In fact, I offended Dante so much he drove off in a strop. But he drove back again later, so we were on good terms again before we said goodbye.' Far too good, damn him. 'It's a pity Bea inherited my disposition, not Dante's.'

Grace smiled wryly. 'He was very taken with her, love.'

Rose shivered. 'I know. But it makes no difference.'

'Are you really sure about that?'

'Yes, Mother.'

'But surely you must have considered telling Dante about Bea once you knew his marriage was over?'

'I didn't *know* it was over. I always refused to listen if Charlotte so much as mentioned Dante's name. You knew, obviously.'

Grace nodded. 'We met him on a visit to Charlotte, but when I tried to tell you about it you shut me up. I understand why now.'

Rose sighed. 'I wish I had listened to you, Mum. I put my foot in it with Dante the first night we met up again in Florence. When he suggested taking Charlotte's place at dinner I practically spat at him and asked if he was bringing his wife along. What a sweetheart I can be when I try!'

Grace gave her a hug. 'I love you just the same.'

When her mother went home Rose got down to work, and did her best to lose herself in it, but it was hard now Grace knew the truth. During the years when the identity of Bea's father had been her own private secret she had hidden it away like an oyster covering a grain of sand. But now it was a secret no longer. She hadn't thought to swear her mother to silence about it, and the relationship between Grace and Tom was so close he would soon know something was wrong and coax the truth out of her. Then probably Charlotte would be the next to know and now she was pregnant and hormonal she was unlikely to be calm and reasonable about it. Rose shuddered as she imagined Charlotte storming into Dante's house, demanding that he did the right thing—whatever that was.

Revelations apart, life went on for Rose in much the same way as usual for the next few days, except for nights disturbed by thoughts of the passionate encounter with Dante, and the fact that her daughter's parentage was no longer a secret. Grace assured her she had not confided in Tom, but found that very hard.

'It's your secret, not mine,' she said unhappily. 'I still think you're wrong to keep the truth from Dante. It would be much better to tell him yourself rather than have him discover it some other way.'

'There is no other way. You're the only one who knows, Mum.' Rose frowned. 'Though you said Tom commented on the likeness. Has he said anything?'

'Yes. But I told him he was imagining it, that Bea's blue eyes came from my grandmother.' Grace pulled a face. 'I just loathed lying to him, Rose.'

'But I'm grateful you did. Think about it! A single mother working hard to provide for her daughter suddenly informs wealthy scion of famous Fortinari wine-producing family that he's her child's father.' Rose's mouth twisted cynically at the thought.

But later than night, when Dante rang after she was in bed, Rose was sorely tempted to tell him the truth when he asked after her little daughter. 'You must be so proud of her. And how is her beautiful mother?' he asked in a tone so caressing Rose's toes curled under the covers.

'Working hard, but otherwise fine. How are you, Dante?'

'I am also working hard, but I cannot sleep for wanting you in my arms again. I need so much to see you, *tesoro*, but for a while this is not possible. I have seen Charlotte,' he added, 'and she is very well.'

'I'm so glad for her and for Fabio.'

'He is looking forward to fatherhood very much—*Dio*, how I envy him!'

A wave of such guilt swept over Rose it was almost like pain. 'You won't when he's walking the floor at night when the baby won't sleep,' she said, deliberately flippant, 'or will he hire a nurse? How do you arrange such things in your world?'

'My world is not so different from yours, Rose. Some people have such help, but if I had a child I would wish to be involved in the caring as much as possible.'

'Sorry, Dante, I must go,' she said breathlessly, 'I think I hear Bea.'

'Then run, little *mamma*. I will ring again soon. *Buonanotte*.'

Rose laid the phone down and slid out of bed to check on Bea, who, as she'd known perfectly well, was fast asleep with Pinocchio and Bear. With her blond curls tumbled over her forehead and the unmistakable blue eyes closed, there was no resemblance to her father at all. But awake it was so marked to Rose that as Bea grew older she had been afraid that everyone involved who knew Dante would some day make the connection. Lying awake afterwards, Rose kept hearing the note in Dante's voice when he spoke of envying Fabio. Her mother was right. It was time to tell Dante he was Bea's father before someone, somehow, got in first. He deserved the truth from her whether he believed her or not.

CHAPTER FIVE

Rose was glad to be abnormally busy the following week, with more travelling than usual. By the time she'd played with Bea once she'd got home, given her a bath and shared her supper, then read to her until she slept, Rose was too tired for soul-searching.

Dante rang to inform her that the following week he would be in London again and would drive down to see her. 'I shall take you out to dinner, Rose, but this time you may choose the restaurant,' he assured her, and laughed softly. 'And I will not come too early.'

Rose braced herself. 'Actually, Dante, perhaps you'd like to come to supper here this time. I'll cook.'

'*Grazie*, I would like that very much,' he assured her, surprised. 'But do not tire yourself with cooking. We can send out for a meal.'

Rose rolled her eyes at a sudden vision of a designer-suited Dante surrounded by foil cartons. 'I'll think about it.'

'I cannot sleep at night for missing you. Have you missed me?'

'Yes,' said Rose simply.

'*Ottimo*, I am very happy to hear it. I will be with you at eight on Wednesday evening.'

'Come earlier than that if you like.'

'I like very much, but won't your Beatrice object?'

'No. Apparently she likes you much more than Stuart.'

'And who,' growled Dante, 'is Stuart?'

'An old school friend I go out with occasionally. Bea disapproves of him because he calls her "little girl".'

'So you allow this man to come to your house?'

'No. But we've met him in the town a couple of times. He feels uncomfortable around Bea and she's picked up on it.'

Dante chuckled. 'I will not be uncomfortable with her.'

Rose bit her lip as she closed her phone. He might change his mind about that once he knew the truth. But she would tell him this time, somehow. She had nothing to lose. If Dante refused to acknowledge Bea she was no worse off than before. Besides, she was only taking his advice. It was Dante who'd insisted Bea's father had a right to know.

Grace's reaction to Rose's decision was a mixture of pride and apprehension. 'At least I can now tell Tom. We can provide backup if you like, darling.'

'That's very brave of you, but this is between Dante and me. You can stand by to pick up the pieces if things go pear-shaped.' Rose smiled ruefully. 'I've always been afraid this would happen one day. Every time Bea smiled up at Charlotte and Fabio I was sure the penny would drop, but it never did.'

'Only because they haven't seen Bea and Dante together.'

'True. They're in for a shock.'

'Not as big a shock as Dante.' Grace patted her hand. 'Are you sure you want to handle this alone, Rose? I'm perfectly willing to play the outraged parent. After all, Dante had no right to seduce you when he was about to marry someone else.'

'Mum, he didn't *seduce* me. One minute he was comforting me, the next minute we were so utterly desperate for each other we didn't even hear his phone ring straight away.' Rose sighed. 'He didn't want to answer it but I insisted, and you know the rest.'

Now she'd made her decision to tell Dante the truth Rose wished she could have done so right away instead of having to wait a week. None of her usual travelling was necessary for the time being, which enabled her to get through a lot of work at home and spend more time with Bea, who was delighted by the arrangement.

'But you like it when Gramma looks after you?'

Bea nodded vigorously. 'And Tom,' she assured her mother, and then gave Rose the smile exactly like her father's. 'But I love you best, Mummy.'

'I love you best, too,' said Rose, clearing her throat.

She was reading to Bea on the sitting room sofa later when the doorbell rang.

'Gramma!' cried the child, sliding down.

'I don't think so. She's gone shopping with Tom. Hold my hand while we see who it is.'

Rose opened the front door to find a vividly attractive brunette smiling at them.

'Rose Palmer? I'm Harriet Fortinari. Sorry to take you by surprise like this, but I'm on a fleeting visit to my mother so Dante suggested I look you up.' She leaned down to the child. 'You are Bea, of course. I've heard all about you.' She smiled so warmly she received one of Bea's sunniest smiles in response.

'How lovely to meet you. Do come in.' Rose ushered her guest inside. 'Dante said you were English, but I didn't realise you came from Pennington.'

Bea looked up at the visitor with far more welcome

than she'd given Dante. 'Want a cuppa tea?' she asked hospitably.

'I'd love one, darling.' Harriet grinned at Rose. 'If that's all right with Mummy?'

Rose laughed. 'You're honoured. Bea doesn't offer tea to everyone.'

'So I gather from Dante!'

'Come into the sitting room; I won't be a minute.'

'I'd rather watch while you make it. Bea will show me where.'

'Let's take our guest to the kitchen, then, pet,' said Rose, surprised to see her daughter take Harriet's hand.

'We had to come home from the park,' Bea informed their visitor. 'It rained. Want to see my paintings?'

Harriet assured her she'd like nothing better, and inspected the artwork in the kitchen with due respect while Rose made tea and took a cake from a tin.

'You're a very good artist, Bea—' a verdict which won another smile '—shall we sit here at the table?'

Bea nodded proudly. 'I don't need a high chair now.'

'Of course not. You're a big girl.'

Rose smiled warmly into Harriet's beautiful dark eyes. 'You've been speaking to Dante!'

'Have you got a little girl?' asked Bea.

'Yes, though she's a big girl, too. A bit bigger than you. Her name's Chiara. And I have a son, too; his name's Luca. I couldn't bring them with me because they're in school.'

'I go to school,' said Bea proudly.

'Would you like some cake, Harriet?' said Rose.

'Gramma and me made it,' confided Bea.

'I'd love some,' said Harriet, and sipped her tea with pleasure. 'Wonderful. I can never get tea to taste the same in Fortino.'

Rose loaded a tray. 'Shall we go back to the other room?'

'Let's make it easy and stay here. OK with you, Bea?'

The child nodded happily.

'It's kind of you to spare the time to visit us,' said Rose warmly.

'Charlotte Vilari suggested it first, seconded by Dante, who gave me your number,' said Harriet, and grinned. 'After which, nothing would have kept me away, of course. I should have rung you first, but I'm on a very short flying visit, so I seized the moment. I hope I'm not interrupting your work?'

'You're not, but it wouldn't matter if you were.' Rose smiled eagerly. 'You've seen Charlotte recently? How was she?'

'Blooming! But she told me to say you'll have to fly there to see her because Fabio refuses to let her travel right now.' Harriet looked at her expectantly. 'Will you go?'

'As soon as I can, yes.' Rose smiled at her daughter. 'You can get down now if you like, Bea.'

'Get Pinocchio.'

'Off you go then.'

Harriet smiled as Bea ran off. 'She's lovely. Enjoy her at this stage while you can. They grow up too fast.' She turned, suddenly serious. 'Look, Rose, while we're alone, I just want you to know that Dante had a really rough deal with his marriage. The family was delighted when Elsa the Witch left him but, although he hid it well, the rejection must have been a blow to his pride. Up to the death of his grandmother, whom we all adored, life had been kind to Dante. Then Nonna died, and he married Elsa. She had chased him mercilessly, desperate to marry a Fortinari, but once she had the ring on her finger she refused to have children. Soon afterwards, thank God, she met a man as old as the hills, but so filthy rich the delightful Elsa left Dante flat and took off with her sugar daddy.'

Rose nodded. 'He told me this when I was in Florence. But why are *you* telling me, Harriet?'

'Because I think Dante's lonely. He's no playboy. He works hard and loves his family. My children adore him. So do I. And he cares for you, Rose. Otherwise he wouldn't have asked me to call in on you. How do you feel about him?'

Rose flushed. 'I like him very much. We met years ago, actually, at Charlotte's wedding.'

'So she told me—' Harriet broke off, smiling as Bea ran into the room brandishing Pinocchio. 'Isn't he gorgeous?'

From then on Harriet Fortinari concentrated on Bea, and a few minutes later got up to leave. 'I must go. It's been lovely to meet you both. May I have a kiss, Bea?'

The child promptly held up her face, beaming as Harriet caught her in a hug and gave her a smacking kiss on both cheeks.

'Thank you so much for coming,' said Rose as they made for the door.

'And for the lecture?'

'Is that what it was?'

'I hope it didn't come across that way. I was just putting in a good word. When you come to visit Charlotte we must get together again. It was good to meet you, Rose.' Harriet dropped a quick kiss on her cheek and smiled down at Bea. 'It was lovely to meet you, too, darling. Goodbye.'

'Bye-bye,' said Bea, so sadly that Rose picked her up and cuddled her as they waved their visitor off.

When Dante rang that night Rose thanked him for sending his sister-in-law to see her. 'Bea was very taken with her. So was I.'

'*Bene.* I thought you might like to meet her.'

'She's very attractive.'

'And the light of my brother's life. It was fascinating to watch Leo falling in love with her when they first met. Before that it was the women who fell for him.'

'Is he as good-looking as you?'

Dante laughed. 'However I answer will be wrong. But Leo is an attractive man, yes.'

'So are you.'

'*Grazie*, Rose, I am glad you think so.' He breathed in deeply. 'I am very impatient to see you again, and not just to hold you in my arms again, but because you have invited me to supper.'

'You haven't tasted my cooking yet.'

'The food will not matter if I am with you, *tesoro*.'

'I bet you say that to all the girls.'

'You are wrong. The only ladies who cook for me are my mother, Mirella and Harriet.'

'And I'm sure they're experts. You're making me nervous. It's just a casual kitchen supper. Don't expect haute cuisine, Dante.'

'I will enjoy whatever you choose to give me, *carina*,' he said in a tone which curled her toes.

Rose would have been nervous enough about merely cooking a meal for Dante, but with the thoughts of their love-making fresh in her mind and the spectre of confession lurking to round off the meal she lived in a state of tension which gradually increased until on the day of the dinner she was wound so tight that Grace took Bea off to the park with Tom so Rose could make her preparations uninterrupted.

'We'll give Bea her supper, too,' said Grace as they left. 'And for heaven's sake give yourself time to get ready, and then sit down for five minutes doing nothing. Try to relax, love.'

'And don't forget,' added Tom with emphasis, 'we're just minutes away if you need us.'

Rose smiled sheepishly. 'I know. I let my inner drama queen take over for a minute, but I'm all right now. After all, he can't eat me, can he?'

But when she opened the door to Dante later, for a moment he gave every indication of wanting to do just that. He said nothing for a moment, his eyes gleaming with a look which brought colour to the face which had been pale with tension most of the day. '*Buonasera*, Rose,' he said huskily, and took her by the shoulders to kiss her very thoroughly. 'You look lovelier every time I see you.'

Since Rose had deliberately dressed down in jeans and a by no means new Cambridge-blue sweater she was pleased to hear it. 'Charmer! Shall I take your jacket?'

Dante shrugged out of the butter-soft leather and handed it to her. '*Grazie*. Where is little Bea?'

'Having tea with my mother and Tom. They'll bring her back shortly. In the meantime, come into the kitchen, where I can keep an eye on dinner while I give you a drink.'

'Something smells very good, Rose!'

'It's my signature dish,' she said, handing him a bottle and an opener. 'Will you do the honours?'

Dante inspected the label and laughed. 'A Fortinari Classico! *Grazie tante*, Rose.'

'When he knew I was feeding you, Tom gave it to me.'

'A man of taste!'

'I hope it's suitable as a partner to chicken.'

He smiled at her as he removed the cork. 'You can drink it with anything you wish, *cara*. Will you drink some now?'

'Just half a glass. I must put Bea to bed before we eat.' Rose tensed as the doorbell rang, and then smiled brightly. 'There she is now.'

Dante was the only one at ease when Grace came in with Tom following behind with Bea in his arms. Once the greetings were over, Tom put Bea down and stood tall and formidable as he looked from the child to Dante.

'Over to you now, love,' he said to Rose.

Bea smiled up at Dante. 'Mummy made chicken for you.'

He smiled back. 'I am very lucky, yes?'

She nodded, eyeing him curiously. 'You talk funny.'

'Bea!' exclaimed Grace. 'That's not very polite.'

'But true,' said Dante, chuckling. 'I talk this way because I am Italian, not English like you, *piccola*.'

'Please don't translate,' said Rose swiftly. 'Bea's a big girl, remember.' She looked at Grace. 'Would you two like a glass of wine?'

'No, thanks,' said her mother hastily. 'I put a casserole in the oven so we must get back to it. Nice to meet you, Dante.'

'My pleasure, *signora*.' He turned to Tom. 'I saw your daughter yesterday, and she looks very well. You are thrilled to have a grandchild, yes?'

'I am indeed.' Tom bent to brush a kiss over Bea's curls. 'Though I look on this one as my own, too.'

Grace gave her grandchild a kiss, then blew one to Rose and Dante and hurried Tom away.

'Signor Morley does not approve of me?' said Dante, frowning.

'Of course he does.' Rose looked down to see Bea eyeing Dante in speculation.

'Bath time,' she announced.

He smiled. 'Then perhaps I shall see you later when
you are ready for bed.'

Bea looked at her mother. 'I want to show him my
ducks.'

'Are you up for that, Dante?' asked Rose.

'I am honoured,' he assured her and smiled down at
Bea. 'You have many ducks?'

She nodded importantly. 'Lots and lots.' She held up
her arms to him. 'Up,' she ordered, then intercepted a look
from her mother and dazzled Dante with her most winning smile. 'Please?'

He lifted her in the practised way of a man used to small
children. 'So tell me where to go, *per favore*—that is how
I say please,' he informed her.

Rose checked that all was well in the oven and then
followed Bea and Dante upstairs to the small bathroom,
which felt even smaller with the three of them inside it.

'Down now,' said Bea as her mother turned on the taps.
She took a jar from the side of the bath and shook it. 'Bub-
bles,' she informed Dante. 'You do it.'

Dante smiled, entranced, as he obeyed, then widened
his eyes in mock awe when Bea showed him a basket
piled with rubber ducks. 'You were right, *piccola*, you
have many, many ducks.'

'Right then,' said Rose briskly. 'Clothes off, Bea.'

Dante backed away. 'I will leave now.'

'No!' ordered Bea. 'Play with me.'

'She likes races with the ducks,' said Rose, 'but be careful or you'll be soaked.'

He smiled. '*Non importa*. I have been wet many times
bathing Leo's children; Mirella's also.'

After a spirited session with a chortling Bea and a flo-
tilla of ducks, Dante's hair was wet and his sweater so
damp Rose took it away to put it in the dryer, and returned

with an old sweatshirt acquired from one of her rugby-playing friends in college. 'This will have to do for a while, I'm afraid,' she said, averting her eyes from his muscular bronzed chest. 'Time to come out, Bea.'

'Mummy reads stories now,' the child told Dante as Rose enveloped her in a bath towel.

'You are a lucky girl,' he told her. 'No one reads stories to me.'

She chuckled, shaking her damp curls. 'You're too big.'

'True.' He glanced down at Rose, who was rubbing so hard her child protested. 'Do you think Mummy will let me listen while she reads to you?'

'A'course,' said Bea firmly.

'Then I will wait downstairs until you are ready,' said Dante.

'I'll call down when we are,' Rose told him, willing her stomach to stop churning.

Bea was so impatient to get the drying session over that Rose was feeling even more twitchy by the time her child was propped up in bed with Pinocchio and Bear.

'Call the man now,' said Bea imperiously, but then bit her lip at her mother's raised eyebrows. 'Please,' she muttered.

'I should think so. And our visitor's name is Dante. Can you say that?'

'A'course,' was the scornful answer.

Rose went out on the landing to call down. 'You can come up now, Dante.'

'*Grazie.*' He ran up the stairs two at a time and planted a kiss on her lips on the way into Bea's bedroom.

Bea had a story-book waiting open on the bed and waved a gracious hand at the basket chair drawn up close by. 'There, Dante—please.'

Dante's eyes, which had widened at his name, were luminous as they rested on the child, who looked like a Botticelli angel with the lamplight haloing her bright curls. 'You are most kind, *piccola*. Which story have you chosen?'

'*Goldilocks*.' Bea wriggled more comfortably against her pillows and smiled as Rose perched on the bed beside her. 'Ready, Mummy.'

Rose was proud of her steady voice as she read the story with the animation her daughter always demanded, with a different voice for each bear and a special one for Goldilocks. As she read, careful not to miss out a single word, it occurred to her that, though none of this had been planned, it was a good warm-up to her big announcement. Dante was obviously delighting in the interlude as he sat perfectly still, more handsome than a man had a right to be, even in the incongruous old sweatshirt. His eyes remained on Bea's face as she drank in every word. Towards the end her eyelids began to droop and when Rose finally closed the book the child made no protest when her mother kissed her good-night.

Dante got up very quietly, a look on his face which told Rose he would have liked to kiss the child, too, but he merely said a very quiet good night and left the room as Rose dimmed the lamp.

Before going down to join him, Rose took a detour to her room to tidy her hair and touch up her face, then ran down to open the dryer. 'I hope you're not sorry I asked you here to dinner now,' she said lightly as she handed his sweater to him. 'Bath time can be an exhausting experience.'

He stripped off the sweatshirt and pulled on the jersey. '*Grazie*, Rose. For you, bath time with Bea comes at the end of your working day, when you are already tired. For me, tonight, it was pure pleasure. Thank you for letting me share it.'

'You're welcome. Will you pour the wine now while I check on our dinner?'

Dante sniffed in appreciation as Rose opened the oven. 'It smells good.' He filled two glasses and with a sigh of satisfaction sat down at the table she'd made festive with a bright green cloth and yellow candles in pottery holders. 'This is much better than a restaurant.'

'Even one as good as your cousin's?'

'Yes.' Dante eyed her flushed face with pleasure as she set a casserole dish on the table. 'Here we are alone with no waiters to intrude. But I can help if you allow.'

Rose shook her head and took a dish of roasted vege-tables from the oven. 'No, thanks. All done.' She took the lid from the main dish. 'This is chicken and broccoli in a creamy sauce, finished off with a Parmesan cheese gratin in honour of my guest. Please help yourself.'

'First we make a toast,' said Dante and held up his glass to touch hers. 'To many more evenings like this.' He paid Rose's cooking the best compliment of all by rolling his eyes in ecstasy at the first bite, then clearing his plate and accepting seconds. 'I hope you were not expecting there to be leftovers.'

'No, indeed; I'm glad you enjoyed it. But no pudding, I'm afraid, though I can offer you cheese instead.'

'I rarely eat *dolces*,' he assured her, 'and tonight I have devoured so much of your chicken dish I can eat noth-ing more.'

Rose braced herself. Confession time loomed. 'In that case I'll just make some coffee to take into the sitting room.'

'While you do that I shall visit your bathroom,' he said matter-of-factly.

She blew out the candles and gathered up the used dishes in a tearing hurry. By the time Dante returned, she had the coffee tray ready and the dishwasher stacked, and could find nothing more to do to delay the inevitable. 'If you'll just take the tray, then.'

Dante eyed her closely as he complied. 'Something is wrong, Rose? Do not worry about little Bea. I took a look through her open door and she is sleeping peacefully.'

'Good.' Regretting the second glass of wine she'd downed for Dutch courage, Rose followed Dante into the sitting room and asked him to set the tray down on the table in front of the sofa.

When they were settled side by side with their coffee Dante eyed her expectantly. 'After such an excellent dinner we should be sitting here relaxed. But you are very tense, Rose. Will you tell me why?'

'Yes,' she said, resigned. 'I will. But I don't know where to start—'

Dante smiled. 'At the beginning is usually the best place, *tesoro*.'

She tensed at the endearment then took in a deep breath. 'Dante, if you'll think back to Charlotte's wedding, you made it plain from the start that you were attracted to me. I was thrilled and excited, and so instantly attracted to *you* I drank so much more champagne than I should have. I was tearful after Charlotte left with Fabio. You comforted me when you took me to my room and you know what happened next.'

Dante brought her hand to his lips. 'The entire day with you had been like the *preliminari* for me. Foreplay, yes? *Allora*, the moment I kissed you I was lost. I have no excuse for what followed. I was no schoolboy to lose control in such a way. But as the climax to that happy day, the joy I felt in your arms, Rose, was sweeter than anything I had experienced before. It was torture to tear myself away from you, even though I was in desperate worry over Nonna.'

He sighed heavily. 'All that day I had banished Elsa from my mind, but later, on the flight home, I felt great guilt because I had not told you about her. When did you learn that I had a *fidanzata*?'

'The next morning, over breakfast. Your friends were worried that your grandmother's illness would affect your wedding.' Rose looked him in the eye. 'The word *wedding* hit me so hard I was numb for a while. Then my temper kicked in. I wanted to punch that face of yours until you weren't so handsome any more. Denied the satisfaction of that, I blocked you from my mind instead, deleted you from my life and refused to listen whenever Charlotte mentioned your name. So she soon gave up trying.'

'And you never knew that Elsa left me,' he said very quietly and took her cup to put it on the tray with his.

'No.'

He frowned. 'Yet Charlotte was most insistent I delivered her letter to you in person in Firenze.'

Rose nodded. 'Fabio sent money for me in the package so she needed someone to deliver it, and you just happened to be on the spot.'

Dante smiled wryly. 'I was most happy to do it, but thought you would refuse to speak to me.'

'I wanted to!'

'Yet you agreed to dine with me.'

She shrugged. 'The thought of eating alone in that rather grand hotel was so daunting I decided to make use of you instead. But why did you offer, Dante?'

'You looked so unhappy when you read Charlotte's letter I longed to take you in my arms and comfort you. Instead, I offered to take her place.' He looked at her steadily. 'You have more to tell me, I think?'

'I do.' Rose sat very erect. 'That was the prologue. Now

we get to the main part. I've decided to take your advice, Dante.'

He frowned. 'What advice, *cara*?'

'To tell Bea's father he has a daughter.'

His eyes blazed in sudden, vehement denial. 'No! I no longer think this a good idea. Do not, Rose. He is probably married by now. You are right; after all this time he will not believe the child is his.'

Rose looked long and hard into the impassioned blue eyes. 'Is that how you would react in such circumstances, Dante?'

'I believe not. I hope I would not. How could any man be sure of his reaction to such news?'

'Now's your chance to find out.' She took in a deep breath. 'Bea is *your* child, Dante.'

He sat like a man turned to stone for several endless seconds, his eyes wild on hers.

'*Cosa*? What are you saying?' His bronze skin drained of all colour. 'It is not a thing to joke about.'

'It's no joke, I assure you. I'm deadly serious.'

'*Dio!*' Dante thrust a hand through his hair as he eyed her incredulously. 'But, even so desperate to make love to you, I used protection that night.'

She flushed. 'It didn't work. After you'd gone I found it had split.'

'Then what you say is really true?'

'You honestly think it's something I would lie about?'

He shook his head in wonder. 'Beatrice is the result of our lovemaking that night.'

Rose sighed heavily. 'I don't blame you for doubting it. I couldn't believe it myself.'

'Why did you never tell me this before?' he demanded with sudden heat.

'How could I, Dante?' she snapped. 'You were already

married by the time I found out. Which is why I was so obstinate about refusing to name the father. But, after seeing you and Bea together for the first time, my mother was sure it was you and said you had a right to know.' Rose slumped back against the sofa cushions. 'So now you do. But don't worry; I'm not asking anything of you.'

He glared at her, incensed. 'You tell me I have a daughter and think I will walk away?'

Rose hugged her arms across her chest, refusing to look at him. 'I don't expect anything from you, Dante. Bea and I have managed perfectly well up to now without you. So by all means walk away if you want. I have no proof that she's your child. If this were a Gothic novel she'd have a birthmark or something to show she was yours, but—'

'I need no proof,' he said roughly and got up to pace the room. 'If you say she is mine I will believe you.'

'Will believe or do believe?' demanded Rose.

Dante turned on her angrily. 'Do not mock my command of English, *per favore*.'

Rose sat very still, gazing at him in such misery Dante sat beside her again and took her hand.

'Why do you look at me so?'

'It was very hard to tell you, Dante.'

'Perche?'

'I was afraid you wouldn't believe me. And it's over four years since that night so you might have forgotten all about it. And even if you did remember you could have thought I was telling you about Bea to get money.'

Dante clenched a fist, as though hanging on to every shred of his self-control. At last he turned to look Rose in the eye. 'I had forgotten nothing. When I saw you again in Firenze I was transported back to the Vilari wedding and my meeting with the entrancing girl who stole my heart.'

'The heart which already belonged to someone else,' Rose said bitterly.

He shook his head. 'Elsa never had my heart. She had no use for it. She wanted my name and my money. But there was less money than she expected. Financially, I was a great disappointment to her.'

'Did you love her?'

'I desired her when we first met. And she desired marriage to a Fortinari.' Dante's mouth twisted. *'Alla fine*—in the end—I was deeply grateful to Enrico Calvi for taking her from me.' He took Rose's hand in his. 'Now, let us talk of important things. How soon can we get married?'

CHAPTER SIX

'HOLD ON!' SHE shook her head decisively. 'That's not going to happen, Dante.'

'*Cosa?*' He pulled her to her feet and stood staring down at her. 'We made a child together—'

'But by accident, not because we were in a relationship.' Rose held her ground. 'I didn't tell you about Bea to force you to marry me, Dante. I don't want—or need— a husband.'

'But this is not all about you, Rose,' he flung at her. 'My daughter needs a father. Soon she will be old enough to ask why she lacks one, no? Other children will ask also. You have not considered this?'

'Are you serious? Of course I have!' She sighed wearily. 'I had no way of providing one for her, or even to meet a likely candidate because I had to work from home so I could always be there for her. Besides, I like being in charge of my own life—and of hers. If I married you, Dante, I suppose you would expect me to uproot us to live with you in Italy?'

'*Naturalmente.* I have a home ready for you, also a family who would welcome you,' he said swiftly.

Rose shook her head firmly. 'It's not the basis for a marriage, Dante.'

'You would find it so hard to be my wife?' he demanded, eyes glittering.

In some ways not hard at all, but that wasn't the point. She should, she knew, be grateful that he'd taken the news of his fatherhood so well, with none of the doubts she'd expected. 'I think it's a mistake to rush into anything, Dante,' she said at last. 'You need time to get used to the idea.'

Dante stood with long legs apart and arms folded as he stared down at her. 'If you do not marry me I will demand to spend time with my daughter,' he said harshly.

'Of course,' she said, secretly dismayed. 'But before we descend to bickering about it perhaps you'll listen to what I have to say?'

'*Allora*, talk, Rose.'

'I'm sorry. I shouldn't have been so abrupt with my objection.' She gazed at him in appeal. 'But you must see that we are, in effect, strangers, Dante. Before we rush into something as binding as marriage, it would be sensible to get to know each other better.'

His eyes softened slightly. 'Is that how you feel, Rose? That I am a stranger?' He raised an eyebrow. 'After what happened here between us the last time, how can you say that?'

She felt her face flame. 'It's obvious that we—we're compatible in that way.'

'Compatible!' He gave a mirthless laugh. 'If you mean I want to crush you in my arms and kiss you until you are helpless to refuse me, you are right. Do not look like that,' he added. 'I will not resort to—to physical coercion, this is right? Instead, I give you no choice. You will marry me and make your home in Italy with me and with our daughter.'

'Oh, will I?' Rose cried. 'Just because you've suddenly discovered you're Bea's father doesn't give you the right to turn our lives upside down.'

'You are wrong. It does,' he retorted, a look in his eyes that sent her backing away. 'My child must grow up knowing she has a father who loves and cares for her. If you do not agree to marriage you must share Bea with me. She will like my house, and she will have cousins to play with her, also doting grandparents and uncles and aunts.' He shook his head in sudden wonder. 'I was resigned to the role of uncle. To discover now that I am a father, I feel great joy.' He glared at her. 'Also great frustration because the mother of my child will not marry me.'

Rose thrust a hand through her hair, her eyes troubled. 'Before I took a giant step like that I'd have to be sure that it would make Bea happy.'

Dante held her gaze in silence for a time and then took her hands in his. '*Allora*, this is what we do, Rose. I will go back to Fortino to talk to my brother, also to my parents. Then I will return here to stay at the Hermitage for a while to spend time with Bea. Later, you must bring her to stay at the Villa Castiglione for a holiday to meet my family.' Dante's eyes held hers. 'You agree with this?'

She thought it over then nodded reluctantly.

'*Va bene*. But first she must be told I am her father.' He closed his eyes suddenly. '*Dio*, I still cannot believe it.'

'If you have any doubts on the subject say so now and we forget the whole thing,' said Rose and backed away as his eyes flew open to blaze into hers.

'I meant,' he said very deliberately, as though he was translating as he advanced on her, 'that I cannot believe my good fortune in possessing this child we created together.'

'By accident!' She stood her ground and met his eyes squarely. 'If we did marry would you expect more children?'

'I would hope for them, yes. So if you have some strange idea of a *matrimonio di convenienza*, put it from your mind. You would share my life. And my bed.' Dante drew her into his arms. 'Would that be so hard to do?'

'No,' she admitted, colouring. 'As you well know, Dante.'

He smiled victoriously and brushed his lips in a feather-light kiss over hers, then stiffened at the sound of an anguished cry upstairs.

Rose bolted away from him to take the stairs at a run, Dante hot on her heels as they raced into Bea's room to find her sitting on the floor beside her bed, crying piteously as she reached out her arms to her mother.

Rose scooped her up and ran with her to the bathroom, where Bea threw up copiously. 'On the bed too,' she sobbed, and Rose held her close, murmuring wordless comfort as she glanced round to see what Dante was doing, her eyes scornful when she saw he'd vanished. Fair weather daddy!

But Dante reappeared in the doorway with an armful of bed linen. 'I took these from the bed and shall put them downstairs. Tell me where to find clean sheets, Rose.'

'Airing cupboard on the landing,' she said, startled. 'Bea's things are on the upper shelves.'

Dante eyed the bowed curly head with sympathy. '*Poverina*! Are you better now?'

Bea shook her head mournfully. 'My tummy hurts.'

'You will soon be better in a warm, clean bed,' he assured her.

By the time Bea was bathed, sans ducks this time, and fragrant in clean pyjamas, Dante had made her bed, complete with Pinocchio and Bear.

'A man of many talents,' murmured Rose as she tucked her daughter in.

'Dante, read to me,' commanded Bea, and smiled at him. 'Please?'

Rose blinked hard at the look on his face, and turned away to sort through some books. 'How about *Pinocchio*?' she suggested, clearing her throat. 'He's Italian, too.'

'A good choice,' said Dante huskily as his daughter nodded in approval. 'Where shall I sit?'

'On the bed,' said Bea, and wriggled back against her pillows.

'I'll pop downstairs and get a drink,' said Rose, and escaped before she did something really stupid like bursting into tears at the sight of Bea with the father she didn't know she possessed.

Rose loaded the washing machine with Bea's sheets and pyjamas and stripped off her sweater, which had suffered in the interlude in the bathroom. She pulled on a T-shirt from the basket of laundry waiting to be ironed and went up to Bea's bedroom, but paused in the doorway, her throat tightening as she heard Dante's voice growing gradually softer as he read his daughter back to sleep. Rose stood very still as he finally closed the book and leaned down to brush a kiss over the bright curls. He turned and held a finger to his lips as he followed her downstairs.

Rose felt suddenly awkward, unsure what to do or say next. 'Would you like some coffee, Dante, or maybe a drink?'

'Coffee, *per favore*, to wake myself up to drive. I almost sent myself to sleep with Bea,' he added wryly. 'I will come into the kitchen while you make it, Rose, then I must leave.'

'Thank you for your help,' she said as she filled the kettle. 'I was impressed.'

'I have helped in such ways before,' he said matter-of-factly. 'Perhaps the little one's *nonna* allowed too rich a *dolce* after supper.'

'Actually, Mum's pretty strict. But Tom isn't, so maybe

Bea conned him into giving her an extra sweetie or two.'
Rose smiled. 'He's putty in her hands.'

'Putty? Ah, yes, *stucco*. I sympathise. It must be hard
to refuse her anything she desires.' Dante chuckled. 'He
will find it even harder with Charlotte's child.'

When they sat facing each other across the kitchen table
with mugs of coffee steaming between them, Rose smiled
wryly. 'I thought Italian men were spoiled by *mammas*
who did everything for them, yet you were very efficient
tonight. Thank you.'

Dante shrugged. 'At home, when young, in Fortino,
where my mother was very much in charge, I did little, I
confess. Now I do many things for myself. After Elsa left
me my family bombarded me with dinner invitations.' He
smiled derisively. 'I wished only to be left alone but this
was never allowed.'

'Your family obviously love you very much—'

'They will love you and little Bea also,' he said emphatically and reached a hand across to grasp hers, but
released it and got up when Rose stiffened. 'I will go now
and let you sleep.'

Rose walked to the door with Dante, her mind in turmoil. Half of her wanted nothing more than to creep into
bed and pull the covers over her head. The other half, the
part of her savouring the warmth and scent of Dante as
they stood together, wanted to pull him into bed with her
and blot out the world.

'Tell me the truth, Dante—how do you feel?' she asked.
'Now I've told you about Bea, I mean.'

'Amazed, but happy,' he said simply, and took her in
his arms. 'I will be even happier when you are my wife,
Rose. It is useless to fight. It is your fate. We were meant
to be together.' He kissed the mouth which opened to protest and let her go. *'Arrivederci, tesoro.'*

Rose watched him stride down the path to the car, then closed the door and leaned against it for a moment, feeling limp. She pushed away from the door in sudden irritation—time to stop behaving like a character in a romantic movie and do her nightly chores. She had work to do tomorrow. As usual. But maybe a day off would be good for once. She was well in hand with the accounts she did at home and had no visits to make next day. Her mother would be desperate to hear how things had gone tonight, so after she took Bea to school in the morning—so long as she wasn't unwell again—Rose decided she would give Grace a full report over coffee.

To Rose's relief, Bea slept the night through and was even more bouncy than usual the next morning as she ate her cereal.

'I like Dante,' she announced when she'd finished.

Rose's stomach did a forward roll. 'Do you, darling?'

Bea nodded. 'Can he read stories again?'

'I expect so.'

'You like him, too, Mummy,' Bea stated.

'Yes, I do. Now, let's get a move on or we'll be late.'

When Rose got back home from the school run Grace had let herself in and had coffee waiting.

She eyed her daughter anxiously. 'You obviously had a bad night. Dante didn't believe you?'

Rose busied herself with filling mugs. 'Oh, he believed me right enough. He was stunned at first, but when the truth finally sank in he was all for marrying me right away.'

Grace's delighted smile faded quickly. 'But you don't want that.'

'No. As I told Dante, we're virtually strangers. Before jumping in at the deep end I made it clear we would need to know each other better, and I would have to be utterly sure that Bea was happy with the idea.'

'Did he agree?'

'Yes. He immediately made plans to go back to Fortino to arrange some leave, and then come back to stay at the Hermitage to spend time with his daughter.'

'Goodness,' said Grace, blinking. 'I take it you're against the idea?'

Rose nodded vehemently. 'The minute I gave Dante the good news he started giving orders. I was to change my life completely, marry him and take off for Italy to live with him and Bea in his house—the Villa Castiglione, left to him by his grandmother.'

Grace downed her own coffee and got up to refill their cups. 'Good for Dante. After all, love, he could have rejected all idea of Bea's paternity.'

'No chance of that; he was entranced with her from the start,' said Rose moodily. 'He played with her ducks with her in the bath, and afterwards sat with her while I read the bedtime story. Then I softened him up even more by giving him a good dinner before breaking the news that Bea was his child.'

'How did he take it?'

Rose blew out her cheeks. 'As I told you, once the truth sank in he ordered me to marry him. Then when I didn't joyfully and gratefully accept he turned belligerent and demanded time with his daughter whether I married him or not.'

'To take her to his place in Tuscany, you mean?' said Grace, startled. 'So what did you say?'

'Bea started crying at that point because she'd thrown up and we both bolted upstairs.'

'How did Dante cope with that?'

'He stripped the bed and remade it while I cleaned Bea up, then he read her to sleep.'

Grace smiled. 'Bravo, Dante! Tell me, darling, quite apart from Bea, how do you feel towards him now? Are you still bitter?'

Rose shook her head hopelessly. 'Fool that I am, I *love* him. I always have. I tried so hard to forget him, but it was impossible with Bea looking up at me with those eyes of his.'

'How does he feel about you?'

'I wish I knew. He still fancies me. Physically, I mean. But that's not enough for marriage, especially with people from such different backgrounds.'

'It works for Charlotte and Fabio,' Grace pointed out.

'True. But they got married because they really love each other. Dante's motive for marrying me is purely to get Bea.' Rose shivered. 'Last night, when I didn't leap at the marriage idea, he said he'd demand time with his daughter. Could he do that legally, do you think?'

'No idea. You didn't name him as her father on the birth certificate and you've never lived together. Also he's not a British national, so I should think it's unlikely. I'll ask Tom.'

'Dante thinks Tom doesn't approve of him.'

'He's right. Tom can't get past the fact that Dante made you pregnant when he was about to marry someone else.' Grace smiled wryly. 'Yet at the same time he can't help liking Dante either.'

Rose nodded ruefully. 'I know the feeling!'

'Have a cup of tea, then go off to bed for a bit. Tom and I will collect Bea.'

'That sounds wonderful. I didn't sleep much last night after all the excitement.' Rose hugged her mother. 'You spoil me.'

'I prefer to think of it as helping. Take a hot shower and climb into bed. I'll give Bea her lunch before bringing her home.' Grace kissed her weary daughter and pointed her at the door. 'Go.'

Rose felt better after the shower, and even managed a short nap. When she got up, she had come to a decision. This afternoon she would take Bea to the park, and then play all her favourite games with her and later watch her favourite cartoon film with her for the umpteenth time. Rose's teeth clenched. Bea didn't *need* a father! She'd done perfectly well without one up to now, and even had the benefit of a male presence in her life in the shape of Tom Morley.

When Dante rang that night, Rose was ready and armed, waiting for him.

'How are you tonight, *carina*?' he asked in the deep caressing tones which still had the power to raise the hairs on the back of her neck—something that infuriated her in the present circumstances. 'And how is my little Bea? Is she recovered now?'

'*My* little Bea, actually, and we're both fine.'

Silence for a moment. 'What is wrong, Rose?'

'I'm afraid the deal's off, Dante. I'm saying no to your demands.'

'*Cosa? Perche*? What has happened?'

'I've given it careful consideration and decided I can't face the upheaval of making a new life in a strange country. I like my life the way it is. There's no room for a man in it, even one as irresistible as Dante Fortinari,' she added with sarcasm.

'And so you will deprive me of my daughter, and Bea of a father? Can you think only of yourself?' he demanded hotly.

Rose suddenly lost it. 'I had to after you left me pregnant and took off to marry someone else,' she spat at him. 'Goodbye, Dante.'

Dante tried ringing back several times but eventually gave up, which made her even more furious. When her phone rang an hour or so later she snatched it up, ready to tell Dante to go to hell until she saw the caller ID.

'When, Rose Palmer,' Charlotte said belligerently, 'were you going to tell *me* that Dante is Bea's father? I had to hear it from Dad.'

'I didn't tell Dante until last night, so you were next on the list. Not even Mum knew, so don't get angry with me.' Rose's voice broke. 'Please.'

'Oh, love, don't cry; of course I won't! But I demand details.'

'First of all, how are you feeling?'

'At this time of night I feel fine; in the mornings not so much. But never mind all that. You said Bea's daddy was some student, while all the time it was Fabio's best friend! So go on. Talk.'

With a sigh, Rose went through her story yet again, with Charlotte exclaiming in amazement at intervals.

'You were so *brave*, Rose, going through all that and never telling a soul, and all the while working so hard to make a living for Bea. Though, thinking back, the clues were there. You would never listen if Dante's name came up, but I thought that was because of Elsa the Witch. I suppose he never mentioned her when he was charming the socks off my bridesmaid?'

'Of course not,' said Rose indignantly. 'Otherwise—'

'You'd have sent him packing! So now he knows about Bea, what happens next?'

'I am ordered to marry him and take Bea to live with him at his villa.'

'How masterful!' Charlotte waited for a moment then sighed. 'But you're not going to do that.'

'No. With help from my wonderful mother and your equally wonderful father, I've managed my life very well up to now. Dante can issue orders as much as he likes, but I'm staying put. And so is Bea.'

'Damn! I wish I could nip over and see you, but Fabio is adamant about no travelling for a while. And, if I'm honest, I'm not up to it right now, anyway. If I send you the fares will you bring Bea here instead?'

The mere thought of being anywhere in the vicinity of Dante Fortinari made Rose want to kick and scream. 'I can't just now, love. Maybe later on.'

Rose checked on Bea and then stacked her pillows and got into bed to lean against them, waiting for the phone to ring. When it remained obdurately silent she removed two of the pillows and tried to settle down to sleep. Instead of issuing orders, all Dante had needed to get her consent was to tell her—and convince her—that he wanted to marry her because he loved her, not because she came as a package deal with their daughter.

When the phone rang later Rose shot upright and grabbed it, then sank back against the pillows when she saw the caller ID.

'You took a long time to pick up,' said Grace.

'I thought it was Dante again.'

'I gather you won't answer when he rings.'

'How do you gather?'

'Because he rang Tom—he got the number from Fabio—and asked to speak to me. He's desperately worried about you, love.'

'Good!' said Rose viciously.

'I assured him that, healthwise, both you and Bea were

fine, and told him it was best he doesn't contact you for a while.'

'And what did he say to that?'

'That he would try to take my advice, but it would be hard.'

'You should have told him not to contact me at all. Ever.'

Grace shook her head. 'I didn't do that because I know you only too well, Rose Palmer. If I had, you'd be utterly miserable. So I gave you the chance to change your mind when your temper dies down, as it always does, in time.'

'This wasn't a childish tantrum, Mum!'

'I know that. I also heard the pain in Dante's voice, love. When he does ring again, promise me you'll speak to him.'

'I'll think about it.'

This was a promise all too easy to keep. It was impossible for Rose to think about anything else. The nights were the worst part, just as they'd been years before, after her first encounter with Dante Fortinari. Even though she immersed herself in her work and spent the rest of the time with Bea, she existed in a constant state of tension, waiting for a phone call from Dante. A phone call which never came.

CHAPTER SEVEN

IT WAS A relief to spend most of the following Sunday at Tom's house. Bea enjoyed her day so much she protested loudly when it was time to go home. She even refused to wave bye-bye to Gramma and Tom and sobbed when she was secured into her car seat for the drive home, but, much to Rose's relief, fell asleep once the car was in motion.

'Wake up, Bea. We're home now,' said Rose as she turned into the drive, then swallowed, her heart thumping, as she saw a familiar male figure standing on her front porch.

Dante strode forward to help, arms outstretched, as Rose unstrapped Bea. 'I will take her.'

Exhausted after a day spent trying to fool her mother and Tom that she was perfectly happy, Rose yielded his daughter to him without protest.

'This is a surprise,' she said coldly.

'We need to talk; you will not take my telephone calls, so I came,' he informed her, then looked down tenderly as Bea woke up with a smile of delight when she realised who was holding her.

'Dante! Read stories?'

He chuckled. 'Of course, *piccola*.'

Rose unlocked the door and switched on lights. Now

Dante was here, he might as well make himself useful. 'Would you take her straight upstairs, please?'

Once Bea was in bed later, flanked by Pinocchio and Bear, Rose handed Dante a selection of books for Bea to choose from, kissed her daughter good-night and, after a moment's indecision, left them to it.

The sitting room seemed small and chilly after the space and comfort of Tom's house. Shivering with nerves as much as cold, Rose switched on the electric fire and drew the curtains, then went to the kitchen to make coffee and took a tray into the sitting room.

Dante joined her soon afterwards. 'Bea is fast asleep,' he said and crossed to the fire to hold out his hands. 'It is cold tonight.'

'Would you care for some coffee?'

His lips curved wryly. 'Yes, Rose. *Grazie.*'

'Why the smile?' she asked as she poured.

'You are so polite.'

She set the pot down with a clatter. 'Only to hide how worried I feel about the reason for your sudden appearance.'

He lifted a shoulder. 'It is nothing to cause distress, Rose. Because my first proposal did not meet with your approval, I came to make a different proposition.'

Rose sat down suddenly. 'What do you have in mind?' If he had some idea about taking Bea away from her to stay in Italy for weeks at a time he could think again.

Dante joined her on the old velvet settee, careful, she noted, to leave a space between them. '*Ascolta*—listen to me, Rose. I feel much guilt that in the heat of passion after the Vilari wedding I took from you something impossible to replace.'

She raised an eyebrow. 'I wasn't a virgin, Dante! I'd had a steady boyfriend in college.'

Dante's lips tightened. 'I meant that by leaving you with child I robbed you of your youthful freedom.'

Rose nodded as she thought it over. 'I suppose you could say that. I certainly had to grow up in a hurry. But, to be fair, I was an equal partner in what happened between us.'

'But if you had known about Elsa you would not have been, no?'

'Absolutely not! I wanted to beat you up when I found out about her.' She ran the tip of her tongue over suddenly dry lips. 'But the possibility of consequences never occurred to me because you used protection, and even though I later realised there had been a problem with the condom I really thought the chances of anything happening were a million to one. It was a huge shock to find out I was pregnant. There was an equally huge fuss when I refused to name the father.'

Dante took her hand. 'Why did you refuse?'

'You were married by then, so what was the point? You're a close friend of Fabio Vilari, so no way was I going to upset Charlotte's newly wedded bliss by bringing your name into it. Anyway,' she added militantly, 'I was determined to take care of Bea myself.'

He nodded. 'And you have done so admirably. But now I shall help you care for her.'

She eyed him warily. 'How, exactly?'

Dante's grasp tightened. 'The best way is to marry and give our child the love and security of a normal family.' He raised an eyebrow. 'But you do not want this. You value your independence too much.'

'Yes,' she admitted unwillingly.

'Even so, you must listen to my plan.'

'I'm listening.'

Dante smiled in approval. '*Va bene*. The plan is simple. Arrange your work to take time off, and then bring Bea to the Villa Castiglione for a little holiday. We can visit Charlotte and Fabio, also my family, *naturalmente*.' He paused. 'My mother is longing to meet her granddaughter, Rose.'

She bit her lip. 'I can't believe she's longing to meet *me*, Dante.'

'You are wrong. I have told her everything, and she has much sympathy for you, also admiration for the way you work so hard to support our daughter.'

My daughter, thought Rose fiercely.

'My house has several bedrooms. You are not required to share mine,' he assured her suavely. 'A week is all I ask, to see how Bea likes life Italian style.'

'Are you saying that if she does like it you'll expect me to let her stay with you there from time to time?'

'She is too young to do that without her mother.' Dante put a finger under Rose's chin and turned her face up to his. 'You would come with her.'

Her eyes fell from the searching blue gaze. 'And if she doesn't like it there?'

'Then I must spend time with her here.'

'You mean stay here in my house?' she demanded.

He gave a mirthless laugh. 'I do not hope for such a privilege. I shall stay at the Hermitage and come here to take her out.'

Rose stared at him in defeat. 'Very well,' she said dully. 'I'll bring her to Italy, but only for a week. I can't take more time off than that.'

'*Bene*. Let me know when you are free.' Dante stood up. 'I will arrange my diary to give me time with Bea. And with you, of course, Rose,' he added silkily.

'Thank you so much!'

'*Prego*. Now I must go.'

Rose went to the door with him. 'When do you fly back?'

'Early in the morning. This was a truly flying visit. And I have much more travelling to do once I get back, but by road, for which I am grateful.'

'You prefer roaring around Italy in your car, I imagine.'

'What man would not?' He took her hand and bowed formally over it. '*Arrivederci,* Rose.'

'Goodbye.' She hesitated. 'Dante, I'm sorry you had to come all this way. I should have let you talk to me on the phone.'

He shrugged. 'It was worth it to gain time with my daughter.'

She winced, hoping he couldn't tell how much that hurt. 'But if I come—'

'*When* you both come!'

'All right, when we come, you must make it plain to your family beforehand that this is just a holiday. It doesn't mean I've agreed to anything permanent.'

Dante nodded, his eyes expressionless for once. '*Va bene.* It shall be as you wish. And if Bea likes it there at my home, what then?'

Her chin lifted. 'Let's take this one step at a time.'

'There is one step you must take before you bring Bea to the Villa Castiglione. You must tell her I am her father.' Dante took her by the shoulders, ignoring the hand that tried to push him away. 'Let us be truthful with each other, Rose.'

'I just wish you'd been truthful when we first met,' she snapped, her eyes stormy. She still couldn't get past Dante's deception in the past. The hurt was still raw for her.

'I did not lie,' he said huskily. 'With you in my arms, I forgot Elsa existed—'

'We spent a lot of time together that day before we reached that point. And while you might not have lied, you omitted to tell me you were engaged, which is as bad as lying.'

'*Davvero*! But it was such pleasure to laugh and dance with you, I could not spoil the day by mentioning Elsa.' He pulled her closer. 'I fell under your spell at first sight and went on falling deeper and deeper all that day, until I lost control as we kissed later in your room. It was such agony to leave you that, even frantic with worry over Nonna on the flight home, I was determined to tell Elsa I could not marry her. That I had met someone else.'

Rose stared at him in disbelief. 'You obviously didn't tell her,' she said at last.

'Ah, but I did.' His mouth twisted in distaste at the memory. 'It was a painful revelation to see someone so physically beautiful turn into a *strega* before my eyes. She spat at me that she was expecting my child, which, as she knew well, gave me no choice. Nonna died the next day and in my grief I felt only relief that Elsa abandoned her plans for a big church wedding. She arranged a hasty civil ceremony instead in her determination to become a Fortinari.'

'So what happened to the baby?' asked Rose, stunned.

'There was no baby. Elsa lied. On our wedding night, she told me there had never been a child and never would be.' He dropped his hands and turned away. 'I was an arrogant fool, she told me, to imagine she would ruin her figure that way, even more fool to think I could jilt Elsa Marino, the supermodel all men lusted after. I stared at this beautiful woman saying these ugly things and felt such revulsion I did not touch her that night or ever again.' He gave a mirthless laugh. 'People pitied me when she left me for another man, but I rejoiced.'

'You never told anyone the truth about this?'

'Only Leo. Therefore, Harriet must know also.' He turned to look at her. 'If I had known that *you* were expecting my child, Rose, nothing would have made me go through with the *farsa* of my wedding to Elsa.'

'You must have found it hard to live with her after that?'

His mouth tightened. 'I did not do so very much. With Leo's help, I made sure I was often away on my travels when she was home, which for Elsa meant her flat in Firenze. She hated the Villa Castiglione.'

'But you love it,' said Rose quietly.

'Very much. After Elsa left with Enrico Calvi—and my fervent blessing—the house was my sanctuary.'

'Yet your family tried to get you out of it as much as possible.'

'To show the world I was not heartbroken. My parents were enraged that Elsa had treated me in such a way. It was my mother's greatest wish that I find someone else as soon as possible.' He rolled his eyes. 'Therefore, every time I dined with my parents, or with Mirella and Franco, even Fabio and Charlotte, there was always some woman invited for me.'

'How about your brother?'

'Leo told me I could find my own woman, and Harriet lured me from my house by asking me to do the babysitting for them—which is when I learned to change a bed quickly! I enjoyed this much more than the socialising. But the one I am most grateful to is Charlotte Vilari. She sent me to Firenze to find you again, Rose.' He paused, his eyes searching hers. 'Are you truly sorry that I did?'

Rose eyed him thoughtfully. 'You really told Elsa the wedding was off because you'd met me?'

'Yes.' He raised a dark eyebrow. 'You do not believe me?'

'I want to,' she said honestly.

'But you still have doubts.' He stood back. '*Non im-*

porta. I shall ring you next week to learn when you are free to leave. I will make the travel arrangements.'

'Right. I hope Bea will take to air travel.'

'With both of us to care for her, there will be no problem.'

Her eyes widened. 'You're coming to collect us?'

He smiled bleakly. 'This surprises you?'

'Well, yes; I expected to cope alone.'

'As always. If you prefer to do that—'

'*No*! Indeed, I don't. Thank you.'

'*Prego.* You will permit me to look in on Bea before I go?'

'Of course.'

Rose watched him leave the room with the swift grace that was such an essential part of Dante Fortinari and felt sudden regret, as though she'd somehow missed out on something important. She smiled brightly when he returned. 'Is Bea all right?'

'She is sleeping like an angel, as all children look when they sleep, even Luca, Leo's son, who is more demon than angel when awake. And now I must go. I will ring you early in the week.' His eyes locked on hers imperiously. 'And this time you will answer me and talk to me.'

'Yes, I will. And Dante,' she added quickly before she could change her mind, 'I'm not sorry.'

'*Cosa?*' He frowned.

'That you found me in Florence.'

'*Bene*, I am happy to hear it!' But, instead of kissing her as she'd hoped, he gave her the smile he shared with his daughter and turned to go. '*Arrivederci*, Rose.'

CHAPTER EIGHT

ONE OF THE highest of the several hurdles facing Rose was informing Bea that Dante was her daddy. Grace advised doing it straight away before Dante rang again, so that evening, after reading a longer than usual bedtime story to put off the moment, Rose finally told Bea she had exciting news—they were going on holiday to Italy, where Auntie Charlotte lived, to stay in Dante's house.

Bea, no lover of road journeys, frowned. 'In the car?'

'Only for a little way. Dante is driving us to the airport to catch an aeroplane.'

The blue eyes lit up. 'Tomorrow?'

'No, not tomorrow, darling, but soon.'

'Gramma and Tom, too?'

'No, just you and me. And Dante. Will you like that?'

Bea nodded eagerly. 'Are there stories in his house?'

'I don't know. We'll take ours, shall we?'

'OK.'

Rose took a deep breath. 'Darling, I've got a secret to tell you.'

'What?'

'Dante is your daddy.'

The blue eyes stared at her blankly for a moment then rounded like saucers. 'A real daddy, like Holly's?'

Rose cleared her throat. 'Yes.'

Bea was quiet for several long, tense moments. 'Will he get me from school?' she said at last.

Rose blinked, taken aback. 'Why, yes, I'm sure he will when he's here.'

Bea smiled triumphantly. 'Dante's *much* nicer than Holly's daddy.'

'You like him then?'

'Yes.' Another pause. 'Why didn't he come before?'

The question Rose had been dreading. 'I wouldn't let him.'

'Why?'

'Because I was silly.' Rose bent to kiss her. 'Now, go to sleep. You can tell Pinocchio and Bear your secret if you like.'

'And Gramma and Tom, too?'

'Yes. In the morning.'

After a hectic week spent in bringing accounts up to date and rearranging client appointments, Rose told Dante that the following week was good for her.

'*Ottimo*. I will make all arrangements and ring tomorrow with details.'

'Don't book a hotel room when you come to collect us,' she added casually. 'It would be more convenient to stay here the night before we leave—if you'd like to.'

He was silent for a moment. 'I would like that very much, Rose. *Grazie*. Is Bea happy about the trip?'

'She's wildly excited, though surprised that Gramma and Tom aren't going, too. I told her they had to do my job while we were away.'

He laughed. 'Is your mother happy to do that?'

'Yes, though I've tried to make sure there's very little for her to do.'

'You sound tired, Rose.'

'Nothing a night's sleep won't mend,' she assured him.

'I will ring as soon as I can. *Buonanotte.*'

Rose was in the middle of an endless ironing session when Dante rang to say he would be with her on Sunday afternoon and had arranged a flight to Pisa the following day.

'Is this good for you, Rose?'

'Yes, fine. Mum and Tom have taken Bea out so I can get our things ready.'

'They are much help to you.'

'Always. I'm very lucky.' She paused awkwardly. 'I'll see you tomorrow, then.'

'Yes, Rose. *A domani.*'

When Dante arrived next day Bea flew to the door to open it, beaming up at him. 'Dante, Dante. I've got a secret!'

'A secret! How exciting.' He put down his bag, smiling fondly as he picked her up. 'Will you share it with me?'

'Come inside first,' said Rose, peering past him down the drive. 'Where's your car?'

'I came by taxi.' He leaned to kiss her cheek. 'It is so good to be here, Rose. How are you?'

'I'm fine.'

'*Bene.*'

Dante followed her into the kitchen and sat down at the table with Bea on his lap. 'So, *piccola*, what is this wonderful secret?'

She beamed at him triumphantly. 'You're my real daddy!'

His eyes snapped shut as he hugged her close. 'That is such a wonderful secret. It makes me very happy,' he said when he could trust his voice. 'Does it make you happy?'

Bea nodded fervently. 'I told Gramma and Tom.'

Dante exchanged a look with Rose over the curly head. 'And did they like your secret?'

'Yes.' She looked up at him cajolingly. 'Will you get me from school now?'

'Like Holly's daddy,' explained Rose, busy with the coffee.

Dante took in a deep breath. 'I will like to do that very much, whenever your *mamma* says I may.'

Bea gave her mother a commanding look. 'Every day!'

'Dante doesn't live here, darling,' said Rose rather helplessly.

'But every time I come to England I will fetch you, *piccola*,' promised Dante, and speared Rose with a look which promised discussion on the subject later.

'Mummy was silly,' Bea informed him.

'Because I wouldn't let you come to see us until recently,' explained Rose, wishing she'd explained more to Dante before he came. But she'd been human enough to want to see his reaction when Bea told him her secret.

He smiled lovingly at his child. 'But now we are going to Italy together tomorrow to stay in my house.'

'Is it a big house?'

'Quite big, yes,' he said, ruffling her curls.

'You got children there?' she enquired.

Dante shook his head. 'You are my only child, *piccola*.'

'But you remember Harriet, the lovely lady who came to see us one day?' asked Rose.

Bea nodded with enthusiasm. 'She's got children.'

'You are so clever to remember,' said Dante proudly. 'Their daddy is my brother Leo, and we shall go to his house to play with Luca and Chiara.'

'Tomorrow?'

'No, but soon,' promised Dante. 'Tomorrow we fly in the aeroplane to Italy.'

Due to her excitement, Bea took longer to get to sleep than usual, and later, after a dinner shared with Dante in determined harmony, Rose's tension began to mount as she went upstairs ahead of him. 'You're in my room,' she informed him, ushering him inside. 'I hope you'll be comfortable.'

Dante closed the door quietly behind them. 'Where are you sleeping, Rose?'

'On the sofa bed in my study.'

He frowned. 'I should sleep there and you remain here, near to Bea, yes?'

'Certainly not. You wouldn't fit on it and, besides, I hear Bea wherever I am.' Rose made for the door, but Dante barred her way.

'I cannot take your bed, *cara*. But there is an obvious solution to the problem.' He took her in his arms. 'Share it with me.'

Rose opened her mouth to protest but Dante kissed her into silence. He held her hard against him and her body reacted involuntarily, savouring the scent of him and the pleasure of the contact with a taut, muscular, male body. He raised his head a fraction, but only to rub his cheek against hers and murmur in her ear in his own tongue.

'I don't understand,' she said hoarsely.

'Ah, but you do, *tesoro*,' he whispered. 'I desire you, Rose.'

Desire, not love, she thought bleakly.

Dante drew her closer, his lips against her cheek. 'I think—I know that you want me, yes?'

'Yes,' she admitted, but pulled away, blinking tears from her eyes. 'But not so much that I'll let you turn my life upside down again.'

'Ah, *carissima*, do not cry, or you'll break my heart.'

'Then you'll know how I felt when you broke mine!' Rose flung away and left the room, closing the door softly behind her.

* * *

Rose's second trip to Italy was very different from the first one. A chauffeured limousine replaced the coach trip to Heathrow, followed by a first-class flight to Pisa. The flight attendants were charmed with Bea, the females among them charmed with Dante, too, noted Rose acidly as she listened to melodic exchanges in Italian. She couldn't blame them. Dante was so obviously enjoying every minute of his time with his child, and so far Bea was behaving so well it was hard to remember she was prone to the odd tantrum or two at home. She was delighted with everything, including the pasta she was given for lunch, but Rose, occupied with thoughts of facing Dante's family, could only manage a cup of tea.

'You are not hungry?' asked Dante.

'No.' She managed a smile across her daughter's head. 'What happens when we land?'

'I shall drive you to the Villa Castiglione in my car. Do not worry,' he added. 'I have installed a car seat for Bea.'

'Thank you; how thoughtful,' said Rose, embarrassed because she hadn't thought of it herself.

To her gratitude, the rest of the flight passed quickly, helped by a peaceful interlude while Dante read to his daughter until she fell asleep. Rose sat, trying to relax, but her mind kept returning to the night before.

After her emotional parting shot, she had dreaded seeing Dante again this morning. To avoid him she'd showered and dressed hurriedly in the downstairs bathroom, and after getting Bea through the same process took the coward's way out by sending her to knock on Dante's door to say breakfast would be ready in a few minutes. She needn't have worried. Dante had walked into the kitchen later, smiling as though the biting little exchange of the night before had never happened. But his eyes had smudges of fatigue that matched hers.

Rose tensed as the plane began its descent. She wondered if Dante's family would be there *en masse* at his house to meet them, or if she'd have a day's grace to prepare herself while she explored the Villa Castiligione. A hand reached out to touch hers and she turned to face Dante's questioning eyes over his sleeping daughter's head.

'You feel ill, *cara*?'

'No, just nervous.'

'Of the landing?'

She shook her head. 'Of meeting your family.'

'You will not meet them today,' he assured her. 'I asked my parents to wait until tomorrow.' He smiled as Bea stirred. 'Wake up, *bella*. We are nearly there.'

They left the plane with much waving and hand kissing from the flight attendants for Bea. Dante would have picked her up to carry her but she shook her head.

'Walk—please.'

So Beatrice Grace Palmer made her entrance into the airport, hand in hand with both parents, her father carrying a shiny pink holdall with Pinocchio and Bear peeping out of it. As the trio reached the baggage carousel Rose saw a young man waving vigorously.

'*Va bene*, it is Tullio with my car keys,' Dante told Rose. 'He will help with the luggage.'

Tullio bowed, smiling, as Dante presented him to Rose and Bea, who grew very excited when she spotted her mother's familiar battered student luggage on the baggage carousel.

'Ours, Daddy,' she said, pointing.

Dante gave Rose a look which turned her heart over. 'So it is, *tesoro*,' he said huskily, 'and that is mine beside it.'

The useful Tullio helped stow the luggage in the car

while Rose fastened her daughter into the smart scarlet car seat. She chuckled suddenly and Dante looked round, smiling.

'What amuses you, *cara*?'

'Your car looks faintly ridiculous with a child's seat on board.'

'It must get used to it, yes?' He had a quick conversation with Tullio, who took his leave of them, blew a kiss at Bea and hurried off.

'Where's he going?' asked Bea.

'To take a taxi back to work.'

'What does he do?' asked Rose as Dante helped her into the passenger seat.

'He works for me. He is good at the selling, too.'

'But not as good as you!'

'He soon will be. He is eager to learn. And as an advantage with the selling he is an attractive young man, yes?'

'Very attractive!' Rose turned round to smile at her daughter, who was cuddling Pinocchio. 'Are you comfortable, darling?'

Bea nodded happily.

'Allora,' said Dante and switched on the powerful engine, 'let us go home.'

'Not fast!' ordered Bea in alarm. 'I don't like fast.'

'Welcome to fatherhood,' murmured Rose. 'Soon she'll ask if we're there yet.'

Dante laughed and drove with care as they left the airport. He touched Rose's hand fleetingly. 'Did you hear what she said?'

'She called you Daddy. You obviously liked that.'

'Very much. Did you tell her to say it?'

'No—her idea entirely.'

He let out a deep breath. 'I wanted to buy her many toys, but I did not.'

Rose nodded. 'You need her to like you for yourself.'

'*Esattamente.* You think she does?'

'Oh, yes. Apparently, you're much nicer than Holly's daddy.'

Dante laughed and reached out a hand to touch hers but put it back on the wheel at the look on her face. 'Do not worry, Rose. I will drive safely with such precious cargo on board.'

Judging by the speed of other traffic whizzing past them on the *Autostrada*, Rose found he meant what he said. Even so, she was relieved when they left the motorway at last to take a winding road lined in places with groups of tall cypress trees like exclamation marks which emphasised the breathtaking views of the rolling Tuscan landscape.

'Are we there yet?' came a voice from the back. 'Pinocchio and Bear want to get out.'

'Very soon,' said Dante, smiling at Rose, and after a while turned off on a narrow road which wound up a steep hill in corkscrew curves he negotiated with care she was sure must be very different from his normal approach to his home. As if reading her mind, he slowed down to a crawl to drive through an entrance flanked by stone pillars and on through tiered gardens to park at the foot of steps leading to a terrace edged with small timeworn statues and stone urns full of flowers.

'Welcome to the Villa Castiglione,' said Dante and turned to smile at the wide-eyed child in the back seat.

Rose was as silent as her daughter as she gazed at the weathered golden stone of a lovely old house fronted by an arcaded loggia.

Dante opened the passenger door to help Rose out. 'Do you like my home?'

She nodded dumbly. 'It's beautiful, Dante.'

'Come out!' demanded an imperious voice and Dante

laughed and hurried to release his daughter from her seat. But as he set her on her feet she reached her arms up to him in sudden alarm as someone emerged from the house.

Rose would have given much to do the same as a regal woman with silver-streaked dark hair came out to meet them.

'Mamma!' Dante laughed affectionately as he kissed her. 'You could not wait.'

'No, *caro.*' Maria Fortinari turned to Rose. 'Welcome to my son's home. Dante said I must wait, but I could not let you arrive with no one to greet you.'

Rose smiled shyly. 'How very kind. Thank you.'

'Will you introduce me to my granddaughter, *cara*?'

Bea had recovered from her attack of shyness. From her place of safety in Dante's arms, she eyed his mother with interest.

'This is Beatrice Grace, *signora*,' said Rose, and smiled at Bea. 'This lovely lady is your other grandmother, darling.'

'Another Gramma?' said Bea, surprised.

'No, *piccola*,' said Dante. 'This is my *mamma*, so she has an Italian name. She is your *nonna*.'

'Can you say that?' asked his mother gently.

Bea nodded. 'Course. Down, please, Daddy.'

A look of wonder crossed his mother's handsome face as Dante set his daughter on her feet. She touched the fair curls gently and smiled down into the blue, unmistakable eyes. 'I would so much like a kiss, Beatrice.'

Rose crossed mental fingers, praying that Bea would cooperate, and let out the breath she was holding when her daughter held up her face for the kiss her grandmother placed on both cheeks.

'*Grazie*, Beatrice.'

Since her name sounded even more unfamiliar pronounced Italian style, Bea shook her head. 'I'm Bea.'

Maria smiled lovingly. 'That is a very small name for a big girl like you!'

Wonderful, thought Rose, as Bea accepted her grandmother's hand to go inside.

'Come,' said Dante. 'Let us follow. You would like tea?'

'I would, please. What a lovely house, Dante.'

'I am glad you like it.' He looked up with a smile as a beaming woman came hurrying across the marble-floored hall to greet them. 'I inherited Silvia with the house,' he muttered in English, and in Italian introduced Rose to the woman, who greeted her with a flood of what were obviously good wishes. But she threw up her hands in delight as she saw the child and came out with another flood of Italian, most of which seemed to consist of *bella, bella*, repeated several times.

'This is my son's house,' said Maria Fortinari, slanting a smile at Dante, 'so I must not give orders—'

'Which means I am neglecting you, Rose!' He gave his mother a kiss. 'Just for today, give your orders, Mamma, *per favore.*'

She nodded briskly. 'Rose, what do you desire most? Tea, coffee or to go to your room?'

'Both of us need a visit to a bathroom, *signora*,' said Rose gratefully, and took Bea's shiny pink bag from Dante. 'But, after a freshen-up, some tea would be wonderful.'

'I will take you up,' said Dante firmly, 'while Mamma arranges it.'

'*Subito, caro,*' said his mother, and brushed her hand over Bea's curls as she smiled warmly at Rose. 'It is very good to have you here.'

'It's good to be here, *signora*,' Rose assured her, and to her surprise found she meant it.

'Come,' said Dante. 'Do you need anything from your luggage now, *cara*?'

'No, thanks—' Rose eyed her daughter, who was beginning to fidget. 'Just get us to a bathroom, please.'

The room Dante showed them into was bright with sunshine, held a large bed and, most vital at that particular moment, an adjoining bathroom. Rose hurried Bea inside and a few minutes later mother and daughter, both clean of face and hands, emerged to find Dante pacing impatiently.

'Do you like the room, Rose?' he demanded.

She liked it a lot now she had time to look at the carved furniture and filmy white curtains moving lazily at the open windows. 'It's lovely.'

'Have I got a room, Daddy?' asked Bea.

'Of course, *carina*, but we shall look at it after we have tea with Nonna on the loggia.'

'What's a loggia?'

'The veranda outside, so you must wear your beautiful blue jacket—yes, Mummy?'

Rose nodded. 'I'll wear mine, too.' She hesitated. 'It was kind of your mother to come here to welcome us, Dante.'

'She could not wait to do so,' he assured her wryly, zipping Bea's jacket.

Maria Fortinari was waiting at a table set for tea when they went outside. 'Come sit by Nonna, *tesoro*,' she said, patting the chair beside her. 'You like orange juice?'

'Yes, please,' said Bea, remembering her manners, to her mother's relief.

Maria smiled in fond approval. 'There is English tea for you, Rose, and coffee for Dante, of course.'

Rose took the chair Dante held out for her next to his mother. 'What a heavenly garden,' she commented.

'We've got a garden, too,' Bea told her new grandmother. 'Tom helps Mummy in it.'

'Tom,' Dante explained, 'is Charlotte Vilari's father.'

'Gramma lives with him in his house,' said Bea, and began on her juice.

'She will miss you, *piccola*.' Maria turned to Rose. 'Forgive my English; it is not so good as my son's.'

'It sounds perfect to me,' Rose assured her. 'I can only claim some schoolgirl French, I'm afraid. I wanted to learn Italian when I was younger, but I never had the time.'

'As I told you, Mamma, Rose was too busy qualifying as an accountant,' Dante reminded her. 'And when she had her degree she studied for more qualifications to run a bookkeeping business from her own home.' He met Rose's eyes. 'So that she could stay with Bea while she earned money to provide for her.'

'After such hard work, Rose, you must rest now you are here.' Maria Fortinari smiled down at Bea. 'Would you like one of the *trammezini*, Bea?'

'That is a sandwich, *carina*,' said her father. 'You like ham and cheese?'

'Yes, please.' Bea took one of the dainty sandwiches eagerly.

Rose sat sipping her tea, amazed that this was actually happening. Here she was in Italy with Dante, in his beautiful house and, strangest of all, taking tea with his mother. In the past, when she was facing up to life as a single parent, working hard to provide for her child, this scenario had never entered even the wildest of her dreams.

'Please eat, Rose,' urged Dante. 'You had nothing on the plane.'

'Thank you. The little cakes look delicious.'

'Silvia made them especially for you and your *mamma*, Bea,' said Maria.

'I make cakes with Gramma,' Bea informed her.

'*Che bello*! Your mother lives near you, Rose?' asked Maria.

'Yes. It's a wonderful arrangement for Bea and me.'

'For your mother, also, I think, yes?' She turned to Dante. 'Bea has finished. Would you take her for a little walk in the garden, *caro*?'

Bea looked at Rose in appeal. 'Can I go, Mummy?'

'Of course. Wipe your hands on your napkin first, please—mouth, too.'

Bea obeyed with alacrity then took the hand Dante held out. 'You got lots of flowers, Daddy.'

'*Allora,* shall we go and count them?'

Maria cleared her throat as she watched her son walk off, hand in hand with his child. 'She is so sweet, Rose. *Grazie tante* for allowing Dante to share her. This is hard for you?'

'In some ways, yes,' said Rose honestly. 'Until a short time ago no one—not even my mother—knew that your son is Bea's father.'

Maria shook her elegantly coiffed head. 'So if you had not met Dante again in Firenze he would never know he has a child.'

'No.' Rose flushed painfully. 'By the time I knew I was pregnant Dante was already married.'

'My heart was heavy the day he married Elsa Marino,' said the other woman forcefully. 'Then one day my prayers were answered and she left him for that wealthy old fool, Enrico Calvi.'

'But until I met Dante again in Florence I didn't know that,' Rose said, and looked Maria Fortinari in the eye. 'It wasn't easy for me to come here, *signora*. I was afraid you'd think I was trying to trap a rich father for my child.'

Maria smiled ruefully. 'I confess I wondered. But then Dante described how you work so hard to make a good life for the little one. I think you are very brave. But now,' she added, suddenly brisk, 'what will you do? Dante says you refuse to marry him.'

Rose felt her colour rise. 'I'm used to running my own life, *signora*. And even though we have Bea as a common factor, Dante and I don't really know each other very well.'

'Yet you were drawn to him in the past, yes? Or Bea would not be here.'

Rose nodded ruefully. 'I fell madly in love with your son the moment I met him, and believed he felt the same about me. I was devastated when I found he had a fiancée, but my world really fell apart later when I found I was expecting his child.'

Maria winced. 'Did you curse him at the hour of Beatrice's birth?'

Rose shook her head sadly. 'No. I wanted him there with me so much I cried. But I still didn't say who I was crying for.'

Maria sighed. 'Your mother must feel much anger at my son, I think.'

'No, *signora*. I've made it very plain that what happened between Dante and me was mutual.'

Rose was glad to change the subject when Bea came running towards them with Dante in hot pursuit. 'Mummy, Mummy, there's a little pool!' Bea launched herself onto Rose's lap, her eyes bright with excitement.

'We shall take Mummy to see it later,' Dante promised.

'And tomorrow,' said his mother, 'you will come to Fortino to meet the rest of the family. We will have a party, yes?'

Bea slid off Rose's lap to look hopefully at her grandmother. 'With balloons?'

'Yes, *carissima*. With balloons!' Maria laughed and

kissed the pink cheeks. 'But now I must go home. *A domani*—until tomorrow.'

Once they'd waved his mother off Dante suggested they go indoors to show Bea her room.

'It's not bedtime yet!' objected Bea as they went upstairs.

He laughed. 'No, *piccola*, it is not. But we must show Pinocchio and Bear where to sleep, yes? Your room is here, between your *mamma*'s and mine.' He threw open the door and waited as Bea ran inside then stopped dead as she saw the doll propped up on the bed.

She looked up at Dante, wide-eyed. 'Whose dolly is that?'

'She is yours.' He caught Rose's eye and shrugged impenitently.

The doll had fair curls and blue eyes and wore jeans and a T-shirt. 'She's got clothes like me,' Bea crowed, picking the toy up to hug her.

'What do you say?' prompted Rose.

'Thank you, Daddy! You get kisses for presents,' she informed him as he picked her up.

'*Davvero*? Then you must kiss me twice because there is another present. Your dolly has a bag.'

Bea obliged with the kisses and wriggled to get down. 'What's in it?'

'Open it and see.'

The holdall, much to Bea's delight, was full of dolls' clothes.

'How lovely, darling,' said Rose, and smiled wryly at Dante. 'You couldn't resist, then?'

He shook his head. 'No. You disapprove?'

'How could I?' Rose smiled as Bea laid out every piece of miniature clothing on the bed, her eyes shining as she showed them to the doll. 'I'm only surprised you had the restraint to wait until now.'

'So am I.' His eyelids lowered. '*Allora*, now I know that presents are rewarded with kisses I shall buy something special for you, Rose, also.'

She shook her head, flushing. 'No need.'

'You mean,' he whispered, moving closer, 'that no gift is necessary for you to kiss me?'

Rose turned away hastily. 'What name shall we give her, Bea?'

Her daughter turned in surprise. 'Dolly, a'course.'

Dante threw back his head and laughed, then seized Bea and spun her round. 'So tell me, *piccola*, do you like your room?'

Bea nodded, giggling as he set her down. She frowned suddenly. 'Is it my room for always?'

Dante exchanged a look with Rose. 'Always,' he said emphatically.

Later that evening, Bea, tired out with all the excitement of the day, made no protest about going to bed in her new room with her growing collection of companions. Once she was asleep, Rose showered and changed into a dress in honour of her first dinner with Dante in the formal dining room, and felt glad she'd made the effort when she found he was wearing a lightweight suit. Dark curls gleaming in the light from the chandelier above a face alight with a smile at the sight of her, he took her breath away.

'You look very beautiful, Rose,' said Dante.

'Thank you.'

'Because this is a special occasion, Silvia has stayed to serve dinner.'

'She doesn't live in?' said Rose, surprised.

'She did in my grandmother's day, but after Nonna died

Silvia surprised everyone by marrying a man she'd known in her youth. So now she comes here for an hour or two in the day, and then goes home to Mario.' Dante eyed her warily. 'She assured me that if we wish to go out any evening she will stay with Bea, but I did not think you would allow that.'

'No, indeed. Not,' added Rose hastily, 'that I don't think she's trustworthy, but—'

'You could not leave your child with a stranger who speaks no English.'

'Put like that, it sounds very cold, but yes, I suppose I do mean that.' She sighed. 'It was a big step for me to bring Bea here at all, Dante.'

'I know this. And now you are here, how do you feel?' The blue eyes lit with heat as they locked on hers. 'For me, it feels so natural, so right, to see you sitting here with me. As we should have done long ago if Elsa had not lied to me,' he said bitterly.

Rose held up a hand. 'Let's not talk about the past.'

He nodded. '*Va bene*. We shall discuss the future instead.'

'No, not tonight, Dante. Let's just sit here and enjoy Silvia's dinner together.'

His eyes softened. 'Does this mean you are enjoying your time here with me, Rose?'

She grinned. 'It beats an evening spent with my computer.'

Having eaten very little all day, Rose was more than ready for the soup Silvia served, and for the chicken roasted with herbs and vegetables that followed. She thanked the beaming woman when she came to clear away, and assured her, via Dante, that the meal had been delicious.

'*Grazie tante*, Silvia,' she said, smiling.

This prompted a voluble response Dante translated as

great pleasure, that coffee and *biscotti* awaited them in the *salone* and Silvia wished them both good night.

Dante led Rose to a sitting room with a painted ceiling and furniture upholstered in ruby velvet. By the abundance of gilt-framed mirrors and pictures, it had obviously remained unchanged since his grandmother's day.

'How lovely, Dante. You've kept everything the same?'

He nodded as they sat down together on the sofa. 'My family says I should buy new things, express my own personality, but I preferred to wait.'

'Until you'd stopped grieving for your grandmother?' she said gently.

'No. Until you and I could make the changes together, Rose. *Perche,*' he said, his voice deepening, 'now I know I have a daughter, nothing will come between us this time.'

CHAPTER NINE

ROSE STIFFENED. 'ONLY because you're so desperate to be her father you're willing to take me as part of the deal!'

Dante stared at her angrily. 'This is not true. When I first saw you at Fabio's wedding I was entranced.' He turned her face up to his. 'It is plain you did not share my feelings.'

'Of course I did,' she said impatiently. 'I fell madly in love with you, Dante. Otherwise, the…the episode in the hotel room would never have happened.'

'The episode that changed your life. When you cried in my arms that night I meant only to comfort you, but the moment we kissed I felt such desperation to make love to you I was lost. When I was forced to leave you so suddenly I felt torn, as though I had left part of myself with you. Which I had,' he said bitterly. '*Dio*! How fate must have laughed when Elsa told me her lies.'

'Tears are something I must try to avoid in future,' Rose said darkly. 'They get me into too much trouble.'

Dante seized her hand. 'You cried the night in your house when we quarrelled, yes?'

'Yes.' She smiled brightly. 'So no more quarrelling, either.'

'This is a good plan,' he agreed. 'So now when I say we must marry you will not argue?'

If he made it clear he loved her for herself, rather than part of the deal that gained him a daughter, there would be no argument at all. He made it crystal clear he wanted her physically, but she would have to be convinced that his heart was involved, too, before she agreed to anything permanent between them. And if that was asking for the moon, so be it. She'd managed without him in her life before and she would do it again rather than enter into a relationship where her feelings were greater than his.

'I still think we should take more time to get to know each other first.'

'Gran Dio!' Dante thrust his free hand through his hair. 'How much time do you need? We have wasted too many years already.' He released her hand and sprang up. *'Scusi!'*

Rose watched, dismayed, as he strode from the room. Did he intend on coming back? But, to her relief, Dante returned quickly, holding out a leather-bound diary.

'Open it,' he ordered.

Her eyes widened as she saw it was dated the year they'd met. As she took it from him, a withered rosebud slid out.

'It fell from your hair at the wedding,' Dante informed her curtly. 'I have kept it all this time, like a sentimental fool.'

She felt her throat thicken and blinked furiously as she carefully replaced the pressed bud. 'I must check on Bea,' she said, getting up, but Dante barred her way.

'I have just done so. She is sleeping peacefully.' He took her hand and drew her down the sofa beside him. 'You say we do not know each other well enough to marry yet, but the best way for this is to live together, the three of us as a family.'

She looked at him squarely. 'And there's the buzz word. Without Bea in the picture, would you be in such a hurry?'

Dante dropped her hand and moved away, his face

drawn. 'What more can I do to convince you? I even embarrass myself by showing you the rose I kept. You say you fell in love with me at first sight, but now your feelings for me are very different, yes?' He shrugged. '*Non importa*. For Bea's sake, we shall marry, and soon. My child shall not grow up believing I do not want her.'

'But what shall I *do* here?' she said unsteadily. 'You're away a lot. At home I have my work—'

'You could work here also if you wish. Harriet helps Leo a great deal. She is very good at taking visitors around Fortino.'

'She speaks Italian?'

'Yes. She taught it at one time. French also.'

Her face fell. 'I don't do any of that. My sole talent is with figures.'

'You could help Harriet by taking over the English-speaking tourists.' Dante turned to look at her, his eyes bleak. 'Also, I will travel less after we marry.'

Will, Rose noted, not *would*. She had known all along that saying yes to the trip was saying yes to marrying Dante. Which was all she'd ever wanted from the first moment she'd met him; even more so now he'd matured into a man who'd suffered enough, courtesy of Elsa. And so had she. For Bea's sake, if nothing else, it was time to move on. Grow up at last. And surely, once they were married, she could make Dante love her for herself, not just as his child's mother. But what, said an inner voice, if he never does?

'I'll think about it,' she said at last.

Dante eyed her suspiciously. 'What are you saying?'

'I can't just walk away from my life at a moment's notice, Dante. I'd have to sell my business first, for one thing. So you'll have to give me more time.'

He shook his head in wonder. '*Dio*, that is not the answer I wanted, Rose.'

'Take it or leave it,' she said, shrugging, then quailed inwardly at the sudden fire in his eyes.

'I will take it! I will also take this,' he added huskily and kissed her with sudden fierce demand that shook her to her toes. He pulled her onto his lap, his lips and hands caressing her into a response which swept through her with such heat he pulled her to her feet and led her up the stairs to the gallery. At the open door of Bea's room, they gazed at their sleeping child for a moment then Dante took away what breath Rose had left by picking her up to carry her along the gallery to his room. He laid her on his bed and began taking off his clothes. She shot upright in protest.

'Wait a minute!'

He shot her an imperious look. 'No. I have waited long enough.' He knelt on the bed beside her and began undressing her. 'You may not love me, but you want me. Do you deny it?'

'No, I don't.' She took in a deep breath. 'But don't do this in anger, Dante.'

His eyes smouldered as he slid the dress from her shoulders. 'No, *bella*, not in anger.' He took down the hair she'd spent so much time over earlier and buried his face in it. 'I want you, Rose.' He removed the last of her clothes and held her shivering body against his hard male nakedness with a growl of pure male satisfaction. 'Tonight,' he said huskily, 'we finish what we began so many years ago, yes?'

'You've made love to me since then,' she said unsteadily as his lips moved down her throat.

He kissed the pulse he found throbbing there. 'But once again only in haste. Tonight I will show you what loving can be for us, *tesoro*.'

Rose felt his heart thudding against hers and looked up

into the brilliant eyes moving over her in open possession. *Yes*, she thought fiercely. *Show me. I want this.* 'You'll have to make allowances, Dante,' she said unevenly, her breath catching as he slid his lips down her throat.

'For what, *amore*?' he whispered.

'You've obviously done this a lot and I…well, I haven't. As you know, I had a boyfriend in college, but there's been no one since Bea was born.'

Dante held her closer. 'And was he a skilled lover, this college boyfriend?'

'No, he was much better at playing rugby,' she said unevenly. 'But I was fond of him and he made me laugh.'

'It is good to laugh together,' agreed Dante, and kissed her with mounting urgency. 'We shall laugh together many times, I hope, but at this moment, *tesoro*, I want you in all the ways a man wants a woman.'

Rose fully expected an onslaught as he sought instant relief for the tension she could feel building in his body, but instead Dante took infinite pleasure in kissing and caressing every inch of her with clever, inciting hands that tuned her entire body to such a pitch of longing she gave a hoarse little cry of protest as he paused an instant to use protection then took her mouth in a devouring kiss as his body fused with hers in a jolt of such pure sensation she fought for breath, her heart hammering against his. She lay relishing the almost painful pleasure of it for an instant before he withdrew slightly then thrust again to what felt like the very heart of her, his eyes like blue fires burning down into hers as he began showing her exactly what the art of loving should be. He kissed her as he made love to her, the rhythm slow at first until he felt her desire mount to match his, but at last he took her hard and fast towards the culmination that finally overwhelmed them both and, with a smothered cry, she came apart in his arms, and he surrendered to his own release.

Dante drew the covers over them and turned her in his arms to hold her close. 'Rose,' he whispered later, 'I do not wish to move, but soon I must take you back to the guest room. Bea might come looking for you and find the bed empty.'

She nodded, flushing. 'You're right.'

'Tomorrow,' said Dante with emphasis, 'we bring your clothes to my room and tell our daughter you will be sharing it with me.'

Rose braced herself as she shook her head. 'I'd rather not do that until things are more settled between us, Dante.'

'Ah!' His face darkened. 'This is my punishment, Rose?'

'Punishment?'

'For my sins,' he said bitterly. 'I did not tell you about Elsa, I left you with child—'

'Since the child is the light of my life, I wouldn't punish you for that, Dante.' She looked at him in appeal. 'I just want you to slow down a little, to give me more time to get used to—'

'To me?' he said quickly. 'Yet, here in my arms, I thought I made you happy, Rose.'

'You know you did,' she said, flushing, and turned her head way. 'That part of our relationship would obviously be good.'

'All of it will be good,' he said with passion. 'But if you want me to wait until you are also sure of this I will do so.' He gave a mirthless laugh. 'I am good at the waiting. I have been waiting for you for years, Rose.'

She turned on him sharply, her eyes flashing. 'If that's true, why didn't you come looking for me once you were free?'

His chin lifted. 'Charlotte told me you had someone else in your life. She would not say who it was, so I believed, *naturalmente*, that it was a man.' He shook his head in wonder. 'While all the time it was the daughter I did not know I possessed.'

'I begged Charlotte to keep my baby secret. So she did.'

'You were ashamed of Bea?'

She glared at him. 'No, I was not! I was merely afraid that if any of your friends saw you anywhere near my child they would know exactly who her father was. And because you were married, it would have been disaster all round.'

'But Bea resembles you, not me,' said Dante, surprised.

'Not the smile and those eyes of yours. They're a dead giveaway. My mother took one look at you two together and knew straight away.'

'*Va bene*, now the whole world will know,' he said with satisfaction, and slid out of bed. 'No. Stay there, *cara*. I have a present for you.' He licked his lips as he leaned over her. 'So I will get kisses, yes?'

Rose laughed. 'Very probably!'

'I have dreamed of this so often, yet now you are really here at last. Where you belong, yes?' Dante gave her a look that curled her toes then turned away to open a drawer and took out a small box before sliding back into bed.

'You don't have to give me presents to get a kiss,' she remarked, eyeing the box.

'Then I will kiss you first,' he said and did so with such lingering pleasure that Rose kissed him back in kind and melted against him, breathing in the scent of his skin as he nuzzled his lips against her neck. 'Open the box, *tesoro*,' he whispered.

Rose obeyed, and breathed in sharply at the sight of a gold ring set with a baguette emerald between two rose-cut diamonds. 'Oh, Dante,' she breathed, tears welling in her eyes.

He sat upright, pulling her up with him. 'You do not like it?'

'Of *course* I like it,' she said hoarsely, and knuckled the tears from her eyes. 'It's just that I can't accept it just yet.'

'Why not?' he demanded, eyes suddenly cold.

She eyed him in appeal. 'Don't look at me like that! I'm just asking you to wait a little longer.'

Dante closed the ring box with a snap and tossed it on the bedside table. *'Va bene,'* he said shortly. 'But I will wait only until I take you back to England. Tomorrow, you will have a taste of what life could be for us here in Fortino. After that, if you still say no to me it will be the last time. It is against my nature to beg and I will do so no more—but then I will make legal arrangements to share our daughter.'

Rose stared at him in horror. 'Dante, listen—'

'No, Rose. It is you who must listen. It is best we are clear on this. Say yes and we live a normal married life. If not, you know what will happen. *Allora,'* he added silkily, 'since I have you here and now in my bed, I will enjoy the privilege while I can.' And he pulled her closer and made love to her all over again. But in the throes of the climax that engulfed her she waited in vain for the words which would have ended all argument, whichever language he chose. *'Ti amo'* was one bit of Italian she would have understood perfectly well.

CHAPTER TEN

ROSE WOKE TO bright sunshine and found her daughter at the foot of the guest room bed with Dante, shaking her head at her mother in disapproval.

'Up, Mummy. Party time.'

'Not yet, *piccola*,' said Dante, laughing. 'First we have breakfast. So let us leave Mummy to her bath and you and I shall walk in the garden until she is ready.'

Rose blinked in surprise at her daughter, who was wearing fresh jeans and T-shirt, her face shining and curls brushed. 'Good morning, darling. Did you get dressed all by yourself?'

Bea beamed up at Dante. 'Daddy helped me. But I washed and did teeth by myself.'

Rose eyed Dante with unwilling respect. He was diving into the deep end of fatherhood with enthusiasm. 'Then I'd better get a move on and do mine, hadn't I?'

'You are tired, *cara*?' said Dante softly, his eyes gleaming.

'Travelling always affects me that way,' she said, and thrust her hair back from her flushed face. 'Now, give me ten minutes and I'll join you for breakfast—I'm hungry.'

After a swift shower, Rose wrapped her wet hair in a towel to style later, slapped on some moisturiser and pulled on jeans and sweater. Something more elegant could be achieved later on before they left for Fortino. She felt a pang of apprehension again at the thought of meeting the rest of Dante's family. But his mother had been kind and Rose already knew Harriet, so she would have support from a fellow Brit among the alien corn. As she hurried downstairs she could hear Bea chattering away to Dante as they came in from the garden and felt a shamed little pang of jealousy of the man who was making her little girl so happy.

Silvia came hurrying through the hall with a tray as Rose went down, and smiled and wished her good morning, but in a different accent from Dante's.

'*Buongiorno,*' echoed Rose, hoping it sounded right, and received such a beaming smile in response assumed it did.

'There you are,' said Dante, getting up as she went outside on the loggia. 'Are you dressed warmly enough to eat outside?'

'I asked Daddy if we could,' said Bea.

'And Daddy said yes, of course,' said Rose, smiling.

He shrugged, grinning. '*Naturalmente.*' He pulled out a chair for her.

'That means a'course,' Bea told her, and smiled at Silvia as the woman poured orange juice into her glass. '*Grazie,*' she said proudly, in exact imitation of Dante. 'Was that right, Daddy?'

'Perfect.' He nodded in agreement as Silvia, smiling fondly at the child, spoke rapidly to him. 'Silvia says you are a clever girl.'

Eating a leisurely breakfast outside in the cool sunlit morning was such a contrast to the normal routine in the Palmer household. Rose suppressed all uneasy thoughts of Dante's threat the night before and smiled as she described their usual morning chaos. 'It takes more effort some days than others, but I always manage to get Bea to nursery school on time.'

'Do you like school, Bea?' Dante asked.

She nodded. 'The teacher reads stories. And we do painting and make things.'

'Did you tell her you were coming to Italy for a holiday?'

'Yes. To Daddy's house.'

Rose eyed her daughter wryly. 'And what did she say?'

'What a lucky girl! Can I get down now?'

By the time Rose had washed her daughter's face and hands and collected Dolly, Pinocchio and Bear, Silvia had brewed a fresh pot of coffee, so Rose sat down to share it with Dante while Bea played with her toys on the steps beside them.

'Sorry about the face and hair,' murmured Rose. 'I'll do something better before we go.'

'I like to see you like this.' He shrugged. 'Elsa drank only black coffee in the morning and refused to leave her room until her face and coiffure were perfect.'

'Who's Elsa?' asked Bea.

Dante shot a remorseful glance at Rose. 'A lady I used to know.'

'Will she be at the party?'

'No, *piccola*. Today is for family only.'

Bea scrambled to her feet. 'Mummy, can I have more juice?'

'Go to the kitchen to ask Silvia for some,' suggested Rose. 'Daddy will tell you what to say.'

'I can get it,' said Dante instantly, but Rose shook her head.

'It's a good way to learn the language.'

He bent down to Bea. 'You must say "*Succo, per favore*, Silvia".'

She repeated it solemnly then went running into the house.

'Forgive me, Rose,' said Dante heavily. 'I did not think. I will not mention Elsa again.'

She shook her head. 'It doesn't matter.'

His eyes flared as he pulled her out of her chair. 'It does matter. Now you and Bea are in my life, I wish to forget she ever existed,' he said, and kissed her fiercely.

But without Bea this would not be happening, Rose thought unhappily, and with iron will managed to keep from melting into his embrace as he crushed her to him.

Dante released her, smiling as Rose picked up the towel she'd lost in the encounter.

She thrust her hair back from her hot face. 'Maybe you should see how Bea is getting along with Silvia.'

'With pleasure!' He went into the house and eventually returned with a plastic beaker of juice, his daughter running beside him.

'This is a special mug for me, Mummy,' she informed Rose, beaming. 'And I said *grazie* to Silvia for the juice.'

'You're a star! Come and sit down by Dolly to drink. Only don't spill anything on her.'

Bea obeyed carefully. 'Mummy, can I wear my party dress today?'

'I've been meaning to ask about that,' said Rose. 'What do you want us to wear today, Dante?'

'My women will look ravishing whatever they wear,' he assured her.

'Only if they're wearing something appropriate and don't feel out of place,' Rose said tartly. 'So are you wearing a suit?'

'No, *cara*. Just ordinary clothes and one of my leather jackets.'

'None of your clothes look very ordinary, Dante.'

'*Mummy!*' repeated Bea imperiously. 'Can I wear my dress?'

'Yes,' said Rose in sudden decision. 'I'll wear a dress, too. But we'll take some jeans and a T-shirt for you, just in case. What time are we due at Fortino, Dante?'

'Noon.'

'In that case I'd better make a start on my hair. You can take a look at the clothes I've brought, Dante, and choose for me.'

'I always do that, Mummy,' said Bea, pouting.

'We shall choose together,' said her father hastily, and snatched her up to give her a piggyback up the stairs.

On the approach to Dante's childhood home through the vast vineyards of Fortino, the house which came into view looked familiar to Rose.

'It's the label on your Fortinari Classico,' she said, impressed. 'I'd assumed it was a reproduction of some Renaissance villa.' She bit her lip. 'It's very grand, Dante.'

'But in bad condition when my parents inherited it,' he informed her. 'Much work was necessary to make it look as it does today. Part of it is used as offices, so Mamma wants a smaller, more private place to enjoy my father's retirement. She would like Leo and Harriet to take over Fortino.'

'Will they do that?'

'Harriet says Leo spends most of his time here anyway, so she is willing to make the change. But Leo is attached to his present house because it is the home he brought Harriet to as a bride.'

'Look, balloons, Daddy!' piped up a voice from the back. 'And lots of people.'

Bea was right. As Dante parked the car, people came streaming out of the house onto a loggia far bigger and grander than the one at the Villa Castiglione, with brightly coloured balloons tied to its venerable pillars.

'Do I look all right?' demanded Rose urgently, and Dante picked up her hand and squeezed it.

'You are perfect,' he said, and got out to help his little family from the car.

Maria Fortinari came hurrying down the steps to greet them and kissed Rose in warm welcome, then planted kisses on her granddaughter's cheeks. 'You both look so beautiful,' she exclaimed, and turned to the distinguished silver-haired man following behind. 'Our newest grand-daughter, *caro.*' She drew Rose forward. 'And this is Rose, her *mamma.*'

Lorenzo Fortinari took Rose by the shoulders and kissed her on both cheeks. '*Benvenuti,* Rose.' He smiled down at the child clinging to Dante's hand. 'Welcome to you, also, *piccola.* May I have a kiss?'

'This is *my* daddy, Bea,' Dante informed his daughter. 'But to you he is *Nonno.*'

Much to Rose's relief, Bea held up her face for her grand-father's kiss, then her eyes lit up and she broke away to dart up the steps to the people clustered there watching. 'Auntie Charlotte, Auntie Charlotte!'

'Honey Bea!' Charlotte Vilari hugged her tightly. 'How's my lovely girl?'

Bea smiled up at her joyfully. 'I got a big secret, Auntie.'

'Have you, darling?'

Bea nodded vigorously. 'Dante's my daddy!'

There was delighted laughter and, to Rose's surprise, a ripple of applause from the people gathered waiting there. Charlotte passed Bea to her husband, Fabio, and hurried down the steps to throw her arms round her friend, both of them too emotional to say a word until Rose drew back, grinning happily through her tears.

'This is a lovely surprise—mind the bump, little mother!'

Dante gave them time to recover then introduced Rose to

his sister Mirella and her husband, Franco. 'This is Rose,' he said with pride. 'And the little angel with Signora Vilari is my daughter—as she has already informed you.'

'And I am his brother,' said a deep voice with a more pronounced accent, and Dante grinned as he turned Rose to meet Leo Fortinari, easily recognisable as an older, more saturnine version of his brother.

'*Il capo*, Rose. My boss,' said Dante, saluting smartly.

'Senior partner, not boss,' said a familiar voice as Harriet Fortinari detached Rose from Dante. 'I'm so glad to see you here. Come and meet my children—they are dying to play with Bea. Will she like that?'

'She'll love it,' Rose assured her, and looked at Dante. 'Will you get her?'

'Yes, *amore*.' He grinned. 'If you think Charlotte will let her go.'

Leo Fortinari issued strict instructions to his son, Luca, and daughter, Chiara, to take great care of Bea, and Franco Paglia did the same with Mario, Renzo and Vittoria, who were older, but just as eager to play with the child as the others, but brought her running back to Rose first.

'I want my jeans,' Bea said urgently, and Maria Fortinari nodded in approval.

'Come with me and your *mamma* to change, *bella*. It would not be good to spoil that lovely dress.'

While the exchange was made, Maria smiled warmly at Rose and patted her cheek. 'Welcome to our home, *cara*.'

Rose blinked hard. 'Thank you, *signora*.'

The striking dark eyes misted over. 'It is so good to see Dante happy again. I am very grateful to you.'

'Nonna!' said Bea, dancing impatiently in her blue trainers. 'Want to play now—please,' she added at a look from her mother.

'*Va bene,*' said Maria, clearing her throat. 'Let us go

out. Come, Rose, join the others for a glass of wine while I return to the kitchen.'

'Can I help in any way?'

Maria patted her hand. 'Not today, *grazie*. I have help in the kitchen. Enjoy the day with the others.'

Rose found it only too easy to enjoy herself in company with Charlotte, Harriet and Mirella on the loggia while she watched a very happy, excited Bea running riot with the other children.

'I'm on lemonade,' said Charlotte, pulling a face as she raised her glass to her husband, who was talking to the other men, but with one eye on his wife.

'It is best for now,' said Mariella with sympathy.

'You still have to keep off the wine if you nurse the baby yourself,' put in Harriet. 'But it's worth it, isn't it, Rose?'

Rose smiled ruefully as she watched Bea trying to catch a ball Luca tossed to her. 'I couldn't do it. I had to resort to bottles.'

'I remember how upset you were about it,' said Charlotte. 'She tried so hard to be the perfect mother,' she told the others.

'You succeeded,' said Harriet, waving a hand towards Bea. 'Just look at the result—oops, she's fallen over.'

Rose surged to her feet but Dante was first to scoop up his daughter and make anxious enquiries.

'Down, Daddy,' she said crossly. 'Want to play!'

Dante obeyed, and exchanged a wry grin with Rose as Bea returned to the ball game. 'It is hard to stand back, yes?'

'Unless they're bleeding you leave them to it,' Harriet advised, and Mirella laughed.

'It took me a long time to learn that.'

'Are you taking notes, Charlotte?' asked Rose.

Her friend smiled contentedly. 'I'm just enjoying the

moment, love. To have you and Bea here like this is just wonderful.'

'Mamma thinks so, too,' said Mirella. 'She has worried much over Dante, but now he is happy, Mamma is happy. I am happy, too,' she added, sniffing hard.

'So when are you going to marry him, Rose?' asked Charlotte bluntly.

'There's a lot to consider before making any decisions. For one thing, I have to sell my business first.' And far more vital than that, before she said yes she needed to be sure that Dante wanted her as his wife rather than just the mother of his child.

'Just put it in the hands of an agent—the house, too.'

'First I need to talk with my mother—and your father, too.' Rose grinned suddenly. 'I was most impressed with *your* mother, Mirella. She didn't turn a hair when Bea told her my mother lives with Tom in his house.'

Mirella laughed. 'She was so delighted her new grand-daughter was talking to her, yes?'

Rose nodded. 'Though to be fair to Charlotte's father, he'd marry my mother tomorrow.'

'Perhaps Grace will finally agree if you marry Dante,' said Charlotte.

'Not "if", Charlotte, "when",' said Dante, coming to join them. 'For me it could be tomorrow, but Rose is making me wait.'

'What for, Rose?' demanded her friend as Mirella and Harriet rushed to settle a squabble among their offspring.

Charlotte's question was hard to answer. Here in Fortino, surrounded by Dante's warm, hospitable family, Rose experienced an urgent longing to become part of it. Grace would understand; it was what she'd always wanted for her girls. 'We've only just got together again,' she said lightly.

'Give me time to get used to the idea. I've been running my own life—and Bea's—for quite a time, remember.'

'But there's a man here who will gladly help you with that if you let him,' Charlotte said. 'Right, Dante?'

'With great pleasure,' he agreed, and smiled fondly as he watched Bea playing with the other children. 'She is a delight. I still find it hard to believe I am her father—'

'You have doubts?' demanded Rose.

'None!' He grasped her hand tightly. 'It is you who have the doubts, not I, Rose. I long to marry you and give you and Bea the life you both deserve. We would be good together,' he added, his eyes boring into hers to remind her how it had been between them the night before.

'So for heaven's sake say yes, Rose,' said Charlotte and smiled up at Fabio. 'If Rose and Dante get married in England you'll just have to let me fly there, darling.'

Fabio flung out a hand to Dante in appeal. 'In that case, *amico*, make it soon, yes?'

'I will do my best,' Dante promised, and sprang to attention as his mother came out on the loggia. 'It is time to eat, Mamma?'

'Subito, figlio mio.' She smiled at Rose. 'I have washed the little one's face and hands with all the others. So now we eat, yes?'

A long table had been set up in the garden with a snowy-white cloth obscured by great platters of food and soon everyone was crowded round it, elbow to elbow, and talking non-stop. The children were seated together at one end, with a parent occasionally jumping up to serve them or settle squabbles. Vittoria and Chiara vied with each other to look after Bea, who was so obviously having the time of her life Rose eventually relaxed, enjoying not only the meal but the feeling of belonging.

Lorenzo Fortinari got up when the wine was poured

and held his glass high. 'A toast to welcome Rose and little Bea to Fortino!'

Everyone surged to their feet to echo the toast, and Rose followed suit, smiling gratefully. 'From Bea and myself, *grazie tante*!'

'Brava, carissima,' said Dante as she sat down amidst cheers.

She smiled. 'Just look at Bea. She's having so much fun.'

He nodded. 'It is easy to see her gold head among her Italian cousins.'

Mirella leaned forward, rolling her eyes. 'Vittoria will want to dye her hair blond now.'

Harriet groaned. 'And Chiara—maybe the boys, too!'

Franco shuddered theatrically. 'Do not even think of it, *per favore*!'

At the burst of laughter which greeted this Maria Fortinari came to join them to make sure Rose was enjoying herself and to press her to eat more food.

Rose smiled warmly. '*Signora*, I couldn't eat another thing, thank you. It was such a delicious meal.'

'I did not make all of it, *cara*. Letizia, my cook, is still with me, *grazie a Dio*.'

'Ah, but you made the *pollo Parmigiano*, Mamma,' said Dante, and kissed his fingers. 'It was superb, as always.'

'I make it with the identical recipe.' Harriet sighed. 'But it's never the same.'

Leo patted her hand. 'It is good enough for me. And you baked the wonderful English apple pies for us today, *amore*.'

'Much too wonderful,' said Charlotte, patting her stomach. 'I was greedy.'

'It is only natural right now,' said Fabio fondly.

At one time Rose would have been painfully envious as she watched the other couples together, but now that she had the chance of Dante permanently in her life, envy could be a thing of the past. Whatever his feelings for her, perhaps it was time to grasp this opportunity with both hands and make their marriage work for Bea's sake. And for her own, she admitted, her eyes on Dante.

'Just look at him,' murmured Charlotte as he went off to check on his daughter. 'He's besotted with her.'

Mirella watched her brother laughing among the group of clamouring children. 'He is such good uncle, but now he can be wonderful father at last.' She smiled ruefully at Rose. 'My English is not like Dante's.'

'But very good, just the same,' said Rose huskily. 'I must try to learn Italian as quickly as I can.'

'My wife can give you lessons,' suggested Leo Fortinari to her surprise.

'Brilliant idea, darling!' Harriet smiled at Rose. 'Don't worry; I'm a qualified teacher—and you'll be a much easier prospect than a classroom of teenage girls.'

'You have enjoyed the day?' asked Dante on the drive back. 'It was so good to watch you eating and laughing with my family—and with Charlotte. I did not tell you she would be there. I wished to give you a happy surprise.'

'Which you certainly did. Thank you. It was good to see a familiar face, though heaven knows your family's welcome couldn't have been warmer.'

'I am glad you were pleased. Our little one played very happily with her cousins, yes?'

'Bea had such a great time,' Rose assured him, and laughed softly as she glanced over into the back seat. 'She's fast asleep, but still clutching the string of her balloon.'

'It is a pity we must wake her to put her to bed.' He shot her a commanding look. 'I am impatient to have you both with me permanently.'

She nodded. 'I know, Dante.' She hesitated, but couldn't quite make herself take the plunge. 'Thank you for being patient with me.'

'Then I am a good actor.' He turned smouldering eyes on her. 'Inside, I am not patient at all. Sleep with me tonight, Rose.' He touched a slim warm hand to her knee. 'If not your husband yet, you want me as a lover, yes?'

Not much point in denying it. Rose nodded silently.

Dante let out a deep, unsteady breath. 'Then tonight we'll make up for all the nights after you leave me alone.'

Why not? thought Rose. If making love with her would make Dante miss her all the more she was all for it. And for her it would make up for the times she'd cried herself to sleep over him in the past. Besides, she wanted him physically in a way she would never experience with any other man, so why fight it?

The silence between them was thick with sensual tension as Dante carried his daughter into his house. Bea never stirred as Rose sponged her face and hands and put her in her pyjamas, nor when Dante laid her gently in her bed and kissed the sleeping face. Then he led Rose outside onto the gallery and seized her in his arms.

'Now I take you to my bed,' he said huskily.

'I should shower—' she began, but he shook his head and picked her up.

'We shower together—afterwards.'

To Rose it seemed so natural, so right to slide naked into Dante's arms in bed she almost said yes then and there to the prospect of doing so for the rest of her life as he rubbed his cheek against hers.

'*This* is where you are meant to be,' he said as though reading her mind. His arms tightened. 'Where you should have been all these years.'

She had no desire to resurrect the past. 'I'm here now, so do we talk or did you have something else in mind?'

Dante's laugh was so joyous that Rose laughed with him as his lips and hands told her exactly what he had in mind as he made love to her with patience which ended abruptly when for the first time she initiated some caresses of her own. Dante surrendered joyously to his hunger and took her to the very peak of physical rapture and held her there, gasping with her in the throes of it before they returned to earth.

'If we get married—' she said later, lying boneless in Dante's arms.

'*When* we get married,' Dante corrected and turned her face up to his. 'What were you going to say, *amore*?'

'I wondered what kind of wedding you had with Elsa.' So they could do something completely different—if her answer was yes. As it was going to be, she realised. There was no way she could deprive her child of the kind of life she'd experienced today.

'Elsa was in such a hurry after I told her about you she changed her plans for the wedding of the year into a brief visit to the town hall—but with many photographers there to record the wedding of Elsa Marino, supermodel, *naturalmente*.' Dante shrugged. 'I was glad of a civil ceremony. It was easier to end our marriage later when she met Enrico and his money.'

'But you must have been in love with her in the beginning, surely?'

'I was attracted by the outer beautiful shell—also she was very skilled in bed,' he said bluntly. 'We knew each other for so short a time I did not discover the true Elsa until our wedding night, when she told me the pregnancy was a lie, and that she had no intention of having children ever.'

'What on earth did you do?' said Rose.

He took a deep breath. 'For the first time in my life I could have done violence to a woman. To avoid this I did something which injured her far more. I went into the *salone* of our suite and locked the door. She screamed and cursed me for rejecting her but, as I told you before, and I swear it is the truth, I never touched her again throughout the sham of our marriage.' Dante shuddered and hugged her close. 'No more talk of Elsa, *per favore.*'

Rose agreed fervently. 'I just asked so we could plan something completely different for *our* wedding.' She felt the graceful, muscular body tense against hers as she turned her face up to his.

'*Finalmente*! You will marry me?'

'You said it's what you want.'

His eyes blazed with triumph. 'More than anything in my life.' He caught her close and kissed her passionately. 'I promise you will never regret this, Rose.'

'I'll hold you to that.' She kissed him back.

Dante rubbed his cheek against hers. 'Now you have said yes at last we must make plans. We could have the wedding at the Hermitage. Tony does these often. Then after the ceremony we have a party like the Vilari wedding.' He reached out a hand to switch on the bedside lamp and looked down into Rose's face. 'But this time you will be the bride and I shall gain my heart's desire of a child at last.'

Tears welled in her eyes, and Dante caught her to him. 'Do not cry, *tesoro*. If you do not like this idea—'

'Oh, but I do, I do—I love it,' she said thickly, and knuckled away the tears which had welled at the mention of a child. Not, she assured herself, ashamed, that she was jealous of Bea. She just wanted Dante's heart's desire to include her as well as Bea.

Dante slid out of bed to take a handkerchief from his

dressing chest and dried her eyes. 'What can I do to dry your tears?'

Rose sniffed inelegantly. 'Just hold me, please.'

'Always,' he said, and slid under the covers to pull her close. 'So why did you weep, *cara*?'

'Because it's exactly the kind of wedding I wanted but didn't like to ask.'

'Perche?' he said, mystified. 'Rose, surely you must know by now that I would give you and Bea the moon if I could.'

'How lovely,' she said unsteadily and grinned at him. 'But a Hermitage wedding with our families around us is all I want—complete with our own personal bridesmaid!'

Dante laughed and held her closer. 'Bea will enjoy that very much, I think.'

'She will,' said Rose fervently, and then frowned. 'Will your mother mind having the wedding in England?'

'No, because she is so delighted that I am marrying again. And to please her—and myself—we can repeat our vows privately later before a priest in Fortino. But we must arrange our wedding very soon, not only because I am impatient, but so Charlotte can be there.' Dante gave a deep sigh of satisfaction. 'I am sure Tony will be happy to make space in his Hermitage schedule for his favourite cousin.'

Rose smiled at him ruefully. 'I can't believe this is all happening. Pinch me, Dante, so I know I'm not dreaming.' She hissed as he gently pinched a nipple. 'I didn't mean there! You'll have to kiss it better now.'

'If you insist.' He sighed and then eyed her sternly as she punched his shoulder. 'Be still while I obey your command.'

CHAPTER ELEVEN

THE REST OF their stay at the Villa passed so quickly in visits to Dante's parents to ask their blessing, and to Harriet and Leo and the Vilaris to give their news, the day of departure was on them all too soon.

'It seems a shame to drag you all the way to England just to take us home,' said Rose the night before.

Dante shook his head. 'I must make sure you arrive safely, then I will stay the night in your bed and try not to think of all the nights when I'll lie in this bed alone until you come back to me.'

'You spent a lot of nights in it alone in the past,' she pointed out.

'But that was before I knew the joy of sharing it with you, *amore*. Now it will be hard to sleep without you.'

'You haven't slept much *with* me!'

'*Certo*. Why waste time in sleep when we can make love?' Dante held her close. 'But it is not just the lovemaking I will miss. It is having you here to talk and laugh with, to share my life with you and Bea.' He tensed as he heard a cry from his daughter's room and shrugged on his dressing gown. 'Stay there, *amore*. I will fetch her.'

'You're in Daddy's bed,' Bea accused tearfully when Dante brought her to Rose.

'Mummy's going to sleep here with me now,' he informed his daughter.

'When I get bad dreams I sleep in Mummy's bed,' she told him militantly.

Dante laid her down alongside Rose and got in beside them. 'But now I will be there, too, to chase the bad dreams away,' he said firmly and smiled at Rose as their child nodded contentedly and laid her curly head on his shoulder.

With the prospect of parting from Dante looming over her, Rose found it hard to smile for Bea on the flight home as her child chattered about seeing Gramma and Tom again. She felt uneasy and oddly tearful. Stupid, she lectured herself. Soon they would be married and could be together for the rest of their lives. A prospect she'd never imagined, ever. And in the meantime she would have enough to occupy her with her normal workload added to the wedding arrangements and finding a purchaser for her business.

'You are sad, *tesoro*?' said Dante quietly as the plane began its descent into Heathrow.

'Yes,' she said honestly and tried to smile.

He clasped her hand tightly. 'I will miss you both so much,' he said as Bea began to stir from her nap. 'Wake up, *piccola*. We are almost there.'

Since Rose had texted her mother on the car journey from the airport, Grace and Tom were waiting at the front door of Willow House, arms outstretched as Bea ran to them, talking at the top of her voice.

'Gramma,' she cried as Grace snatched her close to kiss her, 'Daddy's mummy is *Nonna*, and his daddy is *Nonno*, and I got lots of cousins, and Daddy bought me a doll. Her name is Dolly.' She turned to Tom, arms up. 'Auntie Charlotte gave me a present for you, Tom.' Beaming, she gave him two smacking kisses as he swung her up.

'Thank you, Honey Bea,' he said, returning the kisses with gusto as Rose hugged her mother. 'How was Auntie Charlotte?'

'She's a lot fatter,' Bea informed him as he put her down. She ran to Rose and picked up her left hand. 'Look, Gramma—Daddy gave Mummy a present.'

Grace took a look at the ring and hugged Rose close again. 'How absolutely lovely.' She smiled warmly at Dante as he brought the luggage. 'Welcome back.'

'Thank you, *signora*.' He kissed her hand and turned to Tom. 'Charlotte is looking very well, sir.'

'Good to know. Any hope of Fabio letting her fly over soon?' said Tom wryly.

'As a matter of fact, yes,' said Rose, and exchanged a smiling glance with Dante. 'Let's go inside so we can tell you why.'

Bea was incensed the next day when she found Dante was leaving, and clung to him in tears when the taxi arrived.

'Soon,' Dante promised as he held his child in his arms, 'we shall be together at the Villa Castiglione, but until then you must help Mummy and Gramma plan the wedding, yes?'

Bea's tears dried a little as she looked at her mother. 'Can I, Mummy?'

Rose nodded. 'Of course, as soon as Daddy arranges the date for the party.'

Bea brightened. 'With balloons?'

Dante laughed as he set her on her feet. 'With balloons, yes! Now I must go, but first I will kiss your *mamma* goodbye.' He held Rose close as he kissed her. 'Do not work too hard, and take great care of yourself, *carina*.'

'You, too,' she said and smiled brightly.

* * *

The period that followed was one of the most hectic of Rose's life, but the soonest wedding date possible for everyone concerned was a month later, which made it still possible for Charlotte to come, but did not please Dante. 'Tony Mostyn could not do it sooner, even for me! But this is good for you, Rose?'

'Yes. It's not long. Actually, I'm glad of time to get everything settled.' Secretly, she would have preferred it sooner, with less time to worry about Dante's motives for marrying her. But every time doubts crept in she thought of Bea, and how she had clung to her daddy as they parted. And as Rose had done since her child was born, she did what was best for Bea, which in this case was to get on with marrying Bea's father.

'Rose?' said Dante in her ear, 'are you still there?'

'Yes,' she said hastily.

'I thought I'd lost you. I shall contact Tony right now to confirm and will ring you again later. Or will you be too tired?'

'No. Ring me whatever time it is.'

He sighed. 'Ah, Rose, I wish I was there with you. It is strange that I have survived for years without you, yet now the wait to have you both here with me is intolerable.'

Both. Rose yearned for Dante to long for her alone for once, and felt mortified because she did. 'By the way, I've had some feelers about my business, but I'm going to wait for a while before putting the house up for sale.'

There was silence for a moment. '*Perche*? You feel the need of a sanctuary to run to if I do not make you happy?'

'No. It's just that the market is flat right now, so I'll wait until things improve.'

Dante sounded unconvinced as he said goodbye. Rose wished she hadn't mentioned the subject, and by the time he rang again later to report on his talk with Tony her headache was making her queasy.

'All is arranged, *cara*,' he told her. 'Tony and Allegra are very happy for us.'

'That's good.' Rose hesitated. 'Dante, are you upset because I'm keeping the house?'

He laughed. 'No, I am not. It is your house to do with as you wish. Now, let us talk of wedding dresses. Please allow me to pay for them, Rose.'

'Thank you, but no, Dante. Mum insists on footing the bill for the bride—*and* the bridesmaid.'

When the wedding day finally came—though at one stage Rose had been convinced it never would—she felt a sense of *déjà vu* as she entered the Hermitage. But today she was the one holding Tom's arm, and of the two strikingly handsome Italian men waiting for her, this time round Dante Fortinari was the bridegroom. *Her* bridegroom.

At first sight of the smiling faces turned towards her in the private room used for the ceremony, Rose's heart filled with such mixed emotions she felt giddy and held on tightly to the small hand of the bridesmaid, who grew very excited when she spotted assorted cousins waving at her.

'Look, Mummy,' Bea said, waving back, then beamed. 'And there's Daddy with Uncle Fabio.'

Dante watched the progress of the bride and bridesmaid with pride blazing in his eyes. He received Rose from Tom with murmured thanks and kissed his daughter lovingly before Tom bore her off to sit with Grace and Charlotte.

Dante made the simple vows with such passionate sincerity Rose had to fight against tears as she responded, hardly able to believe this was really happening at last as Dante drew his bride's hand through his arm afterwards to walk past the rows of smiling guests.

'Who is the fair man with Leo and Harriet?' asked Rose.

'Pascal Tavernier, my cousin's husband. Rosa is not here, much to her wrath, because she is about to give birth. Her absence will save much confusion. She is only distantly related to Harriet, but so strongly resembles her she could be her twin.'

'She must be very beautiful then,' said Rose.

'*Certo*, but not as beautiful as my wife,' said Dante in a tone which transformed Rose into the quintessential blushing bride as their daughter came running to join them in a flurry of organdie frills, the chaplet of flowers still miraculously anchored to her curls as she linked hands with her parents and beamed for the photographers.

Among the festive gold and silver balloons in the Hermitage ballroom, Rose could hardly believe this was happening as she stood with Dante to receive their guests in almost exactly the same places they'd occupied years before at Charlotte's wedding. Something Charlotte was quick to point out while Grace and Tom, and then Maria and Lorenzo Fortinari hugged and kissed the bride and groom.

'I am so happy,' said Maria, dabbing carefully at her eyes. 'You look so lovely, Rose—and so does our little angel.' She bent to kiss Bea. 'That is such a beautiful dress, *bella*.'

'I choosed it myself,' said Bea happily, and tugged on Grace's hand. 'This is my gramma, *Nonna*.'

Maria kissed Grace, and then smiled up at Tom and kissed him, too. 'Now we are all family, *tesoro*,' she informed her granddaughter.

After so much hugging and kissing, Rose left her daughter with her two grandmothers and went off with Harriet and Charlotte before the meal to make repairs.

'That's a very clever dress,' said Harriet as Rose straightened the folds of chiffon.

'More clever than you know,' said Charlotte. 'It's a replica of the one she wore as my bridesmaid. How on earth did you find it, love?'

Rose smiled. 'I was lucky enough to find the right shade of fabric and a dressmaker willing to copy the dress in the photograph.'

'From his reaction when he saw you, Dante believes he's the lucky one,' said Harriet.

'That's because I come part of a package with our daughter,' said Rose, smiling as Allegra Mostyn put her pretty freckled face round the door.

'Get a move on, Signora Fortinari—the bride, not you, Harriet. Dante's getting impatient out there.'

'Coming,' said Rose, surprised as Harriet gave her a fierce hug.

'You are so wrong, Rose. Make no mistake, Dante's in seventh heaven because he's finally got *you*. So off you go, sister-in-law. A wedding day goes by fast—enjoy every minute of it while you can!'

Charlotte smiled triumphantly. 'And today you're the bride, not the bridesmaid.'

Still finding this part hard to believe, Rose held out her arms as Grace joined them to kiss her daughter tenderly, her eyes bright with unshed tears beneath the spectacular hat Tom had bought for her. 'Are you enjoying your day, my darling?'

Rose nodded and hugged her tightly. 'Thank you so very much, Mum.'

'What for?'

'Everything.'

Dante was waiting impatiently in the lobby as the others hurried on their way to let the bride and groom make their triumphal entry. 'You look so beautiful, *tesoro*,' he told Rose, his eyes glowing. 'And so like the girl at the Vilari wedding I thought I was dreaming when you walked towards me today.'

'You like my dress?'

'So much I cannot wait to take it off,' he said in her ear, then laughed delightedly at her heightened colour and took her hand as music struck up inside the ballroom to herald the arrival of the bride and groom. '*Allora*. That is our song!'

Later that evening, when they were finally alone in one of the luxury suites at the Chesterton in town, Dante took his bride in his arms and kissed her with a sigh of relief. 'At last I have you to myself, Signora Fortinari.'

Rose smiled wryly. 'Is that really me?'

He nodded and rubbed his cheek against hers. 'It is a title you share with my mother, also with Harriet, so, to be sure you know who you belong to, *sposa mia*, think of yourself as Signora Dante Fortinari.'

'I will,' she assured him and hesitated, wondering whether to give him her news now. No. Best to keep it for later. 'It was such a lovely day, Dante.' She turned her back. 'I should have changed before we left the Hermitage but—'

'You knew I would want to take the dress off myself,' he agreed, and kissed the nape of her neck. '*Mille grazie, tesoro.*'

'You're welcome! Will you undo my buttons, please?'

Dante heaved in a deep breath. '*Dio*, Rose, my hands are unsteady and you have many buttons.'

'Exactly the same number as last time.'

'I do not remember undoing so many!'

'You didn't undo any.' Rose turned her head to meet his eyes. 'I was so eager I did it myself.'

Dante breathed in sharply and buried his face against

her neck. 'This time,' he said through his teeth, 'even though I want you more than my next breath, *I* will do it, *innamorata.*' He began undoing the tiny satin-covered buttons with speed and dexterity which quickly sent the dress into a heap of caramel chiffon at Rose's feet, and he snatched her up in his arms and carried her to the bed, his eyes dancing as he saw the blue silk garter above one knee.

'My something blue,' she said breathlessly.

Dante slid the garter down her leg and took it off to put in his pocket, then, with maddeningly slow care, removed her stockings and the satin underwear that had cost almost as much as her dress. He looked at her in simmering silence for a moment and then, careless of finest designer tailoring, tore off the rest of his clothes. He pulled her to her feet beside the bed to hold her close and kissed her parted mouth. 'I want you so much, Rose,' he whispered.

Not exactly what she wanted to hear, but for now it was enough because she wanted him just as much.

He bent to pull back the covers on the bed. 'I can wait no longer, *sposa mia.*' He picked her up and gave a purring growl of pleasure as they came together in the bed, skin to skin.

Rose melted against him, luxuriating in contact with the lean, muscular body that to her eyes could have been a model for one of the sculptures she'd seen in Florence. When she told him this between kisses Dante stared at her in astonishment for a moment, then saw by the look in her eyes that she meant every word and kissed her hard on her parted, eager mouth before his lips joined with his seeking hands in a glissando of caresses that transformed her entire body into a trembling erogenous zone.

'I know it sounds silly,' she gasped, 'but this feels new, as though we'd never made love before.'

'We have not done so for an entire endless month, and

never as man and wife,' he whispered, and positioned his taut, aroused body between her thighs. 'Now, *tesoro*!'

Rose clasped Dante close, her inner muscles caressing the hard length of him as he thrust home into her welcoming heat. He kissed her endlessly, murmuring passionate loving words into her ear as his caressing hands and demanding body drew such a wild response. As he possessed her she stifled a scream when the almost unbearable rapture of her orgasm overwhelmed her a second or two before Dante gave a triumphant groan and surrendered to his own.

They lay together afterwards in a boneless tangle of arms and legs, Dante's face buried in her hair.

'A good thing the other guests are all staying at the Hermitage,' said Rose at last. 'Sorry I was so noisy, Dante.'

He raised his head, his eyes blazing down into hers with pride. 'It is the greatest compliment you could pay me, *tesoro*. I feel like a king to know I gave you pleasure!'

'Did I give *you* pleasure?'

'Pleasure,' he said with feeling, 'is not a big enough word. I have made love to other women in my life. You know that. But with you there is rapture I have never experienced before.' He frowned. 'You are crying, *tesoro*?'

She sniffed hard. 'That was such a beautiful thing to say, Dante.' But still not quite the words she longed to hear.

'It is the truth,' he assured her and with a sigh of contentment turned on his back to pull her close. 'I hope our little angel sleeps well tonight.'

To her shame, Rose's pleasure dimmed a little after Dante's attention reverted so swiftly to his daughter. 'Since she's safe in Tom's house with my mother, and Charlotte and Fabio are there, too, Bea will be fine.' She smiled up into his relaxed, handsome face as she stroked the slim, strong hand now adorned with a wedding ring, something, he'd informed her, he'd refused to wear during his former marriage. 'It's time I let you into a little secret. Everyone thinks I named her Beatrice for my grandmother, and in one way this is true, but it was also my own private little joke.'

'Joke?' Dante looked down at her in question.

'Beatrice was the love of your poet, Dante Alighieri, so I named my baby for her as my secret connection to you.'

A look of pain swept over his face. 'Ah, Rose, if I had known!'

'If you had you couldn't have done anything about it at the time, but I thought you'd like to know now we're married.'

'I do like it very much.' He raised her hand to his lips. 'It is much happier than the revelation given to me on my first wedding night.'

Rose took in a deep breath. 'Talking of revelations, I've been waiting for the right moment to give you another one.'

'You have a buyer for the house?'

'No, something far more important than that.' She propped herself on one elbow to look into his face. 'We're going to have another baby, Dante. It must have happened the night you came back after our quarrel…' Her voice trailed away as he shot upright, eyes narrowed as they speared hers. He gazed at her in silence for so long Rose felt cold. 'Say *something*, Dante, please!'

'So,' he said heavily, 'this is why you agree to marry me. You had many doubts about giving up your independence and your home and job here in England, then suddenly you say yes and I do not question it. I thought you had changed your mind because, like a fool, I believed you wanted me.' His mouth twisted. 'But it was only because you were *incinta* again.'

'No, Dante, that's not true, or at least not totally. I'll admit that it was the final, deciding factor.' She flushed miserably. 'I already had one fatherless child. It was a shock to find I was about to produce another.'

'Neither child is fatherless,' he snapped. 'They are both mine. But why did you not tell me until now? Were you afraid I would cancel the wedding? You think I could do such a thing to Bea?' Dante flung out of bed to make for the bathroom.

Just once, thought Rose bitterly, it would have been good for Dante to think of her first, before Bea. Petty it might be, but on this particular night it would have been the perfect wedding gift.

Her nudity suddenly embarrassing, Rose opened the suitcase sitting at the foot of the bed and got into the ivory silk nightgown Charlotte had given her. She wrapped herself in the matching dressing gown and tied the sash tightly, wincing as her headache suddenly returned in full force. She should have kept her secret to herself, at least for tonight. With a sigh, she perched on the edge of the bed to wait. When Dante finally came out wearing one of the hotel bath robes, he sat beside her, leaving a space between them, she noted with a sinking heart.

'So, Rose,' he demanded, his voice stern, 'I ask again. Why did you not tell me sooner?'

Suddenly furious, she shot him a flaying look. 'Because I was naïve enough to keep the news as a wedding present to you—a sort of consolation prize to make up for your previous wedding night. So if anyone's a fool, Dante, it's me!' She jumped up and marched into the bathroom, then slammed the bolt home on the door.

'Rose!' ordered Dante hotly. 'Come back to me. Now!'

Rose gulped, feeling first hot then icy cold as she dropped to her knees and parted with what little wedding breakfast she'd eaten. Tears poured down her face as she cursed the fate which scheduled her first bout of morning sickness for tonight of all nights. Shivering and miserable, she ignored the banging on the door until Dante threatened to break it down.

'*Dio*, Rose!' he exclaimed when she staggered to her feet to let him in. He stared in horror at her ashen, sweating face. 'What is wrong?'

'What could possibly be wrong?' she flung at him. 'I've been sick, I'm pregnant again and, just like the first time, I don't want to be. Go away!' she spat in desperation, but Dante ignored her. He mopped her gently with a damp facecloth and picked her up to carry her back to bed.

He laid her down gently. 'Lie very still, Rose.' He took her hand. 'What can I do for you? Would you like water, or I can ring for tea—'

'You don't have to.'

'Of course I have to,' he said roughly, his grasp tightening.

'I meant,' she said wearily, 'that you needn't ring for room service. There's a tea tray with a kettle and so on over on the table by the sofa. You can make the tea for me.'

The relief in Dante's eyes was so gratifying she warmed towards him slightly.

'You will trust me to make it correctly, Rose?'

'Yes. But not yet. I'll have a glass of water first, please.'

Dante helped her to sit up, then piled pillows behind her and settled her against them with care. 'You feel better now?'

Rose nodded. 'Yes, thank you.'

His lips tightened. 'You need not thank me so politely. I am happy to do anything to help you.'

Except tell her he loved her. 'I'll have that water now, then.'

'*Subito!*' Dante said promptly. He filled a glass with mineral water and sat on the bed beside her, watching her sip very slowly. 'You have been suffering much with *la nausea*, Rose?'

'No. This is the first time tonight.' She pulled a face and put the half-empty glass on the bedside table. 'Bad move to get morning sickness on our wedding night.'

Dante winced. 'I think perhaps it was I who made you ill, not our baby.'

Slightly mollified when he said 'our baby', Rose shrugged. 'Possibly. Your reaction to my news wasn't *quite* the one I expected.'

'Mi dispiace!' he said and took her hand. 'Coming so soon after experiencing such rapture together, I was not thinking clearly.'

'You sounded pretty clear on the subject to me. But let's not talk about it any more. Perhaps you could make that tea for me now?'

Dante got up at once and crossed the room to switch on the kettle. *'Allora,'* he said, 'I pour the boiling water on the tea bag, leave it for a little while, then remove the bag and add a little milk. Yes?'

Rose nodded. 'Exactly right.'

'Bene.' Dante went through the process with care and finally brought a steaming cup over to Rose.

'Thank you.' She eyed him over it. 'Not quite the wedding night you'd hoped for, is it?'

He gestured towards the sofa under the window. 'You would prefer me to sleep there tonight?'

'Of course not,' she retorted. 'I assume you intend me to share your room at the Villa Castiglione?'

Dante's eyes locked on hers. 'My room and my bed,' he stated in tones which left her in no doubt.

'Then we may as well start as we mean to go on. Besides,' she added, eyeing the sofa, 'you'll never fit on that.'

'*Davvero*! But I was happy to make the attempt tonight to let you rest.'

'Very noble, but no sacrifice required.' Rose slid carefully out of bed, stood for a moment to make sure she was steady on her feet, then made for the bathroom. 'Just give me five minutes to brush my teeth.'

When she got back Dante had tidied the bed and left only one lamp burning. He looked at her searchingly. 'Were you ill again?'

'No. I think that was a one-off just now—at least for tonight.' She untied her sash and slid the dressing gown off into his waiting hands. 'That bed looks very inviting,' she told him, suddenly almost too tired to speak as she slid into bed.

He drew the covers over her. 'I will be minutes only, Rose.'

It seemed like only seconds before Dante switched off the lamp and got in beside her. He hesitated for a moment, then lay flat on his back and took her hand. '*Buonanotte, sposa mia,*' he said softly.

'Good night, Dante.' Rose closed her eyes thankfully, well aware that he'd wanted to put his arms round her and hold her close, but had opted for hand-holding instead. Good move, she approved hazily. His unexpected reaction to her news had cut deep. Any attempt at cuddling by Dante right now would have met with short shrift.

CHAPTER TWELVE

THE RETURN TO the Villa Castiglione the next day was physically far less of an ordeal than Rose had expected. When she woke up she felt a moment of panic when she heard Dante in the bathroom, but then relaxed when she found that her digestive system was in good working order. No dash to the bathroom was necessary. When her new husband emerged, towelling his wet curls, he eyed her searchingly.

'*Buongiorno*, Rose. How do you feel today?'

'Good morning. I feel better, thank you.'

'No nausea?'

She gave it some thought. 'None at all.'

He relaxed visibly. '*Grazie a Dio*. You gave me much worry last night. But be truthful, Rose—are you well enough to travel today?'

'Yes, definitely.' Postponing the trip, even by a day, would mean explanations to her mother she would rather avoid right now. And a second round of goodbyes would be bad for Bea—and herself, if it came to that. Rose slid out of bed and stood up, shaking her head as he moved swiftly, ready to help her. 'I'm fine, Dante, really. After a shower I'll feel even better. What time do we leave?'

'At ten. I will order breakfast.' He put an arm round her. 'What would you like?'

'Just toast and tea, please.' She detached herself very deliberately. 'I won't be long.'

Dante stood back, his eyes sombre. 'You have not forgiven me.'

'Not yet, but I'm working on it.' Rose busied herself with choosing clothes to take into the bathroom with her.

'You are shy of dressing in front of me?' he demanded.

She turned in the bathroom doorway. 'Awkward, rather than shy. I'm not used to sharing my life with a man, Dante. You'll have to make allowances.'

He smiled crookedly. 'Then, to avoid further awkwardness for you, I will dress while you shower.'

'Thank you.' Rose closed the bathroom door and got to work, grateful to Dante for not pointing out that there had been no awkwardness last night when he was *un*dressing her. But today, illogically, it would have been hard to put her clothes on in front of him in the new intimacy of married life—which was something she had to get over pretty quickly to make that life successful, if only for Bea's sake. She patted her stomach gently. *For you, too*, she added. After all, compared with life as a single mother, she was living the dream as Dante's wife. His physical response to her, at least, was everything she could wish for. She would just have to work on changing that into the more cerebral love she felt for him. Not that hers was totally cerebral. Otherwise she wouldn't be expecting his second child. Whatever her brain felt about Dante, her hormones were utterly mad about him.

The limousine trip to the airport and the flight to Pisa went just as smoothly as the first time with Dante in charge. Worried beforehand that the nausea would return en route at some stage, Rose survived the entire flight without a qualm, and to reassure Dante even ate some of the meal.

As before, Tullio was waiting at the airport and had taken time out of his Sunday to help them collect their luggage and hand over the car keys.

'*Congratulazione*, Signora Fortinari,' he said to Rose and kissed her hand then shook Dante's and congratulated him in turn.

'*Grazie*, Tullio,' she said, secretly thrilled to bits with her new title.

After a quick exchange with Tullio while he helped load their luggage into the waiting car, Dante helped Rose into the car and, with a quick wave for his assistant, joined the traffic leaving the airport.

'I will not drive fast,' Dante assured her, smiling, and Rose laughed.

'Unlike my—*our*—daughter, I don't mind fast!'

'Nevertheless, I have no wish to make you ill again, *carina*.' He gave her a sidelong glance. 'I asked Silvia to prepare the house and leave food for us, but then take a little holiday so we can begin our new life in peace together. But,' he added when Rose made no response, 'if you want her to come as usual I shall call her back.'

'Of course I don't. When Mum and Tom bring Bea to join us, peace will be hard to come by.' She shot him a wry glance. 'Though I know you can hardly wait!'

He shook his head. 'Much as I love Bea, it will be good for us to have time alone together for a little while, Rose, yes?'

Yes, she rejoiced silently.

'And after a while perhaps you will not feel so awkward with me,' he said with a wry twist to his mouth.

'I'll do my best, Dante.'

'I do not doubt this,' he assured her, and smiled as he saw her eyelids droop.

'Sorry,' she said, yawning.

'Take the little nap, *bella*. I will wake you when we are near home.'

Home, thought Rose, closing her eyes. Not Willow House any more, but the Villa Castiglione. Her lips curved. It would be good to be alone there with Dante for a while…

She woke with a start to a screeching, crunching sound, her heart pounding as something hit the car. Cursing violently, Dante stood on the brakes and her head hit the side window with a crack that knocked her out for an instant.

Rose came round almost at once because Dante was crushing her hand as he called her name in anguish, along with a flood of impassioned enquiries she couldn't understand.

'Answer me, Rose!' he demanded frantically. 'Where are you hurt?'

'Only my head,' she said groggily. 'What happened?'

'Some *bastardo* took a bend too fast and made contact with our front wing, then drove off like a maniac.' Dante leaned over her, his face haggard. '*Dio*, your head is bleeding. I must get you to a doctor immediately.'

'I don't need a doctor!'

'You do,' said Dante inexorably, and wiped her forehead with a handkerchief. 'Stay very still now while I arrange this.' He took out his phone and after a pause spoke to someone at length.

Rose listened to the rapid-fire conversation, but was unable to pick out more than the word *incinta*. At least she knew what that meant. It obviously had the desired effect, since Dante thanked someone volubly and turned to Rose. 'We will be seen immediately we arrive. I just need to check that the car is safe to drive then I will take you to the doctor. I will be seconds only.'

In sudden need of fresh air, Rose undid her belt and got out very carefully, relieved to find her legs steady as she watched Dante make a long examination under the bonnet. She whistled as she saw ugly scrapes along the shining crimson paint. 'How bad is it?'

'It is cosmetic only. The paintwork is scratched but there is no damage to the car otherwise.' He closed the bonnet. 'It is safe to drive, I promise. *Mi dispiace*, Rose. Even when I was young and drove very fast I never had an accident, yet today, when I was taking such care, this happened.'

'Only because some idiot was speeding. It wasn't your fault!'

'*Grazie, tesoro*. Does your head ache?'

'A bit. Do I look a mess?'

Dante pulled her close, his heart hammering against hers. 'You are still bleeding a little, but you are beautiful, as always.' He swallowed hard. 'When your head hit the window my heart stopped. It is good that *bastardo* drove off so fast,' he added, eyes blazing. 'I wanted to kill him.'

'Bad idea! I don't fancy visiting my new husband in prison.' She smiled. 'Thank heavens Bea wasn't with us.'

'Amen,' breathed Dante, and managed a smile. 'Though I was not driving fast!'

Rose chuckled then eyed him searchingly. 'Were you hurt anywhere, Dante?'

He shook his head. 'A few bruises and badly injured pride only. I am mortified that you had to experience such a thing, *carissima*.'

'I'll live. And so, in case you were wondering, will our baby.'

'That is good—but in that terrible moment when you hit your head I had no thought for the baby, only for you, that I might have lost you a second time, this time perhaps for ever.' He blinked hard, but tears, Rose noted in wonder, hung on his enviable lashes.

Oblivious of passing traffic, or anyone in the world who

might be watching, she pulled her husband's head down to kiss him fiercely. 'Well, you haven't,' she said gruffly. 'I don't suppose you have a tissue?'

'This handkerchief only.' He gave it to her, his eyes smouldering. 'That was a wonderful kiss. Do it again.'

'Later,' she said. 'Spit!'

He laughed as he obliged, and held still while she scrubbed a bloodstain from his cheek then gave him the handkerchief.

'Now you do the same for me.'

Once Dante was sure Rose felt composed enough to continue their journey he drove her to the private hospital used by the Fortinari family. As promised, they were seen immediately by a doctor who asked rapid questions Dante translated for Rose while the cut on her temple was dressed. When it was established that Signora Fortinari was not suffering from concussion, and a scan later confirmed that all else was otherwise well with her, the doctor told Dante he could take his wife home on condition that he brought her back immediately if she felt unwell.

When Dante finally drove up the winding road to the Villa later Rose gave a deep sigh of relief as the lovely old house came into view. 'Home at last,' she said thankfully.

'It is so good to hear you say *home*,' Dante said with feeling. He got out to help her out of the car, and then picked her up to carry her into the house. 'This is the custom for brides, yes?'

Rose wreathed her arms round his neck happily, surprised when, instead of taking her into the *salone*, he carried her straight upstairs to their room and carefully laid her down on the pristine bed before casting himself face down beside her, breathing hard, his arm possessive across her waist.

She lay still for a while, but then patted his arm. 'I hate to spoil this romantic moment, Dante, but I'm hungry.'

'I also,' he agreed and sat up, smiling down at her. 'So tonight we will have a picnic up here from whatever Silvia has left for us. I will bring it and you do nothing except lie there and look beautiful.'

Her eyes sparkled. 'Oh, well, if you insist! But I'll have more chance of looking halfway beautiful if I can have a shower first, so could you bring up some of the luggage before you start on the picnic? And I'll ring Mum to report in and check on Bea.'

The euphoria of surviving what could well have been a serious accident cast a magical aura over their first evening together at the Villa as husband and wife. Dante, who prided himself on his driving skills, was obviously mortified about the incident, but Rose was deeply grateful for it. His anguished reaction when she was hurt had removed all her doubts about Dante's feelings. He had no need now to tell her he loved her. She knew.

When Dante returned after removing the remains of their picnic supper he raised an eyebrow as he asked why she was so deep in thought. Rose hesitated for a moment then made a clean breast of her doubts and fears, which won her a stare of utter amazement. 'You did not believe I love you?'

Rose tucked her hair behind her ears. 'You never actually said so, though I knew you wanted me, physically.'

'How could you not? At your slightest touch I am on fire, *amore*!' He sat down on the bed beside her and took her in his arms. 'But that is only part of my love for you, Rose. I want to spend every minute possible of the rest of my life with you, raise our children together, and grow old together. That is how I love you. Is it enough?'

She smiled at him through a sudden haze of tears and

hugged him close. 'More than enough—even though you were so horrible to me on our wedding night.'

Dante winced and rubbed his cheek against hers. 'Forgive me, *carissima*, but try to understand. I wanted you to love me as a husband and lover, and for a moment I thought you married me only to gain a father for another child.'

'While I was afraid that you took me on just to get Bea as part of the package,' said Rose, and grinned sheepishly at the incredulous look he gave her.

'How could you believe that? In Firenze I could not hide my delight at meeting you again. And I knew nothing about our child at that time.' Dante laid his forehead against hers. 'So, to avoid all future confusion, Signora Fortinari, I have loved you from the first day we met. *Ti amo, sposa mia*. Do you understand me?'

'I do, I do. So make sure you understand, too, Dante Fortinari. I married you for exactly the same reason.'

'For which I thank God.' Dante slid the dressing gown from her shoulders and tossed it away. 'You forgive me then, *innamorata*?'

She pretended to think it over. 'I'm working on it.'

Dante pulled her close. 'Always I am the peacemaker, in the business and with my family,' he said bitterly. 'Unlike Leo, who can be abrasive—that is right? I am the one who pours the oil on the troubled waters. Yet on my wedding night I accuse my bride of sins she has not committed.'

'True. You'll just have to spend the rest of our honeymoon making it up to me,' she ordered.

'With much, much pleasure, *amore*! I have given instructions to my family to leave us in peace at the Villa Castiglione for a while when they return from England tomorrow.' Dante raised his head to look down at her. 'They were surprised that you did not want somewhere exotic for our honeymoon.'

'I just wanted to start our life together at the Villa without our little darling for a couple of weeks.' Rose sighed as she stretched against him. 'You know, even with the marriage vows to prove it, I can hardly believe that we're here together at last, Dante.'

He drew her closer. 'To have you here in my arms as my wife is a dream come true, *tesoro.*'

'I never dared to dream anything so unlikely!' She smiled up at him. 'Even though the first day we met I knew who you were before we were even introduced.'

'I knew at first sight that you were the love of my life, *carissima,*' he said huskily. 'So who did you think I was?'

'The man of my dreams. But dreams were all I had for years, Dante.'

'Now we have the glorious reality, yes?'

'We certainly do. Shall I tell you something else, Dante?'

'Anything you wish *amore.*' His arms tightened. 'Will I like this something?'

Rose nodded and rubbed her cheek against his, which, she noted lovingly, was already showing signs of needing a shave. 'I used to tell myself that one day my prince would come, and now here he is at last, right here in my arms.'

'Where he intends to stay,' said Dante with emphasis and then shook his head. 'But I am no prince, *tesoro.*'

'You are in *my* fairy tale!'

He gave her the smile he shared with his child. 'And because I have read many fairy tales to our daughter I know exactly how they end—we live happily ever after!'

By the end of the fortnight, blissfully happy though her honeymoon had been, Rose was in a fever of excitement at the airport in Pisa as she saw her child running towards them with Grace in pursuit and Tom, laden with luggage, following behind.

There was a laughing collision as Rose seized her child, and Dante caught them both in his encircling arms and kissed his daughter's beaming face as she talked non-stop.

Rose gave Bea a smacking kiss and then hugged Grace. 'How's Gramma?'

'Doing fine,' her mother assured her. 'Bea was no trouble at all except for the odd tear when she realised she was missing you.' She turned to Tom. 'We enjoyed having her to ourselves, didn't we?'

Tom dumped down the luggage to kiss Rose. 'We had Charlotte and Fabio's help for the first week, but the rest of it was excellent practice for when the first little Vilari arrives.' He held out his hand to Dante, smiling. 'No need to ask how *you* are!'

'Davvero,' agreed Dante, surrendering Bea to her mother. 'I am a very lucky man. Welcome, Tom,' he added, picking up some of the luggage. 'The car is outside.'

Bea frowned as Dante fastened her into her seat. 'I don't like this car, Daddy. I like your shiny red one.'

'It needed painting, so your Uncle Leo lent me this,' he said, kissing her nose. 'But this is your very own red car seat.'

Bea lay back in it like a queen on a throne with Rose and Grace close together beside her. 'Can we go and see Luca and Chiara tomorrow, Daddy?' she demanded.

'Possibly.' He exchanged a gleaming look with Rose over his shoulder. *'Andiamo,* let us go home.'

'Not fast!' warned Bea.

'No, *piccola,'* Dante assured her, laughing. 'I will not drive fast.'

Because he kept his word, Bea soon nodded off, leaving Rose to enjoy Grace's company.

'I've no need to ask how you are,' said her mother, squeezing her hand. 'You glow.'

'I enjoyed these two weeks alone with Dante,' Rose admitted. 'I missed Bea, naturally, but it was good to have time together before we get back to parenthood.'

Bea woke as Dante turned up the steep, winding road to the Villa. 'Gramma,' she said in excitement, 'Daddy's house is up here—ooh,' she squeaked in delight as he drove up through the garden. 'Balloons! Is there a party?' She jumped up and down in her seat. 'Look, Tom, Auntie Charlotte's on the loggia.'

'And not just Auntie Charlotte,' said Grace with misgiving, and grasped Rose's hand. 'Do I look all right?'

'You look gorgeous,' Tom assured her.

'Daddy, Daddy, get me out,' demanded Bea, as an assortment of cousins came streaming from the house. Dante unbuckled his impatient daughter and set her on her feet so she could run to join the youngsters who surrounded her, laughing, then delivered her onto the loggia into the embraces of her *Nonna* and *Nonno*. The senior Fortinaris gave Tom and Grace a warm welcome, smiling as a radiantly happy Charlotte kissed the new arrivals then handed them on to Fabio and Leo and Harriet, and finally to Mirella and Franco.

Rose hung back for a moment with Dante just to breathe in the noisy, laughing chaos of the scene. He put his arm round her, smiling down into her flushed face. 'You are happy, *amore*?'

'Yes,' she said simply. 'At this moment I have everything in the world I never dared wish for. A beautiful home, a loving, welcoming family, and my mother here with me to share it all today—but most of all, Dante, I have you.'

'Ah, *carissima*!' He took her in his arms and kissed her

in passionate gratitude, a move which won much applause and laughter from the crowded loggia.

'Come, *mio figlio*,' said Maria Fortinari, smiling. 'Release your bride for a moment. She will want to show Grace and Tom to their room to do the freshening up, and then we eat, yes, Rose?'

A few minutes later everyone crowded round the table laid in the garden, the noise level high as they enjoyed the food Maria Fortinari and her cook had helped Silvia prepare.

Under cover of the joyful hubbub, Grace took Rose's hand. 'I've no need to ask if you're happy, love.'

Rose gave a deep, relishing sigh. 'I'll be even happier if you—and Tom, of course—promise to come and stay with us as often as you can.'

'I can safely promise that, especially when Charlotte's baby arrives—I won't be able to keep him away!' Grace looked up at the house. 'I'm so glad I've seen your beautiful home. I'll be able to picture the three of you here.'

Rose eyed her husband in surprise as he got up to rap a spoon on his glass.

'Listen carefully, everyone, because I make my speech in English so Grace and Tom understand how happy I am to welcome them both here today and thank them for taking care of Bea these past two weeks.' At the mention of her name Bea left her place between Chiara and Luca and went running to her father. He picked her up and kissed her in a way which brought tears to his mother's eyes and to a few others round the table, notably Charlotte's.

'Hormones,' she apologised, blowing her nose into the handkerchief Fabio had ready.

'So now,' continued Dante, 'I wish to thank my mother-in-law for giving her daughter and her granddaughter into my keeping, also Tom, for taking such good care of Rose and Bea in the past.'

To Rose's surprise, Grace exchanged a look with Tom and got to her feet. 'Thank you, Dante, and everyone here for giving us this wonderful welcome. I shall go home—'

'Not yet, Grace,' called Charlotte.

'Not yet,' agreed Grace, smiling, 'but when I do I shall look back on today and feel happy because I know my girls are happy.'

'*Davvero,*' said Dante with feeling, and put his arm round Rose. 'After the years apart, it is now time we live happily ever after!'

'Like in my story book,' said Bea with satisfaction, and Dante laughed as he set her down.

'Only this is better because it is our story, yes?'

'Much better,' said Rose with feeling, and smiled all round to lighten the mood. 'Now, then, Harriet's made some gorgeous apple pies and I've made a very British trifle, so hands up. Who wants a *dolce*?'

* * * * *

A sneaky peek at next month...

MODERN™

POWER, PASSION AND IRRESISTIBLE TEMPTATION

My wish list for next month's titles...

In stores from 18th July 2014:

- ❏ Zarif's Convenient Queen – Lynne Graham
- ❏ His Forbidden Diamond – Susan Stephens
- ❏ The Argentinian's Demand – Cathy Williams
- ❏ The Ultimate Seduction – Dani Collins

In stores from 1st August 2014:

- ❏ Uncovering Her Nine Month Secret – Jennie Lucas
- ❏ Undone by the Sultan's Touch – Caitlin Crews
- ❏ Taming the Notorious Sicilian – Michelle Smart
- ❏ His by Design – Dani Wade

Available at WHSmith, Tesco, Asda, Eason, Amazon and Apple

Just can't wait?

0714/0

Special Offers

Every month we put together collections and longer reads written by your favourite authors.

Here are some of next month's highlights— and don't miss our fabulous discount online!

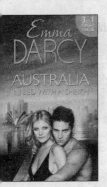

On sale 18th July

On sale 18th July

On sale 18th July

Save 20%
on all Special Releases

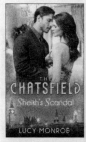

Make it a summer to remember with the fantastic new book from Sarah Morgan

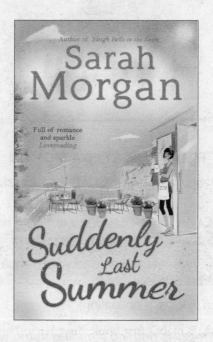

Fiery French chef Elise Philippe has just heard that the delectable Sean O'Neil is back in town. After their electrifying night together last summer, can she stick to her one-night rule?

Coming soon at millsandboon.co.uk

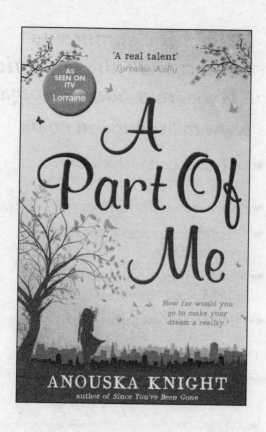

Anouska Knight's first book, *Since You've Been Gone*,
was a smash hit and crowned the winner of Lorraine's
Racy Reads. Anouska returns with *A Part of Me*,
which is one not to be missed!

Get your copy today at:
www.millsandboon.co.uk

Discover more romance at

www.millsandboon.co.uk

- ❤ WIN great prizes in our exclusive competitions
- ❤ BUY new titles before they hit the shops
- ❤ BROWSE new books and REVIEW your favourites
- ❤ SAVE on new books with the Mills & Boon® Bookclub™
- ❤ DISCOVER new authors

PLUS, to chat about your favourite reads, get the latest news and find special offers:

- Find us on facebook.com/millsandboon
- Follow us on twitter.com/millsandboonuk
- ❤ Sign up to our newsletter at millsandboon.co.uk

M&B_WEB